D0539144

That'll be the Day

FREDA LIGHTFOOT

That'll be the Day

HODDER &
STOUGHTON

Copyright © 2007 by Freda Lightfoot

First published in Great Britain in 2007 by Hodder & Stoughton
A division of Hodder Headline

The right of Freda Lightfoot to be identified as the Author of the
Work has been asserted by her in accordance
with the Copyright, Designs and Patents Act 1988.

A Hodder & Stoughton Book

I

A CIP catalogue record for this title is available from the British Library

ISBN 978 0 340 89738 6
ISBN 0 340 89738 4

Typeset in Plantin Light by Palimpsest Book Production Limited,
Grangemouth, Stirlingshire
Printed and bound by
Mackays of Chatham Ltd, Chatham, Kent

Hodder Headline's policy is to use papers that are natural, renewable and recyclable
products and made from wood grown in sustainable forests. The logging
and manufacturing processes are expected to conform to the environmental
regulations of the country of origin.

Hodder & Stoughton Ltd
A division of Hodder Headline
338 Euston Road
London NW1 3BH

1958

I

Betty

After today Betty Hemley would forever associate the scent of chrysanthemums with the shock of seeing again that face. Which was a pity because she loved these stately flowers. Unlike carnations, which always reminded her of weddings and funerals, events she disliked with equal loathing, chrysants, as she liked to call them, were vibrant with colour and positively bounced with vigour. She loved their large showy blooms in golden yellow, pink, bronze or brilliant white; they were perfect for flower arrangements being erect and strong stemmed; a flower to admire. Now, whenever she looked at these beautiful plants she would be reminded of this long-dreaded moment when her past came back to haunt her.

'Are you okay, Mam? You look like you've seen a ghost.'

She heard the voice of her own daughter as if coming from a great distance and fear bloomed in her like a stain of hot blood. It was imperative that Lynda didn't see him standing there. Who knows how she might react?

Yet Betty could do nothing to prevent it, could neither speak nor move. She'd been putting the finishing touches to the display preparatory to making a sale. Now she was grasping the flower far too tightly but felt powerless to unclasp her fingers. It was as if frozen fire were flowing through her veins, her limbs oddly flaccid and unresponsive, her brain a mush of confused emotion.

She was transfixed by the shock of seeing that all-too-familiar face, all other sounds from the bustling market around her fading into insignificance. Betty could hear nothing but his voice:

whining, complaining, criticising, coming back to her like an echo through the years, hearing again those pitiful excuses, those bare-faced lies.

Maybe he *was* a ghost. Maybe he hadn't just walked across the cobbles of Champion Street and smiled at her with that sardonic curl to his lip. Perhaps she was hallucinating and he wasn't standing leaning against the wall of the Dog and Duck at all, watching her with those nasty beady eyes. Perhaps he didn't even exist except in her fevered imagination.

This might all be some sort of nightmare because of that cheese she'd eaten for her supper. She might still be at home in bed, not seated at her stall surrounded by her beloved flowers which she'd risen before dawn to buy, spending hours arranging them in an array of metal vases and baskets.

Yet even in the nightmare Betty was able to savour every nuance of their differing scents: some sweet and cloying, others earthy and moist, or spicy and herblike, each one an individual and at this instant overwhelming her senses.

Betty had never been the kind of person prone to sudden attacks of panic. She prided herself on being a calm, unruffled sort of woman, steady and easy-going, although she was willing to take anyone on if she saw someone being bullied or picked on. She was a familiar figure on Champion Street Market where she had run her flower stall since before the war, bringing up her two children largely single-handed. She had always believed that although human nature may be frail, if you keep your heart strong and your spirits high everything will come out right in the end.

But who could blame her if she was scarred by a bitter resentment, against her own ex-husband in particular? Ewan Hemley had totally messed up her life, and it looked as if he might be about to do the same again.

The stem of the chrysanthemum snapped between her fingers and sound rushed in upon her like an express train. People talking and laughing, traffic roaring by, a baby crying, yet still Betty couldn't move.

'Oh, you've broken it,' Lynda said, taking the crippled flower from her useless fingers. 'It's not like you to be so clumsy. Do you think I should call a doctor, Judy? Mam looks like she's about to keel over.'

'I'm not sure. Mrs Hemley, are you all right? Can I get you something? A glass of water perhaps?'

'Do you want to take a tea break, Mam? Why don't you go over to Belle's caff for a cuppa?'

Betty became vaguely aware of a gentle touch upon her arm, and of anxious voices drowned out by the pounding of her own heart. She forced her trembling lips into a smile. Sweet strong tea sounded good. That's what you took for shock, wasn't it?

'Aye, I might just do that, love. I am feeling a bit queer. Maybe I'm coming down with a cold.'

'Let me help you, Mrs Hemley. You seem a bit unsteady on your feet.'

Betty looked up into a pair of gentle, cornflower blue eyes fringed by long, curling lashes. Judy Beckett, one of her regulars. The poor girl really should take better care of herself instead of always looking faintly worn out and a bit shabby, as if she'd thrown her clothes on or bought them at Abel's second-hand stall.

But then her husband Sam who ran the ironmongery shop inside Champion Street Market, bought her a suspicious number of bouquets. In Betty's opinion their marriage was almost bound to fail so was it any wonder if she always looked so gaunt and ill?

All of human nature passed by Betty's stall, the good and the bad, allowing her the opportunity to speculate, rightly or wrongly, on the lives of her neighbours: to share in their celebrations, their weddings, birthdays and special occasions, and in the sadder events of their lives such as hospital visits and funerals, their squabbles, their guilt, and even their apologies.

She knew that the brand-new marriage of Amy and Chris George had almost been destroyed by a family feud, yet when Amy presented her young husband with a baby daughter, he bought her the biggest basket of flowers Betty had ever seen in her life. Cost him a small fortune that he could ill afford, but then Chris was that rare breed – a loving husband.

Unlike Leo Catlow, for instance, owner of a large distribution depot down on the docks and occupying the big house on the corner of Champion Street. He was a demanding, restless, deep-thinking sort of man who called at her stall once a month to buy carnations for his mother, yet rarely bought his wife so much as a single rose. Nor will he, Betty construed, until she did her duty and provided him with a son.

Hadn't she also watched with a heavy heart as the young hopefuls came courting her lovely daughter Lynda, roses in hand? And seen how the poor girl spurned each and every one of them, not able to trust a man after her own father had so callously deserted her.

Men! Betty didn't have a good word to say for any of them. If only all marriages could be happy, and divorce rendered unnecessary.

That'll be the day . . .

Betty directed her level brown-eyed gaze across the street. He was still there, looking as cocky as ever. Damn him to hell!

'Mrs Hemley? Can you hear me, Betty? Did you forget to have breakfast in your rush to get up early to collect the flowers this morning, and then were too busy preparing them to find time? You're looking really washed out. I think a cup of tea would do you a power of good.'

Judy was petite and pretty with a warm easy smile. Betty liked her a lot and often enjoyed a chat with her about her two children, and encouraged her in her hobby of oil painting which she did so well. It was Judy who had wanted the chrysanthemums. She called at the stall every Friday morning to buy flowers for the weekend, as she was doing today. Often one of Betty's specially made basket arrangements which Sam fondly imagined she did herself.

Husbands, so demanding of wives and yet so flawed themselves. Useless lumps the lot of them, in Betty's opinion. Again she glanced across the street but the pavement was empty this time. The unwelcome intruder, if indeed he'd been there at all, had gone.

Once inside the café taking sips of scalding sweet tea, Betty began to feel faintly foolish. This was no way for a middle-aged mother to behave, coming over all peculiar because of some imagined sighting of an ex-husband. She raked blunt-tipped fingers through cropped grey hair, rubbed the flat of her hand over the soft pads of her cheeks as if to wake herself from some nightmare, then sank her face into her hands with a weary sigh. If that really had been Ewan Hemley and not a figment of her imagination, then it couldn't be good news, not good news at all.

Judy appeared at her side. 'I've brought you a slice of toast and marmalade as well. I often feel a bit odd myself if I've forgotten to eat when I'm painting.'

Betty pulled herself out of her reverie and managed to find her voice sufficiently to thank the young woman for her thoughtfulness.

'Yer a good lass. That might be just the ticket.'

If only it could be so simple. If only a slice of toast, warmly offered, could resolve all her problems. Betty knew in her heart that she hadn't suffered a nightmare, nor an hallucination brought on by her fondness for Welsh Rarebit.

As she nibbled on the toast, the constriction in her throat making it hard for her to swallow, Betty kept glancing anxiously about the busy market hall, worried lest the ghost from her past might again appear like the demon king in a bad pantomime.

Ewan Hemley, the husband from whom she'd escaped and finally divorced in 1945, seemed to be back in her life and that could mean only one thing. Trouble!

What could he be doing on Champion Street Market? She hadn't set eyes on him in thirteen years or more, so why would he suddenly turn up now?

Money! Why else?

Was he still around? Was he following her now that he'd found her again? Yet everything looked perfectly normal: stacks of yellow cheeses beneath striped awnings, women in headscarves buying strings of Ramsay's pork sausages or patiently queuing for one of Poulson's pies. There were the Higginson sisters gently squabbling over how best to display a hat. Racks of gaily coloured skirts standing before the fabric stall and Winnie Watkins as was, Mrs Barry Homes as she should now rightly be addressed since her recent marriage, skilfully measuring out several yards of net curtaining for a customer.

Winnie smiled across at Betty, giving a little jerk of her head by way of acknowledgement and making the bob on her woollen hat quiver. She was rarely seen without that hat, even on a warm September day like today.

Betty put back her head and stared up at the blue sky through the dome of windows high in the iron frame of the Market Hall roof. The sunlight slanting in was as bright and golden as any other ordinary day. Everything perfectly normal, exactly as the market had always looked in all the long years she had occupied it.

Yet for Betty, nothing would ever be normal again.

What if Jake, her nineteen-year-old son, still filled with anger even after all this time, and blaming her for his father's apparent desertion, returned unexpectedly early from his delivery round and discovered what was going on? Lord above, that would never do. That would be even worse than Lynda finding out.

Yet if Ewan Hemley was indeed back in her life, how could she keep it from them? He was still their father after all, even if he was a pain in the backside and hell-bent on making trouble.

Betty drew in a long shaky breath. Good hearted and caring she might still be but not so trusting nor half so stupid as she once was. That innocent young girl who had been so easily taken in by a man's charm and seen her life ruined as a result, was long gone. Betty had seen too how he'd damaged her two children, and had made a private vow to put him six feet under rather than allow anything of the sort to happen to them ever again.

2

Lynda

It was an hour later and her mother still hadn't returned to the stall, which was worrying Lynda. She couldn't even see any sign of Judy. Where were they? Had Mam been taken ill? She was about to ask Barry Holmes to keep an eye on the stall for her while she went to find Betty when a customer came up. 'I'll take a dozen of them roses. Yellow ones, long stemmed.'

'Yellow roses for lost love. I do hope not,' she teased. The man raised his eyebrows but said nothing.

Embarrassed by her *faux pas*, Lynda concentrated on selecting the tightly folded buds, wrapping them in tissue paper while she surreptitiously examined him from beneath her lashes. He was a man in his late fifties, dark haired and of a thin wiry build, no doubt reasonably good looking in his youth but now rather well used; his grey striped suit seemed a bit frayed around the edges, worn with the collar turned up despite the warmth of the day. He didn't look as if he could afford a jam buttie let alone long-stemmed roses.

Frowning slightly she asked him to repeat his order. 'Did you say a dozen? They're two shillings a bud, you know.'

'A special purchase for a special lady,' he said with a smile and Lynda considered him with keener attention.

There was something vaguely familiar about him. She felt certain that she'd met him before but couldn't remember when or where, then gave a mental shrug as she took the notes he offered and dug in her apron pocket for change. No doubt this old codger was one of her mother's regulars. After nearly twenty years she'd built up a loyal band of customers.

The man smiled at her. 'Am I right in thinking you're Betty Hemley's daughter? I would've known you in an instant. You're every bit as attractive. You have her hair and eyes.'

Lynda was used to men flirting with her, particularly old ones like this who should know better, but she'd never been compared to her mother before. Lynda saw Betty as plump and really quite old at fifty-three, her cap of short grey hair which framed her round wrinkled face nothing like Lynda's own abundant auburn tresses.

She'd elected to wear her hair loose today, allowing it to curl upwards where it rested on her shoulders, though she did like to ring the changes, perhaps putting it into a chignon or a French pleat. But then that was one of the advantages of having long hair and, as with boy-friends, Lynda did so love variety.

Despite a fondness for flirting yet she hesitated, not quite sure how to respond, and far too worried about her mother to raise more than a faint smile. She certainly had no intention of encouraging dirty old men to leer at her quite so lewdly. 'My eyes are hazel. Mam's are brown,' she coolly remarked.

'Of course. Yes, I can see they are, now that I look more closely.'

Lynda wasn't sure she wanted this old geyser to gaze quite so intently into her eyes. For some reason he made her feel uncomfortable and her pretty rosebud mouth slid back into its accustomed sulky pout as she counted six shillings on to his palm. It was smooth and white, she noticed; not a working man's hand, and with the hint of a tremor to it. Maybe he hit the bottle a bit hard. 'Your change. Good day to you, sir,' she said, offering a practised, dismissive smile.

Lynda thought he might have been about to say something more but a short queue had formed behind him and she was able to turn her attention to the next customer without appearing rude.

But even as she helped Joyce choose a begonia plant for her hairdresser's shop, and made up a bouquet of asters, freesias and gypsophila for Amy George to give to her mother-in-law on her birthday, she couldn't help but be aware of the man still hovering in the background. After a while he disappeared through the doors of the Dog and Duck, so maybe she'd been right about the drink problem.

By dinner time, her mother still hadn't returned from her tea break and Lynda had forgotten all about him. He wasn't, after all, any of her concern.

Lynda guessed Terry Hall was coming over to speak to her long before he appeared. She heard the swell of Buddy Holly's 'Oh Boy!' grow suddenly louder when he opened the door of his father's little music shop that stood on the perimeter of the market hall, and some instinct warned her he was approaching.

She watched him walk towards her, surreptitiously admiring his long-legged stride. Terry always wore black, generally tee-shirt and jeans, his smooth dark hair combed high at each side of his brow to form the required fashionable quiff. This morning he also had on his biker's jacket. He looked fit and muscular and her mouth watered at sight of him.

Lynda Hemley was a lively, warm-hearted, sexy young woman who liked a good time and plenty of fun in her life. She viewed love as a delightful game. Delicious fun and not to be taken too seriously. She really rather enjoyed the excitement of the chase, the enticing moments of seduction. It made her come alive to feel emotion pulsing through her blood like electricity, as if every caress proved how beloved she was, how cherished. Of course, she realised it was all flim-flam, nothing but shallow pleasure and didn't mind in the least.

She saw nothing wrong in making the most of the attributes with which nature had endowed her: a slender figure going in and out in all the right places, glossy auburn curls that fell in rich waves to her shoulders, and a face that was a near perfect oval with high cheekbones, small pert nose and round strong chin. Admittedly her mouth might be a bit smaller than she would have liked, but she saw its perpetual pout as sexy rather than sulky. Lynda laid no claims to being a ravishing beauty but knew herself to be sufficiently attractive for men falling in love with

her to be considered a natural occurrence. Terry Hall was one
such in thrall to her charms, but then she'd been aware for some
time that he was smitten.

She half turned away, pretending not to notice as he
approached, glad suddenly that she'd opted to wear a new pink
blouse with a Peter Pan collar this morning, and a swirling navy
blue cotton circular skirt with white polka dots. She guessed that
he intended to pester her for another date and found great difficulty in suppressing a giggle when she was proved to be right.

'Hiya, Lynda.'

'Hiya, Terry.'

'What you doing this evening?'

Terry could never be accused of subtlety. Nor did he ever
have much in the way of small talk. With numerous false starts
and offhand shrugs, he finally managed to convey that he wanted
her to go to a dance with him at the Ritz. Lynda fluttered her
lashes, automatically turning on the charm even as she declined
the invitation.

She curled her mouth into a slow sexy smile for the benefit
of this, her latest conquest, hazel eyes sparkling with instinctive
seductive appeal. 'Terry love, I think it would be best if you
picked someone your own age. I don't go in for cradle-snatching.'

A painful flush spread from his neck up over his jaw and
Lynda felt a momentary burst of pity for him, yet she was surely
right to refuse? He was only nineteen, nearly six years younger
than herself.

Six years! She gave a silent inner groan. How she hated to
remind herself of her own great age. At twenty-five, okay nearly
twenty-six, as her mother kept constantly reminding her, she
should be married and with children of her own. Secretly, Lynda
wished that she was but somehow Mr Right had so far refused
to put in an appearance. A good man, she'd discovered, was hard
to find.

Once, when she was very young, no more than seventeen
or eighteen, she'd fallen passionately in love with a man almost
ten years older than herself. Lynda had imagined he would be

more reliable than her usual here-today-gone-tomorrow boy-friends and had allowed herself to believe his protestations of undying love. Then quite out of the blue he'd announced that he couldn't see her any more as he was getting married the following month.

'But I thought you loved *me*,' she'd cried, like some sort of love-sick fool.

'Don't be silly, sweetheart, you know that we agreed from the beginning that what we had together was fun and nothing more.'

For the sake of her pride she'd pretended to agree, saying that of course she'd only been teasing and wished him every happiness in his coming marriage, but her heart had been utterly broken. It had taken weeks before she could even bear to look at another man.

The experience had left her even more wary of commitment. She still dreamed of meeting a man she was willing to give her all to, someone she could trust implicitly and wish to be with for the rest of her life, but beneath the dream lay a growing panic that he might not even exist.

On the other hand, she certainly had no wish to repeat her mother's mistake of rushing into marriage with the wrong man and spending the rest of her life regretting it.

Terry was talking about the band now, promising there was a supper included, doing his utmost to persuade her to go to the dance. Lynda found herself giggling over his intensity. He really was keen, poor boy. What if Mam did sometimes accuse her of seeking attention? Where was the harm in that? There was nothing Lynda loved more than to bask in masculine admiration.

It was true that she could also be moody and difficult, and feel quite vulnerable and emotionally insecure at times. Lynda was aware that most of her boy-friends, and she'd had several, saw her as an enigma. One minute she would be all over them, openly affectionate, perhaps too much so; the next cool and distant, or casually off-hand.

Perhaps, like her mother, she really didn't care for men at all.

Yet unlike Betty, just as a moth is attracted to flame, Lynda simply couldn't resist them.

'Bit gullible, that's me. Indecisive and flirtatious,' she would laughingly explain. 'A typical Libra.'

The true cause of the confusing signals she sent out was far more prosaic. As a child, until the moment he'd walked away, Lynda had believed Ewan to be a loving father. She remembered him bringing her presents; a rag doll one of his comrades had made, a pretty brooch which she still had to this day. She would excitedly pull them out of his kitbag and he would swing her up high in his arms and tell her she was his most precious gift of all.

And then one day he simply stopped coming and she never saw him again. There were no more presents, no letters, not even a card on her birthday.

If her own father could so easily turn away and reject her, suddenly stop loving her with such callous heartlessness, it must be because she wasn't a nice person. If even *he* couldn't find her lovable, what hope was there of any other man doing so?

A shiver of fear ran down her spine at the prospect of turning into a sour old spinster like Annie Higginson, whose only excitement in life was a game of bridge every Thursday at the mission hall. But then why should she when she was still so young and full of life? She simply hadn't found the right man yet and until that glorious day arrived there were plenty of others to be enjoyed, lots of fun and sex and excitement to be had, so long as she held on to her private vow not to fully engage her heart until it was safe to do so.

With this in mind Lynda again considered Terry Hall's dark good looks and his fit young body, telling herself there was no harm in being cautious where men were concerned, none at all. Although it didn't do to be overcautious. Six years difference in their ages was nothing, surely? The poor boy looked so downcast by her refusal and she didn't have anything else planned for this evening.

'Okay, why not? Pick me up at seven,' she said, and almost

laughed out loud as she watched his eyes widen with surprise and joy.

'Really?'

'Yes, really. But leave your tricycle at home, love. I prefer real men who can afford to provide a taxi, not little boys.'

She knew this was an unkind, insensitive remark to make even before she saw the colour in his cheeks deepen with fresh embarrassment, but something inside always compelled her to damage a relationship right from the start.

'I've got a motor bike, will that do?'

'I suppose it'll have to.' Lynda rather liked motor bikes and he went up a little in her estimation. At least the leather jacket wasn't simply for show. 'Seven o'clock it is then. Shall I wear my tight jeans for the bike, then change into a skirt at the dance? I mean, I don't want the wind to blow it up and embarrass you by revealing next week's washing.'

'Stop teasing the poor lad,' said a voice in her ear. 'He's breaking out in a cold sweat at the thought.'

'Oh, hello, Winnie. I didn't see you standing there.' Damn, she should have known a person didn't have a minute's privacy on this market. When had Winnie Holmes ever missed a trick? Biggest gossip on the street, for all she might deny it.

In a show of defiance, Lynda reached up to place a soft kiss on Terry's cheek, sending him back to work in a daze of desire, before turning to Winnie to ask in her coolest tones, 'Did you want something?'

'Aye, a few marguerites. Where's your mam?'

'The marguerites are all finished now, but we've some beautiful blue delphiniums. Mam's gone for a cuppa at Belle's caff. She's got a cold coming on.'

'Oh aye, I saw her there a while back. I thought she looked a bit peaky. She should watch out, it could be that old cow Belle Garside trying to poison her. Hey up, it might be none of my business but isn't Terry Hall a bit young for you, chuck?'

Lynda concentrated on wrapping half a dozen of the tall blue flowers, still in tight bud, refusing to rise to Winnie's snide remark.

The woman was forever poking her nose in where it wasn't wanted. Besides, her mind was fully occupied wondering if dating a vibrant male six years younger than herself who owned a motor bike might turn out to be far more exciting than she'd first thought.

3

Betty

B etty was snoring gently on her green moquette sofa, quietly recovering from the worst day she could remember in a long time. She'd meant to be back at her flower stall by now but had fallen asleep listening to *Woman's Hour* on the wireless. Now she was brought rudely awake by a knock on the door.

'Who can that be? Not Constable Nuttall, thank God, he always hammers the door down.' Betty groaned. 'I hope it's not Winnie Holmes come poking her nose in where it's not wanted.'

Rubbing the sleep from her eyes she shuffled down the passage to the front door in her carpet slippers, the little bobbles on the front bouncing as she walked. The knock came again, louder this time. 'All right, all right, keep your hair on, I'm coming.'

He was standing on her doorstep, a bunch of yellow roses clutched tightly in his hands, bought no doubt from her own flower stall. Betty was filled with a sudden unexpected rage at the sight of him, and, as if guessing her intention, he put a foot in the door.

'Don't try closing it. I just wanted a word. There's no harm in that now, Betty love, is there?'

'Every harm, I should think, judging from past experience,' Betty snapped. 'And don't call me love. I haven't been that for many a long year.'

'Ten minutes of your time, no more. Then I'll be out of your life again, just like before. Here, I fetched you these. I know roses are your favourite.' He pushed the bunch into her unwilling hands and was over the threshold striding along the passage into her home before she could gather her wits fast enough to stop him.

'Nice place you've got here. Must be doing all right on that stall of yours?'

Betty found she was shaking as she scuttled after him and, resolving not to be intimidated, flung the offending roses on to the table from where they skidded off on to the linoleum-covered floor. She stood four-square before her ex-husband, arms folded and a dangerous glint in her eye. 'What is it you want? If it's money you're after, you've come to the wrong shop. I owe you nowt.'

'Dear me, what a low opinion you have of me.'

'I wonder why?' Betty watched with helpless indignation as Ewan Hemley glanced about the small room then settled himself in her son's favourite chair, just as if he owned the place.

'Don't worry, I won't take offence at your rudeness. Not this time. I dare say you know me better than most and my finances are a bit squeezed at the moment, it's true, but I have hopes of improvement in the near future. Great hopes!' He allowed his gaze to roam, taking in every detail of his surroundings.

What the room lacked in smart furnishing was more than made up for in cleanliness, as he would have expected from Betty. The cream and green paint looked new and fresh; the dark green rug set before a brown-tiled fireplace was well brushed if somewhat well worn. A black and white cat clawed briefly at the sofa, looking faintly annoyed at having been disturbed, before curling up again on a small sigh.

'Lazy sod, just like that other cat we used to have. Tiddles, wasn't that its name? Wonder what happened to it?'

'It left home after it had felt the toe of your boot once too often, same as I did.'

He smiled at her, a thin cold smile that chilled her to the bone. 'I believe I told you not to allow animals to sit on the furniture,' and reaching forward he knocked the cat with the flat of one hand on to the floor where it yowled in protest before scampering for cover under the table with the roses.

'Here, you leave my Queenie alone!'

Ignoring her, Ewan got up from the chair and moved over to the sideboard to study a collection of framed photographs, picking one up to examine it more closely. 'So these are the kids, eh? Jake looks as if he's made a fine young man, and Lynda is lovely. I met her earlier when I bought those flowers and . . .'

Betty was by his side in a second. 'I hope you didn't tell her who you were?'

He gave a snort of amusement as if she'd said something funny, black eyes stretched wide in mock innocence. 'As if I would, what do you take me for? I don't see any pictures of me anywhere though. What happened to our lovely wedding snap?'

'I threw it on t'bonfire. Spit it out, Ewan, what are you doing here?'

'Can't a man call and see his family once in a while? You're looking good, Betty love, for your age, though I don't much care for that tatty old jersey and corduroy trousers. A woman should dress like a woman, in my opinion.'

'Fortunately I never did care what you thought.'

'True. And it's not as if I've pestered you over the years, is it? Surely I've a right to call and check on you all, make sure that my children are well?'

'You lost all rights to the kids when you treated them so badly.'

Betty considered him with open distaste, wondering what she'd ever found to like in this scrawny, bean-pole of a man with a face very like that of a ferret. His grey striped suit looked as if it had been slept in and his shoes were filthy. She had a great urge to remind him to wipe them on the mat next time, except that there wouldn't be a next time, not if she had any say in the matter.

He set the photograph down with reluctance. 'Nay, I wasn't that bad surely? I was a good caring father who always brought his kids presents home.'

'Don't flatter yourself.'

'Oh, I don't know. I seem to remember Lynda as a real little darling who loved to be cuddled on her daddy's knee. Jake was admittedly more of a handful.'

A shudder ran down Betty's spine at the images his words evoked. She swallowed hard, pushing them firmly away again. 'Jake didn't have a father capable of showing him any better. You never did take the role seriously, or ever paid a bean towards their upkeep. They could've both starved for all you cared.' Betty moved quickly towards the door. She was getting those palpitations in her heart again and could take no more. 'If you don't say what you have to say and get the hell out of here, I shall call Constable Nuttall.'

'And he'll come running will he, riding to your rescue on his white charger?'

'He will if I ask him to.'

'I don't think so. Not quickly enough to do any good.' The small dark eyes narrowed to slits as, hands in pockets, he rocked back and forth on his heels and laughed down at her. 'I'll go when I'm good and ready and not before. You know me, Betty, I don't take kindly to being given orders.'

Betty swallowed back an angry retort as images of her past life flashed painfully before her eyes: Ewan in the throes of one of his drunken rages beating her senseless; or locking the kids in the under-stairs cupboard because they'd refused to eat the kippers he'd brought home for tea, or for no reason at all, come to think of it. He seemed sober today, at least.

But even though she was no longer his wife, and her precious children no longer victims of his violent mood swings, she must take care not to allow her irritation at finding him back in her life lead her into dangerous waters. Ewan Hemley was not a man who took kindly to independent-minded women.

She decided on a more pragmatic approach. 'I can't see that you and I have anything left to say to each other. Thirteen years is a long time and we never had much in common even in the early days.'

'Hmm, pity that, I always thought. You were an attractive woman in your day, Betty. Still, circumstances, shall we say, have kept me away from you all these years, but now I'm free to please meself what I do.'

'And there's nothing you'd like better than to ruffle my feathers and stir up trouble.'

'These are still my children and I've never quite forgiven you for depriving me of them, nor for grassing on me to the law. But you're right, of course, I never did put me family first, nor cared a jot for them, but it would be worth putting up with the little bleeders for the pleasure of seeing you sweat, as you're doing now.'

There was a silence in which a cold sweat did indeed form on her brow and under her arms. Betty felt sick. She'd believed herself to be safe here in Champion Street, many miles from Blackburn where they'd lived as man and wife together. Now it seemed he was back in her life simply to take vengeance over her escape from him all those years ago.

Betty licked her lips but there was no spittle left in her dry mouth to moisten them. Nevertheless, she found her voice somehow. She had to make a stand or he'd walk all over her. 'We're divorced, remember?'

He crossed the short space between them as if making for the door and for one heady moment Betty thought that he might be about to leave them in peace after all. But then she saw by the glint in his eye that this was mere wishful thinking on her part.

He stopped inches from her, so close she could smell the beer on his breath, and a musty dankness from his clothes which seemed to indicate that he'd been sleeping rough. Now why did that not surprise her?

His long lean frame towered over her short, round body as he smiled down at her with a false geniality. 'That was your choice, not mine. You didn't ask my permission, Betty love, and that's not nice, not nice at all.'

'You signed the papers.'

He shrugged. 'My matrimonial state wasn't high on my list of priorities at the time, being locked up at His Majesty's pleasure. Thanks to you. But papers don't make a marriage, nor do they end one. Remember that, Betty love. I'll call again on Sunday, and I shall expect better hospitality next time. You haven't even offered to put the kettle on today,' wagging a finger in her face as if she were a naughty child. 'I always did enjoy your roast beef and Yorkshire. Shall we say twelve o'clock prompt? And make sure that our Lynda and Jake are at home this time. You need to appreciate that I will have my way in this, so don't try any funny business or you may live to regret it.'

And on this threat he strolled back down the passage and left the house, closing the door quietly behind him. Betty found that she was shaking and collapsed on to the sofa as her fat knees threatened to give way beneath her.

All these years she'd protected her children, wanting them to put out of their minds all that had happened, deliberately never mentioning their father so that they would forget him. How could she begin to explain to a much loved daughter that the father who'd smacked and abused and treated her so badly as a child was back on their doorstep wanting to see her again, demanding to reclaim his rights, not out of love but revenge. And how Jake would react, Betty really didn't care to think.

'Over my dead body!' she muttered to herself.

4

Lynda

Having finally got rid of Winnie, Lynda kept her mind off worrying about her mother's continued absence by setting out pots of scarlet geraniums all in a line, their vivid colours catching the September sun and glowing like balls of fire. Betty would call them pelargoniums, of course, but whatever their name, when one day Lynda bought that cottage in the country she dreamed of, she'd fill her window boxes with this robust and dazzling plant. Every one of them a brilliant scarlet. And this ivy-leaved variety in glorious pinks and mauves she would put in hanging baskets all along her porch. Lynda could picture it perfectly, a tranquil haven far removed from Champion Street.

She was carefully watering the last plant, admiring the five-petalled flowers with their darker veined centres when Clara Higginson appeared.

'Aren't geraniums beautiful, Lynda? I really don't think I can resist buying one. I shall have one of the pink variety with splashes of white. They look as tempting as strawberries and cream.'

Clara and her sister Annie ran the hat stall with the help of their new protégée, Patsy. Not quite so tight-lipped or sharp-tongued as her sister, and with softer curves and rounded cheeks, full lips and a small nose, Clara might have been pretty in her youth, Lynda thought, back in the dark ages of the war. And there was a rumour that she might once have had an illicit affair.

Even so, Lynda shuddered at the thought of ending up like her, a lonely middle-aged spinster, as she wrapped the plant in a torn-off scrap of newspaper sporting a picture of a living room declaring the end of chintzy and advocating clean-cut, angular 'contemporary' lines.

'And how are you this fine morning, and your dear mother? She looked rather strained when I saw her earlier.'

'She's got a cold coming on,' Lynda said. It was often remarked upon that you only had to cough on this market and the rumour would flash round in seconds that you had pneumonia. But the elderly spinster was really quite kind, if a bit old fashioned, and Lynda guiltily told herself she should welcome the woman's concern, not mock it.

'Oh, what a nuisance,' Clara was saying. 'Is there anything I can do?'

Judy chose that precise moment to hurry back to the flower stall rather out of breath and with a heavy basket of shopping on her arm. 'I've just dashed over to let you know your mam's feeling much better, Lynda. She's comfortably ensconced on her own sofa with strict instructions that she keep her feet up for an hour or two. I've told her no dashing about till she's properly recovered from her funny turn. I've also warmed her a dish of soup for her dinner.'

'A funny turn was it?' Clara enquired, looking troubled. 'I thought you said it was only a cold coming on?'

'Well, that's what caused the funny turn, I expect. Thanks, Miss Clara, I'll give her your best wishes, shall I?'

'Oh, yes, please do. I'd best be off. Annie will wonder where I've got to, but I meant it, Lynda. If Betty isn't well, I don't mind popping in on her when you're busy with the stall.'

'Thanks, I appreciate the offer,' and the two girls smiled as the older woman bustled off.

'She isn't such a bad old stick,' Judy said. 'Here, I've brought us a sandwich each, and mugs of coffee. I guessed you'd be stuck here so thought I'd join you for a bit of a chin-wag.'

'Bless you! I can't think how I would have managed without your help this morning. You must take home one of these geraniums. According to Mam, and she knows about such things, geraniums are for friendship, and you've certainly proved yet again to be my very best friend.'

'I wouldn't dream of robbing Betty of her stock. What are neighbours for, if not to help each other?'

'Nevertheless, I insist. I don't know how I come to deserve a friend like you.'

Judy gave a wry smile. 'Because you've listened patiently to all my feeble moans and groans, from my mental arithmetic test with the dreadful Mrs Donaldson to the joyless state of matrimony, not to mention my endless fretting over my blessed children.'

'Feel free. You don't moan nearly enough, particularly about Sam. He's a selfish pig and you're an absolute saint.'

'Don't exaggerate! Just because you don't trust men doesn't mean I should be the same. I saw you talking to Terry, did he ask you out? And did you accept?'

Lynda saw the determined little smile and accepted the abrupt change of topic with resignation. It was none of her business if Judy insisted on turning herself into a doormat and believed everything her philandering husband told her. If Lynda had one unselfish wish for her friend, it would be that she dumped the bastard.

Lynda had pulled up an orange box for Judy and the two young women were enjoying their snack lunch together. They'd been friends since schooldays, although Judy was three years older and would turn twenty-nine just two months after Lynda's own coming birthday in October. There were no secrets between them as they were entirely comfortable in each other's company and Lynda was only too ready to tell her friend all about her date with Terry Hall.

'He's really quite dishy so why the hell shouldn't I go out with him?'

Judy laughed. 'No one can say you don't grasp life with both hands, love. I envy you. I wish I had half your courage.'

There it was again, that faintly wistful note. 'Is it my courage you envy, or my freedom?' Lynda tentatively enquired.

Judy laughingly shook her head. 'Why would I, a happily married woman, want freedom? Far too frightening.'

'Oh, I don't know,' Lynda protested with a secret smile. 'The single state has its advantages.'

'I can see that you enjoy your independence, but I quite like having a man look after me.'

'Sam, look after you?' Lynda looked at her askance. 'I'll believe that when I see it.'

'He does, in his way. He's certainly a good provider, and good with the kids.'

Lynda never had liked Sam Beckett, considering the union a bad one from the start, but had been far too young at the time to understand why the man made her flesh creep, or to say as much. Not that Judy would have listened. She wouldn't hear a word said against him, though God knows why. He didn't deserve her, he really didn't.

Sadly though, Lynda's fears had been proved correct. Despite her friend's efforts to disguise her unhappiness, anyone would need to be blind, deaf and dumb not to see how things stood between them. Judy obediently did his every bidding, waited on him hand, foot and finger, and it made Lynda furious to see her so much under his control while he spread his favours where he pleased.

'And is that your only criterion for a good husband, that he be a good provider? I would want so much more. A sexy lover, his undivided attention, and complete and utter fidelity.'

Judy didn't answer immediately but concentrated on taking a bite of her egg sandwich. At last she said, 'And if you didn't get those things?'

'Then either shove the bastard in the canal or divorce him. Life is too short to spend it dreaming of what might have been.'

'Easy for you to talk when you're not faced with the problem, but I'm not sure I could cope on my own.'

'You're stronger than you think, girl, and should stand up to him more. I've told you so a million times. Over those wonderful pictures you paint for a start. It's a crime, it really is, to hide them away in the attic. Why don't you set up a stall on the market? They'd go like hot cakes.'

'You know Sam doesn't like me working. It's my job to look after the children and the house, though he has no objection to my little hobby. He's not nearly so selfish as you make out.'

'*Little hobby*, how patronising! Why can't he see that you have real talent? He's so selfish. I think he likes having you chained to the kitchen sink, but it really is time you started putting yourself first. The kids are older now, and settled at school. How much time does it take to clean one small terraced house which *he* is rarely in, anyway?'

The warning look was cooler this time and Lynda saw that she'd gone too far.

'It's all right for you,' Judy said. 'Being single you can do as you please. Sam may not be the best of husbands but he *is* a good father. You don't understand how badly it would affect the children if we split up.'

'Now that's where you're wrong. I understand perfectly.'

Judy's cheeks coloured slightly. 'Sorry, I tend to forget.'

'Don't fret, I survived, didn't I? Mixed up though I may be.' Lynda frowned. 'I freely admit that much as I love and support my mother, I'd give a great deal to have enjoyed a normal upbringing with two loving parents but their separation was probably for the best and certainly inevitable.' She reached for a second sandwich, allowing her mind to drift back to those years, painful though it still was to remember.

'Mam didn't see my dad for months on end because of the war, and whenever he did get leave I think she wondered what on earth she'd let herself in for. He would bark out orders, expect her to deliver meals at the drop of a hat and she'd resent it, too used to pleasing herself and living life in the sort of muddled disorder she enjoys. Waiting on a man didn't appeal at all. They were constantly at each other's throats. Then he'd accuse her of seeing Yanks, which I'm sure wasn't true, and she'd call him a bully. Young as I was, I can still remember the rows, the frozen silences, the chilling atmosphere, secretly resenting the fact that those few precious days of Dad's leave always seemed to be spoiled. And then he just stopped coming altogether.'

Lynda hadn't set eyes on her father since she was eleven years old when he'd gone back off leave in the autumn of 1943. She hadn't realised, at the time, that she would never see him again and had kept waiting for him, wondering why he no longer came to see her. He even stopped answering the carefully penned letters she sent him.

'Was he a good father?' Judy asked, blue eyes soft with sympathy.

Lynda stifled a sigh. 'I think so. How can I tell? My memories of him are so hazy, so confused. I can't even properly remember what he looked like, his face is a complete blank. I think I deliberately shut it out as it was so painful to remember. I do recall a stranger once standing in the kitchen and Mam telling me that he was my dad and I should kiss him. He was very tall and smelled funny and I didn't want to, so he told me not to bother as he liked boys better anyway.'

'Oh, Lynda, what a thing to say.'

Lynda blinked, as if even after all this time the tears were still stuck at the backs of her eyes. She gave a resigned shrug. 'He was in the Merchant Navy, so of course he'd prefer boys. Jake was always his favourite. I tried hard to make him like me but never felt confident that I'd succeeded. Then when he stopped coming home, I was quite certain it was my fault. I would sit at the parlour window for hours on end, afraid to move in case he suddenly appeared and I missed the moment.'

Lynda remembered her mother explaining that it was because of the war, that he was away fighting the enemy. When hostilities finally ended she'd excitedly expected things to return to normal, to be as they once were when she'd been seven and the war just beginning. Every night she'd include him in her prayers and try desperately to be a good girl, like when she wanted Father Christmas to bring her presents. But nothing she did made the slightest difference.

Some of her friends' fathers hadn't come home from the war either and finally Lynda had plucked up the courage to ask, 'Is Dad dead?' dreading her mother's answer.

'No, love, he came back from the war fit and well. The truth is, he doesn't care about us any more. I expect he's got himself a new wife and children by now.'

That was a day Lynda would ever remember: the day her innocence and her faith in fathers, in men generally, was destroyed for ever. The world became a less safe, less secure place after that.

'Is it my fault, Mummy? Was I too naughty? Did I do something wrong to make him go away?' she'd sobbed, but her mother had hugged her tight and denied any such thing.

'Course not, love. It's not your fault at all, it's his, the dirty bastard. Pardon my French.'

Lynda knew it had been hard for her mother with little money coming in and two young children to support. Divorce was disapproved of, seen almost as a sin, although there was plenty of it going on following hasty wartime marriages.

She remembered being a rather solitary child with a tendency to depression yet perversely fond of showing off, probably in a desire to be noticed. It wasn't that Betty didn't love her but having to carry out the roles of both parents, being bread winner as well as nurturer, she was often too tired to play games with her children and have fun.

Lynda had partly resented this and yet was deeply protective of her mother, always feeling she should understand why this dreadful thing had happened to them, but never quite managing to do so.

With Jake being six years younger and missing his father badly, he had suffered even more. There had been the bed wetting, the insomnia and his temper tantrums for Mam to deal with on top of working full time on the market. No wonder she was always exhausted.

Yet they had survived, and Lynda really didn't know why these old issues were dwelling so much on her mind today. Perhaps it was seeing Judy's valiant attempts to cover up her own unhappiness.

'Mam's mistake was that she refused to talk about Dad, wouldn't even let us see him. If she had, then I'm sure it would have been much less painful for us both. If Tom and Ruth still had regular contact with their father, they'd be perfectly happy, even if you did split up.'

'I never said anything about us splitting up,' Judy said, a slight edge to her tone.

'No, course you didn't. Sorry!'

There was a silence, one that stretched out between the two old friends for several long seconds until Lynda gave an expressive little shrug. 'I just care about you, Jude, that's all.'

The frozen look thawed a little. 'I know you do, but I'm all right, really I am. Marriage isn't all frosted icing and moonlight dinners, you have to work at it. Like life, most of it is fairly dull and boring.'

'But . . .'

Judy raised one forbidding eyebrow. 'Have another sandwich. I'll listen to no more lectures or advice, however warmly offered. What will you wear tonight? Where is Terry taking you?' And the two young women retreated into a far safer discussion about the dance, the band, what Lynda would wear and whether she was too old to adopt the current fashion for hooped petticoats.

5

Judy

Have dinner ready. Plan ahead to prepare a delicious meal for his return from work and see that there are fresh flowers on the table. Wear your prettiest dress, perhaps put a ribbon in your hair, and of course touch up your make-up and refresh your lipstick. Do remember to smile and welcome him home. Let him know that you have been thinking about him all day.

Judy could recall every word of the article in the magazine, even without re-reading it. She pushed it under a cushion, tweaking at her shirt and slacks with frantic fingers as she glanced anxiously at the kitchen clock. She might just have time to change, if she was lucky. A quick wash and brush-up would have to do. She rarely wore make-up, didn't much care for it, much to Sam's continual disappointment.

Judy groaned. Oh, but why hadn't she washed her hair this morning? There certainly wasn't time to do it now, and she'd just wasted ten precious minutes rubbing cerulean blue oil paint out of her fringe. As a result she stank of turpentine instead of Evening in Paris.

It served her right if she was in a dreadful rush. Her concern for Betty had made her late enough but then she'd exacerbated the problem by spending far too long chatting to Lynda. Worse, this afternoon she'd taken it into her head to start painting a still life of the chrysanthemums while they were still fresh, enraptured by the idea to lay one glorious golden globe beside a brilliant blue glass. Fatal! Once she became engrossed in her painting every other consideration went right out of her head.

Why had she allowed herself to be so stupid when she knew there were a score of jobs still waiting to be done, ironing Sam's shirts for a start? He liked to wear a clean one every day. Perhaps it was to prove, to herself at least, that Lynda was wrong in implying Sam was in control of her life, and that she could do as she pleased.

But where was the point in such defiance if, in the hour before he was due home, she was running around sweeping up crumbs and plumping cushions, cooking with one hand and tidying with the other as if she were a naughty schoolgirl afraid of incurring the wrath of the headmaster?

Maybe Lynda was right, after all, and her marriage was a total disaster. Perhaps, Judy thought, she should have concentrated on her dream to become a famous artist instead of allowing herself to be overwhelmed by Sam's indisputable charms?

Oh, but then she wouldn't have had her lovely children and Judy simply couldn't imagine life without them. They were her reason for living. Her children were the best things that had ever happened to her, the very core of her existence. More prosaically, they were also the reason she put up with this far from perfect marriage.

But where was the point in chewing over the old bones of her life? Her decisions had been made long ago. She'd fallen headlong in love with Sam Beckett and, for better or worse, had married him within months of meeting him at just eighteen. He'd reminded her so much of her own father, since they were both soldiers, except that Sam wasn't a regular and had offered her a home and stability, something she hadn't known as a child constantly moving to different barracks. The idea of being in one place, able to put down roots and make proper friends had seemed like heaven, even if it was a scruffy old market.

She'd also been three months pregnant with Ruth at the time.

How young and foolish she'd been. How naïve! Still believing in love at first sight, fairy tales and happy endings.

She caught a glimpse of herself in the mirror over the tiled fireplace, at the tired face and the weary resignation in those eyes that Sam had once called a patch of blue heaven, and shivered.

'Mum, is something burning?'

'Oh, drat! Ruth, do please go and wash your hands and face. Daddy will be home any minute.'

Judy flung open the oven door and gazed in dismay at the singed crust of the steak and onion pie, flapping away the hot smoke as she hastily turned off the gas, grabbed an oven cloth and flung the pie dish on to the draining board. Don't panic, she told herself, heart fluttering nonetheless. If she cut off the charred edges and smothered it with gravy he'd hardly notice. You could cover a lot of sins with sufficient gravy, so long as it was tasty. Sadly, hers had a tendency to break out in lumps at the last moment.

'Ugh!' Ruth, increasingly critical of her mother, stood condemningly at her elbow. 'I think you've really done it this time, Mum. Dad won't be pleased.'

Judy wanted to reply that Dad could take a long jump, but she was again recalling the words of the Good Wives Guide: *Remember he is the master of the house and as such will exercise his will with fairness. A good wife will always know her place.*

Sam may well consider himself to be master but when had he ever been fair? Oh, she knew her place right enough, a long way down the list when compared to the other women in her husband's life, of which she dutifully feigned ignorance.

'I love *you*, Poppet, not them,' he had blithely remarked when, in the early days of their marriage, she had ventured to protest. 'Chasing a bit of skirt adds a touch of spice to life and does no harm to us at all.'

Judy had been desperately upset by his betrayal in those innocent days of her youth, but nowadays Sam's fondness for women troubled her scarcely at all. She'd grown accustomed to his philandering, accepted it as an inevitable part of his character. She knew that he would never leave her. Sam needed the stability of a solid home life every bit as much as she did, and he loved his children, of course.

Judy cut and scraped away the blackened parts of the offending crust, turned down the gas then pushed the pie back in the oven to keep warm along with a dish of mashed potatoes and one of carrots.

'I've just got time to change, if I hurry. Set the table for me please, love. Tom, put those soldiers away. At once, if you please and help your sister! Yes, you do know how to lay a table. You can fetch the knives and forks, and spoons for the rice pudding,' which thankfully she hadn't burnt. 'You know how Daddy likes things to be just so when he gets home. Where is your tie, Tom? No, don't argue, just find it and put it on.'

Children are such little treasures. He will want to see them looking their best.

'Ruth, remember to stir the gravy occasionally. It's all ready but I don't want it to go into lumps when I'm not looking.'

'Daddy says I make the best gravy,' said the self-confident nine year old. 'I'm not a child, Mum.'

'Of course you aren't, except to me, of course. You will always be my precious baby.'

Judy dropped a kiss on her daughter's brow, trying not to be hurt when she wiped it quickly away. 'If Daddy arrives while I'm upstairs pour him a beer and whatever you do, *don't let him see that pie*! It looks oddly naked without its crimped edging.'

It seemed wicked that she should ask her children to aid and abet her in these little deceptions, but one had to survive as best one could. Both were only too aware that their father was not an easy man to live with, being an ex-POW with an unpredictable temper. Ruth was very like him in many ways, so full of herself and rather headstrong, tending to take his side since Sam spoiled her dreadfully. She also had the same light brown hair and freckles.

But these reflections weren't getting her anywhere. She really must hurry and change.

In her bedroom Judy quickly splashed cold water on her face, ran a comb through her dark, unruly hair and added a dab of pale pink lipstick. One had to use every defence . . .

A wife's duty is to show interest in her husband, to lift his spirits after a long hard day. Learn to listen and be attentive to his needs.

Oh, and she would, she really would be far more attentive this evening. She wouldn't fall asleep in the chair or lose herself in a book. She'd fetch his slippers and the paper, plump up the cushions and, as the article instructed, speak in a soothing and pleasant voice as she asked him to tell her all about his day which he spent selling nails and screws in his ironmongery shop. Not a particularly fascinating environment and he rarely wanted to talk at all. Sometimes they'd sit in silence for hours on end.

But despite his failings, Judy still loved him, still needed him. Didn't she? Overwhelmed suddenly by tiredness after all her rushing around, she slipped out of her grubby shirt and slacks and lay down on the bed with a sigh, trying to ensure that she didn't crease the green silk counterpane or Sam would complain.

Not that Lynda would approve of the magazine's advice, Judy thought, smiling wryly as she recalled how her friend had urged her to start putting her own interests first, such as taking her painting more seriously. They'd very nearly quarrelled over that, which was most unusual for them.

Of course, it was Judy's own fault if Lynda had overstepped the bounds of their friendship by feeling compelled to make such a remark. She'd made the mistake of saying she had to dash back home to rush round with the vacuum cleaner, pick up the kids and slave over a hot stove. Lynda would rather be found naked in a snow storm than be seen waiting on a man. More like her mother than she cared to admit.

Nevertheless, her friend's words had brought a surge of rebellion soaring through Judy's veins, as if she might take it into her head to walk out of a kitchen which at times felt more like a prison than a home, grasp life with both hands and do something totally different and exciting. A heady thought which even now lingered beguilingly in her head.

Judy was only too aware that she hadn't been entirely honest in saying Sam encouraged her in her hobby. He tolerated her painting only so far as it didn't conflict with his own needs, so perhaps Lynda did have a point.

And it would be fun to try to sell her pictures on the market. Judy wouldn't have the time to go every day, naturally, but Wednesdays and Fridays when the farmers and craft people attended wouldn't impinge too much on her housewifely duties, surely? It might also provide her with a small income of her own, which would at least off-set the expense of her paints and canvasses if nothing else.

Maybe she'd look into the costs involved, tentatively broach the idea with Sam. If he was in a good mood she might even mention it this evening.

Judy was instantly overwhelmed by a sense of deep despair, knowing this to be a hopeless dream. Discussing money with Sam was an impossible exercise. He would never tolerate the idea of an independent wife working beside him on the market. He'd see it as some sort of failure on his part, as if he couldn't afford to keep her, as if it made him appear less than a man.

Judy sat up to stare bleakly at her own face in the dressing-table mirror, recognising the all-too-familiar expression of hope-lessness, the pale skin stretched far too tightly over high cheekbones, seeming even more translucent and delicate than usual. Was life passing her by? Was she growing old and missing valuable opportunities?

She noted that the shadows beneath her blue eyes were almost purple and wondered why she even listened to Lynda. Her dear, well-meaning friend dripped dangerous rebellious thoughts into her head which did her no good at all.

Judy picked up the hair brush and began to sweep it slowly through her tangle of dark curls, desperately trying to tame them to the kind of sensible bob Sam approved of, while her mind drifted back to the chrysanthemum still life. The shadows weren't deep enough. The picture was too flat, still needing much more work while the paint was wet. But where was the point in spending hours on the task if it was to moulder for ever in the attic, unseen and unjudged along with all the rest of her efforts?

Surely there must be some way to get round Sam?

The front door banged and giving a little gasp of dismay Judy was jolted from her musings. She quickly pulled on a straight black skirt and pink jumper, slipped her feet into the pointy-toed stilettos that Sam insisted she wear, and flew down the stairs.

The table was set, and, despite instructions to the contrary, Ruth had placed the pie in the centre. It looked even worse than she remembered. Tom had spilled the precious gravy on the blue checked tablecloth and Sam's face looked like thunder. Judy reluctantly shelved the remnants of her dream and adopted a conciliatory smile.

6

Betty

Betty had at last abandoned the sofa and was on her way back to the flower stall to help Lynda pack up for the day. Despite having a blinding headache and still feeling most peculiar, she was resolutely determined not to be bullied by Ewan Hemley as she had been in the past. And she most certainly had no intention of cooking him lunch, not this Sunday, nor at any other time. She'd done all the kow-towing to the likes of that piece of muck.

Turning the corner of the market hall Betty skidded on a cabbage leaf, partly due to the fact she was still unsteady on her feet and stopped to give Barry Holmes a piece of her mind for his untidiness. Betty Hemley may not be the tidiest person in the world herself but she hated mess in others.

Barry looked up from packing cauliflowers, deeply apologetic. 'Sorry, love. I haven't had a minute to sweep up today.'

'Well, see that you do, afore someone breaks their neck.'

She spotted Patsy Bowman on her way to her millinery course and paused to ask the girl how she was getting on with it.

'It's going great,' Patsy said. 'Thanks for asking, Mrs Hemley.'

What a problem Patsy had been when she'd first appeared on the market with not a good word coming out of her cheeky mouth, and now look at her. She'd transformed the Higginsons' hat stall and was going steady with one of the Bertalone boys. It gave a body hope for the future to see young people turn out so well. Betty wished, not for the first time, that her own lovely Lynda would settle down and find a nice young man, if such a creature existed who could cope with the girl's moods.

She could see Lynda now, surrounded by a glorious array of flowers, chatting away to a customer. It was worth all the pain and hard work she'd been forced to endure over the years to see her daughter smiling and happy.

But then she was confronted with the less edifying sight of her son in the grip of the local constabulary. Constable Nuttall had Jake by the collar and, seeing Betty, stopped before her with a sad shake of his head.

'This lad of yours can't go on like this, Betty. He's not a nipper any more who I can clip round the ear. He's a grown lad, nearly a man.'

Betty's heart sank. She couldn't take any more trouble, not today. She really couldn't. 'What is it this time?'

'Nowt! I were doing nowt!' Jake protested, as he always did.

'I'm asking Constable Nuttall, not you, lad. Well?'

'Aye,' Bill Nuttall agreed. 'She's talking to the organ grinder not the monkey. Same as last time, Betty love: loitering with intent is the official word for it. In other words casing one of them big doctor's houses on John Street, clearly with the intention of breaking in. If Jake and his mates didn't have burglary on their evil little minds, then I'm a Dutchman.'

Jake snorted. 'And I always thought you come from Bolton.'

'Less of your lip, son. You're in enough trouble already.'

Betty shook her head in despair. 'What am I to do with him, Bill? He's beyond my control, never does a thing I tell him.'

'Nay, don't say that, lass, or I'll have to take him in, come what may. He could end up at one of them Borstal places. Not good.'

Jake snorted with derision. 'Be cool, man. I'm innocent, right?'

Constable Nuttall grasped the lad's collar tighter still, pulling him up close so that they were almost nose to nose. 'You're a pain in the backside, lad, that's what you are. One more clever remark and you'll be viewing your miserable little life from the inside of a police cell. So this is what you have to do if you're going to escape that horrible fate. Get yourself some honest employment, find some new friends, and listen to your ma. Got it?'

'Get knotted!

'Right, that's it. You're—'

Betty hastily intervened. 'No, no, don't say it, Bill, I beg you. Give him another chance, please. He's not a bad lad, not really, just a bit mixed up.'

'Well get him unmixed and straighten him out. Fast!'

'I will, I will. I'll see he gets a good talking to. He's doing some deliveries for me at the moment so's I can keep an eye on him. But he's looking for a better job, aren't you, son?'

'Yeah, that tin can you call a van is falling apart, Ma. I'm gonna get me a job with proper wheels, and big bucks. I need to work for the kind of cool customer who appreciates my particular skills.'

'Which are what exactly?'

Seeing Constable Nuttall's look of disbelief, and his amusement at her son's idiotic lingo, Betty desperately intervened before Jake could make things any worse for himself.

'Don't worry, Bill, I'll see he knuckles down to some real work. It won't happen again, I swear it.'

There was a long pause while the policeman considered, long enough for the cynical smile to slide from Jake's face.

Constable Nuttall scowled at the lad through narrowed eyes. 'Don't think for one minute that I'm letting you off the hook because I've gone soft. I like your mam. We go back a long way, her and me, to the war, so you can thank your lucky stars for that bit of history between us. She's champion is our Betty. You don't know how lucky you are to have her for a mother and you'd do well, son, to hearken to what she tells you instead of turning yourself into a character from one of them daft American filums, or it'll be the magistrate who doles out the orders next. Got that?'

This time Jake said nothing.

'Got it?'

He gave a mumble that might have passed for agreement.

The constable released the boy's collar with reluctance. 'Good. At least we're both singing from the same song sheet now. Watch him like a hawk, Betty. He's living on borrowed time.' And to

Jake, 'This is your last warning, understand?' Whereupon he left Betty to grasp her recalcitrant son by the ear and after giving him a furious shake, drag him off home, oblivious to his loud protests.

Chuckling to himself Constable Bill hooked his thumbs in his breast pockets and went about his business, content that he'd dealt with the matter fairly but firmly. Whether young Jake was capable of turning over a new leaf was really up to him. Only time would tell. But he'd be watching and waiting, just in case he didn't.

Later that same evening Betty was still worrying over the problem of her ex-husband when Lynda came sailing in, her pretty face wreathed in smiles and the kind of bounce to her walk that warmed Betty's heart.

'Had a good time, love?'

'Not bad, not bad at all. Terry is really quite sweet when he gets over his shyness, but how about you? Are you feeling any better? I feel awful leaving you here all on your tod all evening.'

'I wasn't on me tod. Queenie has kept me company.' Betty indicated the cat, curled peacefully on her lap and purring like a small motor.

Lynda came to sit next to her mother, enveloping her in a big hug. 'How do you feel now?'

'All the better for seeing you. I'll put t'kettle on and make us a nice cuppa.'

'No, you stay right where you are. I'll do the honours tonight. We don't want to disturb Queenie unnecessarily.' Lynda tickled the cat, chuckling as it stretched out its chin for more petting. 'Or would you prefer cocoa?'

'Eeh, that'd be grand.'

Mother and daughter were sitting contentedly together sipping steaming hot cocoa and nibbling Garibaldi biscuits, Lynda idly chatting about the dance and catching up on gossip when she suddenly spotted the roses lying on the floor under the table. Jumping to her feet she went to pick them up.

'What are these doing here? These must be the yellow roses I sold to that tall untidy sort of bloke. Why have you got them? And what are they doing under our table, all wilted?'

Betty felt a roaring in her ears. Dear heaven, why hadn't she remembered chucking the damn roses on the table and seeing them fall? Now what could she say? If she told Lynda the truth about who the stranger really was, she might get all excited and want to see him. She'd certainly want to know why her father had called after all this time, what he wanted, and if he was coming again. Oh, it could all get very tricky.

'He was an old friend who decided to look me up,' Betty fabricated. 'Haven't seen him since he was billeted in Manchester during the war.'

'Really? Do I know him? I thought there was something familiar about him.'

'No, love, I don't see why you would know him.' Betty crossed her fingers and sent up a silent prayer for forgiveness over her deception.

Lynda was frowning. 'But that doesn't explain why the roses were on the floor?'

Betty could feel the colour rising in her cheeks as she avoided Lynda's penetrating gaze. 'I think I must have come over all funny peculiar again. It was the surprise at seeing him after all these years, I suppose. We got talking about old times and I clean forgot all about them. I didn't much care for him being here, to tell the truth, so got rid of him as fast as I could. Then I forgot about them.'

'Even so, it's not like you to treat flowers so badly. Are you still feeling peculiar? Do you need a doctor?'

'No, course I don't. I'm fine and dandy.'

Betty was saved from further questioning by the arrival of her son. Jake flung himself into the small house rather like a tornado might blast its way through town, scattering jacket, shoes and Slim-Jim tie before slumping in a chair and propping his stockinged feet up on the fender. There was a hole in one toe, Betty noticed, making a mental note to darn it.

'I'll have one of those if you haven't supped the pot dry,' he said, issuing the statement rather like a command.

'It's cocoa, not tea, and you can get it yourself,' Lynda tartly informed her brother. 'I'm off to bed. You too, Mam, you look all in and I don't want you waiting on this useless layabout. I know what you're like, you'll be buttering bread and making him chip butties at midnight if I don't watch you.'

'He's my son, who else would look after him if I don't?'

'Who indeed?' Lynda dryly remarked, and returning her gaze to her young brother asked what he'd been up to that evening.

'Nowt!'

'That doesn't sound very likely, knowing you.'

'Cut the gas, you're allus getting at me,' Jake protested.

'And you can cut this stupid hot-rod slang. I hate it, and you don't even have a car.'

Jake smirked. 'I'm working on that, and me mates certainly do. We've been burning rubber down on the rec. I'm not a kid you can boss about any more. I'm nineteen for goodness sake, so lay off, will you?'

'Someone has to look out for you.'

'I don't need two bloody mothers, ta very much.'

Betty only half listened to their banter, with which she was all too familiar. Jake had always been a worry to her and she feared that he never would free himself of the bad company he'd got himself tied up with. But she'd done her best and he didn't take kindly to her continued fussing, as he called it. Sometimes her nagging made him worse, not better. He'd suffered badly from not having a father around, a steady hand to guide him. Not that Ewan could ever be accused of having one of those.

Jake had just turned five when they'd separated back in 1943. As a small boy he'd worshipped his dad and felt his loss keenly, sometimes shouting at Betty in a childish temper that it was all her fault for making his daddy leave. She rather thought he still blamed her to this day. Betty remembered him clinging to a grubby bit of blanket for years, stuffing it in his mouth whenever he went to sleep.

As he got older he'd grown boisterous and aggressive, insisting that he was the man of the house and could do as he pleased. And there was a period as an adolescent when he'd become obsessed with wanting to know where Ewan was, had kept on asking questions and somehow turned against her even more when she couldn't supply the answers he wanted.

'Are you sure you're all right, Mam?'

Betty came out of her reverie with a jerk, finding Lynda studying her with concern. 'Sorry, I was miles away. What were you saying, love?'

'That you still look a bit peaky to me. There's nothing else worrying you, is there, Mam?'

'Why would there be?' Betty was on her feet in a second, anxious to avoid too close an inspection from her daughter. 'You're right though, I am tired, so I'm off up them apples and pears to me bed. You youngsters see you lock up properly, back and front.'

'Don't worry. Jake can do that while I put these roses in water, then I'll be up myself,' Lynda said.

The decision seemed to have been made. One look at her troubled son and Betty just didn't have the heart to tell him that only hours before his father had occupied that very same chair. Nor did she have the energy for that 'little talk' she'd promised Constable Nuttall she'd give her erring son. Tomorrow was soon enough. She'd had just about enough for one day.

As for Ewan Hemley, she would make sure that none of them were at home on Sunday when he called. Betty hoped and prayed that when he found the door locked and bolted against him with no answer to his knock, he would think better of it and go away for good.

7

Betty

Betty was back at her stall bright and early the next morning, happily setting out her flower buckets, filling them with red and pink gladioli, a glorious array of dahlias and great bunches of michaelmas daisies. She made up a bouquet of her favourite brick-red chrysanthemums which were surely for love, together with dark blue-veined veronica for fidelity, and added a few sprigs of fragrant jasmine for elegance and grace.

And while she worked, a plan formed in her mind on how to deal with the problem of her ex-husband. Betty was now even more determined that none of them would be at home when Ewan called on Sunday. It really didn't matter where they went so long as all three of them were out of the house. She meant to put this plan into effect just as soon as Lynda joined her later.

She set down the duck board which kept the damp of the hard pavement from her booted feet. Lynda hadn't scrubbed and swept it clean enough to her liking from the day before, a point she'd remind her daughter of when she got the chance. Oh, but the girl was a hard worker, and Jake wasn't a bad lad, not really, she told herself, as mothers do.

She'd given him a bit of a lecture over breakfast, since she didn't have to dash off this morning to Smithfield wholesale market, about this tendency he had for getting into mischief. Betty had made it very clear that one more step on the wrong side of the law and she'd leave him to sink in his own mire.

'You listen to what Constable Nuttall says, son, because this is your last chance,' she'd warned.

Jake had avoided answering by stuffing his mouth with corn-
flakes but then Betty had been careful not to antagonise her son
too much. She could have told him that he was taking after his
father, that if he carried on along this road then he too would end
up spending half his life in t'clink, but that would mean revealing
the kind of truths she'd spent all of *her* life protecting him from.

The lad would sort himself out, given time, and although as
he'd headed out the door he'd mumbled that he still intended
going out with his mates that night, some of her words must
have stuck because he'd promised to be home at a decent hour
and not to get into any more bother.

Betty could only hope that he'd keep that promise.

Now she opened up her folding chair and settled herself to
the pleasing occupation of observing people. There was nothing
Betty enjoyed more than indulging in her favourite sport of trying
to assess folk, to guess and sometimes cheekily enquire who a
particular gift of flowers was for, and speculate on the true nature
of their relationship.

Right now she could see Sam Beckett chatting to that Fran
Poulson. No better than she should be that lass. God knows what
she'd got up to when she went missing for months on end.
Rumour had it she'd been earning a living down under the arches
with that prossy Maureen. Not that you'd think so to listen to
her mother Big Molly talk, who thought the sun shone out of
her elder daughter's backside.

Betty's lip curled with disapproval as she watched the girl pat
her bleached blond curls and stick her breast out in that too-tight
sweater. Sam Beckett wasn't above enjoying the show. Why young
Judy put up with him Betty couldn't imagine. She'd put rat poison
in his soup if he was her husband. That would soon cool his ardour.

Something not very nice was undoubtedly being hatched
between the pair of them, or she wasn't Betty Hemley, a shrewd
judge of character if ever there was one. Generally speaking her
guesses were uncannily accurate, although with some customers
it was more difficult and Betty knew she could at times be wildly
off the mark.

Leo Catlow, for instance, was one who fell into the more enig-matic category, notoriously difficult to assess. Smiling graciously as he requested his usual bouquet Betty pretended to misun-derstand. 'Are these for the wife then?'

A slight puckering of the brow between a pair of penetrating dark brown eyes. 'For my mother, Betty. I always visit my parents every month around this time, as you well know.'

'I do, aye. And they're enjoying the sea air in Lytham St Anne's, I hope?'

'I hope so too. Put in some of the pinks. Mother does so love carnations.'

Betty selected a dozen, together with three reflex chrysan-themum blooms and the same number of euphorbia with their long, elegantly curved branches for focal interest, slipping in a few stems of leatherleaf fern as greenery before wrapping the bouquet carefully in pale green tissue. Whatever you might say about Leo Catlow as a husband, he certainly didn't stint when buying flowers for his mother.

Was that because he loved her, Betty wondered, or simply out of guilt because he didn't visit very often? This trip to the coast to see his parents was cancelled more often than not, which Betty surmised was probably because Leo and his father, old Jonty Catlow, never had got on.

'Retirement suiting your poor father, is it? He's much improved, I trust? The dear lady must be worried sick about him.'

'Yes, she must,' Leo said, handing over several notes without asking the price.

Tight-fisted he may not be but tight-lipped he most certainly was, Betty thought.

She'd dared to speculate at the time about how his dear mother would cope when Leo's father had suffered a massive heart attack and been forced to retire from the family business. Old Jonty Catlow had become increasingly irascible and in need of constant care, and everyone knew the poor lady was losing the thread. She tended to get confused, perhaps doing her shopping twice over, or boiling the kettle dry because she'd forgotten she was making herself a cup of tea. A fact which saddened all of Champion Street since Dulcie Catlow had been a familiar figure in her twin-set and pearls, and the kindest of ladies, always with a ready smile and time for a chat. Leo, however, had refused to accept there was anything wrong.

Betty, on the other hand, ventured to suggest that Leo and his wife had moved into the family house with his parents in order to keep a better eye on them. 'I expect your wife will be glad of the larger place, once the babbies start coming, and your mam will enjoy doing a bit of baby-sitting and dangling her grandchild on her knee.'

'You don't know everything, Betty Hemley, for all you may think you do,' he'd snapped. 'Some things are not always what they seem.'

Now what had he meant by that?

But then the old couple had upped and retired to the coast, leaving the family home to his son, something Jonty Catlow had sworn he'd never do.

Ever since that day Betty had adopted a little more caution with her questions, but she was feeling particularly perverse this morning. 'So what about the missus then? What sort of flowers does she get on this fine autumn day?'

Betty couldn't recall him ever buying his wife a similar bouquet. Word had it that the couple were at odds because Leo was desperate to start a family, and his wife had not yet managed to fulfil her duty of providing him with the much-needed son and heir to carry on the family business. How true this was Betty had no idea but she couldn't resist provoking him at every opportunity, good customer or no.

Truth to tell she didn't much care for Helen Catlow. Elegant and sophisticated she may be, exactly like jasmine, and every bit as fragrant and delicate, but the woman was a snob, far too full of herself. She always spoke in a low-pitched gentle voice as if she couldn't quite bring herself to address a lowly flower-seller.

'How about one of these pots of African violets, or a single long-stemmed rose for the good lady?'

He didn't rise to the bait, but then he never did. Leo Catlow was what you might call 'close'. He was a private person who liked to keep his opinions to himself. Quite good looking in a conventional sort of way with that strong square chin of his, ears flat to the side of his head, a long straight nose and wide mouth with even white teeth. And oh, those smouldering, deep-set brown eyes. Had she been twenty years younger Betty might have fancied him herself. As it was, he was simply a well-heeled customer, a man who, like others of his sex, neglected his wife and treated his parents with appalling callousness.

Betty counted out his change, giving him a sideways glance of condemnation as she did so. 'Happen the younger Mrs Catlow will be lucky next time, or when her birthday next comes round, eh?'

Leo moved his mouth into what might have passed for a smile but the gesture didn't reach those wonderfully enigmatic eyes, and with a brief nod of his fine regal head he was gone.

Betty chewed on her lip and tried to work it all out. Something wasn't quite right, but she couldn't put her finger on what it was.

In her somewhat prejudiced mind she couldn't find it in her heart to lay the blame for Leo Catlow's all too evident unhappiness on his wife. Maybe the woman spoke in a half-whisper because she was scared witless. Who knew what went on behind closed doors?

Nevertheless, as she watched him walk away, shoulders hunched, head down, she felt a stirring of unexpected pity for him. That wasn't normal behaviour for such a proud, upstanding bloke, a man who owned one of the largest warehouses on Salford Docks and was used to dishing out the orders and expecting to be obeyed. There were moments when he looked so sad Betty had the urge to put her arms around the man and give him a cuddle.

'Get away with you, Betty Hemley,' she sharply scolded herself. 'You must be going soft in your old age feeling sorry for one of the enemy! You'll be inviting that ex-husband of yours to come home for good next.'

8

Helen

Helen Catlow didn't normally frequent the Dog and Duck. With an air of disdain she ignored its brave show of window boxes stuffed with snapdragons, French marigolds and scarlet geraniums and saw only its smoke-blackened brick façade and cracked panes of glass.

A plump woman stood at the door, a basket of violets on her arm, no doubt in case some guilty soul should wish to buy a bunch as a sop to his wife for the state of his inebriation. Two Teddy Boys lounged against the wall, looking very much the worse for wear, and if the men Helen had seen staggering out were anything to go by the place must be heaving with drunks.

'Buy a bunch of violets, lovey?'

Helen shook her head. She'd seen the woman before, seated by her flower stall, but hadn't the faintest idea what her name was. 'No thank you.'

'Just suit your colouring, madam, they would. Nothing nicer than a rich purple next to porcelain skin, and violets are for faithfulness and modesty, which I'm sure you are, lovely young lady like yourself. Only sixpence a bunch.'

'Oh, very well. I suppose they might at least distract me from the smell of this dreadful place.'

Helen barely tolerated living in Champion Street with its jumble of stalls and Victorian iron-framed market hall, its stacks of orange boxes and rotting vegetables. It was an on-going grievance between herself and Leo that he wouldn't even consider living anywhere else but in the corner Victorian three-storey terraced house where he'd been born. The house might well have been in the family for generations and handy for the warehouse on Potato Wharf, but was highly *in*convenient so far as Helen was concerned.

Leo was a lovely caring man, a good husband and employer, sensitive to the feelings of others yet not afraid to take risks or to live on the edge were it necessary to do so. He was his own man, which was what she loved most about him. It was a pity therefore that with so many natural attributes and undoubted success at his fingertips, he consistently failed to appreciate how she, his own wife, might sometimes see things differently and have utterly diverse needs and desires in life.

As for public houses, they were, in Helen's view, strictly for layabouts and drunks. Leo might wax lyrical about the character of the place and the friendliness of the locals, but such places were anathema to her.

She hesitated before going in, hovering by the door as she tried to peer through the stained-glass panels in the hope of seeing him, protectively holding the violets to her nose. She'd hate to arrive early and have to hang around with the riff-raff.

Leo had insisted she meet him here for a bite of lunch because it was 'handy' after a long morning at the warehouse, allowing her no opportunity to refuse.

It wasn't difficult to guess the reason. Hadn't he offered, almost threatened, to make her an appointment with the doctor, adamant that if something were preventing her from conceiving then they should go together to find out the cause of the problem? It would be just like him to have made such an appointment, for Monday morning perhaps, and choose a very public place to tell her of this fact in order to avoid her making a fuss.

Why could he not be satisfied with their life as it was, or at least pour his energies into something far more worthwhile than children? He knew of her ambitions for him, her desire to see him succeed as a man of note in the community, with her by his side.

He'd been offered the opportunity to stand for parliament at the next by election but where was the point in her winning favours from the people who mattered, if he refused to take the offer seriously?

Despite the worries over the H-bomb and the Aldermaston marchers who of course were either student idealists or communists in Helen's view, Britain was rapidly recovering from its post-war malaise. People had money in their pockets at last. The credit squeeze was coming to an end and, as Harold Macmillan frequently reminded them, they'd never had it so good. Even the likes of Harold Wilson, himself from a relatively modest background, was being tipped as the man to watch for the future.

Helen dreamed of Leo joining this noble rank, though on the Conservative benches, naturally.

So why did Leo constantly harp on about his desire to become a father as if that were the only thing that mattered in life?

A man pushed by her, jostling her elbow. 'Sorry, love, are you going in?'

'No . . . at least . . . yes, I suppose I am.'

Helen pushed open the swing door, carefully avoiding the man who had spoken to her in that over-familiar way, and yet another ruffian who swayed past her out into the street, no doubt to be sick in the gutter. She neatly side-stepped both and strode purposefully into the lounge bar, expecting heads to turn as she did so. Helen did so love to make an entrance, priding herself on her innate sense of style, which generally succeeded in getting her noticed. She was not disappointed.

Today she was wearing a neat, pale blue costume with a pencil-slim skirt, teamed with a cashmere sweater of the same shade, and a divine hat with the widest brim imaginable.

She heard a snigger, a muffled comment about Ascot and something far more ribald. Really, these people! Simply no manners at all. Why did Leo have to be quite so egalitarian and insist on mixing with these peasants? The Midland Hotel would have been far more appropriate for their lunch, and the food so much better. She was hardly likely to be offered smoked salmon in this establishment, more likely one of Poulson's pies. Nor would they meet anyone here remotely useful for her husband's future in politics, yet more evidence of his stubbornness.

Helen spotted him the moment she entered. How could she not since Leo was the most handsome man in the room? So tall, so proud, energy emanating from him in almost tangible waves. He was leaning against the bar, one foot resting on the brass rail, a pint glass in his hand as he talked animatedly to a tight-knit group around him. Much to her annoyance he hadn't noticed *her* yet.

She only had to glance at him to feel that familiar curl of excitement, that gripping ache of need. It had been this way ever since they'd met during the war when he'd been a young flight lieutenant and she an innocent young girl determined to make her mark on the world, and striving to distance herself from a very ordinary family.

Her father, Jack Irwin, had been a cheese-maker, quite a successful one in his way since he owned his own business but then work, when he wasn't cavorting with other women, was all he ever thought about. All men ever thought about. Helen could never understand how her mother could have been content with so little. She'd died far too young, with hardly anything to show for her loyalty. Helen had hated cheese ever since.

The one thing in her father's favour was that he made sure his two daughters had a good start in life, paying for a private education for them both. Helen's older sister Harriet had failed to take full advantage of his generosity but Helen had decided quite early on that she deserved something far better than living behind a shop.

She'd known instantly that Leo Catlow was the man to further those ambitions, because he was so clearly going places. She'd recognised this fact instantly, and of course he possessed the added benefit of a secure family business.

There were some rough edges to him admittedly, but nothing that Helen couldn't smooth to suit her own needs. However, there were one or two problems, not least the fact that Leo attracted girls to him like moths to a flame.

Getting him to the altar had been like stepping through a minefield, with any number of other eager candidates lining up for the chance. But she'd won him in the end, by dint of clever manipulation, and by not being quite so prissy about sex as other girls. What man could resist attempting to crack her ice-cool exterior to savour the enticing heat within?

And what woman could resist Leo?

He hadn't noticed her today because he was happily engaged telling some amusing yarn to the most attractive woman in the place. Whenever she saw him talking to another woman Helen felt a sharp stab of jealousy, as she did now. It was really too bad of him. Why couldn't he behave? She hadn't the first idea who this woman was but she certainly intended to find out.

'Darling!' Marching right over, Helen lifted up her face to be kissed, firmly elbowing the woman out of orbit as she slipped between them and pressed herself possessively against her husband's chest.

Dutifully Leo kissed her on both cheeks, accompanying the gesture with a friendly slap on the back and a vigorous hug. Helen had taught him to kiss her in this polite way quite early on in their marriage, otherwise he was constantly ruining her lipstick. Besides, it was so continental and much more upper class. Unfortunately she never had cured him of this annoying habit of hugging her at the same time. So common! She pulled away from him, making a great show of straightening her hat to make the point.

'Darling, let me introduce you to Lynda Hemley. She works on the flower stall where I bought this delightful bouquet for Mother.'

Helen glanced briefly at the lavish bouquet lying on the bar counter and felt a further nudge of jealousy before sketching a smile which barely parted her lips. 'I'm afraid all you stallholders look alike to me. I find it far too confusing to try to remember everyone's name.' Then deliberately turning her back on the young woman without allowing her the opportunity to respond, blithely continued, 'Are we really staying here, darling, or should we move on to somewhere else?'

A flash of irritation, quickly stifled, flickered across Leo's face. 'I've ordered cottage pie for us both.'

'Oh dear! Soup or a sandwich would have been quite sufficient. Still, never mind. What more can one expect from a humble hostelry of this sort?' Helen straightened his tie which seemed to have worked itself loose. 'Shall we sit in the window corner then you can tell me what is so urgent that prevents us from escaping this dreadful place and slipping away early to the country?' As if she didn't know.

No doubt he'd eat the cottage pie at record speed before expecting her to rush off with him to Lytham St Anne's to see his parents. It utterly defeated her why he should always choose Saturday afternoon for this dratted duty visit when they could be at Ashton, their pretty country retreat in the Ribble Valley. He could just as easily take a day off during the week. Wasn't he the boss, for goodness sake, free to choose his own hours?

Helen considered that, as his wife, she had first call upon his time and deeply resented anything or anyone that deprived her of his company. Weekends were precious, and weren't married people meant to spend every moment they could together? A philosophy which Leo obstinately and frequently failed to understand.

She certainly intended to make her displeasure felt on this occasion. Having ruined her weekend completely she would do her utmost to ruin his.

Leo did not notice the malice in his wife's eye as he was still simmering over her condescending remarks to Lynda, damping down his ill humour with exemplary patience, a skill he had perfected over the years. But his response was brusque.

'You choose where you wish to sit. I'll join you in a moment.'

Much to her chagrin Helen was forced to seek out a table by herself while Leo lingered on for a few more quiet words with his very attractive friend. She felt mortified, the burn of jealousy inside her almost unbearable.

How she loathed to see that famous charm in action, to watch him flirt so outrageously with any woman who chanced to cross his path. She simply wouldn't tolerate it.

Helen despised the way Leo dismissed her concerns over his rapacious behaviour with other women, this claim of his that there was nothing more to it than natural friendliness. She hated his casual attitude towards matrimony, his cheerful bonhomie which he claimed to be perfectly innocent. Not for a moment did she believe the tale.

Perhaps she would cry off the Lytham trip and find something more interesting to do with her time. Revenge could be so sweet.

In the opposite corner of the bar, Betty was treating Jake and Lynda to their Saturday treat of steak and kidney pudding and chips, the basket of violets beside her on the bench seat, when she put forward her suggestion for a trip the following day. 'I thought happen we could go to Belle Vue, or else take the train to Blackpool or Morecambe. We haven't done that in years. It would be a real treat, and do us a world of good to get a bit of sun before winter sets in.' Jake looked as if she'd suggested he swing from a tree like a monkey.

'Why would I want to go to Belle Vue?' he scoffed, his handsome face twisting into an expression of absolutely incredulity. 'That's for school kids and old folk like you.'

'Oh, ta very much.'

'You know what I mean. It's Dullsville.'

'You used to like the boats on the lake, and the elephant rides.'

'When I were a kid,' Jake scorned. 'Not now I'm a grown man.'

And growing more and more like your father every day, Betty thought, a tremor of disquiet touching her like a breath of cold air. Not only did he have the same high-bridged bony nose, long face and hollow cheeks but he was every bit as pugnacious, as difficult and as awkward. She half glanced around, anxious suddenly that Ewan might be close by, watching them, waiting to pounce.

Jake pulled out a comb and began to groom his dark brown hair as he often did when upset, sweeping it back from his scowling brows. But he was still protesting, his voice high with outrage. 'Do you think I'm soft in the head, a goof or summat? If my mates saw me on an elephant I'd be the laughing stock of Manchester. You two do as you like, but count me out.'

'Put that greasy comb away, it's unhygienic at the table and eat yer dinner, for God's sake, afore it goes cold.'

Jake happily obliged, piling pudding, chips and mushy peas into his mouth all at once so that Betty had to avert her eyes. Where did he get his manners from?

'So where will you be tomorrow?' she persisted, wanting to be sure.

'Out!'

'That's good.' She was tempted to say more, to insist he stay out all day but that would only arouse his suspicions. Betty consoled herself with the thought that her son never had come home early in his life. Why would he change a life-time's habit tomorrow?

'What about you, Lynda love? We could go to Southport if you prefer. Some of the shops around Lord Street might well be open, even on a Sunday, since it's a holiday town. We could buy us-selves summat nice and have a slap-up meal.' Loving clothes as she did, Lynda had never refused a day's shopping in her life. Look at her now, pretty as a picture in a striped shirt-waist dress, winkle-picker shoes, and her lovely hair caught up in a pony-tail.

'Sounds great, Mam, but I've arranged to see Terry. He's taking me for a spin on his motor bike tomorrow afternoon, so I've invited him to share Sunday lunch with us first, before we go, if that's all right.'

'What?' Betty couldn't believe her ears. Everything was going wrong for her at the moment. 'You can't do that!'

'Why can't I? It's all arranged. You've never minded me bringing friends home before. Anyroad, it seemed only fair. He's providing the petrol, so I provide the food.'

'I think you mean *I* provide the food, don't you?'

Lynda smiled, 'Sorry. You know what I mean.'

'No, actually, I don't. I don't care to be taken advantage of. I've made other plans for tomorrow so you can unarrange it,' Betty almost shouted, desperation in her voice.

9

Betty and Helen

'By heck,' Winnie Holmes remarked, coming upon the three of them unexpectedly. 'It's like one of our Barry's boxing matches in here. You Hemleys in the red corner yelling yer heads off and getting all hot and bothered, and the Catlows in the blue about to murder each other, if I'm not mistaken. I'll bet you five bob she's trying to get out of going to visit his blessed mother.'

'What would you know about it?'

Lynda snorted. 'Because our Winnie is a nosy old cow. Well, you can stick your nose out of our trough. Bugger off!'

'Lynda!' Betty scolded, while Jake merely sniggered, thankful that someone else was in the wrong for a change.

'Can I have some apple crumble?'

'You can shut your face,' Betty told her son. 'You too, Winnie, me old mate. I may not approve of my daughter's choice of words but she does have a point.'

To Winnie it was like water off a duck's back. She merely sniffed and said, 'I'll take me Guinness over here then, if you don't mind, so's I can watch the entertainment. But if you need a referee, Barry'll be here himself in a minute.'

'Do you have to be so rude to people?' Leo demanded, when they were finally settled at a table which suited her needs.

Helen appeared shocked. 'I have never been rude to anyone in my life! But you can't expect me to actually enjoy coming in here. The place smells.'

'Of course it smells – of beer. It's a pub.' Leo loosened his tie, feeling it might choke him at any minute.

'Quite!' And folding her gloved hands Helen sat in rigid disapproval, making her disdain all too apparent as the barman placed two heaped plates before them. Leo fell upon the meal like a starving man, tucking in with gusto, while Helen watched him with undisguised distaste. Really, there were times when she wondered what kind of man she'd married.

'Aren't you even going to try it?' he asked her, through a mouthful of food.

Helen grimaced. 'I told you, I'm not hungry. I rarely eat anything at lunch time.'

'Dinner time. The folk in this pub call it dinner. They are not like your posh friends who nibble on a crustless cucumber sandwich and call it lunch.'

'Cucumber sandwiches are eaten at tea time, Leo, as you well know.'

'Oh, for God's sake, eat the damn food, Helen. It won't kill you and everyone is looking.'

'Please don't swear in my presence.' A flush appeared high on each cheek but Helen's innate fear of making an exhibition of herself compelled her to lift a fork and take a mouthful, although she did not remove her glove as she did so, almost as if the cutlery itself might be contaminated.

But while she outwardly obeyed him, she wanted to make Leo pay for bringing her here. It really was too humiliating. Not another soul in the place was even wearing a hat. That girl Lynda was sitting with her mother now and they seemed to be arguing. So common!

Helen recognised the older woman as being the one who owned the flower stall, the one who'd sold her the violets. Harmless enough, she supposed, and her apron was at least clean, but she was clearly none too bright otherwise she'd find something worthwhile to do with her life, wouldn't she? And there was no husband in evidence, so who knew what her background was? No wonder the daughter was such a shameless flirt. And the boy, her son presumably, looked something of a tearaway.

After several delicate mouthfuls and finding the pie really rather more tasty than she'd expected, Helen returned to their more accustomed point of conflict.

'So that little floosie you were talking to so eagerly just now, how come you know her so well? You certainly seemed most reluctant to leave her.'

Leo sighed in exasperation. 'I told you, I buy flowers from her mother Betty.' He nodded in the direction of their table, as if he too had been watching them. Transfixed by the girl's crossed legs, no doubt, which were long and shapely. 'And I wasn't in the least reluctant to leave her, I merely stayed to chat a little longer because you were so rude . . . so . . . offhand towards her.'

'I hope you didn't feel the need to apologise.'

'No, I merely had no wish to be quite so abrupt as you were, Helen. I felt I should at least allow the girl to finish what she was saying before you interrupted us.'

'Dear me, I'm sorry I disrupted your little tête-à-tête, I'm sure.'

'That's not what I meant, and you know it. She was telling me a rather sad tale about losing touch with her father when she was quite a young girl, and how it has badly affected her brother. Sent the lad a bit off the rails, apparently, but trusty Constable Nuttall is keeping a beady eye on him.'

'I should hope so. We want no trouble-makers on this street. You don't deny she's one of your floosies, then? Your latest *mistress*, I suppose.'

'I don't have a mistress. I have never had a mistress. I am content simply to have a lovely wife.' Leo was wearily asking himself, not for the first time, why he bothered. There were times when he thought he might as well acquire a mistress since he was presumed to be guilty of having one anyway. His fidelity and loyalty were neither recognised nor appreciated.

But how could he do that to Helen? Despite all her insecurities and flaws, he still cared about her and wanted to make their marriage work. He wanted a normal family life, was that so wrong?

Perhaps he didn't feel quite the white heat of their early passion, but he was her husband and would remain loyal and loving.

When they'd first met he'd been bowled over by her elegance, her serenity which was so utterly beguiling, and by her very evident fascination with himself. He'd found her intensity immensely flattering, her long thoughtful silences intriguing. She had fine blond hair cropped very short with a feathery fringe, and neatly trimmed eyebrows that winged upwards over cool clear grey eyes.

Once safely ensconced within the bounds of marriage the coolness had soon thawed and she'd proved to be an ardent and passionate lover. Even now, after eleven years, she was always eager for sex, making it abundantly clear that she was readily available. Almost too available. As a young newly wedded husband her response had thrilled and excited him. Now he found it very slightly disturbing and far from satisfying, in fact almost shallow and insincere. There were times when he would have enjoyed more mystery and have her play a little hard-to-get.

Marriage to Helen had seemed to offer peace and tranquillity. He'd hoped for warmth and affection, and the kind of family life he yearned for. Unfortunately it had turned out to be anything but tranquil, and with precious little in the way of affection. The reverse side of this delightfully robust sexual appetite was a cool and unemotional personality.

Leo had always sought to physically show his love for her with warm smiles, a touch to the cheek, a kiss on the lips, and huge bear hugs. None of this was ever forthcoming from Helen and, little by little, she had managed to curb this desire in him too, indicating that it was really rather childish on his part to need such demonstrative proof of her affection.

Helen seemed to see emotion as weakness, and the slightest conversation he might exchange with another woman as evidence of flirtation at the very least, and more likely adultery.

A crippling loneliness was creeping over him, as if by not being allowed to mar her lipstick or disturb her expensive coiffure, to touch or to hug her, he was becoming imprisoned in a cold and isolated shell. He was only allowed out when she needed him to satisfy these constant cravings of hers, this passion that could suddenly explode all over him, as if that was the only way she could prove how important he was to her.

Perhaps it might have been different if they'd been blessed with children but although Helen insisted she wanted them too, she kept putting off the moment for starting a family, and Leo was growing increasingly frustrated.

'If there's a problem let's get it looked at and sorted out,' he'd offered, more than once.

But she always resisted, refused even to see a doctor. 'There isn't a problem. I've only just turned thirty so where's the rush? I'm sure it will happen when the time is right.'

Leo was less sure, beginning to wonder if indeed it would be right to bring children into such a shaky marriage. He surely needed to somehow solve the problem of her terrible jealousy first.

Lynda was staring at her mother, fork poised mid-air in shocked surprise. It wasn't like Mam to be so adamant and difficult. Soft hearted to a fault where her children were concerned, she'd always been the sort to keep open house should any of their friends feel like popping in. 'I can't just break my promise to Terry, and let him down like that. It would be rude. What's got into you, Mam? Not having another of your funny turns, are you?'

'I just fancied a day out with me own family. Nowt wrong in that, is there?' A shiver rippled down Betty's spine, as if she heard the distant chuckle of her ex-husband enjoying her discomfiture.

Lynda's pretty mouth fell into its habitual sulk. 'Now you're making me feel guilty. Oh, Mam, I'm sorry, I really am, only it's all fixed up. It's one of those club outings, a sort of rally, and I've promised Terry faithfully I'll go with him. All the other guys will have their girl-friends with them and it wouldn't be fair to stand him up at the last minute. Besides, like I say, I've promised him a Sunday lunch. His mother's dead don't forget, and his dad's a dreadful cook so he's really looking forward to it.

Look, I'll do the cooking if you're still not feeling well, and we could go next Sunday to Southport instead. How would that do? As you quite rightly say, I do love Lord Street. And for once little brother here could make the effort to come with us. A real family outing, eh?' She dug him in the ribs. 'Couldn't you?'

'Next Sunday's no good,' Betty said, before Jake had time to do more than glower, difficult as that was through a mouthful of steak and kidney pudding.

'Why isn't it? What difference does it make?'

'Because I feel like a break *now*, not next week, that's why. I'd set me heart on us going out tomorrow,' Betty repeated, and once more glanced nervously about her.

'What's got into you at the moment? You're like a cat on hot bricks, constantly looking around as if you expect the devil himself to emerge like a puff of smoke out of the cobbles.'

'The demon king you mean,' Betty mumbled, before she could stop herself.

'What did you say?'

'Nowt! Just tell Terry Hall it's all off tomorrow. You're coming with me to Southport!'

'*Mam!* Stop this. I've said I'll cook the flamin' lunch. I really don't understand why . . .' Lynda stopped talking and her eyes narrowed with suspicion. 'This hasn't anything to do with that old friend of yours, has it? The one who brought you those roses? You haven't made plans for him to come with us tomorrow, have you?'

Jake made a retching sound at the back of his throat. 'Hells bells, I refuse to be seen out with me own mother and one of her boy-friends.'

'Don't talk daft, I don't have any boy-friends,' Betty sharply retorted. 'And no, I haven't planned anything of the sort, the very idea.'

'Who is he then? What's his name? Why do I feel as if I've met him bef— Oh, my God, it can't be!'

'What?' Jake said, momentarily putting down his knife and fork to watch the colour drain from his sister's face.

'It's him, isn't it?'

'Who? I don't know what you're talking about.'

'Yes you do. It's Ewan. It's me dad, isn't it?' Realisation was bringing excitement to Lynda's voice, in contrast to her earlier annoyance. 'That's why you want to rush us off to Southport tomorrow. He's coming to the house isn't he and you don't want us to meet him? That's it, isn't it? No, don't bother denying it, I can tell by the expression on your face that I'm right. And you weren't even going to tell us, were you? Oh, Mam, how could you be so cruel? Shame on you.'

And having heard all she needed, Winnie went back to her stall, well satisfied.

IO

Lynda and Helen

L ynda spent the rest of that Saturday afternoon looking for her father. The flower stall had been packed away for the weekend, what was left of the stock put into cold storage in the lock-up they rented at the back of Champion Street. She washed the duck boards and locked them away too, together with her mam's folding chair, baskets, buckets and pot plants.

Normally Lynda would be revelling in her freedom and going round the shops, to Lewis's or Kendals, trying on clothes and testing the make-up on the big cosmetic counters. She fancied one of those new chemise-style frocks with the low slung waistline and flounced skirt, one with a low V in the back. But instead she was filled with only one desire: to find Ewan Hemley, her father.

She couldn't believe her mother's attitude. They'd had a big row when they'd got back home after their Saturday dinner at the pub, with Lynda insisting that surely enough time had passed for her to at least act civilised towards him. Betty had yelled that hell would freeze over before she allowed that man ever to step over her doorstep again.

'It's only Sunday lunch, for God's sake! No one's asking you to sleep with him.'

'I should bloody hope not!' Betty had retorted, forgetting her disapproval of swearing.

Betty was feeling utterly desperate, blaming herself entirely for this mess. She should have moved them farther away, emigrated to Australia, anywhere but Manchester. If it weren't for her, Ewan would never have popped up like a bad smell out of the drains looking for them. 'Give that man an inch and he'll take a flaming mile!'

'Well, maybe you should at least have asked our opinion on the matter. We can't go on never being allowed to so much as mention his name, never seeing him or having the chance to talk things through. He's still our father, after all.'

'No he's not, we're divorced.'

At which point Jake had joined in the heated debate. '*You* divorced him. *We* were given no say in the matter.'

'You were too young to understand. You still are. You know nowt about it.'

There was nothing Jake hated more than being told he was too young or too stupid to understand, even if it was true. 'I know we have rights too, and when I'm being deprived of them.'

'Oh, for goodness sake, don't talk to me about bloody rights. What rights did *I* have when he was making all our lives a misery and nobody to help? Everything I've done has been for your benefit.' *Why* couldn't they see that?

'So you say, but you never even let me see him, never let me write to him. You said me dad had abandoned us, gone off with another woman, but I think you chucked him out.'

'Aye, well, you might be right there, son, and I might've had good reason.'

'But you won't say what it was. I don't even *know* him, me own dad.'

'Do you want me to box your ears, because you're not too old for a cluttering, no matter what Constable Nuttall might say to the contrary?'

'Mam, calm down!' Lynda hastily intervened, fearing the squabble might deteriorate into fisticuffs. 'Jake does have a point though. You've never allowed us to so much as mention Dad's name.'

Betty winced. 'Don't call him that.'

'I can quite understand that you weren't getting on and you did what you thought best at the time, but *we* should at least both be given a say in any decision made about him in the future. Have you considered that we might actually want to meet him at last?'

For a moment she thought her mother might be about to collapse, or explode with fury as her face went purple, then white to the lips. Lynda made her sit down, draw in deep breaths while she sent Jake scuttling to put the kettle on.

Only when Betty had a mug of strong sweet tea in her hands did Lynda begin, very gently, to press home her case, kneeling on the rug to cradle her mother's hands between her own.

'I'm twenty-five, Mam, twenty-six next month. Even Jake will be twenty soon, nearly a grown man. We don't need your protection any longer. We're not children any more and can look after ourselves.'

Betty gazed into her daughter's face and felt her entire world slipping away from her. She tried to speak calmly, to be reasonable and objective but a small sob escaped her throat as she said, 'You know nothing. You certainly don't know *him*. Listen to me, Lynda. He's a hard, selfish man, a complete wastrel. He took every penny I had, even broke your piggy-bank to put a bet on a horse. You don't know what he's like. I won't have him come anywhere near either one of you.'

'Don't upset yourself, Mam. We won't let him touch our money, not that we have much anyway.' They both instinctively glanced at the green rug under which their small savings were hidden, beneath a broken floorboard.

Panic rose in Betty, hot and sour. Was she going to be forced to tell them everything? Dear heaven but she hoped not. What would that do to Jake? 'Aye, but it's not just about money. There's other things too . . . things I don't like to talk about . . . things best forgotten. Just take my word for it, he's bad news.'

'What things?'

'All sorts of stuff that you won't remember, praise the Lord . . .'

Lynda was plumping up cushions, patting her mother on the shoulder, trying to make her lean back upon them and relax. 'There always is a lot of bad feeling left after a divorce, I can understand that, Mam, but you must stop fretting. It'll be all right. Look, I'll go and find him, he can't be far away, and we'll have him in to lunch in a sensible, civilised fashion.

'And it'll give us all a chance to talk things through as adults. I hope it will help Jake and me to get to know our father at last and make up our own minds about him. Where's the harm in that? You too will probably feel much better if things can be put on a better footing between us. Jake might even start forgiving you for messing up his life,' giving a little chuckle, as if to make light of her brother's neurosis.

'Oh, Lynda. Oh, love. I'm begging you not to do this.'

But Betty could tell by the obstinate expression on her daughter's face, by the way she smiled and patted her hand, that she was wasting her breath.

Ewan Hemley had won just by turning up. He would get his revenge, and all she could do was sit back and watch the tragedy unfold.

It was exactly the kind of Saturday Helen loathed. Taking tea with her in-laws in their boring little bungalow with lace doilies on every polished surface and the ubiquitous flight of ducks up the flock-papered wall. Even her own parents, living behind the cheese shop, hadn't been quite so predictable. Worse, she would be compelled to listen to her husband pandering to their every whim.

Determined to have him all to herself for once, Helen did her utmost to persuade Leo to cancel. 'Ring and say something has come up.'

'But it isn't true. Something hasn't come up, and Ma and Pa so look forward to my visit.'

'You've had a tiring week at the warehouse. You deserve a rest. We both do. We need some time together.' She leaned against him, sliding her hand down his inner thigh as he sat beside her in the driving seat of the Jag. 'We could be at Ashton in less than an hour. We need some time alone.'

Her voice was heavy with promise and yet all he could feel was sadness that she couldn't find it in her heart to care about his old parents. 'We'll go next weekend, I promise.'

Helen flounced back in her seat, her tone with a bitter edge to

it. 'You never can make time for me, only for work and those
floosies of yours. I suppose you're sleeping with that Lynda woman.'

Leo sighed. 'This isn't helping, Helen. I love only you. How
many times must I say it?'

He had a great urge to shake her but was far too much the
gentleman to do any such thing. Why did she always want things
her own way? Why couldn't she find some small sympathy, some
warmth and consideration for others in that cool, logical heart
of hers? Even her porcelain skin which he had once so admired,
bore an ice-like coldness. Did he really still love her, or was he
simply used to having her around? If only she would relax and
laugh a little then everything might be different between them.

'I don't think I shall come.'

He looked at her with infuriating patience. 'They would be
sorry if you didn't. They always like to see you.'

'No, they don't. Your mother will start dropping heavy hints
about my failure as a baby machine, and your father will endlessly
cross-question you over the business. I really can't stand it. Nor
would *you* care if I didn't come. It would give you the perfect
opportunity to call and see this Lynda person on your way home.'

'Stop it, Helen. You're becoming ridiculous. And what would
you do all on your own here for the entire day? Come with me,
darling. We'll walk on the sands, take a tram ride, perhaps stay
overnight and enjoy a leisurely drive home tomorrow. Stop off
for Sunday lunch at some tucked-away pub in the Ribble Valley.
It could be fun.'

'You think it *fun* to sleep in your mother's guest room with
those dreadful candlewick bedspreads, listening to your father
snoring through the paper-thin walls?'

In the end she'd been unable to get out of it. She simply
couldn't bear the thought of what Leo might get up to by himself,
even in Lytham St Anne's. Much safer if she go with him, and
grin and bear the dreaded in-laws, as always.

It certainly wasn't that she couldn't find some other way to
amuse herself over the weekend. With a husband like Leo you
had to learn to play the man at his own game. She'd decided

upon that little strategy at a very early stage in their marriage. As the song said, anything you can do, I can do better.

And if her first transgression had been out of a need for petty revenge, to her surprise Helen had discovered that no matter how much she loved Leo, a little excitement on the side really quite spiced up her life. It seemed to satisfy a deep craving within. Rather like reading *Peyton Place*, which she loved to do in quiet moments when no one was around.

Helen had more sense, however, than to allow these little treats with which she indulged herself to intrude upon their life together, nor to flaunt them in her husband's face. She was nothing if not discreet.

As Helen had predicted, they hadn't been in his parents' house five minutes before Leo's father was finding fault. Even before Dulcie had poured the Earl Grey from her silver teapot, Jonty was barking orders and questions at his son. Today he was interrogating Leo about the accounts, wanting to be sure that he was keeping the business up to scratch.

'I hope you're looking after the Kenyons, they're one of our oldest customers.'

'Of course I am, Pa.' Leo painstakingly and with immeasurable patience answered every question, trying to make allowances for his father, knowing how the state of his health had deteriorated, making him more irascible than ever.

Old John Catlow, Leo's grandfather, had started the distribution business back in the days of the industrial revolution by building the warehouse on Potato Wharf. Leo's own father Jonty had expanded it still further by adding a second depot, building it right in the heart of Salford Docks. He'd bought large delivery vans and acquired more accounts in the way of shipping companies who used the firm regularly, importing and exporting goods along the Manchester Ship Canal.

Jonty had lived for the business, spent every waking hour at the docks and, being quite unable to delegate, had never allowed his only son to take much of the load from him. He'd paid for this obstinacy with his health and had suffered two minor strokes and finally a heart attack which even he had been forced to take seriously. Yet he continued to be critical of anything and everything his son did.

'I hope you haven't lost the Whittaker account. You were slow making those deliveries last month.'

Leo frowned. 'There was a slight hiccup at the depot over the paperwork but how would you know about that, Pa?'

Jonty Catlow tapped his nose. 'Nothing slips by me. I make it my business to keep myself informed. I can still use a telephone to speak to those useless warehouse managers you insist on employing.'

'You really shouldn't be concerning yourself about such details,' Leo said, irritated almost beyond his patience.

'I'm still a major shareholder, I'll concern myself as much as I damn well choose, boy.'

'Pa, I'm not a boy and . . .'

Leo's mother, ever the pacifier, hastily intervened and attempted to change the subject. 'Do have some Battenburg cake, Leo, I bought it especially for you, knowing it's your favourite, dear. I'm sure you work far too hard, just as your father did, so you deserve a few treats. We'll go for a nice walk later, on the sands, to blow the cobwebs away. And what have you been up to recently, Helen? What good works are you involved with at the moment, I'm afraid I lose track.'

Helen stared at her mother-in-law with cold distaste, hating her composure, her security in the love of her son. 'As you do of everything these days, Dulcie.'

The older woman looked slightly startled and then gave a trilling little laugh. 'Well, I can't deny that none of us are getting any younger, are we? Our brains become rather tired, I dare say.'

'Assuming we had one in the first place,' Helen said.

'Ah, yes, I suppose you are right there too.'

'The clock is ticking for all of us, which is why we should take our family duties more seriously.' Jonty snapped, leaping to the defence of his wife.

Helen flushed, only too aware of her father-in-law's disapproval of her socialising and 'gadding about', as he called it, which in his opinion detracted from her main role which should be to provide his son with an heir.

Leo handed his plate to his mother. 'I think I will have another slice of Battenburg, it's delicious, Ma.'

'Oh good, yes it is, isn't it? Helen?'

Helen set down her half-eaten cake. 'No thank you. It's rather too sweet for me.'

In Helen's view, Dulcie was a rather silly woman with no education and fewer brains, always happy to do whatever her husband asked. Sitting there in her twin-set and pearls with her white hair curling neatly about her round smiling face she had never known a moment's worry in all of her sheltered, spoiled life, save for a couple of miscarriages before she had Leo, and what did they signify? Quiet and unassuming, sweetly compliant, she was adored by her husband and fussed over by her son *ad nauseum*.

Yet whenever her mother-in-law and she were alone Dulcie would rest a gentle hand upon Helen's arm and whisper, 'Any sign yet? I do hate to intrude upon your personal affairs, dear, but time is of the essence, is it not? How old are you now, dear, thirty-one, thirty-two?'

'No, thirty.'

And she would shake her head with deep sadness. 'It is so much more difficult to get pregnant once you are past thirty. I can confirm that from my own experience. I tried so hard for more children, as I'm sure you are trying.'

'It really doesn't trouble me in the slightest.'

'No dear, that is exactly the line to take,' accompanied by another comforting pat on the hand. 'Relax, and who knows, it could just happen. Better luck next month, I hope.'

Helen hated her.

11

Betty

There was no sign of the yellow roses when Ewan arrived in good time for his Sunday lunch. He knew better than to be late, of course, or to ask what she had done with her gift. But if there was one place Betty had never wished to see her ex-husband ever again, it was seated at the head of her table. When he made a move to do so, she quickly stopped him. 'Jake sits there, you can sit to one side, opposite our Lynda.'

'Righti-o, Betty love. Whatever you say.'

'Let's have matters clear from the start, shall we? I'm not your love and this is a one-off. You'll get Sunday lunch and nowt more. You eat up, see the kids like you wanted, then make yourself scarce. There won't be a repeat performance, not ever.'

'Mam, don't start,' Jake said, all too familiar with that sleeves-rolled-up tone of voice.

Lynda smiled brightly around the table in an effort to inject some warmth into the chilled atmosphere. 'This is nice, isn't it? The whole family together again after all this time.'

Ewan hadn't been difficult to find. He'd come wandering into the Dog and Duck late Saturday afternoon. Lynda was thrilled to at last have the opportunity to get to know her father but this was not at all how she'd planned it, with her mother sitting there all sour-faced and the pair of them replaying World War Two.

Guessing it was going to be a difficult meal she'd felt compelled to tell Terry not to come, which was a great shame. But she was still meeting him later to go with him on the biker's rally. She'd probably be glad of an excuse to escape by then. She'd wear her new plaid Capri pants which would make her bottom look all pert and sexy on the bike.

'It's certainly interesting to be here with you all,' Ewan dryly remarked. 'And I'm most grateful to be invited,' carefully avoiding a withering glance from Betty. 'Them Yorkshire puddings look spectacular. You've not lost your lightness of touch with the baking then?'

Betty didn't even trouble to answer this pathetic attempt at a compliment. She recalled too well how even on the morning he'd walked out on her, he'd casually remarked that he'd miss her cooking, particularly her Yorkshire puddings.

His eating habits had not improved over the years. He still chewed with his mouth open, and insisted on a slice of bread to mop up the gravy.

'It's too good to waste, Betty love.'

Betty sucked in her breath and made no comment as they all addressed themselves to savouring prime roast beef, no one quite willing to break the silence. It was Jake, naturally, who eventually fired the first shot.

'So why did you split then? And why have you never tried to contact us since?'

Ewan half glanced at Betty but by the tightness of her expression it was plain she had no intention of helping him out with that one. He cleared his throat. 'Why I left isn't really important, lad, not after all these years. As to why I didn't keep in touch, you'd need to speak to your mam about that. I did write, at first, but I doubt she showed you my letters. I certainly never got a reply.'

Jake's mouth fell open, revealing an unsightly amount of unchewed beef. He gulped, swallowing the mouthful whole before shouting across at his mother, 'You kept his letters from me? I don't believe it. It can't be true. You *knew* how much I wanted to see me dad. You *saw* how many pathetic attempts I made to write him a decent letter, young as I was, even sending him daft pictures of meself playing football just to make him proud.'

'I wrote too,' Lynda put in, her voice oddly strained and quiet.

Ewan leaned across the table and stroked her hand. 'I'm sure you did, chuck. I only wish I'd got them.' As one, three pairs of eyes swivelled in Betty's direction.

She got briskly to her feet. 'I'll fetch the pudding. It's apple pie, your favourite, Jake love.'

'I don't want it. I've lost me appetite.' He pushed his half-eaten meal away. 'I should've known I couldn't trust you, you stupid cow.'

'*Jake!*' Lynda scolded. 'There's no need to be rude.'

Betty blinked away the threat of tears. This was what she'd most dreaded: Ewan putting his side and she standing dry-mouthed, unable to explain or defend herself. But what could she say? How could she tell them what it had really been like living with this man? Why should she subject her lovely children to remembering all of that pain, thereby destroying years of effort on her part to help them forget?

But Jake wasn't done with her yet. 'Well, what've you got to say for yourself?'

'Nothing. I've nothing to say except I did what I thought was right.'

'*Right*? You thought it was right to deprive me of me own father?' He turned to Ewan. 'Did you leave of your own accord or did she ask you to go? Just tell me that.'

Ewan almost smiled. 'Things were a bit difficult at that time, it's true, but yes, Betty made it very clear that the marriage was over and I had to go.'

'You *bitch!*'

Jake was on his feet, fists clenched and Lynda, white faced and in something of a panic, was desperately trying to calm him down.

'Don't speak to Mam like that, Jake. Don't use such awful words, it's not right. Anyroad, he's here now. Let's all try to stay calm, shall we? Why don't you tell . . .' Lynda stumbled, wondering what to call him. A part of her wanted to call him Dad but she knew her mother wouldn't like that. 'Why don't you tell Ewan how well you did in football at school, how you nearly got picked for City? I'm sure he'd like to get to know a bit more about what you've been up to all these years.'

'Aye, true enough, I would. Manchester City, eh? That's summat, that is.'

'I didn't get bloody picked though,' Jake muttered, reluctantly resuming his seat and gazing mournfully at the food on his plate. He loved beef and Yorkshire pudding. Could he eat it without losing face? he wondered.

'Aye, but to be given the chance to try for a place is an achievement in itself, it really is.'

Jake preened himself before the praise. 'I suppose it *was* pretty cool – Dad,' and picking up his knife and fork, he got stuck in.

Hearing Jake use this word for the first time brought a jolt of shock like kilowatts of electricity running through Betty and she gripped the edge of the table in panic. What should she do? There must be some way to rid themselves of this man for good and all, but if so, she certainly didn't know what it was. Ewan, she noticed, was looking mighty pleased with himself, a smirk of pure satisfaction curling his lip. All she could think to do was to gather up the dirty plates and dash to the kitchen.

Lynda followed, hustling her brother to finish his dinner and helping to clear the table while Betty concentrated on breathing slowly and slicing the apple pie.

'Are you all right, Mam?'

Betty couldn't think of a thing to say. How might Lynda react if she said, 'Your dad's only being nice to you to make me mad. He only wants revenge for what I did to him and doesn't give a tinker's cuss about either of you two.' Would Lynda believe her? Not on your nelly. Nor would Jake. Listen to the stupid lad laughing at one of Ewan's sick jokes even now.

When Lynda brought the warmed pudding dishes, Betty said, 'How can I possibly be all right with that dreadful man sitting at my table looking like a cat what's swallowed the flaming cream, and our Jake attacking me like that.'

'I know it's hard but Jake has to be given the chance to sort things out in his own mind. You'll need to be patient with him, Mam, with both of us.'

'Patient? You think I don't understand what it means to bite your lip and be patient?' Betty made a sound of disgust deep in her throat then, grabbing the dishes, she slung a slice of hot apple pie into each one. 'Here, take them through. I'll be with you in a minute, soon as I've thrown some cold water on my temper.'

Lynda put her arms about her mother's comfortable figure and held her close for a moment. 'It'll be all right. Trust me. You know I wouldn't let anyone hurt you, not for the world. Haven't we always stood by each other?'

Betty sniffed, wiping a tear from her eye. 'Yer a good lass, get on with you.'

But running cold water over her hands and wrists Betty knew in her heart that nothing would ever be *all right* ever again. Her sanctuary had been invaded. Her escape had ended the moment she'd spotted him leering at her from across the street. Rinsing her face to wash away the unshed tears and attempt to cool the anguish in her heart, she drew in a steadying breath. Children! Why was it they could never see beyond the end of their own noses?

But then to be fair to both Jake and Lynda, Ewan always could put on this clever act, as if butter wouldn't melt on his lying tongue. Why should today be any different? He was somehow managing, by dint of saying very little, to put himself in the right with Betty herself seen as the difficult one. As if she were the one who had created the problems and called an end to this imagined idyllic life they'd led together. A fantasy Jake clearly believed.

Well, not even Ewan Hemley could keep up the pretence for too long. All Betty could hope for was that her son didn't suffer too much when he saw his father for what he really was.

Then she picked up a jug of custard and went to join her family.

It was after the apple pie had been eaten and the dishes all cleared away, washed, dried and stacked on the kitchen dresser that Ewan revealed a glimpse of his true colours.

He got up from the table, belched loudly, then went to sit in the winged fireside chair. Betty saw the private battle taking place in her son's face: the urge to order this stranger out of his chair warring with the desire to make friends with his father.

Ewan sat contentedly picking his teeth. 'What a treat that was. I'd forgotten what an excellent cook you are, Betty love.'

Betty winced, averting her gaze. 'I only made the Yorkshire puddings, our Linda cooked the rest. And I've told you before, I'm not *your love*.'

Ewan beamed at his daughter, a look of pleased surprise on his face. 'Better and better. What talented children I have. Oh, and I've told you, Betty, me old love, me old faggot, that I'll call you whatever I damn well please.'

Jake snorted, stifling the sound quickly when he caught his mother's furious glare from where she stood, unmoving, by the kitchen door.

Betty spoke through tightly compressed lips. 'Lynda, fetch your father's coat will you? Sunday lunch is over. Everything has been said that needs to be said, now I'll thank him to take his leave.'

Jake looked as if he might be about to protest, but then glancing again at his father reclining in *his* chair as if he owned the place, changed his mind and seemed to think better of it.

Ewan watched this conflict of emotion on his son's face with some amusement, then allowed his gaze to follow Lynda as she went to the under-stairs cupboard to reach for his overcoat. But he made no move to rise.

Instead, he casually took a pipe from his pocket and proceeded to fill it, tamping the tobacco down with meticulous care. Taking his time over the task, he drew on it till the tobacco flared hot and red, then glancing in mock surprise at Lynda, and using the stem of the pipe to indicate the coat she was holding out for him, softly smiled.

'Thanks, love, but I don't think I'll be needing that till the morning. I've no intention of leaving, d'you see? I've come home and I mean to stay, so fetch me the Sunday papers and a stool for me feet. I fancy an hour or two of peaceful perusal of the *Sporting Chronicle* before tea. Then I reckon an early night after all this emotional upset, don't you? No, don't panic, Betty love, your virtue is quite safe. I'm sure our Jake won't mind sharing with his old dad. Time we got to know each other again, isn't it, son?'

12

Helen and Judy

They did indeed enjoy a 'nice' walk on the sands to 'blow the cobwebs away'. Jonty, Leo and Helen walked in uneasy silence for what seemed like miles before returning home to partake of the tinned salmon and cucumber salad which Dulcie had prepared, as usual, for their evening meal; her son's bouquet of carnations and lilies on proud display in the centre of the table so that no one could quite see over or around it.

After the peaches and Nestlé's milk had been enjoyed and the washing-up done, Helen endured a long dull evening listening to an orchestral recital on the Third Programme, twiddling her thumbs while the two men talked business and Dulcie crocheted, fingers flying as she hummed softly to herself.

When she could bear no more and grew tired of listening to Jonty verbally batter her husband with Dulcie acting as occasional referee, Helen escaped to bed. Not that there was much hope of any hanky-panky sleeping in the narrow twin beds with their pink eiderdowns and matching candlewick bedspreads.

Helen was aware of the moment her mother-in-law retired as she paused to tap softly on the bedroom door. 'Goodnight, dear, sleep tight.'

Of course she could see the light on under her door since Helen was reading, but it irritated her all the same. Helen chose not to reply.

Later she heard voices raised in argument coming from the living room. Jonty was claiming that Leo allowed people to take advantage of his good nature, that he was weak and useless, which he vehemently refuted. Helen listened for a while, itching to go in and do battle for her husband. How anyone, particularly his own father, could accuse Leo of being weak was quite beyond her. He was kind and loving and affectionate, certainly, but nobody could deny that Leo wasn't a strong, capable man.

He radiated high levels of energy, was bold and daring, yet was decent and honourable. He'd been a fighter pilot during the war, joining at just eighteen in 1940 so no one could ever call him a coward either. Her husband possessed admirable qualities, gave his all to the business, often to the detriment of their personal life together since he was so determined to take the distribution business into the modern world.

The only problem was that Leo was too attractive for his own good and positively drew predatory women to his side. Helen never felt quite able to trust him. How could she? Even her own father had strayed once or twice. Men did that, it was in their nature. Hadn't her mother told her so a thousand times? To be fair to Leo, Helen guessed she was the only woman whom he truly loved, and she was certainly the only one who could manipulate him.

But she needed to be the only woman *in his life*, not simply the one he cared for the most. Although whatever rules she applied to Leo, did not necessarily apply to herself.

Jonty's voice intruded into her thoughts, loud and clear. 'You'll damage your cash flow if you allow creditors too much leeway. Never mind thirty days, I never gave them thirty minutes. Cash on the nail, that's the best way.'

'That's not how business is conducted these days, Pa.'

'Stuff and nonsense. Don't be dictated to by idiots, make up your own rules . . .'

And so it continued. Drat this bungalow, far too small for comfort. Pulling the covers over her head, Helen snapped off the lamp and tried to get some sleep.

Helen was woken by the sound of a door banging, of voices shouting out in panic, and of running feet. A light snapped on, momentarily blinding her and then everything was mayhem. Dulcie was sobbing, Leo was leaping from his bed and charging about in his pyjamas, one moment making frantic telephone calls, the next pounding his father's chest where he lay sprawled on the hall floor. Apparently Jonty had gone off to the bathroom and collapsed before he reached it.

'At least put your dressing gown on,' Helen ordered Leo. 'You look ridiculous swanning about in your pyjamas. What will the ambulance men think when they arrive?'

For once Leo had no patience for her sensitivities. 'For God's sake, Helen, does it matter? Pa has had a heart attack. He could be dying.'

Jonty Catlow passed away early that morning without ever regaining consciousness. Perhaps his final disagreement with his son had been too much for him, but even Helen dared make no mention of this possibility.

When a pale sun emerged over the horizon Dulcie was sitting motionless on her chintz sofa, a cup of tea gone cold in her hand and Leo was still on the phone, now dealing with undertakers and solicitors.

During the course of that endless Sunday neighbours and relatives called to leave their condolences; more tea was brewed than was actually drunk and Helen sat and watched it all unmoved. She'd never liked her father-in-law and really saw no reason for her to weep and wail as the rest were doing. It would simply be hypocritical to pretend she grieved for the difficult old man.

Sam Beckett liked to enjoy a peaceful weekend. Once he'd closed up his ironmongery shop, carrying inside all the boxes of second-hand tools, the buckets and shovels that he stacked all around, his one wish was to go home, put up his feet, and relax. He wasn't the kind of man who liked to spend hours in a pub, drinking. He felt perfectly capable of entertaining himself with his various hobbies: his fishing, his running and boxing, and his collections of badges and memorabilia which he was cataloguing and displaying on shelves he'd made himself.

He naturally expected his wife to provide him with a good meal, a warm hearth and a smiling face, plus a willing body when it was time to go to their bed. That went without saying. Where was the point in being married otherwise? A man had his appetites after all.

He was, Sam believed, a man who asked little from life but somehow he constantly met with disappointment and failure. Judy seemed quite incapable of achieving any sort of order or comfort in their home. She left everything to the last minute, constantly forgot things and forever either had her head in a book or her fingers covered in oil paint from those dratted daubs of hers.

But she'd really done it this weekend, had completely ruined any hope of relaxation. Sam could hardly believe what he was hearing and stared at his wife in total disbelief. 'You want to what?'

Judy cleared her throat nervously. 'I'd like to have a stall of my own on which to sell my paintings.'

She'd spent days making her plans, hours and hours going through her paintings and choosing those she perceived most suitable for sale, coming up with quite a good selection. Judy had spoken to Belle Garside who was now Market Superintendent and really had been most helpful, assuring Judy that she was more than welcome to have a stall in the Farmer's section of the market. Craft stalls, Belle said, were always popular and because they were held only two days a week, required very modest rents.

The only obstacle remaining was Sam, and Judy had known instinctively this would be the hardest of all to overcome.

She'd chosen to show him the still life of the golden chrysanthemum lying beside the blue vase as a demonstration of her skill and talent, but he'd scarcely glanced at the painting. Seeing his lack of interest, Judy had stuffed the picture quickly out of sight behind her back, feeling very much as if he'd slapped her.

Now she drew a steadying breath and tried again. 'I thought that selling some of my pictures might help to finance my little hobby,' she said, carefully using the same phrase Sam himself had adopted to describe her work.

'Are you suggesting that I keep you short of money?'

Judy was appalled. 'Of course not! Heaven forbid. You are the most generous of husbands,' and she kissed him on the cheek to prove it. He hadn't shaved yet this evening and it was prickly with bristles, nevertheless she bestowed upon him her warmest smile. 'But oil paint and canvasses are expensive, and since it's my little indulgence I feel I should finance it myself.'

'I don't see why.' Sam considered her carefully, face devoid of expression, pale eyes hooded.

'It's only two days a week and won't intrude on the children. I'll make sure I finish in good time to meet them after school, as usual. They won't even know I've been out of the house.'

'*I* will know. So will everyone else.'

Judy tried a little laugh, to cover up her attack of nerves. He must agree, he simply *must*. Ever since Lynda had made the suggestion she'd become more and more excited by the prospect of having a stall of her own. Now she'd quite set her heart on it. 'I should hope everyone *would* know, otherwise I'd have no customers, would I?'

Sam was not amused by her little joke. 'I won't have people thinking that I can't afford to keep my wife and family, that my ironmongery business is failing in some way.'

'But you'll think about it? Please?'

'I'd like my Sunday dinner now, if it isn't too much trouble.'

The meal, roast chicken followed by Queen of Puddings, was eaten in silence, Judy feeling far too nervous to risk mindless chatter. Even Ruth and Tom said very little, casting each other warning glances as they recognised the frigid atmosphere between their parents.

When the meal was over Sam slept for an hour or two in the chair with the newspaper over his head. When he woke he demanded a cup of tea, then put on his grey duffle coat and announced that he was going out. He could tell that Judy was disappointed even before she begged him not to go.

'Not now, please. I was hoping we could talk some more about the possibility of my having a stall, now that I've got the children off to bed. I could perhaps show you more of my pictures.'

Sam didn't trouble to respond to this suggestion, merely announced that he had far more important business matters to attend to than listening to 'silly dreams'.

Ten minutes later, thankfully safe from the threat of being disturbed since Big Molly and Ossie were, predictably, in the Dog and Duck at this hour on a Sunday evening, Sam was peeling off Fran Poulson's baby-doll nightie up in her back bedroom and pounding out his furious frustration into her willing body.

There was no question of them going home, naturally, not until after the funeral, which passed with unconscionable slowness and pomposity. Jonty Catlow had been a noted figure in the community, a man of business and therefore greatly respected. The local press must have their interviews with the bereaved, the vicar was zealously consoling and the family solicitor insisted upon reading the will in the traditional manner, even though everyone was aware of its predictable contents. The bungalow, together with a modest income from her husband's shares in the family business, was left to Dulcie, and the company itself to his son in its entirety.

Helen drew a heartfelt sigh of relief when the whole performance was complete, the relatives had gone on their way with the usual meaningless remarks to let them know if there was anything they could do. Then she closed the door with a firm click on the last.

'May we now go home?' she asked Leo, with what she believed to be exemplary patience.

'As soon as Mother is ready.'

Helen stared at him, hoping she had misunderstood. 'Perhaps Dulcie should have asked one of your aunts to stay with her for a while. *We* certainly can't stay any longer. I have a committee meeting for the new leisure centre fund-raising committee on

Thursday, and I'm sure you have a great deal of business to attend to in the office.'

Leo sighed. 'Of course I do, and I'm as anxious as you to get home, but there's no question of leaving Ma here alone. You could speed things along by helping her pack.'

'Pack? She's coming with us? You can't be serious. You surely aren't expecting me to open up my home to your mother?'

Leo gave a sad little smile. '*Our* home, I think, would be a more accurate term, or even *my home*, but yes, I am. Not, however, your heart. Even I do not ask the impossible, Helen.'

'But it *is* impossible. Utterly! Your mother and I simply don't get on.'

'Well, you'll just have to try to do so in future. Go and help her to pack, Helen, please. She's still in shock and doesn't know how to cope. Don't forget, charity isn't simply about fund-raising.'

'Oh, for goodness sake!'

Dulcie's quiet voice intervened in their heated argument. 'I should be perfectly all right staying here. It's very sweet of you to offer me a home, Leo, but I think I'd rather stay in my own. The last thing I want is to be a nuisance to you and Helen. You have enough on your plate already.'

Leo strode over and gathered his mother in his arms. She felt so frail suddenly, so – old. 'Nonsense, I won't hear of you staying cooped up all alone in this bungalow. It would do you no good at all. You need people around you, people who care about you at this dreadful time. And you won't be a nuisance, don't even think that. We want you to come with us, don't we, Helen?'

Helen drew her lips into a tight little smile. 'Of course we do, Dulcie. At least until you feel fit enough to manage on your own, which I'm sure you will in no time at all.'

'Of course, whenever you feel ready,' Leo conceded. 'Maybe later, in a few weeks or months perhaps you could try coming back home, once I'm sure that you are over the worst of the shock and have had time to adjust. But you must give it time.' He stroked his mother's white hair, kissed her paper-soft cheek. 'Let *me* look after *you* for a change.'

'You're the best son in the world,' Dulcie said, blowing her nose rather loudly. 'I'd better get packed then, but only for a few weeks, you understand. I can't leave this place unattended for too long.'

'Don't worry about the bungalow. I shall ask Joe next door to keep an eye on it for you.'

And so it was decided. There was to be no picturesque tour of the Ribble Valley on their journey home, no stopping at a tucked-away country pub for a cosy lunch. That dream had been swallowed up by days of family duty, and it made Helen shudder to contemplate what lay ahead with their privacy threatened and the future looking decidedly grim.

The car was packed with several of Dulcie's fine leather suitcases and they drove straight to Manchester, stopping only once for a cup of tea along the way.

The weekend had turned into a week of hell, far worse than Helen could ever have imagined.

13

Betty and Lynda

Betty was in her favourite spot, standing on her duck board watching the world pass by her stall. Her feet were frozen despite the fur-lined, zip-up suede boots she wore, but she was smiling as she made up a bunch of miniature zinnias for Molly Poulson. Her life might be falling apart but these were such glorious little flowers with their padded heads in brilliant jewel colours. As she wrapped them, she was listening with only half her attention to a long-drawn-out sob story about the other woman's worries over her elder daughter, Fran. The girl hadn't been seen around the market in months but was now back home creating more worry for her mother.

'She's never in the house more than five minutes, and when I complained she threatened to run off again. What can I do with her, Betty? I'm sure she entertains men on the sly in that bedroom of hers. The other night when we come home early from the pub I could hear all sorts of funny goings on. I told our Ossie to knock on her door but he wouldn't, daft cluck. Reckoned he couldn't hear nowt and says it's none of our business anyroad, that she's of age and I should be grateful that the lass has at least come home. What cowards men are!'

'Well, he does have a point, Molly. You were out of your mind not so long since, wondering where she was.'

'Aye, well happen I were better off not knowing.'

Betty tried to sound sympathetic, making suitable noises about the benefits of Fran making a fresh start, since things had gone so badly wrong for her when her fancy man had gone back to his wife. Not that she put it quite so bluntly to Molly, trying at least to sound tactful over a girl who was said to have earned her living under the arches with the likes of that prossy Maureen.

'If she goes on like this she'll be up the duff again, you mark my words,' Molly mourned.

'I'm sure she'll take better care of herself in future,' Betty commented.

Molly was less mealy mouthed. 'I'd say serve the little tart right if I didn't love the bones of her.'

Touched by her old friend's genuine distress, Betty presented her with a begonia in a pot as a free gift, just to cheer her up. Sometimes she thought she gave away more profit than she actually made, soft fool that she was.

And all the while her gaze was fixed on a small drama unfolding across the street. She could tell by the way young Judy was standing so defensively before her husband that the conversation was not going well. She seemed to be drooping, her head bent and submissive as a blue harebell, every bit of her as fragile and as delicate. The more robust Betty pulled her thick cardigan tight about her plump breasts and worried for the girl.

She'd clip Sam Beckett round the ear if he ever hurt Judy, big bully that he was.

What could the problem be, she wondered? Was she asking him for something? Begging more like. Pity it wasn't for a divorce. There was one young lady who'd do far better on her own. Betty could only pray that the poor lass had more strength in her blood than was evident in the anaemic quality of her tired skin.

Course, he should be the one begging for mercy. Didn't Betty recognise a lying man when she saw one? She could spot a straying husband at twenty paces, even without her specs on. Being cock-of-the-hoop was what they enjoyed most, and it usually cost women dear.

By heck, but if she could put a rod of iron in that girl's spine she'd do it. The lass was certainly going to need it, if she was any judge.

To Betty, the night her ex-husband stayed on had seemed like the longest in her life. She'd adamantly refused to allow Ewan up the stairs or to go anywhere near either her son or her daughter's rooms. He could sleep on the sofa, if he must, but it would be for one night only. She insisted he wash in the kitchen and as the lavvy was down the yard that wasn't a problem, or so she imagined.

The next morning, and to her great relief, he was gone when she came down to make breakfast. By the end of the day, when he still hadn't materialised, Jake was complaining that his father had abandoned him yet again, Lynda was sulking and Betty was almost smiling with relief. But her happiness was short-lived. By night-fall when hunger struck there he was again, expecting to be fed and watered and lay his weary head on her comfy green moquette sofa.

Betty confronted him, plump arms folded. 'Whatever little game you're playing, it's got to stop. In case you've forgotten, you and me are history. We're divorced. This can't go on.'

'It'll go on as long I say it'll go on.'

'This is *my* house, not yours, so I'll thank you to go back to whatever miserable little hole you crawled out of.'

As Ewan eased himself into Jake's chair he smiled with the easy confidence of a man who believed himself in control of his own destiny. 'You always were one for the fighting talk, Betty. I loved that in you. Lynda, chuck, fetch your dad a cuppa, and a pair of slippers would be good if you can find any to fit me. A pair of Jake's will do nicely. These old boots of mine have seen better days and me poor old meat plates are frozen. You can wash me socks overnight at the same time. What a little treasure you are. Oh, and three sugars don't forget.'

And so it began.

Day after day he would sit in the chair issuing orders as if he owned the place, and Lynda and Jake would carry out his every bidding without a murmur. They even sat at his feet to talk to him and ask questions. None of which he answered with truth, Betty noticed.

It turned her stomach just to have him near. He'd fart and belch at the dinner table, slurp up his tea out of the saucer and throw bits of bread at the poor cat, laughing and telling raucous jokes to Jake as he did so.

He'd come home roaring drunk, often with Jake in tow every bit as much the worse for wear. Then pee just outside the kitchen door in the back yard because he couldn't be bothered walk the length of it to the privy. The living room stank of tobacco smoke and he'd hawk and spit in the fire, leaving gobbets of brown juice on her shiny brass fender. He'd even blow his nose without a hanky.

It made Betty want to vomit just to watch him and hatred simmered inside her to boiling point, searing her throat and making her fingers itch. She'd strangle him with her own bare hands if he didn't leave soon, she would really.

'What sort of an example is this to set for the lad, coming home drunk every night? Don't you think I've had enough bother trying to keep him on the straight and narrow, and here you are making him ten times worse.'

'You sound like a flaming Methodist. Shut your noise, woman, and get t'supper on the table.'

'Get it your flaming self,' she would shout back, then Lynda would be beside her, urging her to hold on to her patience, saying it was hard for them all but they had to try to get on, and that Jake was only sowing a few wild oats.

'Where is the harm if he gets a bit tight occasionally? At least he's got the chance now to spend some time with his father. It certainly doesn't help, Mam, if you and Ewan are at each other's throats the whole time. We're just trying to get to know each other a bit better, that's all, and to be a family.'

'Family? He's not in our family any longer. I divorced the nasty old bugger.'

Lynda momentarily pressed her lips together in annoyance,

her longing for a quiet normal family life seeming to be further away than ever. She drew her mother to one side to whisper fiercely in her ear. 'He's still my dad, so lets just try to get along, shall we? I don't suppose he'll stay long but while he's in the area Jake and me want to see him, right?'

Betty felt helpless, caught in a trap, alienated not only from her ex-husband whom she loathed and feared with a venom, but also now from her own children as well. She tried her best to understand their point of view but it felt as if they'd turned against her.

Worst of all was Ewan's behaviour towards Lynda. 'Come and sit on Daddy's knee, pet,' he would say to her, a leering smile curling his ferret-like mouth.

'Leave her alone, she's too big for such nonsense. She's not a child any more, she's a grown woman,' Betty would protest, but to no avail. Even Lynda herself would argue against her.

'Don't be so prickly, Mam. Why shouldn't I have a bit of a cuddle with me dad?'

So Lynda would sit on Ewan's knee and lean her head on his shoulder, and Betty would watch his bony hands stroke her soft curls, smooth her slim young back or pat her firm round bottom. Betty would see the look of triumph in his black beady eyes as he smirked at her over his daughter's shoulder, making Betty want to retch.

Oh, she'd make him sorry for this, she would really.

Lynda was too caught up in the excitement of the new love in her life to take her mother's concerns over having Ewan Hemley back in her life too seriously. Night after night she'd doll herself up, put on the lipstick, fold her abundant hair into a French pleat or tease it into bouncing curls falling loose about her shoulders. Then she'd slip into her tightest raglan-sleeved sweater with a deep slashed neckline, her sexiest trews or jeans, and take great delight in making young Terry's heart pound and his blood pressure go up.

They couldn't afford to go to the pictures every night, so

much of the time they'd spend snogging up back alleys, or sitting on freezing park benches while they went in for a bit of heavy petting. Lynda was determined that this time she'd hang on to her virtue, such of it as she had left, she would tell herself wryly.

She was no virgin, having given her all in the fond belief that marriage would surely follow, only to be betrayed. Now Lynda was more cautious. If this was just some silly fling, she'd make sure she was in the same condition at the end of it as she was at the start. No shotgun wedding or unwanted pregnancy for her. He'd get nothing more than necking without a ring on her finger first.

Oh, but it was hard. Terry was a dreamboat and they really got on well.

He'd kiss her till her lips were all pink and swollen, her face sore from friction burns, and she'd tease him to shave a bit closer next time. Then Terry would gently caress her breasts and it would be Lynda urging him on to do more, Lynda who would unbutton her blouse so he could slip his hand inside and press bare soft flesh.

'God, Lynda, I want you so much.'

They'd both get very heated and flustered, breathing hard and desperate to take things further, and they would, going just as far as she dare, touching and caressing, stroking and teasing, each exploring the other with fresh and thrilling delight. But after a while she'd call a halt and Terry would have to leap up and pace about for a bit till he'd calmed down.

It would be so easy, Lynda thought, to succumb.

The argument with his wife had given Sam a raging headache, which left him in a foul mood for days. Judy had turned stubborn over this stupid notion of hers to sell her pictures on a stall, a request he'd paid little attention to when she'd first mentioned it. And to make matters worse Fran had had a row with her mother and taken herself off some place. She'd be back of course, daft cow, but it left Sam kicking his heels with frustration.

But then he was a man with more than one iron in the fire.

He certainly had no intention of being dependant upon the likes of Fran Poulson, or his silly wife.

Later that afternoon he met up with his latest lady friend and he was more than ready for her. He needed to expel his aggravation on someone. Sam had known, of course, that she would be waiting for him up the back alley, as she always was around tea time.

No time was wasted on social chit-chat, but then being such a classy lady she no doubt had enough of that sort of nonsense in her everyday life. Nor was she much of a one for foreplay which suited Sam perfectly. From him she obviously expected something more earthy and fundamental than her usual diet of politely amorous encounters, something dirty and exciting, and Sam had no intention of disappointing her. He slammed her up against a back-yard wall, lifted her skirt and, finding her naked and ready for him beneath, as always, was pounding into her within seconds.

Some greasy tar from the wall came off on to her fine wool skirt which fired the blood in his veins to an even greater heat. There was nothing Sam liked more than seeing her pale skin bruised, her immaculate clothes marred by their fevered passion. Didn't it prove that he was a man, the one in control as she whimpered and begged for more, only too willing to debase herself. And who knew what she might agree to do for him in the future?

When they were done to their mutual satisfaction, she kissed him lightly on the nose by way of thanks. Then adjusting her skirt and swing-backed jacket, somewhat creased and grubby after their hasty coupling, she retrieved her basket from where she'd abandoned it on the cobbles and coolly walked away to resume her shopping as if they'd done nothing more than pass the time of day. What style!

14

Judy

'You wouldn't mind if I took a little job, would you, darling?' Judy asked her daughter.

Ruth appeared taken aback, as if the thought of her mother actually working was the craziest thing she'd ever heard of, then screwed up her small face in disgust. 'Why would you want to? Anyway, what sort of a job could *you* do?'

The child was so like her father Judy found herself smiling even as she stifled a weary sigh. She explained about her paintings and Lynda's idea that she should try to sell them on a market stall.

Ruth considered this for a moment, looking mildly interested but then frowned. 'Would it mean I have to baby-sit Tom?'

'Of course not.'

'Or do more chores in the house? I do far more than Tom already. Boys are hopeless at washing up *and* setting the table, but I'm not doing it all by myself. He'll just have to learn even if he is only a baby.'

'Tom isn't a baby, he's a big boy and of course you won't be asked to do any more chores. This isn't about my wanting to escape what I do for you as your mother,' Judy told her, not too accurately.

'What is it for then? Are we hard up? Do we need more money?'

'No, Daddy earns plenty for us all, but . . .' Judy was fumbling for an explanation. How did you explain the need for independence, that desperate searching for who you once were, to seeking an identity, to a nine year old? 'The stall will only be open while you two are at school. I shall still pick you up on the dot of four, so it will make absolutely no difference to your lives at all. I just want something of my own, something for *me*. Can you understand that?'

Ruth's frown deepened as she struggled to see her mother's point of view. 'What does Daddy think? Won't he mind your not being here?'

How astute the child was. Of course Sam would mind. They both knew that. 'Daddy is thinking about it, but I'd like your opinion too. I don't want to do anything that would upset you.'

'What if Tom gets a cold on his chest like he did last winter, or measles or something and has to stay home?'

'Then I wouldn't be able to open the stall that day, would I? It's my stall, I can please myself. I think it would be fun.'

Ruth brightened. 'I suppose it would. Could I help serve on it?'

'How could you, sweetie, when you'll be at school?'

'I mean during school holidays and stuff.'

Judy hadn't thought that far, had pushed the problem of school holidays from her mind. 'It might be possible, we'll see.'

'Well,' said Ruth, struggling to be magnanimous. 'I don't think *I* mind, but Daddy probably will. You know, Mummy, that he won't *really* like you having a job. He'll probably say no.'

Judy rather thought her daughter might be right.

Judy wrapped her arms about her husband, stroking his chest and striving to relax the military-hardened muscles. 'Have you thought about what I asked you the other day? Please say yes, it would mean so much to me.'

She knew him for a stubborn man, tense and highly strung, and not in the least little bit flexible. He laid down a schedule of work for her to complete for each and every week, one she was expected to keep to if she was to avoid a humiliating interrogation.

She could never say, 'Oh, but Lynda popped in for coffee and we got chatting so the ironing will have to wait until tomorrow.'

If Monday was marked as washday, then Tuesday must be the day for ironing, and windows cleaned every Thursday, come rain or shine. Polishing the fire brasses and tidying out the under-stairs cupboard was set down for Friday afternoons. The list was long and detailed, always with something new or unusual thrown in just to keep her on her toes, like the time he insisted she take down the washing line every evening to wash and bleach it before tying it up again the very next morning. Laborious, mind-numbing tasks which he would always check had been done, rather like a sergeant-major inspecting the troops.

And if she made a mistake Judy would be punished. Put on jankers was the term Sam used, when she'd be made to do extra chores, usually unpleasant, such as white-washing the out-house, or scrubbing the window sills and front step every morning for a week. Or she would be kept in on what he termed detention, confined to barracks, which meant she couldn't even slip out to chat with Lynda or idly wander around the market choosing something nice for tea. She couldn't walk in the park or see an afternoon matinee at the Odeon.

Her mother-in-law would be instructed to do all essential shop-ping, and to collect the children from school in her place, on the grounds that Judy had to catch up on her housewifely duties and couldn't leave the house.

Judy hated these petty punishments with a venom but however much she might protest she knew there could be no escape. As Sam frequently told her, far easier to carry out the chore or duty correctly in the first place, rather than be obliged to repeat it over and over again until he was satisfied. It made life so much easier.

He was no less disciplined with himself. Sam constantly strived for perfection, polishing his shoes every night without fail and placing them correctly by the side of his bed where he could slip them on first thing in the morning when he woke up. Sam was not a pipe and slippers man.

And he was militant also in his fitness routine. He ran for two miles along the canal bank every morning; worked out regularly at Barry Holmes's boxing club. And was most particular about what he put into this lean fit body of his. Not a scrap of fat must be found on his meat or there would be hell to pay.

He drove her mad with his lists, his collection of badges and army memorabilia which must be dusted and labelled and kept in the right boxes. Judy came to loath this obsession for order and schedules, his cleanliness and need for perfection.

Sam also insisted that she keep an itemised list of the contents of every cupboard. Labels were stuck inside every kitchen door listing the items within and woe betide Judy if she forgot to cross off a packet of caster sugar or PG Tips she'd removed, or worse still, forgotten to add it to her shopping list for immediate replacement.

Conversely he could be as sentimental and soft as a baby, and beguilingly romantic should he choose to be so. He would think nothing of blowing ten pounds on a meal out, or surprise Judy with an unexpected gift. And he regularly came home with huge bunches of flowers that must have cost him a small fortune. Judy was always deeply touched, striving not to think of the guilt which must lie behind the gift.

Most important of all he absolutely adored his children, always finding time to play with them of an evening, and endlessly patient over helping Ruth and Tom with their homework. In return, they clearly adored him, cheerfully tolerating his room inspections and his silly rules about how the soap should be left dry in the dish, or how their socks should be folded neatly together. So sweet! Maybe that was why she stayed, because he was such a good father, even though Judy had long since stopped loving or wanting him as a husband.

Tonight Judy hoped he was in one of his gentler, more sentimental moods. Her first effort to remind him of his promise to consider her request had met with a brick wall and an embarrassing argument right in the middle of the market with everyone looking on. Now, in the peace and quiet of their own home she was ready to try again. She'd taken care to dress smartly in her 'At Home' fashions, as her magazine recommended: a paisley print cotton shirt worn under a coachman corduroy vest with big shiny buttons, and tapered matching pants in a bright pillar-box red. Sam loved to see her in bright colours. She'd even put on a little make-up – scarlet lipstick, mascara and blue eye shadow. Judy cuddled beside him on the sofa, letting him kiss and fondle her, doing her best 'to keep her man happy'.

'I was thinking that people do love to buy something from someone they know, such as a local artist. Aren't you proud of what I do?'

Sam made no reply, as if the thought had never occurred to him.

Judy gently persisted. 'Come on, love, admit it. You must be just a little pleased for me, otherwise you would object to the cost of all that oil paint and canvasses.'

'Money is not a consideration. You are my wife, so it's my responsibility to fund your little hobbies.'

He made her sound as if she were a charity case but Judy smiled anyway, trying not to mind. He did not return the compliment but then Sam was not a naturally cheerful character, rather soulful in fact, prone to dark moods and long silences. He'd endured a tough war, about which he refused to speak, so she'd learned to be tolerant of his sudden anxieties, his insecurities, his need for mindless sex whether she were in the mood or not, and count her blessings. Some men had come back from the war a whole lot worse, and some not at all.

'You know I wouldn't do anything you didn't want me to,' she said, noting how her words softened the rigid line of his jaw just a little. But did she really mean it? Lynda would never say such a thing, Judy was certain of it. 'Don't you see, I *want* you to be proud of me. You are so good at everything you do. I value your high level of ability, as I would like you to value mine.' She knew that he was ridiculously susceptible to flattery.

Sam had a broad, square face with a smattering of freckles which he hated but Judy rather liked, his nose slightly hooked on the ridge, the nostrils flared. But it was his chin which was his most striking feature. Jutting and square it had a pugnacious quality to it and he would thrust it forward as he walked. Judy placed a kiss on it now.

'You could send your customers along to view my pictures, and I could send mine to you to buy the picture hooks they'd need to hang them up.'

She felt him stiffen. 'I don't need anyone to send me customers, thanks very much. I have a regular and loyal clientele.'

Oh dear, she'd said the wrong thing. Again! 'Of course you do, darling. I only meant . . .'

'I know what you meant, Judy, but I really think you'd be taking too much on. You have enough to do already looking after the children, the house, and me, of course. I doubt you could cope with any more work.'

She could feel freedom slipping away from her and Judy snatched at it, grimly determined to hold on. 'Of course I can cope with more work. The children are growing up and well settled in school. You are out working on the market all day, and it really doesn't take the entire week for me to keep one small house tidy and clean.'

'Small? Are you trying to say that I don't provide you with decent living accommodation?'

'Of course not.' Heavens, he was becoming increasingly touchy.

'I always understood there was more to being a wife and mother than simply cleaning,' he snapped. 'What about being there for me? I don't want a wife who's tired every evening. And what if either of the children were ill?'

'Then I would stay home and look after them, of course I would. Or perhaps your mother would help?' Judy wasn't on particularly close terms with her mother-in-law but Lillian was good with the children and would often take them for an afternoon to give her a break, even when she wasn't on jankers.

'Go to bed, Judy,' he told her, abruptly ending the conversation. 'I'll be up directly.'

'But . . .'

'Do I have to repeat myself?'

Judy went. Later, he took her with his usual lack of finesse, but then Judy didn't expect anything more. She gazed bleakly over his shoulder at a cobweb on the ceiling while Sam grunted and gasped and satisfied his needs, or however he might choose to describe the sex that took place between them. It always seemed to Judy like an act of physical necessity, a part of his regime rather than something you could call love-making. Judy's own needs were never discussed. It would probably surprise her husband to discover she actually had any. Intimacy was certainly not a part of their relationship but at least he never took long over the act. As with other matters he was brisk and efficient, and blessedly swift.

He lifted himself off her and Judy gently drew down her nightdress. She wouldn't make a move to the bathroom until she heard his snores, which wouldn't be long in coming. If she moved too soon he'd claim she was accusing him of being unclean by immediately going to wash herself. He was so vigorous she always felt a little sore afterwards despite having learned to comply on demand.

But she was still worrying over her request. Judy simply couldn't let it go, not after it had taken her so long to pluck up the courage to broach the subject.

Tentatively she stroked a hand over his brow, the light brown hair cut close to his head, military style. 'Have you thought about what I asked you, Sam? Will you agree to let me try and see if I can cope with a little stall, just part time? If it gets in the way of the children, or your routine, then I'll stop at once, but allow me to at least have a go. Please. It might be fun and you do want me to be happy, don't you, darling? I don't object to your little hobbies, after all.'

It was the nearest she dare come to reminding him of how much he expected *her* to put up with. He lay beside her, saying nothing, but Judy could see that he was considering the point behind those hooded eyes.

Sam was in fact thinking of this new love-interest in his life, a liaison fraught with danger, although that was the part he relished the most. Where was the point of it otherwise? If Judy was around the market more, mightn't she catch them unawares? He wondered if that would matter or if this further threat of discovery might simply add to the thrill of their encounters?

Perhaps, since this lady didn't frequent the market a great deal, it wasn't such a problem. She was far too classy, yet possessed a curious proclivity for having sex in interesting and unsual places. Then again, a refusal might make Judy suspicious and she complained very little, unlike most wives.

Perhaps, in view of these considerations, he could afford to cut her a little slack and be generous. After all, he could put a stop to her little scheme any time it suited him to do so.

15

Helen and Judy

Helen Catlow was being driven demented by her mother-in-law. She tried to make allowances, constantly reminding herself that the woman was recently bereaved, that she had loved her husband even if no one else had. But then Helen would come home and find newspapers and magazines scattered all over her beautiful silk brocade sofa, her mother-in-law happily reading with her glasses perched on the end of her nose, oblivious of the mess, and Helen would have to go round whipping them up in a frenzy of temper before the print marked the cloth.

Or she would go into her pristine kitchen and find the gas jet on and a pan burned dry. She would open a cupboard and discover that all her precious crockery had been put back in the wrong place, lace doilies placed beneath her gold ormolu clock, or a table moved.

'I thought it might look better there,' Dulcie would say when she challenged her on the matter.

'If I had wanted the table against that wall, I would have put it there myself.'

'Of course you would, dear. Sorry! It's being at such a loose end, I really don't know what to do with myself. Perhaps we could go out somewhere this afternoon? Do a little shopping and have tea at the Midland Hotel? Or we could have a nice game of draughts by the fire. Wouldn't that be nice?'

Nice! Everything was nice in Dulcie's world. How Helen hated the word, and the woman who used it. Didn't it just prove her total lack of education? Helen clicked her tongue with impatience. Sympathetic she might be for her mother-in-law's situation, but nursemaid she was not.

'I'm sorry, I really don't have time. I'm heavily embroiled in organising a coffee morning to raise funds for Leo's campaign. You will just have to amuse yourself.'

'Yes, yes, of course, silly me. I didn't even know he'd agreed to stand. He's never really shown any interest in politics.'

'Of course he will stand,' Helen snapped. 'Would you like him to run you home to Lytham St Anne's next weekend, before he gets too busy with the campaign?'

'Oh . . . I really hadn't thought. How long is it since . . . ?'

Too long, Helen thought. 'Six weeks.'

'It seems like only yesterday when my darling Jonty . . . Dearest Helen, how generous of you to put up with me for so long. I find it surprisingly pleasant to be back here in what was once my old home, if you remember, since this used to be our house before you and Leo took it over.'

'Yes, I do remember,' Helen acidly commented, grinding her teeth with barely restrained impatience. 'How could I ever forget?'

'I do so enjoy living in the city again, and being close to the market, just like in the old days before Jonty retired. I'd forgotten how very much I always loved the old place. It still feels like home, do you see? I know I ought to go back to Lytham, although the bungalow will seem cold and damp having not been lived in for so long.'

'You've only been gone a short time, Mother-in-law, so I hardly think that likely.'

'Well, it will certainly feel lonely without my darling Jonty.'

Helen wanted to scream at the woman that her darling Jonty had been a difficult, over-critical, officious pain in the backside but she managed to hold her tongue.

Dulcie was still talking. 'Perhaps I'll speak to Leo about going home, see what he thinks.' And she fled to her bedroom from which, minutes later, emanated the sound of heartbreaking sobs.

Helen hardened her heart and left the house, determined not

to be blackmailed into feeling sorry for the silly woman, or allowing her to stay a moment longer than absolutely necessary.

Judy couldn't believe her good fortune. He'd agreed! Over the next week she made all the final arrangements for the stall with Belle Garside and spent many happy hours in the attic sorting through her paintings again. Some she framed, while others seemed better suited to their simple canvas state. Were they even good enough to sell? she worried. Were they too photographic, a bit too chocolate box perhaps? She mainly painted flowers, cats playing on the cobbles, or children. She loved doing figures best of all, and the dark industrial landscape, but generally people wanted something pretty and colourful to hang on their wall and Judy didn't presume she could ever hope to reach Lowry's brilliance.

Even Ruth showed an interest and helped her to carry the final selection downstairs.

'This is my first morning and I'm so scared,' Judy admitted to her children over breakfast. Tom paused in eating his shredded wheat to look at her, as if the very idea of a mummy being afraid was beyond his comprehension. Ruth gave her a bracing smile, as her father might have done had he cared sufficiently.

'Just think that *you* painted the pictures, not anyone else. If they criticise, let them see if they can do any better.'

Judy looked at her daughter in surprise, so young, so determined, so sure of herself. 'Sometimes, darling, you are so very wise,' and this time when Judy kissed her, Ruth actually giggled and didn't wipe the kiss away.

Sitting at her stall in the early-morning sunshine of a bright autumn day was not unpleasant yet Judy's nerves were so twitchy she kept rearranging the display, and almost cringed with embarrassment whenever anyone came near. A woman wandered over, picked up a canvas to examine it, then considered Judy with equal intensity.

'Did you paint this?'

'Yes, actually, I did.'

The woman put the picture down and walked away. Judy's heart plummeted. What had she been thinking of to imagine anyone would wish to buy her work? She had a great urge to hide some of her less effective efforts under the table. What was she doing here? Setting herself up for ridicule, that's what.

Several more people came by, but no one else touched a single picture. They would study them with interest, often from different angles, some would even smile at her and nod as if in praise, but then walk on. It was almost dinner time and she still hadn't made a single sale.

And then Dena Dobson came over. 'Hi, are these yours, Judy? I never realised you were so talented. How much are they? They look very expensive.'

'Oh, my goodness, I haven't put any prices on.'

Dena burst out laughing. 'First rule of a market stall – always price your product. The customer might haggle since there's nothing they enjoy more than a bargain, but they need a starting point to get them going, otherwise they'll assume they're too expensive.'

'Oh, Dena, you're right. How stupid of me. Thank you so much.'

'You should have seen the mistakes I made when I first got started with my dressmaking. Bought fabric that was far too expensive, stitched the left sleeve in the right armhole, and gave myself far more work than I could cope with. If it hadn't been for Winnie's belief in me I'd never have survived. Look, I could keep an eye on your stall while you go and buy some postcards, if you like. They'll do as price tickets for now.'

Half an hour later Judy made her first sale. It was the golden chrysanthemum, bought by old Mrs Catlow who seemed enchanted by it.

'I've never seen anything so lovely in my life. Did you paint this, dear, all by yourself? Well done! I shall treasure it. Look at the gloss on that flower, and the light on the blue vase. I feel as if I could pick it up, fill the vase with water, and just drop the chrysanthemum right in.'

Judy rather thought this delightful lady could well be her friend for life. She was in business.

'I really shouldn't be here,' Helen said as Sam hoisted her up onto the work-bench in his tiny stock-room. 'And it is somewhat claustrophobic.'

Sam wasn't listening to her complaints, he was too busy admiring her French silk panties even as he struggled to understand how the little ribbons operated on each hip so that he could get them off. Growing impatient, he tugged harder, resulting in a ripping sound.

Helen gave a little squeal. 'Now you've ruined them, ohhh . . .' Whatever other complaint she might have been about to make was forgotten as she threw back her head, flung back her porcelain-pale arms and gave herself up to ecstasy. The work-bench rocked beneath them as the pace of their rhythm increased, but all Helen cared about was the glorious sensation cascading through her body, as if she were soaring up through the clouds to a bright exploding star.

She really didn't mind at all making love in a room little bigger than a cupboard, nor lying on a work-bench among the screws and nails while Sam plunged into her. These interesting places he found seemed to make their trysts so much more exciting, and the words he whispered in her ear so very appropriate.

'You know you love it when I do this, and this – and how about this,' making her gasp with shock as he licked her in places he really shouldn't. Leo would never do anything of that sort!

Helen felt no guilt. Whatever naughtiness she got up to with Sam Beckett, or anyone else for that matter, really didn't impinge upon her marriage with Leo one little bit. After all, what he didn't know wouldn't hurt him.

Besides, she was utterly convinced that this other, secret part of her life added an extra dimension to their relationship. It wasn't that Leo didn't satisfy her as a lover, of course he did, it was simply that she needed so much more than he could possibly provide, especially as he was working such long hours. He would often come home exhausted and be asleep in seconds, and what good would it do for him to have an unsatisfied, lonely wife? Far better for her to be content and fulfilled. Where was the harm in that?

And there was often a lovely bonus to her little escapades, as her liaisons sometimes proved to be most useful, like her little dalliance with David Barford for instance, which had resulted in the offer to ask Leo to stand as the next parliamentary candidate in the borough. So exciting! If she could but persuade Leo to appreciate how beneficial such a position would be to him. How much *power* it could bring.

Helen moaned with pleasure as Sam suckled her breast, sending sharp little pains shooting deep down inside her, increasing her excitement to fever-pitch. Goodness knows what he'd done with her bra but she truly hoped he hadn't ripped that too. Not that she minded too much as she had plenty more, and she too had popped a few buttons on Sam's shirt as she'd fought to get her hands on that powerful muscled body of his, slick with the sweat of their coupling.

She wrapped her legs about his waist and concentrated on the glory of the moment, her head spinning and her teeth cutting into her lower lip in her efforts not to make any noise. The very thought that Barry Holmes or even his wife Winnie could at this very moment be the other side of the stock-room door riffling through Sam's myriad of boxes in search of curtain rings or cup hooks, made her want to scream out loud with laughter. The very danger of their situation greatly added to the thrill of it.

What would these people say if they opened that door to be confronted by the sight of Sam's bare backside, trousers round his ankles, and the ice queen of the market with her legs in the air? Helen almost choked with glee as she imagined their shocked faces.

With a last shuddering gasp Sam withdrew and Helen slumped on to the hard, uneven surface. She experienced a nudge of regret that it was over but she'd reached her own climax long since, several in fact, so felt delightfully sated. Sam was, after all, a most diligent and skilled lover, if not particularly considerate or gentle. But then, she didn't expect him to be. That's why she enjoyed herself so much. She wasn't seeking emotional involvement or love. She got both of those in spades from her marriage with Leo, more than enough in fact.

Nor was Sam seeking emotion either. The attraction between them was purely physical, you could say almost businesslike, which was how she liked it. That's why they got on so well. Sam was brimming over with aggressive energy so why shouldn't she channel a little her way?

Helen was quite sure she must be covered in bruises and scratches from all the nails lying about on the bench, and she felt suddenly desperate for a bath.

She put back her torn knickers, pulled down her skirt, dusted her hands and ten minutes later was walking innocently across the market, basket swinging on her arm with only a slight flush on her cheeks to reveal that anything untoward had taken place.

Helen glanced about her in open contempt. What fools these people were, what boring little lives they must lead. Content with nothing more than manning their sad little market stalls day after day, while she was perfectly in control of her life, and of Leo's too, if she had her way.

Save for the presence of her dratted mother-in-law, a situation that was merely temporary, Helen reminded herself. Of that she was quite certain. One way or another, and no matter how often the woman might express her pleasure at being back in her old home, Dulcie would soon be returned to her bungalow by the sea and life with her flying ducks and dreadful pink candlewick bedspreads.

Helen arrived home to find the painting of a still life: a chrysanthemum lying beside a blue vase, for goodness sake, hanging on her lounge wall cheek by jowl with her precious Constable. Admittedly the masterpiece was not an original, only a print, but even so it surely deserved not to be sullied by an amateur daubing, which this other painting most clearly was.

When Helen challenged Dulcie on the matter the older woman sounded almost belligerent, as if she'd every right to put pictures up on what had once been her wall, if she'd a mind to.

'I thought it lovely. I bought it from a very pleasant young woman on the market. It looks delightful there, don't you think?'

'I have to say that no, Dulcie, I really don't care for it at all.'

'But that wall looked quite bare with just the one picture.'

'It's meant to be that way, to show off a single worthwhile painting, not clutter the place up with any old rubbish.' Helen took the painting down, annoyed to find that Dulcie had driven a picture hook into her brand new imitation Chinese silk wallpaper without even asking permission. 'Why don't you put it away until you go home? I'm sure it will look very well in your bungalow.'

'You're probably right, dear. Our tastes are not quite the same, I will admit,' Dulcie agreed in a stiff little voice.

'And I'm sure you'll be going home quite soon. Perhaps I could help you to pack?'

And then the stupid woman came down with a stomach infection. She was sick half the night, ruining a pair of perfectly good Irish linen sheets. And when the next morning Helen insisted she take a walk, in the certain belief that fresh air never hurt anyone and would be sure to bring a little colour back into her pallid complexion, Dulcie had the gall to collapse in the street and shame them before everyone.

The doctor had to be called, giving his opinion that her mother-in-law was suffering from a bronchial infection. There was certainly no question now of her returning home to Lytham St Anne's, not for the foresseable future.

Worse, when it later turned out that Dulcie was also diabetic, the woman actually needed to be nursed and cared for, tablets and injections given, her food carefully weighed, her diet monitored. It was all so desperately trying that Helen thought she might scream.

16

Betty

It was a lovely spring day and the market looked brighter and cleaner than usual, the sun glistening through the market hall's big windows. A stiff March breeze was blowing and the older women were closely wrapped in head scarves and the dullness of winter coats while young girls were more optimistically decked out in puff skirts, rainbow petticoats and Capri pants in striking tartans; many purchased from Dena's own stall where she sat happily whirring her sewing machine, always ready with a smile or her tape measure to make something for a special occasion, or to help her customers choose exactly the right garment to suit them.

The sight of all this blaze of colour made Betty feel drab in her grey linsey-wool skirt and white blouse, although she'd never felt it right for a flower seller to compete with the glory of her precious chrysanthemums, her beautiful and proud daffs and tulips.

As the weeks and months had slipped by, Betty had become more and more depressed. Christmas came and went and apart from doing well on the stall selling dozens of holly wreaths and pots of cyclamen and hyacinths, there was little in her life to cheer her. The weather hadn't helped, being the coldest foggiest winter in nearly a decade. Now, with spring coming even the familiar scents of the market, the enticing aroma of Poulson's pies, the sharp tang of Barry Holmes's stack of rosy apples and the sweetness of her flowers failed to lift her spirit.

Much of the time her heart was racing and she felt all shaky inside, really rather ill. Betty felt out of control, as if she were stuck on an express train that was heading straight for the edge of a cliff. She couldn't concentrate on her work, the displays and bouquets she made up for her customers showing less flair and imagination than they had come to expect from a Betty Hemley arrangement.

'Nay, what do you call this, a funeral wreath?' her friend Winnie Holmes said to her one morning in that blunt way she had of saying exactly what she thought. She'd asked for a bunch of something cheerful for a sick friend and Betty had handed her six white lilies wrapped up in white tissue. 'Is that the best you can do? She might not be feeling so grand but she'll be at death's door if she sees that lot.'

'I'm doing my best.'

'Well it's not good enough. One look at that lot and she'll expect the hearse along any minute.'

Betty looked at the ethereal waxy flowers and flushed with embarrassment. 'Sorry, I wasn't thinking. How do you feel about freesias? Lots of pretty colours there. I'll put in a few chincher-inchees an' all. Expensive they are but I'll give you a good price, and they last well. Known as Star of Bethlehem.'

'Aye, well, at least the poor lass won't want to cut her throat soon as she claps eyes on them. You don't look much better yourself, chuck. Like a wet fortnight in Blackpool without a stick of rock in sight, and yer as prickly as an hedgehog. It might be none of my business but you're not yourself, Betty lass, that much is very plain.'

Betty made some excuse or other and sent Winnie on her way with an extra large bunch of her most colourful spring flowers but inside she did indeed feel bleak. She could see no way out. If only he'd never come back.

If only she'd moved the children miles away, down south, or emigrated to America. If she could've flown to the moon to avoid him, she would have done so. Betty blamed herself entirely for Ewan's reappearance in their lives. If he weren't so set on taking out his revenge on her he wouldn't be bothering them at all.

Each morning when she woke, Betty would pray that this would be the day he'd grow tired of the game and be off on his travels again. Ewan Hemley never had been able to stay put for more than five minutes; his years in the Merchant Navy had increased his wanderlust rather than satisfied it, so surely he'd grow bored, go on his way and leave them in peace.

Or she'd pray that the kids might ask him to leave, though so far there was little evidence of that happening. They were too wrapped up in themselves as all youngsters were, Jake pestering her for a new van since the old one kept breaking down and Lynda out every night with young Terry.

But how much longer could she be expected to put up with Ewan's presence in her house, listen to his criticisms, take his flaming orders, and daily witness the evidence of his vile manners? And Betty sensed that he was watching her just as closely. Some plan was being hatched in that evil little brain of his. She just wished she knew what it was.

Looking around this place that she loved, it seemed to Betty that people were relaxed and happy, taking their time as they strolled around the stalls, pausing to browse through dusty copies of Arthur Mee Encyclopedias, to examine a piece of cracked china, or gossip with friends. Betty envied them this freedom.

Gossip, of course, was the life blood of the market. Even Dena, loved as she was, remained a hot topic for speculation. She was still living with Winnie and Barry Holmes, still seeing Belle Garside's boy and still causing outrage by refusing to marry him, even though she had one illegitimate daughter already.

Were people talking about her, Betty wondered? Did they imagine she'd happily welcomed her ex-husband into her home? At that opportune moment she spied Constable Nuttall on his walkabout and caught the young policeman's attention by handing him a carnation.

'What's this?' he laughed. 'Bribery?'

'It's for later, when you go out on the town.'

'A nice thought, Betty, but I'd never hear the last of it from my sergeant if I took to wearing flowers in my buttonhole. What is it you want? Is something wrong?'

'Aye, you could say that. I've got a problem, Bill, and I thought you might be able to advise me on how best to deal with the matter.' She told him then how Ewan Hemley, her ex-husband, had suddenly walked back into their lives and into her home.

'Aye, I did notice you had a visitor.'

The constable listened patiently to Betty's tale of woe, her plea for help, all about how he'd parked himself upon them and insisted on being waited on hand, foot and finger. 'He's been here for weeks – months – and shows no sign of leaving.'

'Is your complaint that he refuses to contribute towards household expenses?'

'No, it's not just about money, though I'm sure he would start dipping into my purse if I was stupid enough to leave it lying around. I don't want him here, living in my house. I hate the bastard, pardon my French. I need you to give him his marching orders, to get him out of it and make him leave. That's the point, d'you see, it's *my* house, not his, and I don't want him here. I don't want him anywhere near my kids.'

Constable Nuttall looked troubled. 'But they're *his* kids too, Betty, and if he claims he wants to get to know them a bit better, then surely that's a good thing. Really quite a worthy cause.'

Betty battled against an instinctive urge to shout that there was nothing worthy about a man who put his hand down his daughter's knickers when she was only five years old. But there were some things that were too private, too *dreadful*, to bring out into the cold light of day and share with strangers, even if they were the law.

'He wants to plague *me*, to take his revenge on *me* for the fact I took them away from him, and got him into trouble at the time with the police. He doesn't give a toss about them really.'

The policeman instantly became alert. 'What sort of trouble?'

'Petty thieving, illegal gambling. He's not bright enough to do anything really bad, or to get away with it, but the police searched our house and found our cellar stuffed with the gear he'd nicked, so he says I shopped him.'

'And did you?'

'Happen! What difference does it make now? I wanted him out of our lives. Now he claims he's served his time, probably more than once since I last saw him, and he's going straight. If you believe that, you'll believe pigs can fly.'

Constable Nuttall chewed on his lip for a moment, then drew Betty into the shadows behind the dustbins, out of the mêlée of customers and the noise of stallholders calling their wares. The smell of rotting vegetables was sharp in her nostrils but Betty paid not the slightest attention, her gaze riveted on the policeman, anxious to hear his every word.

'I can certainly keep an eye on him, bearing in mind what you've just told me, and if you hear anything further about any current activities he becomes involved with, I'd be interested in that too. It goes without saying that all confidences would be respected. Anything you tell me is perfectly safe. He'd never hear from me that you'd grassed on him. No one would.'

Betty had a struggle not to let her impatience show. 'I appreciate all of that, but this isn't about Ewan's career as a small-time crook, it's my children I'm concerned about.'

'Course you are, but you could be doing him a disservice, Betty love. I have to say that divorce is a tricky area and not one I'm expert in, to be honest. It's not like this is a question of custody, is it? If he really is going straight and they are still his children, after all, his renewed interest in them must be seen as a good thing, so unless he's actually assaulted someone or hurt them . . .'

'He's far too cunning for that, not till he's got his feet well under our table, but a leopard doesn't change his spots, as they say. He certainly *did* hurt them in the past when we were all together. That's one of the reasons I divorced him, and it could all start all over again if we don't get rid of him.'

Constable Nuttall sucked in his breath. 'Tricky! I mean until he actually does do something . . . and, as I say, it's not really my field. Have you got a restraining order against him to make him keep away?'

'No, could I get one, even though Jake and Lynda are adults now?' Betty felt a kindle of hope, which the policeman swiftly quenched.

'Probably not. The judge would say that since Lynda's . . . how old . . . in her mid-twenties anyway, that she was mature enough to make up her own mind. As is Jake in theory, although I accept that's a harder one to swallow. Have you tried asking Ewan to leave?'

'Course I have,' Betty snapped.

'And he refuses?'

'He won't bloody budge an inch, and he's talked Lynda and Jake round into taking his side. He's biding his time, I tell you. Once he feels secure he'll show his true colours and how will we stop him then, when it's too late? You have to help me, Bill. You must. I'm desperate!'

'I'm sorry, Betty, I can understand and sympathise with your distress but there's nothing I can do. He isn't breaking any laws, d'you see?'

Oh, she saw all right, because that's where the problem lay, with the law. No policeman was interested in a 'domestic', not in Betty's experience. Women might have been considered worthy of helping to win the war but a man still maintained all the rights, over them and their kids.

When had anybody ever helped her? Certainly not the first time when she'd been in even more desperate straits with her children distressed and abused, and herself more battered than a piece of fried haddock. All of them: doctors, solicitors, magistrates, social workers and the police might have made all the right noises, but where was the practical assistance that a desperate woman needed in such a situation? Where were the shelters for a battered wife to go in order to escape from a violent husband?

Why was the only solution for abused children to take them into care away from the mother too, just because she didn't have a safe place to take them to or money to feed them, even when she was innocent of any crime against them? And how could she possibly have any money when her husband didn't give it to her and the state didn't give a toss?

That was the kind of predicament Betty knew only too well, the one she'd been in the first time and got out of by shopping her husband to the police. Ewan Hemley had gone to jail and she'd sold every stick of furniture she possessed, then taken her children and run for it.

Now here she was, thirteen years after fondly believing she'd finally succeeded in getting rid of him, and still running. The whole frightening scenario was starting up all over again.

'Bloody men!' Betty shouted at the shocked policeman. 'You all support each other. I hate the flaming lot of you!' Whereupon she stormed off in a fury, only to hide up a back alley and sob her heart out into her clean hanky.

When she was done crying and had mopped up her hot tears, Betty pushed back her shoulders and made a private vow. She'd battled and won against him the first time, and would do so again. She'd protect her precious kids, no matter what the cost.

17

Leo

Flowers were not much in evidence on Salford Docks where Leo was working. The canal was too slow a method of transport for anything which needed to be kept so fresh and sold before the tightly furled buds opened. But the business was not short of other products in need of shifting from place to place. These were boom times and Leo always felt stretched to the limit.

The docks were crowded with vessels and first thing every morning fleets of buses would arrive to unload hundreds of workers, not to mention a unending stream of men on bicycles, canvas bags strung across their backs carrying their sandwiches in a bait box. Unofficial visitors to the docks were strictly forbidden, because of the danger of overhead cranes and the unexpected movement of transport, or the operation of dangerous machinery.

All manner of businesses occupied the dockside. Leo's own wasn't involved in manufacturing but with distribution. He stood now beside dusty stacks of timber, the smell of seasoned wood mingling with that of the normal dockside smells of rope and warm tar as he examined the bill of lading on his foreman's clipboard, checking the cargo, destination, order of loading, and weight.

'Everything seems to be going smoothly.'

'Aye, boss, it should reach Liverpool in time for the evening tide.'

'Excellent!'

Leo loved his work and enjoyed good relations with his work-
force. Oil, cotton, electrical goods and foodstuffs regularly
appeared on their export lists. The other day they'd shipped out
a large consignment of Austin Seven cars to the West Indies and
Panama. But then he was responsible for importing and exporting
goods to every corner of the world from Canada to New Zealand.
Each day was different, and brought a new challenge.

Helen didn't share his passion for the place. He never even
brought her here, but then she'd never shown any inclination to
come. She rarely asked him about his day, or took the slightest
interest in his work.

There was little sign of a slowdown in trade which made Leo
very content. He should be getting back to his office but he stood
for a moment or two longer watching a tug progress unimpeded
beneath the swing road bridge, going about its regular dredging
duties. Ships couldn't be too large in order to negotiate the locks
on the Ship Canal.

His mother had always loved watching the ships, but then
Dulcie was entirely different from his wife, working in the firm's
office beside his father throughout the war when most women
of her age would be content to stay at home with their knitting.
Leo wished Helen could see this other side to her personality,
this puritan work ethic that had been in both his parents.
Something he'd always admired and respected as a boy, and still
did. He supposed it was all too evident in himself too.

Helen filled her life with other matters, largely social functions
and committees. So long as she didn't attempt to rope him in
on these, or reorganise his life to suit her, Leo really didn't mind
in the least what she did with her time.

How he was ever going to get it through to her that these
high-flown ambitions she held for him were a non-starter he
really didn't know. In the end, he would simply have to put his
foot down and refuse to go along with it, though he dreaded the
tantrum which would surely erupt as a result.

The thought reminded Leo that he should ring her to explain
he might be late home tonight. He wanted to see this latest load

of timber safely dispatched and then he had a great deal of paper-work to catch up on. He pushed open the office door, making a mental note to do something about the flaking paint and found the phone was ringing even before he reached it.

His secretary took the call and seconds later held the receiver out to him. 'It's your wife.'

Leo thanked her, feeling guilty over the familiar sinking feeling that came into his stomach as it always did these days whenever she rang him. Her voice came over loud and clear, resounding in the quiet office.

'Darling, I'm *so* glad I caught you. I do hope you've remembered we're having the Barfords over for supper this evening? Anyway, I didn't have time to pick up the wine and champagne after my hair appointment, so could you do that for me, then dash over with it.'

Leo was instantly irritated. He'd quite forgotten about the Barfords, if indeed he'd ever known they were coming. Or maybe he simply hadn't listened in the first place when Helen had told him. With so much work to do, he really didn't have time for social chit-chat today. 'Helen, I've told you a million times that I can't simply drop everything I'm doing to run errands for you.'

'But I need it *now*. The champagne has to be put on ice, and you know how small our refrigerator is. If you would only agree to buy me a decent large one, these sort of problems might not arise.'

He recognised this as an excuse to make another dig at him, a way to manipulate him into doing as she asked by accusing him of being an inadequate provider. However much money he lavished on Helen, or allowed her to spend on the house, she could always find fault and think of a way she could have managed better if only he'd been more generous.

'Sorry, you'll just have to pop out and get the wine yourself, I'm far too busy.'

Her voice rose several decibels. 'Why do you *hate* me so much? I'm sure you run errands for *her*, for your *mistress!*'

Leo tried to move away from the desk but it was too late, his secretary must have heard Helen's screeching voice down the phone as she was so obviously trying not to react to it. Other heads turned and stared at him in open curiosity, but then they were all familiar with his wife's constant demands and always found them entertaining.

Leo sighed, raising his eyebrows in comic resignation for the sake of his embarrassed staff. 'Would four o'clock suit you? I have an appointment with a new client around then and could possibly fit in a dash to the wine merchant.'

'If that's the best you can do, then I suppose it will have to.'

The sound of the phone going down seemed to echo around the small office like a clap of thunder. Leo thanked his secretary, though for what exactly he wasn't sure, the unexpressed sympathy in her eyes perhaps since she was never fooled by his pantomimes.

The smile slid from his face as Leo returned to his desk, and Helen's call seemed to put him in a foul mood for the rest of the morning. No wonder no one came near him, being naturally wary of the black mood which generally descended after one of his wife's calls.

By four o'clock Leo's temper was worse than ever as he abandoned some tricky accounting in order to dash to the off-licence on Deansgate before it closed and collect the champagne. Why couldn't Helen attempt to be more understanding and cooperative? Not only would he have to be home early this evening, but he'd wasted half his afternoon as well. What an infuriating woman she could be.

He was driving back along St John's Place, far faster than he really should, when he saw the boy. He'd clearly been set upon by three bullies, all much bigger than himself, although the child was doing his utmost to stand up to them and give as good as he got. Nevertheless, Leo could see at a glance that it was a hopeless task. He couldn't be more than six or seven and the boy's puny little fists rarely connected with their target, the three bigger boys pushing and punching with fierce gusto, tossing him between them like a rag doll.

Leo could recall being bullied himself as a young boy, until he'd thankfully grown sufficiently tall to make his oppressors think twice before taking him on. Any minute now they'd fling the boy into the road right in front of Leo's Jaguar.

He screeched to a halt, flung open his door and leaped out to put a stop to the unfair battle.

'What the hell do you think you're doing? Pick on someone your own size, you great bullies.' Long before he reached them, the three had turned tail and run, leaving their young victim sprawled senseless on the pavement. Even as Leo bent down to check on his pulse and gently probe several shiners that were already appearing on his small pale face, a woman ran up and fell to her knees beside him.

'Tom, are you all right, darling? Oh, please speak to me, Tom. Oh, my God, they've killed him!'

'I don't think so,' Leo reassured her. 'But he is unconscious. Ah, good, he's showing signs of coming round already. Excellent! All right, son, don't try to move for a minute till you get your bearings. You'll be feeling a bit woozy I should think.'

Frantic with anxiety the young woman was half gasping, half sobbing, in addition to being clearly out of breath from having run to save her son. 'Who were they? How dare they pick on someone so much smaller than themselves?'

Leo put a gentle hand on her shoulder to calm her. 'He'll be fine, don't fret. Boys, even small ones, are tougher than you might think. But I agree that it was an unequal contest, and bullying should always be stopped. I suggest you speak to his headmaster tomorrow.'

'No, Mum, don't do that.' The boy seemed now to be sufficiently recovered to speak. 'They'd only hit me again if you told on them.'

'Oh, Tom, you're alive,' and she burst into floods of tears, hugging him and smoothing his soft brown hair from his ashen face, smothering him with kisses.

Leo waited until natural relief and emotion had spent itself and the woman turned to him with moist eyes. 'I haven't thanked you yet for helping. That was very remiss of me. Tom owes his life to you.'

'I doubt the fight would have gone that far, and young Tom here was making quite a fist at holding them off all by himself. Are you one of Barry Holmes's young stars?' Leo asked him with a grin.

It was the woman who answered. 'Oh, indeed yes. He attends regularly with his father, every week, and would never miss a session.'

'Well, it looks as if it has stood him in good stead. You've nothing to be ashamed of, lad, because you lost the battle. There were three of them after all, and you gave them quite a pasting.'

A touch of pink crept into the boy's cheeks and he managed a small smile. 'I did, didn't I?'

'You certainly did. They'll think twice before tackling *you* again.'

A shadow of doubt flickered across the child's face, one his mother saw too as she helped him gingerly to his feet. 'I think I'll just pop into the doctor's and make sure there are no other injuries.'

'Aw, Mum . . .'

'No, don't argue, Tom. I intend to have you fully checked over.' Back in control of her emotions she turned to face Leo and held out a hand to him. 'I really don't know how to thank you enough.'

Leo got up from his crouched position and stretched to his full height. He found himself smiling warmly at her, his earlier bad temper having completely dissipated. She was petite and slim, her face bare of make-up and all the lovelier for that, with the kind of gently smiling mouth he had a sudden and unexpected urge to taste. Her shoulder-length dark hair flew about her head in a tumble of wild curls and she lifted one slender hand to push it back from her face in an attempt to tame it. But what he felt most in that moment was a jolt of recognition, as if he'd met her somewhere before.

'Do I know you? You seem very familiar.'

'My husband is Sam Beckett. He has the ironmongery shop inside Champion Street Market.'

'Ah, of course.' He thought it rather curious that she should identify herself by naming her husband, as if she had no identity of her own. Not something Helen would ever do. But that must account for her familiarity. He'd seen her around the market, nothing more than that.

Yet Leo knew, as he took her hand in his and savoured the small warmness of it, that there was a great deal more to it than that. 'Leo Catlow,' he said, and they smiled into each other's eyes.

In that moment it came to him that this was the woman he'd been waiting for all his life. The trouble was, he'd found her far too late.

18

Lynda

Lynda was taking her turn on the stall while Betty enjoyed a late breakfast of toasted crumpets in Belle's café. She was hammering the hard stems so that they would properly take up water, filling up the black galvanised buckets with clean cold water, stripping off the leaves from below the water line. Each day it was growing warmer and keeping the flowers fresh demanded endless spraying with cool water at intervals throughout the day. The daffodils were flown in every morning from Jersey and the Scilly Isles to Covent Garden and from there came by train to Manchester. Some flowers, such as tulips, were grown in Lincolnshire, miniature roses in pots travelled down from Scotland, and primroses and violets came from the woods of Devon and Cornwall. Lynda cupped a hand around a sprig of lavender to draw in the full aroma of its scent.

Lavender for distrust. Betty was no nearer to trusting Ewan, her ex-husband, but did *she* feel the same way about him? Lynda asked herself. Was she too beginning to have doubts over the wisdom of having her father come to live with them?

Lynda had naturally been thrilled when Ewan had first announced his intention to stay on for a while, if surprised by the sudden decision. He didn't even ask if her mother minded. This hadn't troubled Lynda at the time, but now she recognised it as a lack of respect on his part.

She'd always known that Ewan Hemley wasn't an easy man. Lynda thought of him as an eccentric, a free spirit, and at first had been annoyed by her mother's lack of patience with him, and by their constant back-biting.

But even she was beginning to find his manners and general behaviour disturbing. There was something not quite right about the man, something not particularly pleasant, and Lynda's earlier irritation with her mother was beginning to fade and change to one of sympathy. It couldn't be easy to have your ex-husband show up after all this time, let alone march into your home and attempt to take over.

'Come on, chuck,' Ewan would say. 'Come and sit on your old dad's knee.' Lynda had done so because she'd always longed for a father, to be part of a proper family and assured of his love.

Yet she was becoming increasingly uncomfortable over these excessive displays of affection. After only a few moments of feeling his hands on her back, or his tobacco-stained fingers twisting in her auburn curls, Lynda would experience the slightest sensation of a shiver running down her spine. Now why was that?

At first she told herself it was because they were still virtual strangers, not having seen him since she was a young girl. Naturally he wouldn't *feel* like a father, would he?

And although she would never tell her mother, he had a strange habit of fondling her bottom, which Lynda really didn't care for at all. It had only happened once or twice, but he'd slide his hand over her buttocks and knead the softly rounded flesh in an oddly intimate fashion. The first time she'd thought it a mistake, or her imagination, but the second time it had happened Lynda had got quickly to her feet and made some excuse that she'd promised to go over to Judy's place, and fled. The sound of his laughter had followed her all the way out the door, which somehow made it even more chilling.

It was that same night she'd first had the dream.

The fear was the most prevalent part of it, that, and a desperate need to escape. Then there were the hands. They were huge and very white, fluttering at her in the dream like a pair of avenging angels, or pigeons flying at her in Albert Square, something which she'd always found frightening.

Exactly what a pair of huge white hands had to do with Ewan Hemley, Lynda couldn't understand, but a small worm of doubt was growing inside her that perhaps she didn't like him quite so much as she'd hoped she would. And watching Jake make a fool of himself getting drunk night after night in order to gain his father's attention didn't seem to be such a good thing either.

So maybe her mother did have a point, after all, and it was time Ewan moved on. Lynda still couldn't bring herself to call him Dad, even though her brother used the word regularly, casting sly glances of triumph at Mam as he did so.

It went without saying that she would want to stay in touch with him after he left. He was still her father, after all, no matter what his idiosyncrasies. But attempting to reunite them as a family had probably not been such a good idea. Too late, maybe, after all these long years apart.

The trouble was that Lynda felt nervous of actually telling him so. What was even more worrying was that not a day passed without Betty demanding he leave. On one occasion her mother had even packed a bag for him, with sandwiches and a flask of coffee. He'd picked the bag up, looked inside, then thrown it at her. The flask had smashed and the coffee formed a dark stain all over the pretty flowered wallpaper.

'I'm bloody going nowhere, so you can stuff this up your own arse and shout lost, Betty my love.'

It was in that moment Lynda realised how her own over-eagerness to get to know her father might perhaps have been a bad mistake, resulting in more problems for her mam, whom she'd always tried to protect. Her eagerness for this long-dreamed-of family life had inadvertently landed them all in a mess. Therefore it was surely her duty to put it right. The trouble was, Lynda hadn't the first idea how to set about the task.

'What can I do, Judy? It's all gone terribly wrong.'

'Just a minute, Lynda. Let me finish wrapping this picture for Dena.'

It was a Wednesday and her friend was busy at her stall selling pictures of cats and flowers. Lynda was suddenly filled with pride for her friend, and suffused with shame over her own complaints. Judy had a much more difficult life than she, living with that controlling husband of hers who'd sleep with any woman who so much as glanced in his direction. And here she was moaning about a few clumsy cuddles from a father whom she'd spent her entire life craving to know, and all because he still felt like a stranger. What was wrong with her?

'You look rushed off your feet,' Lynda said when Dena had happily gone on her way.

'Oh, I am. I would never have believed a stall selling my little pictures could be so successful. I can't thank you enough for suggesting it. It means I can afford to spend so much more time painting, if only to keep up with demand, which I love.'

'And how about himself? What does Sam think of your efforts?'

Judy pulled a face. 'He's still not particularly thrilled about my working, but seems willing to put up with it. Mind you, I take good care always to be home in good time to see to the children, clean the house and . . .'

'Make it look as if you've never been out of it?' Lynda finished for her, making Judy laugh.

'That's about it. Silly, I know, but it keeps him happy and makes life much more comfortable for us all. I'd want to pick them up from school in any case. I love my kids and enjoy spending time with them. But this special time for me is important too, and it's only two days a week.'

'The change in life-style must be suiting you. You're looking so much better.' Judy had in fact never looked prettier. Her blue eyes sparkled even more than usual, her dark curls were shining with healthy vigour and her skin didn't have that dingy, tired quality to it any more. She seemed to have come alive. Even her shirt and slacks looked tidier than usual, although still bearing tell-tale signs of oil paint here and there.

'So what were you saying about something going terribly wrong?'

Lynda shrugged her shoulders. Not for the world could she

bear to unload her own petty problems on to her friend, not right at this moment when Judy was looking so happy and relaxed at last. 'Oh, nothing important. Mam still isn't getting on with – with Ewan, that's all. But what would you expect?'

'Are you getting on with him okay? You enjoy having your father around at last, don't you?' Judy asked, her voice soft and caring.

'Oh, yes . . . yes, of course I do,' Lynda agreed, pasting a brisk smile on her face. 'I'm delighted.'

Lynda had made her decision. Seeing her friend standing up for herself at last seemed to give her the courage to do the same. Wanting to get to know her own father was all well and good, but it shouldn't be at the expense of her mother who'd brought her up, and whom she loved dearly. And there was no doubt that having Ewan in the house day after day was making Betty very unhappy.

With this in mind, she plucked up the courage to tackle Ewan on the subject of his leaving.

'So you see, I think it would be best if you were to move out. I know there aren't many houses or flats to rent in the area but if you can't find one, there are plenty of people who take in lodgers. And we could still keep in touch, of course we could, and see each other regularly. But you must see how it's upsetting Mam having you here. The pair of you aren't getting on at all, and why should you? You're not even man and wife any more.'

'And whose fault is that?'

Lynda didn't know how to answer that one. 'Hmm . . . so I think you should live some place else. It was a big mistake for us to expect it to work, don't you think?'

'I'll go when I'm good and ready and not before.'

'Look . . . Dad . . .' The name sounded awkward on her tongue but Lynda wanted to reassure him, to let him see that she wasn't rejecting him in any way. 'I feel bad about it but this is a small house. Mam works hard on the flower stall and when she comes

home she needs a bit of peace and quiet, not tension and arguments. Jake and I can't bear to see the pair of you at each other's
throats the whole time. You're divorced, and that's that. We all
have to accept that fact and you need to make a new life for
yourself. I just want you to know that we will still be a part of
that life, as you will still be a part of our family. But you can't
stay here.'

He hit her. One minute he was smiling at her in that sardonic,
I'll-do-as-I-please sort of way, the next he'd smacked her across
the face with the back of his hand. The violence of the blow sent
Lynda reeling. She fell against the table and slumped to the floor.

Ewan stood over her, knuckles clenched. 'The best way to stop
the arguing is for you all to do as you're told. That's not too
difficult to understand, is it? Good, now we've got that sorted
you can make my tea and stop your blathering.'

Lynda gladly escaped to the kitchen where she leaned against
the door in a state of total shock. Finding her legs were shaking
uncontrollably, she half collapsed into a chair, leaned her elbows
on the table and put her head in her hands, feeling ice-cold
tears slide through her fingers. Dear God, what had she done?
She'd brought a monster into their home. So this was the reason
her mother had left him; this was what Betty had always refused
to talk about. Ewan was violent and had probably beaten her
too.

A surge of hot fury soared through Lynda's young veins. Well,
he damned well wasn't going to bully her. She grabbed a knife
and as she peeled potatoes, sliced and cooked chips and fried
him an egg, Lynda wished she could chop him into little bits
and throw him away with the potato peelings, even as silent sobs
and tears wracked her body. How could she have been so foolish
as to imagine he could love her? He might be her father but he
was still a stranger to her.

Ewan Hemley had ignored them for years and now thought
he could simply walk back into their lives and order them about
to suit himself. Worst of all, her mother had protected them from
him for years and now she, Lynda, had thrown that care in her

face by inviting him in for that dratted Sunday lunch. If she hadn't done that, they wouldn't be in this terrible situation.

When Betty came home, her daughter's tear-stained face told her at once that something was wrong and she turned on Ewan. 'What have you done to her? What have your mucky hands been doing to her now?'

That was the phrase she used: *your mucky hands*! Words that electrified Lynda.

The hands in her dream, were they her father's hands? Did he use to hit her before, when she was a small girl? Did he do other things too? Oh, dear God, let that not be the case. But if so, why couldn't she remember?

Lynda knew the answer even as the question formed in her mind: because Mam had made sure that they *didn't* remember. She'd been determined that they forget all about their father and his nasty ways. Betty had taken them to what she believed to be a safe place here on Champion Street in the heart of Manchester, and shut Ewan Hemley out of their lives.

Oh, why hadn't she listened when Mam had begged her not to allow him home for Sunday lunch? Why hadn't she tried to understand?

Lynda longed to hear the full details of the marriage now, so that she could understand everything, but how could she ask with him sitting there like – like a king of his own domain? A demon king, wasn't that the word her mother had used? And it was true. Lynda was ashamed to discover that a part of her actually hated him, for all he might be her own father.

19

Judy

S am was not sympathetic over his son having been bullied
and told the boy he should have been able to give a better
account of himself. 'Haven't I paid for you to have boxing lessons
at Barry Holmes's club? I'm surprised you didn't see them off.
Look at you, covered in bruises. I can see I've wasted my money.
You're nothing but a weakling.'

Judy gasped, drawing her stricken child protectively to her
side. 'But there were *three* of them. How can one six-year-old
boy stand up to *three* bullies?'

Sam ignored her as he again addressed his son. 'Your failure
to stand up for yourself means you're going to need extra training.
Let go of him, Judy, you'll turn him into a mummy's boy, and
I won't have that.'

'The man said that I did well.'

'What man?'

'The one who came to help me.'

Sam's flint-like gaze slid from his son to his wife. 'Do I take
it you weren't even there?'

'I arrived within minutes – seconds.'

'Go to your room, lad. I'll deal with you later.' When Tom had
gone, dragging his feet and glancing back anxiously at his mother,
as if to make sure he wasn't in trouble with her as well, Sam
rounded on Judy.

'The fault for this episode is entirely yours. Had you been
there on time, as you should have been if you'd been doing your
job as a mother correctly and not playing at running market
stalls, then this would never have happened.'

Judy was stunned by the accusation. 'Oh, Sam, that's a cruel thing to say. I was only seconds late, mere seconds. I told Tom to wait for me by the school gate but he'd set off home alone.'

'And where was Ruth through all of this?'

'Her class were at the swimming baths having a lesson. We picked her up on the way home.'

'So you were late for her too. Right, that's it, the stall will have to go.'

'What? But I can't . . . Oh, don't make me give it up now, when it's doing so well.'

'It's exactly as I predicted. The stall, and that bloody hobby of yours, is standing in the way of your proper duties. I'll give you a week's grace, but I shall expect to see you back home being a proper mother again by this time next week. I've no intention of putting our children's lives at risk for one of your selfish fancies.'

'But that's not fair. It's not me or my stall at fault because some bullies beat up our son. It's theirs and theirs alone. I intend to say as much to the headmaster.'

Sam slammed his fist down on to the table. '*You will do no such thing!* Apart from the fact he will think exactly as I do, that it wouldn't have happened if *you*, his mother, had been there; complaining to the school will only make Tom's situation worse. It'll make him look a real namby-pamby, needing his teacher's help.'

'But we can't let those boys get away with it. We have to—'

'That's *enough*!' Sam roared. 'There's no more to be said on the matter. I will allow one week for you to sell off those stupid pictures of yours for whatever you can get for them, then close the damned stall down.'

Judy couldn't believe her bad luck. She'd only been held up for a matter of minutes, selling a rather special picture to a customer.

Perhaps Sam was right though. She should have been there to protect Tom. Oh, she was filled with such guilt. Was she a failure as a mother? Was she selfish? Surely not. How could she have imagined that such a thing might happen? And she'd made a point of telling both her children to wait by the school gate should she ever be held up for any reason. What had possessed Tom to set off home alone? She rather thought that he'd had no choice in the matter. Perhaps he was running from the bullies, hoping he would meet up with her, and it had all gone badly wrong.

But for Sam to accuse Tom of being a mummy's boy was equally unfair. Why should he be made to feel a failure because he couldn't take on three big lads? This was a hang-over from Sam's own childhood. Lillian, his mother, had always been a fussy woman, constantly ailing and complaining, and neither parent had shown their young son much in the way of affection. Sam's father had insisted the apron strings be cut early to make sure the boy grew into a strong man, and now Sam, in turn, was behaving in exactly the same way with his own son.

But punishing her by insisting she close the stall was unfair. What had that got to do with anything? How cruel Sam could be sometimes. Why couldn't he see that she needed a life of her own, in addition to motherhood? She needed some freedom to express her creativity, to be herself, and where was the harm in that?

He would say there was a great deal of harm, if it meant that she neglected her children.

Oh, but she hadn't neglected them, not knowingly, and despite everything she'd been through with Sam, all the times he'd cheated on her, Judy had studiously accepted the way things were between them. She had learned not to complain, not to expect him to change, or to give up what was an intrinsic part of his personality. Hadn't it been made clear to her from the start that there was little point in her trying?

She'd tolerated his iron control, his need for perfection, his lectures and his orders, as did the children, just as if they were all privates in the army and he was their sergeant. But she was tired of it, tired of feeling guilty, tired of obeying his every whim, tired of failing to meet his exacting standards.

Now, for the first time, Judy began to question her own loyalty. Where was the point in her putting up with all of that if Sam allowed her no freedom whatsoever, gave her no love, nor showed even the smallest degree of kindness and understanding?

Why couldn't he have been as sympathetic and understanding as Tom's rescuer, Leo Catlow, had been?

It came to her in a moment of rare clarity that not only was her precious child being bullied at school, but she too was being bullied by her own husband in her own home, even if he never had laid a finger on her. And she would tolerate it no more.

Judy made a private vow that from now on she would somehow make an effort to take charge of her own life. If he was free to enjoy his women, then she should surely be allowed some freedom of her own to make her own life tolerable.

Damn it, she wouldn't close down her stall. She would go on running it for as long as she possibly could.

It was on Friday morning that Leo strolled casually over to Judy's stall to ask how Tom was. He really should have been in his office by now but something had caused him to linger over breakfast in the hope of catching sight of Judy Beckett before he left. He told himself it was nothing more than concern for the hapless victim. It was the polite thing to do.

'Has the little chap got over the shock of being used as a punch-bag?'

Judy smilingly nodded. 'I think he'll live, but it was a stiff lesson for him to learn.'

'Hardly his fault though. I hope you've made a strong complaint to the school.'

Judy paused, not quite meeting his eye. 'My husband doesn't seem to think that's a good idea.'

'I see.' A short pause while he studied her. She was even lovelier than he remembered, and more fragile. He could see something was troubling her, the usually warm smile seeming somehow strained. 'But you don't agree with him.'

'No, I don't.' She looked up at him then and it was exactly as before. There was an instant rapport between them, a sort of recognition, almost as if he could read her mind which was perhaps what allowed her to make this frank confession. It was the strangest experience, comforting and yet exciting all at the same time. Dangerously so. Just looking into those sparkling blue eyes brought a tightness to his chest.

'Perhaps you could have a quiet word with the boy's teacher, without your husband knowing. Ask her to keep an eye out for any trouble.'

Judy was shocked. 'Oh no, I could never go behind my husband's back. Never!'

'Never?' Leo gave a half-laugh. 'I thought women were well practised in the art of getting their own way.'

She shook her head. 'Not me.'

'My wife certainly is. I am married too, you see.'

The phrase seemed heavy with meaning but she couldn't seem to drag her gaze from his. 'Yes, I know.' Another telling silence followed, which neither seemed able to break. After a beat Judy cleared her throat, frantically saying the first thing that came into her head. 'Your wife is a lovely, elegant woman.'

'Oh, very stylish, yes, and truly female. If she wants something, she believes it is my role in life, as the man of the household, to supply it.' He was smiling again, making light of his words but Judy recognised a hint of bitterness underneath.

'I could never persuade my husband to do anything he didn't want to.'

'You could, if you were as single-minded as my wife.'

'Oh no, I can't imagine a situation where I would ever go against his wishes, in anything.' And Judy blushed, wondering what on earth had possessed her to make such a foolish remark since she was doing exactly that by refusing to close down the stall.

'Never?'

'No, never.'

'I see.'

There seemed to be a vibration in the air between them, some hidden meaning to the words as if they were speaking about something other than whether or not she should talk to Tom's teacher without Sam knowing.

The smile faded and Leo's expression became unusually solemn as he continued to hold her gaze, his voice soft and filled with compassion. 'That must make life quite difficult.'

She shrugged. 'Sometimes. But that's how it is, isn't it, when you're married?'

'Is it?'

Leo longed to say something that would bring back that lovely warm smile, make it light up her face again but he felt as tongue-tied as a raw youth. What on earth was happening to him?

The moment was broken by Lizzie Pringle coming over in search of a gift for her mother's birthday, and with a last brief nod Leo turned on his heel and walked quickly away. Perhaps he'd been saved from making a complete ass of himself, yet in truth he resented the interruption deeply.

Judy steadfastly turned her attention to the task in hand, although she felt a surprising regret at seeing him go.

More than a week later she learned the cost of daring to defy her husband. Sam was furious when he discovered that she had disobeyed his instructions and her stall was still operational. He said nothing to her there and then, in front of everyone on the market, but she could tell by the way his jaw tightened and his fists clenched when he saw her setting up as usual, that he was filled with rage. Sergeant Sam Beckett was not accustomed to insubordination, particularly from his own wife.

Judy got through the day as best she could, but it was not until later that evening that she learned the full extent of his anger. He marched into the house and ignoring the carefully set table, the flowers in place at its centre, his wife and children beautifully dressed and welcoming, he stormed up to the attic and slashed all her pictures to pieces. There wasn't any question then of Judy continuing with her stall, as she'd nothing left to sell.

20

Betty and Lynda

In Betty's little book of flower meanings, marriage was asso-
ciated with ivy which seemed highly appropriate in the circumstances. Ivy would cling to anything and choke the life out of it,
rather as Ewan Hemley was trying to do to her. And even though
she'd chopped their marriage off at the roots, just as ivy did with
brickwork he continued to cling and hang on week after week,
month after month, when really he should give up and accept
defeat.

On her stall today she had branches of golden broom, known
for humility, as was the sweet-scented lilac. If she took a bunch
home to stand on her dresser, would it remind her to exercise
more of that virtue herself? Somehow Betty doubted it. Hadn't
she learned long ago that humility and patience could easily turn
a woman into a doormat, a role she never intended to play again.

Ewan had struck Lynda. The girl might deny it but Betty had
seen the fear in her eyes and the bruise on her cheek. Wasn't she
familiar with the signs, the kind she'd hoped never to see again?

Later, when they'd gone upstairs to bed, mother and daughter
had exchanged a few whispered words of comfort. Lynda
admitted that she'd asked him to leave, and he'd refused.

'It's all my fault that he's here,' she'd sobbed.

'No, it isn't, love. If it's anyone's, it's mine. I should have taken
you further away, to the other side of the world if necessary.
Ewan Hemley is bad news. Look at what he's done to our Jake.
The lad still hasn't come home again tonight, so where the hell
is he? Out with them rapscallion mates of his, I'll be bound, up

to no good. Having a father around has made him worse, not better.'

'He's just seeking attention,' Lynda said, as if they didn't both know that already.

The two women were silent for a long while, sitting huddled together on the edge of Betty's bed with their arms about each other.

'What can we do, Mam?'

'I don't know, chuck, but I'm thinking about it. We'll get no help from Constable Nuttall, that's for sure, I've already tried down that road. So it's up to me, lass, to sort this one out. All I've ever wanted out of life is for you and Jake to be happy and safe. Now wipe your eyes and get some sleep. We'll talk some more tomorrow.'

Now Betty stared about her at the smoke-blackened brick of the terraced houses, each door brightly painted, the windows glistening from regular applications of soap and water and liberal quantities of bleach and washing soda, the sills given their twice-weekly coating of cream rubbing stone. Who'd want to go to Australia when she could live here in Manchester? Betty loved her home and nobody, not even Ewan Hemley, was going to chase her out of it.

Lynda was still seeing Terry, and that evening they were going dancing at the Co-operative Rooms. They'd been dating for almost six months now and she'd bought herself a new dress to celebrate. It was shantung blue cotton in the new Trapeze line with elbow-length sleeves and a bow just under the breast. Terry whistled softly when he saw her in it. He never failed to appreciate the trouble she took to look nice and Lynda liked that in him.

Terry belonged to a skiffle group and was playing for part of the evening while Barry Holmes, who operated the record player, took a break. He was naturally musical, since his father Alex owned Hall's Music Stall, and played lead guitar in the group. Much of the winter had been spent in rehearsals at the back of the shop and Lynda didn't mind missing out on a few dances as she loved to sit listening to him, entranced.

He finished with 'Sweet Little Rock & Roller,' a Chuck Berry number, and Buddy Holly's 'Rave On', which Lynda loved. Lynda had adored Buddy Holly and still wept when she thought of his tragic death in February.

She was also still stinging from the blow her father had given her. She'd felt compelled to lie to Terry when he'd first seen the bruise, pretending she'd banged it against a cupboard door when she was making tea. Lynda hated to deceive him but was fearful Terry might go straight round and thump Ewan, which would do no good at all. She was the one who had to live with him and Terry couldn't be there to protect her all day, so, as Mam said, they had to sort this one themselves.

Tonight Lynda had put make-up over her bruises and was determined to be happy so she smiled up at Terry when he returned to her side. 'You really are quite talented.'

'I was singing it specially for you, my own sweet little rock and roller.'

'Oh, that's the nicest thing anyone's ever said to me,' and Lynda kissed him, a long, demanding sort of kiss that brought whistles and cheers from their friends and made Terry blush.

Later, on their way home, she let him do a great deal more than kiss her. But then she was fancy free and single, so why not? She let him fondle her breasts, then slide his hand beneath her net petticoats and press it against that secret, private part of herself. She groaned with pleasure but that was as far as she let him go. She was still being cautious, still needing to be sure of him.

'Hey, don't think you can do as you please just because I'm old enough to have been round the block once or twice.'

Terry gazed into her hazel eyes, his face oddly serious and wearing that wounded-little-boy look that turned her heart over. 'As if I'd think such thing. Why do you put yourself down in that way, Lynda? Don't you know by now how I feel about you? That you're very special to me.'

'Oh, Terry, you're special to me too.' Lynda could hardly believe it of herself but despite her efforts to remain cool and detached she was falling for him, good and hard. She'd never met anyone so caring, so loving, and yet so exciting. She loved tearing around the countryside with him on the back of his motor bike, but was equally content to walk with Terry by the canal, or sit and watch him play his guitar. And even though she daren't ask him over to her place, because of Ewan, she was welcome any time at his house, and called in regularly on a daily basis, if only to see his gorgeous face.

'My word,' Judy had said, when she'd told her all of this. 'You have got it bad.'

'I know, and it's great. You don't think he might be *the one*?'

Good friend that she was Judy had advised caution, urging Lynda not to rush into anything. 'Marriage and all that stuff is such a commitment. Give yourself time. I wish I had,' and such a pained, bleak expression had come over her lovely face that Lynda had reached out to hug her.

'Yeah, I know, but I'm twenty-six now, not getting any younger.'

Judy laughed. 'There's plenty of time yet.'

'I suppose so. Anyway if I ever start to get broody I only have to look at Mam and Ewan to see the mess marriage can bring. It's hell on earth in our house at the moment.'

'I thought you were happy to have your father living with you at last?'

'It's not quite so straightforward as it might seem,' Lynda had said, and quickly changed the subject.

Tonight, Terry would have walked with her right to her front door but Lynda told him there was no need. 'Look, this is your house here, and mine is just twenty yards away.' Terry lived on Quay Street, along which they'd walked from the corner of Deansgate after they'd got off the bus.

'More like a hundred-yard dash along two more streets,' Terry said. 'I'm coming with you.'

She gathered his face in her hands and kissed him again, long and hard. 'You're a sweet boy but don't fuss. I'm a big girl now.

I can negotiate a couple of streets, do a hundred-yard dash if necessary.'

'Please don't call me boy. I'm twenty, nearly twenty-one, and I don't care if there are a few years between us, I like you, Lynda, and that's all that matters.'

'Oh, you're right, it is. I didn't mean to sound – well – so patronising.'

'I know,' he said, kissing her some more.

It was several moments later before Lynda finally broke away from him, her cheeks rosy and with not a scrap of lipstick left on her swollen mouth. 'I've got to go. See you tomorrow. We'll meet up for coffee in Belle's caff at eleven as usual, right?'

'Right.'

And with a cheery wave she turned and hurried away, aware of him standing at the bottom of Gartside Street watching her until she reached the corner of Grove Street. Here she turned and waved one last time, calling out that she was fine now before setting off to run the last few yards to Champion Street.

The night was dark with few stars and no sign of a moon to light her path, only the pale yellow glow from the old-fashioned street lamps that had once been operated by gas but were converted to electricity before the war. Champion Street looked oddly naked with all the market stalls stacked away and a few stray chip papers blowing about. A chill wind made Lynda draw her coat closer about her and quicken her pace, though it didn't quench the warm glow in the pit of her stomach.

But she felt less brave walking home alone than she'd expected. Maybe she was growing too used to having a regular escort? Lynda almost fell over her own front doorstep on a sigh of relief, pushed her key in the lock and flung herself inside. Home safe at last. What a softie she was!

Betty was waiting for her when she got inside, sitting with Queenie in her lap, and with her head in her hands. Ewan wasn't in yet, and neither was Jake, no doubt off on the razzle together like a couple of daft teenagers.

'What's up?' Lynda asked, but her mother quickly shushed her.

Betty shooed Queenie gently on to the floor then went to make hot cocoa for them both. They sat sipping it side by side on the sofa, the biscuit barrel between them. 'He's been at it again,' Betty eventually confessed, her round face creased with anxiety.

'At what?'

'Me purse. There's a five-pound note missing. Last week it was two pounds and the Friday before that one pound ten shillings. I thought happen I'd miscounted, but there's no mistake this time because I kept a careful note. He's nicked it.'

'Oh, Mam, you can't be certain it's him.'

'Aye, I can, if only by the way he laughed for no reason when he saw me totting up the day's takings. I work, and he steals and drinks, that's how it's allus been. I'm scared he might find my secret hoard, you know – me tin box what I keep under the floorboards?'

Mother and daughter both stared down at the green rug which hid Betty's hoard.

'Shouldn't you move it then, if you're worried?'

Betty frowned, looking deeply concerned, and Lynda put her arms about the soft cosy shoulders and hugged her beloved mother close. 'We'll think of something, somewhere safe to hide your stash. Don't you and me always solve our problems in the end? Remember that time our Jake started stuttering in order to get attention. We tried everything under the sun, then we threatened him with some nasty-tasting medicine and it stopped overnight.'

Betty chuckled at the memory. 'But Ewan Hemley isn't a seven-year-old child, and getting rid of him will take more than a spoonful of cough mixture. He's got to go, Lynda, or there'll be blue murder done in this house, and then where will we be?'

Next morning, at eleven, Lynda was waiting as promised in Belle's caff but it was Alex Hall and not his son who came to meet her.

'Terry asked me to come and apologise for his absence but he's had to stay home today. After you left him last night someone jumped him and gave him a real going-over. Beat him up so bad the poor lad is covered in bruises. He looks like he's gone nine rounds with Tommy Farr.'

'Oh, my God, is he all right? Who would do such a thing?'

'I don't know,' Alex said, a frown of anxiety etched into his face. He sat down opposite her and thoughtfully sipped his frothy coffee. 'Probably some nasty little tyke out of his skull on booze. But when I find him, Terry won't be the only one seeking retaliation.'

'Are you sure he's all right?'

'He'll live but he's got some badly bruised ribs. I've told him to go to the doctor but will he listen?'

'Can I go and see him during my dinner hour? Maybe I can persuade him to go.'

Alex grinned at her. 'You seem to have got it as bad as him.'

'Maybe I have,' Lynda admitted, a sheepish smile hiding her concern. 'And when you find out who did this terrible thing, give him one for me too, will you?'

Lynda spent as much time as she dared with Terry, promising she'd buy herself a packet of crisps later to make up for missing her dinner. She couldn't stay nearly as long as she would have liked as she was working on the chocolate stall this afternoon, to give Lizzie Pringle a break.

'Who was it, did you see who hit you?'

Terry shook his head. He was strangely quiet, clearly not keen to talk about the experience which Lynda could quite understand. 'I thought he might not stop, that he'd go on till he killed me.'

'Oh, Terry, don't say such a thing. You must have been terrified. I can't bear to think of it.'

'Why, would you miss me if anything happened to me?' He gazed up at her with such hope and adoration in his eyes that she chuckled softly at him.

'If you weren't covered with such horrendous bruises I'd think that maybe you were deliberately trying to make me feel sorry for you.'

He grinned then, a rather crooked, one-sided sort of smile but at least with some warmth to it. 'You could kiss the bruises better, and I'll kiss yours. I'd have no objection to that.' Lynda readily did as he asked and they both felt considerably better by the time she got up to go.

Terry held on to her hand for a long, telling moment. 'No matter what, Lynda, nothing and nobody can change the way I feel about you.'

Lynda failed to pick up on the hint that the beating-up might have something to do with their seeing each other. She was too keen to ask another question entirely, a teasing note in her voice. 'And how *do* you feel about me, exactly, Terry Hall?'

'I'll tell you some other time, when I don't feel like I've been kicked all over by an elephant.'

'See that you do. I shall hold you to that promise.'

21

Helen and Judy

Helen was lying sprawled on the bed, one linen sheet only half covering her naked body, the curve of her breasts enticingly on view. Leo found he could hardly bear to look at her, as if for some reason he felt ashamed of what they'd just done together, and of her willingness to do it all over again. She'd been the one to initiate it, as was so often the case these days, taunting and teasing him until he'd been quite unable to resist.

No matter how prickly their relationship in everyday life, there seemed to be no problems between them sexually, and, knowing himself to be a good lover, powerful and demanding, Leo had never felt his manhood threatened in any way if Helen should choose to take the lead.

Today, however, had been different. He wasn't able to concentrate on her needs at all, wasn't really *with* her as his mind was elsewhere, seeing a different face altogether.

He even found himself half listening for his mother. Not that Dulcie would ever simply walk in upon them, being far too polite and middle-class for that, but she would often tap on the door and whisper through the pale oak panels as if wary of disturbing them even as she did so. It infuriated Helen to the point of distraction and made Leo jumpy, as he was now.

He was only too aware that relations between his wife and his mother were far from easy. Only the other day Dulcie had approached him, suggesting it was perhaps time she returned home to Lytham, but he could tell that her heart wasn't in it.

She'd only moved there in the first place in an effort to force her stubborn husband into retirement. She was much happier here, in the city. He was delighted to see that she was meeting up with old friends again, had rejoined her church groups and was living a much fuller life. Why would he condemn her to life alone in a silent bungalow?

It certainly didn't trouble Leo having his mother live with them, it was a large enough house for them not to intrude upon each other. Unfortunately he couldn't persuade his wife to share this viewpoint. He'd suggested they make a separate flat for Dulcie, with her own kitchen built into the old conservatory, but Helen wouldn't hear of it.

'What, ruin our lovely home? Over my dead body.'

He was rarely allowed to forget the long-drawn-out war that was raging between the two women in his life. Mostly it was conducted in polite undertones, Dulcie treading on egg-shells with Helen cutting the frosty atmosphere with her famous barbed remarks. Occasionally tempers would erupt and he'd hear doors being slammed and voices raised, although rarely his mother's. He was more likely to find Dulcie sniffing into her hanky while Helen was the one who had the tantrum. It was all very troubling.

Nevertheless he'd be fooling himself if he said that his mother was the only concern occupying his mind at present. If he was too preoccupied to be interested in their love-making today, the cause lay in quite another direction altogether.

Ever since that moment when he'd rescued her son from the bullies he couldn't get Judy Beckett out of his head. Nor later when he'd talked to her at her stall and she'd made those enigmatic remarks about not disobeying her husband. He remembered how she'd first introduced herself by identifying herself through him. Yet she was clearly a talented artist so why did she have so little confidence in herself? And why should the woman matter so much to him anyway?

'It's all right, Dulcie is asleep,' Helen was saying, guessing his thoughts, at least partially. 'I heard her snores on my way back from the bathroom.'

'She's a very light sleeper, particularly since my father died.'

'But *we* aren't dead, *we're* still very much alive, and I need you, Leo. Don't you need me?'

'Of course I do, I'm just a bit down that's all. Not only because I'm worried about Ma but I still feel swamped by grief, so sad that my father died before ever we'd bridged our differences. I can't seem to properly relax.'

'Utter tosh! That happened months ago and it's long past time you got over it. Come here, I'll soon make you feel *much* better.'

She rode him hard, bringing him to the peak of fulfilment, but then he flunked it at the last moment, hating himself for this show of weakness.

Desperate not to admit failure, Helen scrambled to her feet and stood above him on the bed, naked and proud, wanting him to see every inch of her finely toned body. 'Don't tell me this doesn't set your blood pumping?'

She smiled down at him, cool and calculating, laughing softly as she saw the effect she still had on him. And of course her brazenness produced the desired effect.

Leo pulled her down beneath him, and, determined to rid himself of this other image haunting his consciousness, he drove into her with a greed that shocked and repulsed him even as the blood roared in his ears and the sweat slicked his body. Helen was like a wild cat in his arms, biting and licking, spurring him on to greater heights.

When it was over she turned from him to coolly walk away, presumably to wash the smell of his sweat from her lovely body as she always did. There were never any post-coital cuddles with Helen. Talking was never part of their love-making. Sex, so far as she was concerned, was all consuming, not to be interrupted by soft words or romantic discussions.

Instinct told him that making love to Judy Beckett would be very different.

The thought of love-making was not, at that precise moment, high on Judy's list of concerns. She sat amongst the remnants of her slashed canvasses and wept. How could he do this to her? How could Sam be so cruel, just so that he could get his own way?

Even Ruth, not the most sentimental of girls and deeply loyal to her father, sat grasping her mother's hand in speechless horror.

The child should have been in bed, of course, but she'd heard the row and the crashes, heard her mother run upstairs in a flurry of panicking sobs. The moment Sam had left the house, slamming the door behind him, she'd crept up to the loft to see what was going on.

'Oh, Mummy, all your pretty flower pictures have been spoiled. And that one of me and Tom in the back garden. He's ripped that too. Why would Daddy do such a terrible thing?'

Judy was struggling to steady herself. She felt as if she might actually vomit as she looked at the wreck of months of hard work, but the last thing she must do was to allow her children to hate their father. 'Daddy lost his temper. People do bad things sometimes when they're angry, like when Tom broke his fire engine by flinging it at the wall that time when I told him to put it away.'

'Is Daddy angry because you didn't close down your stall? Doesn't he like you doing so well?'

Ruth was far too astute for her own good and at least deserved an honest answer. 'He thinks I should stay at home and be a better mother to you and Tom, and I suppose he's right.'

'I said he wouldn't like it,' Ruth agreed, her small face thoughtful. 'I could always make the gravy in future, would that help?'

'Oh, Ruth, this isn't about gravy, sweetheart.' Ruth never ceased to surprise her, one minute being deliberately difficult and objectionable, the next as soft hearted and kind a daughter as any mother could wish for. She was growing quickly into a typically confused adolescent, and Judy had no wish to have her caught up in the back-fire between two warring parents. 'Daddy just wants me to concentrate on being a good mum.'

'Can't you do both?'

'I thought I could, but perhaps I shouldn't have tried. Perhaps he doesn't think my pictures are any good.'

'*I* like your pictures, Mummy,' Tom said, rubbing the sleep from his eyes as he came into the room.

'Tom, you should be in bed asleep.'

'I couldn't because of all the shouting. Are you going to paint new ones?'

'I don't think I can,' and when a tear trickled down Judy's cheek, it was Ruth who wiped it away.

'I think you should, Mummy. You think so too, Tom, don't you?'

The little boy nodded, then clambered up onto his mother's knee, not quite able to understand all the nuances of the discussion but anxious to show that he cared. He stroked his mother's cheek. 'I love you, Mummy, even if Daddy doesn't.'

'Daddy does love me, sweetie. You mustn't think that. He's just . . . concerned, that's all.'

Ruth said, 'But you mustn't give up your painting. Remember when I didn't get picked for the netball team and I said I wasn't going to practise any more? You told me that would be wrong because God had given me a special talent to run and catch a ball, and I should use it. And look, they picked me for the team this year, didn't they?'

Judy could hardly see her daughter's face for the tears in her own eyes. 'Yes, my darling, they did indeed.'

'So there we are then. You'll just have to paint better pictures next time, and make him see how important they are to *you*. We'll explain to Daddy that you have a special talent, and that's why you have to paint.'

If only it were so easy, Judy thought, hugging her children close.

Helen returned from the bathroom looking immaculate, as cool and enticingly beautiful as ever. She lay upon the bed with the clear message that she was sufficiently refreshed to start all over again, should Leo wish to. For some reason her very eagerness revolted him.

Leo stood staring blankly out of the window into the darkness of night, seeing nothing of the street beyond. 'I'm thirty-six years old, my father is dead, my mother increasingly frail, and it's long past time I justified my own existence. I feel as if time is running out for me too.'

A chuckle from the depths of the bed behind him. 'Don't talk silly, darling. You're a man in his prime.'

He half turned to glance at her over his shoulder, savouring the pale outline of her shapely figure in the shaft of moonlight that slanted in through the window. This was how she had always appeared to him, like a moon goddess: distant, remote, untouchable unless she allowed him the privilege. He half smiled, still distracted by his own thoughts. 'I'm growing older by the day. We all are. Beautiful though you undoubtedly still are, my sweet, you too are not immune to the passing years.'

Helen stiffened, dragging the sheet higher. 'What a horrible thing to say. Are you implying that I'm growing old and ugly?'

Leo chuckled. 'I wouldn't dare.' He came to sit beside his wife, taking her hand in his to stroke the long elegant fingers. 'But if we are to have a family, it should be soon. I'm trying to say that time doesn't stand still.' Even as the carefully chosen words were spoken he felt her hand jerk away from his.

'Don't start that again. You know how I feel about babies.'

'Did you use something tonight?'

He was looking at her with such sadness in those deep brown eyes that Helen felt obliged to look away. 'Of course I did, I'm not a fool. Why won't you accept my decision? My sister has ruined her health by having children, four of them for God's sake, as you well know, and at least two more that she lost.' A shudder ran down her spine. 'And look at the result.'

'Harriet seems very content with her brood.'

'How can she be content living with a jobbing building who is struggling to keep a roof over their heads?' Helen snapped, irritated that Leo refused to understand her point of view. 'They live in that untidy, overcrowded little house in Atkinson Street and she has never taken a holiday in her life.'

Leo smiled softly at his wife, drawing her hand back into his and kissing her fingertips. 'I've never heard her ask for one. Anyway, I doubt such a fate would happen to you, my darling, were you to become pregnant.'

Helen lifted a determined chin. 'I am not as strong as Harriet. I might not even survive the pregnancy. The doctor has told you how very delicate I am.'

'Doc Mitchell is an old fuddy-duddy. He told you what you wanted to hear, and it's absolute nonsense. You're a fine healthy woman and there's no reason on earth why you shouldn't have a beautiful healthy baby. Wouldn't you like that, Helen? Wouldn't you love to hold your own child in your arms?'

She looked up at him from beneath her lashes with cool indifference. 'Why would I? Babies are such messy creatures, always screaming and crying, judging by my many nieces and nephews. Dreadfully demanding.'

Helen never tired of pointing out to him the mess and bother babies caused. In fact, Leo would have welcomed a little more disorder, some disturbance to bring this immaculately presented house to life. 'I am reliably informed that one's own children are far less obnoxious than other people's.'

Helen suddenly got to her knees to grasp his face between her hands, flickering sensual fingers over his wide mouth. 'There are so many *other* things we could do with our lives that are far more important, far more *useful* than producing noisy little brats. Power is what really counts in this world.'

He pushed her hand aside. 'You're not still trying to persuade me to aim for political glory? I thought I'd made it clear that I wasn't interested? I have no desire to present myself as a rival to Harold Macmillan.'

'Don't be so damned stubborn.'

'I'm perfectly content running my distribution business on the docks, which more than fulfils me.' If there was a gap in his life, it wasn't one that could be filled by politics. Leo wanted to be a family man, not stand for Parliament. Why could she not see that?

Helen shrugged off his protests as not worth listening to. 'Nonsense! You'd make an excellent MP. I've said so a million times. Why were you so difficult when David Barford was attempting to make you change your mind the other evening? Did you have to be quite so blunt?'

Leaving her to drone on, all about how she was quite certain he could be the kind of politician who would appeal to the vast majority of electors and rise quickly to the very top, Leo got up from the bed to again take his stance by the window. He'd heard it all so many times before.

Now she was reminding him how he would never have been considered as a possible parliamentary candidate in the first place, if it weren't for her own efforts on his behalf. 'You simply don't appreciate how much I have done for you, or how much *you* could achieve if you would only put your mind to it.'

When she finally ran out of steam Leo allowed the silence to lie between them for some moments before he responded. 'Quite frankly, I wish you would cease making efforts on my behalf, Helen. The answer is no, and will ever remain so. I have no objection to becoming involved in community affairs, would in fact be happy to stand for the *local* council, but have no interest whatsoever in the national, let alone the international stage.'

'But, my darling, you would be wonderful and I . . .'

Leo turned to offer her a wry smile which didn't quite reach his eyes. 'And there's an end of the matter.'

'Are you deliberately trying to upset me?'

'No, my dear, I simply need you to listen occasionally to what *I* have to say. I will *not* be involving myself in any parliamentary by-elections, this May or at any time. That is completely out of the question.'

Helen knew when he used that particular tone of voice she'd been bested. Even so, she must have the last word. She knelt up on the bed, her milk-pale limbs draped beguilingly in the sheet, her beautiful face sour with temper. 'How could you *possibly* consider refusing? It's a *wonderful* opportunity, and not one given to just anyone. You could be *such* a success, and naturally I would be more than happy to continue to work on your behalf. That goes without saying.'

Leo made no response. He'd made his position clear. There was no point in arguing further. When did his wife ever listen to any opinion but her own? Silence, he'd discovered, was the best way to shut her up.

But it didn't work tonight. She came to him, curling her arms about his neck, pressing herself against him. 'We can talk about this some other time, darling, when you're feeling less morose. I'm sure you'll come round to accepting David Barford's offer once you've got over your father's death and start thinking more clearly. In the meantime, I've decided, Leo, that I need a car of my own. Having my own transport will allow me the freedom I need. I have so many functions, so many committee meetings to attend these days. All vitally important if we are to keep the right people sweet.'

'Indeed.' Leo's tone was dry.

'I believe I shall soon be adopted as chair of the resources committee for the new leisure centre. Then once you've got over your sulks and been elected as MP there may be times when you are tied up with constituency affairs while I could drive myself down to the country on my own, should I choose to. You can afford to do this little thing for me, couldn't you?'

Leo drew in a rasping breath through gritted teeth. 'I do a great deal for you already, Helen. When are you going to do something for me in return?'

She slipped her hands between the folds of his dressing gown, seeking to bring him to hardness once again. 'I will do anything for you, Leo, you know I will.'

'Except have my child.'

She gave a tiny, disinterested shrug. 'Except that.'

22

Betty and Lynda

'So what kind of flowers do you fancy, Belle?'
'Something to cheer me up.'

'You do look a bit down.' Betty selected a bunch of narcissi. 'How about these? That's what they're called, Cheerfulness, and such a lovely creamy colour.' Privately, Betty thought it a perfect choice for the market superintendent since in Greek legend Narcissus fell in love with his own reflection, and nobody could say that Belle Garside wasn't full of her own importance. 'And how about a few daffs to go with them?' She added a dozen daffodils with bright orange trumpets.

The entire market was aware that Sam Beckett had dumped Belle yet again for this new woman of his, whose identity remained a mystery. The pair of them had enjoyed an on-off relationship for years, which had kept the stallholders in thrall. But then Belle Garside was a glamorous, attractive widow so could do as she pleased and generally did. Sam was another matter entirely, although nobody was prepared to risk expressing their opinion on the way he treated his wife, not to his face, that is.

'There you are, chuck, how about these?'

'Beautiful, thank you, Betty, I appreciate the trouble you always take. No one quite understands how difficult my life is.' Belle patted her hennaed curls into place with razor-sharp scarlet nails. 'Having a son in jail is not easy, though *you* more than anyone must understand how I feel about that. How are you getting along with that ne'er-do-well husband of yours? Still creating havoc, is he? Can't think why you let him back in.'

Betty stared at her. Glamorous she may be with those Elizabeth Taylor violet eyes of hers but nobody could accuse Belle Garside of being strong on tact or diplomacy. 'I didn't exactly put a welcome mat at the door. Anyroad, he's not my husband any longer, as a matter of fact, and no, I don't understand what it's like to have a son in jail. Ewan's petty crimes never did involve killing people.'

Belle was sufficiently thick skinned to accept this remark with a philosophical shrug. 'It was an accident. You know it was. My son never meant to kill the boy. That Dena Dobson should have taken more care of her little brother.'

'Let's leave all of that in the past, shall we? The lad is doing his time, and I agree it can't be easy. But my problem is the opposite of yours, Belle. While you want your son out of the clink, I want my ex-husband back in.'

'Fix it then. There are always ways and means.'

'I don't have your connections, Belle.'

The other woman laughed, a rich smoky sound, accepting the apparent slur on her good name without rancour. 'And what about your Lynda and Jake, how do they feel about having their dad back in their lives? I'm not sure my boys would care for it, too used to having their own way.'

'I'm surprised you know who their father is.'

Belle shrugged. 'There are times when not knowing can be an advantage.'

'Aye, you might have a point there. Our Lynda hasn't yet made up her mind what she feels. She's a bit confused by it all, and our Jake is running more wild than ever. Constable Nuttall is keeping a beady eye on him, and seems to think our Jake has taken up with a crowd of petty thieves. I've promised to make him knuckle down and do some proper work but I can't give him full employment, and he never stops in a job more than two minutes. How do you cope with rebellious sons, Belle love, tell me that?'

Belle snorted. 'I'm the last person to ask for advice on that one.'

'Aye, silly of me to ask, but I dread to think what he might get up to next.'

Later that day when the stallholders were packing up for the day, Jake came tearing up Champion Street in a beat-up old Ford. He screeched to a halt beside his mother, revving the engine furiously just in case she hadn't noticed him.

With a patient sigh Betty set down the empty flower buckets she'd been in the process of washing and walked over to her son. 'What the hangment have you got now?'

'I've bought myself some wheels, Mam. Ain't this some cool machine? Don't you just dig it?'

'And where would you find the money for a car?' Betty stared at the vehicle, somewhat dazed by its sudden appearance, as was half the street judging by the crowd gathering about them. The car might once have been black, but someone had painted it a bright shocking pink.

'Folk'll see you coming a mile off in that thing, lad,' commented Jimmy Ramsay as he walked around the car in his striped butcher's apron, kicking the tyres and examining the bodywork, which seemed to be pitted with rusted holes or filled with patches of a lumpy cement-like substance.

Jake positively purred with pleasure. 'Some classy chassis, huh? That old van were knackered so I traded it in, and before you complain I put some of me own money to it.'

'That must be a first.'

'Want a spin in it, Mam?'

'I don't think so, I plan on living a bit longer yet.'

'It goes like crazy, really leaves a patch.'

Betty didn't understand one half of what her son was saying but she was nonetheless troubled by this sudden acquisition. 'You've found yourself a new job then, is that it?'

'Aw, Mam, don't be square. I do the deliveries for you, and a bit of work on the docks shifting stuff now and then, but this is Smallville. I'm not stopping in Castlefield for much longer, I'm gonna make it big in the music business. I've bought a guitar too, see.' He indicated the instrument lying beside him on the front passenger seat.

Betty was even more surprised, not having heard anything of this dream before. 'Can you play that thing?'

Jake pouted. 'I can learn.'

'I'll believe that when I hear it, at least I'd rather not. There's enough racket in our house already.'

Winnie Holmes had wandered over, never being one to miss a drama. 'Hey up, somebody must have come into a bit o' brass. Have you taken up our Barry's offer of work then on his vegetable stall, lad, or come into a win on "Double Your Money"?'

Betty shook her head in despair. 'The poor sod thinks he's Stirling Moss.'

'Don't start, Mam, you think I'm some goof who can't make it on me own? I'll make it big all right, you'll see. I just wanted to show you me new hot rod. Don't know what time I'll be home. I've places to go, people to see.'

Betty's cry that he should take care which places and which people he get involved with was lost in the roar and rattle of the engine and the cloud of black exhaust fumes as he put his foot down and drove the old bone-shaker as fast as he was able out of the street.

'Think yourself lucky,' Jimmy Ramsay said at her elbow, 'that he can't afford a proper car. That one won't last five minutes.'

'That's the trouble though, isn't it? When it coughs its last, will my son go with it?'

Lynda missed the entertainment her brother had provided for them all, as she'd been chatting with Terry, busily making plans for the evening. It was a choice between going dancing or seeing Kirk Douglas in *The Vikings*. Lynda would have preferred to see the big new movie *South Pacific* with its special sound effects, but Terry thought it might be a bit too soppy for him. She didn't really care what they did or where they went, so long as they were together. Ooh, she liked him, she did really. Best decision she ever made was to go out with Terry Hall.

As she waltzed into the house, happily singing 'You Got to Have A Dream', her good humour was instantly destroyed by a barked question from Ewan.

'How's that boy friend of yours? Has he got over his headache yet?'

She stared at her father, the very smallest hesitation before she answered. 'Why do you ask? What are you talking about?' Terry seemed reasonably well recovered so far as she could tell, but remained strangely reluctant to talk about the beating he'd suffered.

They were alone in the living room, Betty engaged in making tea in the kitchen and Jake out, as usual. Ewan was slumped in the big fireside chair with his feet propped up on the fender. He hadn't even taken off his boots, and his pipe, clamped tight between his teeth, was shedding bits of hot ash down the front of his filthy jersey, rather like a mini volcano. Lynda experienced a shudder of revulsion at the sight of him.

What was happening to her? This was the father she'd spent her life longing to meet. Why couldn't she just walk up to him and give him a kiss on the cheek as any ordinary daughter would?

Ewan put down his feet and leaned closer, then dropping his voice to a whisper spoke to her through gritted teeth, the pipe bobbing furiously up and down. 'Maybe that'll teach the little bleeder to keep his filthy little hands off *my* girl.'

Lynda stared at him, dumbfounded. '*Your* girl, what are you talking about? I don't understand.'

'I saw the pair of you together, him slobbering all over you, and with his hands where they shouldn't be. No young man is turning a daughter of mine into a whore, so see you don't behave like one.'

Realisation slowly dawned, and with it came understanding as to why Terry had refused to do anything about the assault. 'My God, it was *you*! You were the one who beat Terry up. *How could you*? What has he ever done to you?'

'I've just told you. He's not putting his mucky hands on *my* little girl. That's the last time you'll be going out with Terry bloody Hall.'

'*What?*'

'I thought I'd made it clear enough to him but obviously not, so I'm putting a stop to it now. I hope you haven't made any plans to see him this evening because if so, he's going to be disappointed. Mark my words, Lynda love, you and him are history. You can do better. I'll not allow you to go out with that useless tyke ever again, or you'll feel the back of my hand if you do.'

Lynda couldn't believe what she was hearing. She was appalled, but, ignoring the crawling fear that was making itself all too apparent in her stomach, ploughed stubbornly on. 'I'm not *your little girl*, I'm a grown woman, and it's no business of yours what we were doing. I can see who I like. What right have you to say who I can go out with?'

'I have the right because I'm your dad, and don't you ever forget that fact, or a worse fate might happen to that biker boyfriend of yours. And you wouldn't like that one bit, now would you?'

Lynda cancelled her date with Terry, much to his disappointment and distress, and sat through the evening meal quite unable to eat a thing. Jake still wasn't in, as was so often the case these days. Mam told her about the pink hot-rod car he'd bought, which made Lynda laugh till she saw how worried her mother was. Jake had been driving since soon after he turned seventeen, but certainly couldn't be called the responsible type. Presumably he'd taken the car out on a trial run, desperate to avoid the increasingly depressing atmosphere in his own home, for which she could hardly blame him. But his absence put Ewan in an even worse mood.

'That boy is the very devil. A lad after me own heart! Still, car or no car, he should be here on time for his tea.'

Ewan redirected his snapping and snarling to Lynda, watching her move her food about her plate before ordering her to be grateful for it, and eat up.

Lynda pushed her plate aside. 'I'm not hungry.'

Betty was concerned. 'You aren't coming down with summat, I hope?'

'No, Mam, I'm fine.' She sent silent glances across the table urging her not to ask any more questions. Betty took the hint and silently finished her own meal, deliberately keeping her gaze averted as Ewan picked at his teeth with a grubby fingernail.

Later, in the kitchen, the two women had a whispered conversation over the washing-up, Lynda hastily trying to explain to her mother how Ewan had banned her from seeing Terry.

Betty was appalled. 'He can't do that! Terry's a grand lad and you're a grown woman, not a child who needs to do her father's bidding. I shall tell him so this very minute.' So saying, she wiped her hands on the tea towel and made to march into the living room there and then.

'No, leave it, Mam. I'll deal with it in my own way. I've certainly no intention of obeying. It's none of his business who I see, and I've already told him as much.'

But Betty was incensed by the thought of her ex-husband issuing orders to her daughter, and in her own house, at that. 'Who the bleeding hell does he think he is? I'm having no more of this. He's going to get his marching orders once and for all.'

She got no further as she heard voices raised in anger. Jake had finally arrived home, flinging his boots and coat on the floor as was his wont, and Ewan, who tended to do exactly the same, was telling him to pick them up.

'And what time do you call this to come in for your tea? What have you been up to till this hour, shagging your girl friend on t'back seat of your new jalopy, eh?'

Betty stormed in to stand before her ex-husband, hands on hips. 'Don't you use such foul language in front of my son. Not in my house.'

Ewan spat in the fire, chortling to himself as if he'd done something clever. 'I'm sure he's heard worse, haven't you, lad? Not that he's capable of doing anything of the sort. You're a bloody poofter, that's your problem, son. You're queer. You always were and always will be. Wouldn't know what to do with a woman if she stripped off naked in front of you.'

'That's not true!' Jake's voice rose in anguish. 'You'll bloody take that back,' and the boy suddenly launched himself at Ewan. The next minute father and son were rolling on the floor, throwing punches at each other and sending chairs and furniture flying.

Taken completely by surprise, Betty did her best to intervene. 'Stop it, the pair of you! Ewan, lay off, you'll kill him. Jake, stop hitting your father, for God's sake!'

By way of response Jake gave Ewan a crack on the jaw and then the older man grabbed the boy by the hair and shook him, as if he were a rat.

Jake yelled out in such anguish Betty was certain the neighbours would hear and come running. Somehow the boy managed to extricate himself and lifted his fist ready to plant another punch on his father's chin when Betty shoved him to one side. The result of her action was that Ewan's fist came crashing down on her own head instead, knocking her sideways.

'Bloody woman, why can't you learn to keep your nose out of men's business? He's *my* son and I'll deal with him as I choose.'

'No, you flaming won't! Nor will you tell our Lynda what to do neither. She's a grown woman, free to live her own life. If she wants to go out with young Terry, it's none of your flaming business.'

The rage in his eyes was terrible to see. Lynda watched what happened next as if a black and white movie was operating in slow motion right before her eyes, the horror unfolding within as she was helpless to prevent it.

Reaching behind him Ewan snatched up the poker and swung it hard right across Betty's knees. She went down like a felled tree, and her scream of pain and terror would echo forever in Lynda's head.

23

Lynda

Lynda continued to run the flower stall alone as best she could, wishing she'd paid more attention to the things Mam had tried to teach her about flower arranging and plant care. She remembered to spray them regularly, to deal with the stems and to take the thorns from the roses, a job she hated, but they all seemed to wilt so much quicker without Betty's green fingers to look after them.

Lynda thought she would never forget the night her mother was injured as long as she lived. She ran screaming into the street, yelling for someone to call an ambulance. Champion Street looked deserted, doors shut fast and not even a net curtain twitching. If neighbours had heard the commotion, as they surely must have done, they were keeping their own counsel. She ran from house to house hammering on doors, shouting for someone to come, then raced back to her mother's side.

Betty lay at the foot of the stairs, her face a sickly shade of green, eyes closed and clearly in tremendous pain. Lynda spun round and glared at Ewan. 'Why have you moved her?'

He didn't answer.

The first person to arrive on the scene was Constable Nuttall, rushing into the house calling, 'What's going on here?'

Lynda was all for telling him, for blurting out how Ewan had bullied them, fought with her brother and then assaulted her mother. But Ewan was standing with his hand firmly planted on Betty's shoulder and she only had to look at the fear in her mother's eyes to know that she couldn't do any such thing.

The words dried in her throat, and it was Ewan himself who produced some cock-and-bull story about Betty falling down the stairs.

Lynda could see that Constable Nuttall wasn't entirely convinced by the tale but when he turned to her and asked, 'Is that right, Lynda? Is that what happened?' she didn't need to so much as glance at Ewan to know that the risk of defying him was too great. If he could do this to her mam over a silly argument about Jake going out for a spin in his new car and coming in late for his tea, what might he do if she really turned against him?

And her brother was no help. Jake sat hunched in a corner, seemingly in shock as he no doubt imagined the whole episode to be his fault.

Lynda managed to nod her agreement while crouching beside Betty and hugging her close. She saw gratitude as well as pain in her mother's eyes and knew she was saying what was expected of her, though whether it would turn out to be a wise decision, or one she would later come to regret, was quite another matter.

Lynda had gone in the ambulance with Betty to the hospital, sitting alone for hour upon hour in the waiting room while they found a doctor and dawn crept up over the city horizon, and then for several more hours while the surgeons operated on her leg.

In the days since, she'd gone every afternoon, Judy minding the stall for her while she visited her mother in hospital. Most of her neighbours in Champion Street visited too, taking turns in an effort to keep Betty's spirits up, presenting their old friend with get-well cards, bunches of her own flowers and any number of grapes. Winnie Holmes took her in a few magazines and Big Molly smuggled in a hot meat and potato pie, on the grounds that you didn't get 'proper food' in a hospital.

Betty would thank them, tolerate their company for ten minutes or so, then turn her face to the wall or close her eyes and pretend to be asleep.

'I'll come when you're feeling up to having visitors, love,' they would say, and creep quietly away.

When she wasn't at the hospital Lynda was working on the flower stall, or attempting to maintain some sort of order in the house. And when Jake didn't return home, she also spent hours hunting high and low for her brother, finding neither sight nor sound of him. His car was still parked where he'd left it in the back street, which wasn't like Jake at all. He'd been so proud of this new acquisition, why would he go anywhere without that beat-up pink jalopy of his?

Lynda was at her wits' end and close to exhaustion, yet no matter how tired she was she couldn't sleep.

Desperately concerned about her mam, whose recovery was worryingly slow, Lynda would sob her heart out night after night so that her head throbbed the next morning. Three times a week she needed to get up early to fetch the flowers from the whole-sale market but was forced to beg a lift from Barry Holmes, now that she had no transport of her own. Not that Barry minded but it was no way to run a stall. She'd kill that brother of hers for selling the old delivery van, if ever she got her hands on him again, that is.

Oh, God, what a mess! Where was he? Where could her stupid little brother have gone? Would Mam recover? Would she ever walk again? Their little family had been torn apart and here she was doing nothing about it.

But Lynda didn't have the energy to keep on looking for Jake. Nor did she waste any more time on Ewan. What he did with his time Lynda had no idea and didn't ask. He'd collected a few cronies at the Dog and Duck and she would sometimes see him hanging about street corners, smoking and talking with them, no doubt furtively putting bets on the dogs or the horses.

Unable to bring herself to even speak to her father, Lynda pointedly ignored him. Far easier to place his meal on the table and then slip out and spend the evening with Judy where at least she could relax for a little while, returning only when she was certain Ewan would be out.

She longed to see Terry, of course, but was nervous of doing so in case Ewan should hear of it.

And every night when she came home, Lynda would want to ask if he'd found himself a job yet, or somewhere else to live. But always her courage failed her at the last moment.

Why hadn't she listened to her mother? If she'd only done that, then Betty would still be at home, fit and well, instead of stuck in a hospital bed fearing she might never walk again.

Lynda was missing Terry badly, taunted by the sight of him around the market, so near and yet utterly beyond her reach.

It was no good trying to explain to Terry why she could no longer see him. That would involve telling the truth about her mother's alleged accident and who knew where such a confession might lead? The last thing she wanted was for him to start some war of attrition against her father on their behalf. Lynda shuddered at the prospect. Ewan would be bound to win because he played dirty. Her mother's injuries and his fight with his own son had proved that to her beyond question, and as he'd beaten Terry up once already, he wouldn't think twice about doing so again.

Lynda decided that she had no choice in the matter. For Terry's own safety, she must finish with him. Until she succeeded in getting Ewan out of the house all she could do was try to protect those she loved the most. Better a broken heart than a broken head.

She asked him to meet her in Belle's café and Terry came eagerly, thinking this must indicate that all was well again between them. Instead, she told him bluntly over their steaming cappuccinos, without any soft words or apologies, that it was all over.

'I don't understand. I thought you loved me,' Terry said, his handsome face stricken. 'I thought you and me were going to stick together for ever.'

Lynda struggled to swallow the lump that came into her throat at his words, but couldn't bear to look at him as she openly mocked his simple sincerity. 'Don't be daft! When have I ever stuck with a man? Can you see me as a blushing bride? I don't think so. I told you from the start I didn't go in for all that marriage and commitment stuff. Love them and leave them, that's my philosophy.' The pain in her chest was threatening to choke her.

'I don't believe you.'

'Please yourself.' Lynda finished her coffee in one single gulp and got up quickly, desperate to leave, half turning away so that Terry couldn't see the anguish in her face. Why hadn't she stuck to her vow not to get involved in the first place? Hadn't she always told herself a thousand times that it was far better to hold herself aloof?

Lynda remembered how she'd once actually enjoyed the freedom of being able to move on when she grew tired of someone. She'd think, why commit yourself girl, when there'll be another gorgeous male along any minute? But for some reason it felt almost impossible to keep such a vow where Terry was concerned.

Tossing back her auburn curls she deliberately hardened her tone. 'Like I told you once before, I take every care to protect myself from emotional and physical damage. I've always been determined that there'll be no unwelcome little accidents, no broken hearts for me. None of my lovers last very long, a few weeks at most.'

'We've been together over six *months*, Lynda,' Terry quietly reminded her, his face ashen.

Lynda gave a casual shrug as if she really couldn't care less. 'Well then, you've done better than most, Terry love. So now you can go home and play with your train set.'

And she walked quickly away so that she wouldn't see the pain in his lovely dark eyes.

She didn't go back to the stall right away but ran straight home. Once behind her own closed door her knees buckled and Lynda sank to the floor in a flood of tears.

It was late the following afternoon, and, after visiting Betty as usual, Lynda left her mother sleeping comfortably to return to an empty house feeling utterly exhausted. Overwhelmed by emotion and worry she ran herself a bath and lay in the hot water sobbing her heart out. What had possessed her to invite Ewan in for that dratted Sunday lunch? If she'd left things as they were instead of chasing a foolish dream, none of this would have happened. Her mother would still be fit and well, Jake would be home where he belonged, and she and Terry would still be together.

What would happen when Mam did eventually come home she really didn't care to contemplate. How would she react to find her ex-husband, the one who had crippled her, still occupying her house?

Lynda felt she was failing her mother if she didn't kick him out, yet how could she? Ewan obstinately refused to recognise that he'd done anything wrong. Yet, appalled by what her father had done, Lynda knew she couldn't let him get away with it.

Ewan staggered in very much the worse for drink later that evening, stinking of beer and as merry as if he hadn't a care in the world. In that moment, father or not, Lynda hated him.

Hands on hips she bluntly ordered him to leave. 'If you've any sense you'll pack up and go right now. Mam'll kill you if you're still here when she gets home. She certainly won't tolerate having you stopping on a minute longer than necessary, not after what you've done.'

Ewan hiccupped loudly then rolled his eyes to the ceiling. 'Nag, nag, nag. I thought we'd had this out already.'

'Well, I'm bringing it up again.' Lynda drew in a shaky breath, holding tight to her nerve. 'How could you do such a thing?'

He looked at her all hang-dog, maudlin with drink, as if he hadn't the first notion how any of this could have happened. 'Me temper gets the better of me at times, lass. I'm right sorry. Aw, you'll forgive me though, chuck, won't you?'

'How can I forgive you? Mam could be crippled for life, and all because of your blasted temper. You've got to go. Now!'

'Nay, you wouldn't be so cruel as to throw your old dad out on the street, would you, lass?' He blinked owlishly at her. 'Not till I've had time to get meself sorted anyroad.'

'You've had ample time to get yourself sorted. I want you out of here by Friday.'

'Don't you know how good it feels to have me family round me again, having my little girl close at last.' He smoothed the heel of one thumb over her flushed cheek and Lynda jerked away, taking a half-step back, not comfortable with the familiarity of his touch.

Her loyalty to her mother still warred with her desire to capture that elusive father figure of her dreams. It was all so difficult, so unlike how she'd imagined it would be.

She tried again, 'You could at least start looking for a job so that you can make a contribution to expenses, then set about finding yourself alternative accommodation. Like I say, you can't stay here forever. It wouldn't be right.'

Something glinted behind his eyes which Lynda couldn't quite put a name to. She'd call it nasty, even vicious, were it not for the fact that his voice sounded so calm, almost pleasant as he smiled at her.

'I've asked around, put out a few feelers, but I'm not optimistic. Accommodation that I can afford will not be easy to come by. Eeh, I never thought you'd grow up to be so hard, Lynda love, and you used to be such a sweet little girl. I've made a bad mistake, all right, and I'm sorry for it. I won't do it again, I swear.'

His voice was all soft and wheedling, his expression so pitiful that Lynda felt herself start to weaken as she thought how lonely he must have been over the years with no family to call his own. But then she remembered the sight of her poor mother in pain after that long operation and hardened her heart.

'I doubt you mean that. I'm beginning to think Mam was right about you. You're nothing but trouble.'

'Nay, don't say such a thing, chuck. I know you like having me around really. We were getting on fine, you and me, getting to know each other at last. I'm right sorry I lost me rag, I am really.'

He did sound genuinely sorry for what he'd done, so pathetic, almost shrunken before her eyes. Lynda felt confused. How should she deal with this man she called father? Could she trust him? Should she force the issue, or not?

In her heart, Lynda knew there was much more to her reluctance to act than the pity she felt for him. There was something about Ewan Hemley that warned her not to challenge or defy him too strongly. His manner disturbed her, perhaps because his self-pitying words didn't quite match the defiant stance he was taking, the way he hooked his thumbs in his thick leather belt, or the sidelong leering glances that followed her about as she paced the room in her agitation. Whatever the cause he made her nervous, and Lynda could feel herself beginning to weaken.

She didn't have the power to order him out of the house. He knew it, and so did she.

Lynda made excuses, told herself that Ewan Hemley was still her own flesh and blood after all, the father she'd always wanted; that maybe later, when her mam was home again and on her feet, they could face him together and persuade him to leave then.

She salved her conscience, and her pride, by ending the conversation on a warning. 'Well, keep off the booze then and try to behave better in future. And don't think I'm going to wait on you hand, foot and finger while she's laid up, because I'm not.'

Then Lynda went back to the kitchen to make him a cup of tea to sober him up so that he wouldn't be sick on the green moquette sofa. What more could she do? She'd grown weary of arguing with him, and had far too many other concerns on her mind.

24

Helen and Judy

So long as she and Leo didn't actually split up Helen saw no problem in continuing with her affair. She always made a point of choosing married men because apart from adding to the danger and thrill of the liaison, by the very nature of their situation a married man was obliged to be more discreet. Other than this requirement she wasn't too particular who it was, nor did she object to the somewhat common sort like Sam Beckett. Sam might be a bit short on charm and conversation but he was fit and strong with good muscles, reasonably attractive, and certainly never left a woman dissatisfied.

And since Leo was still resisting the political plans she'd made for him, and had grown really quite distant and cool towards her recently, he was only getting what he deserved. All he did was either neglect her, or complain about not having any children. Too, too tiresome for words. Even if he did discover her secret, which was unlikely since she took every care, Helen was perfectly certain he would never risk the scandal of a divorce. She was therefore safe to enjoy herself as she pleased.

This morning she and Sam had made love in the back of his van among the detritus of tools: the hammers, pickaxes and shovels he'd bought at the wholesalers before picking her up on the corner of John Dalton Street and driving to a quiet corner of Salford Docks. She'd made him spread out an old car rug, so that she didn't mark her new Mary Quant dress, but it was certainly a fascinating way to end a shopping session, and so very clever of her to manage her life so perfectly.

Afterwards, and for the sake of discretion, Sam dropped her some distance from the market on Water Street, which seemed ideal until she unexpectedly ran into Dulcie on her way home.

'Have you been down to the docks to see Leo?' her mother-in-law smilingly enquired, seeing this as an odd direction to be returning from the city centre.

Helen was momentarily at a loss for words. How could she agree that she had been to the docks when she'd been nowhere near her husband's office? Nor could she deny she'd been into the city when she was carrying shopping bags with Kendal Milne splashed all over them. 'Actually no, I was given a lift part-way home by a girl-friend.' Hoping that she hadn't put too much emphasis on the word girl.

At precisely that moment Sam's van drove past them and rounded the corner into Champion Street to park beside the market hall entrance.

'Isn't that Sam Beckett over there, just parking his van?' Dulcie mildly enquired, giving her daughter-in-law a rather arch look. 'Was he the one who gave you the lift? Are you sure it wasn't a *man*-friend who brought you home, dear, and not a girl at all? I can't see you walking very far with those bags on your arm.'

Helen was furious. The woman was too nosy for words, clearly suspicious and if she mentioned any of this to Leo could spoil everything. 'What fantasies you do have, mother-in-law. Anyway, where have *you* been? What were *you* doing wandering so far from the market? Not lost again, were you?'

'I was going to see my friend Doris.'

'Doris lives in Whitworth Street, nowhere near here. Are you sure that's where you were going. Not lost, are you?'

Doubt came into Dulcie's eyes and she looked momentarily confused. 'I *was* going to see Doris. Or did I decide to call on Alice instead?' It took only the fierce glare of her daughter-in-law's gimlet eyes and she practically forgot her own name.

'I'd better get you home and put the kettle on. I think you're in need of a little lie-down, don't you? Besides, I need a rest myself. Spending your son's money always tires me out.'

Judy was waiting at the door of the little ironmongery shop when her husband drew up in the van. She'd arrived early, hoping to make one last effort to persuade him to allow her to reopen her stall.

She'd had a quiet word with Tom's teacher about the bullying, although not the headmaster. The woman had really been most understanding of Judy's dilemma, agreeing that men often viewed these matters differently and she promised to be discreet, to say nothing to Tom but keep an eye out for any sign of future problems.

After a week or two of toeing the line, of picking her children up regularly and on time, providing beautiful meals for her husband and making every effort to be pretty and welcoming, Judy had hoped to win him round.

Judy longed to get back to her painting but daren't, not without Sam's say so. She couldn't bear the thought of painting new pictures only to have those slashed too. Besides, he'd thrown away her oil paints and even broken her easel. She'd have to start again from scratch which would cost more than she could afford just at present, unless she were certain of selling her work.

So it was that this morning Judy had again spoken to Belle, asking if it might be possible for her to start up the stall again. Belle had given her lazy, knowing smile, carefully licking her crimson-coated lips before replying.

'Not without Sam's agreement, dearie. I heard what happened, along with everyone else on the market, and your husband isn't a man I'd care to cross. We certainly don't want him wrecking your pictures in public next time, now do we? We've enough problems in that direction with the Poulsons' frequent feuds and dramas. Family squabbles of that nature do tend to give the market a bad name.'

'Sam would never do such a thing.'

Belle lit up a cigarette, narrowing her eyes against the curl of blue smoke. 'Well, as his *wife*, you know him better than me, lovey.'

Judy inwardly squirmed. Painfully aware of the one-time relationship between this woman and her husband, Belle's body language seemed to be telling her the exact opposite, that she knew Sam only too well.

Now here he was, and as he walked past her with scarcely a glance, his arms full of new tools wrapped in brown paper and string, she caught the unmistakable scent of expensive perfume.

Judy followed him into the stock room and closed the door. 'You're late opening this morning. It's nearly twelve o'clock.'

'So?'

'You've been with *her*, haven't you?'

'What are you twittering on about now?'

'You've been with your latest woman. Who is she? Anyone I know? Who is making a fool of me now?'

Sam gave a heavy sigh. 'As you've just pointed out, I'm late. I took a morning off. So what? If you don't mind, I'll open up and get on with earning our living.'

'Don't walk away from me, Sam. I've had enough, do you hear? I'm a person in my own right, not just someone to do your every bidding, someone with no other purpose in life but to skivvy for you and care for your kids while you sleep with whoever you choose.'

He glanced down at her then, a sardonic curl to his lip. 'Don't tell me you're jealous?'

'No, I'm not jealous as a matter of fact. I'm just heartily sick of being used. You can't keep me a virtual prisoner in my own home, expect me to be satisfied with cooking and cleaning, denying me any chance of a life and yet treat our marriage with such complete contempt. It's not fair! I have rights too, you know. Marriage is a democracy not a dictatorship.'

He laughed. 'And when did you suddenly start learning such big words?'

'Don't patronise me, Sam, I'm not stupid. It's time you treated me with more respect.'

'You're wrong! Marriage is not a democracy, or a partnership, so you can banish that modern rubbish from your head right away. Didn't you agree to love, honour and obey when we stood at the altar together? When you married me we became *one* person, and *you* don't have any say at all. So what are you going to do about it, eh?'

Fury roared through her veins. 'I'll show you what I'm going to do. I'm leaving you, and I shall take the children with me.'

'You wouldn't dare!'

She strode over to the door. 'Watch me.'

'Don't do this, Judy. You'll regret it.'

'I know you love them, that you're a good father to your children if not a good husband to me. The choice is simple, either you let me have my stall, allow me to do my painting and live my life as I choose – *and* agree to give up all your *other women* – or it's over between us.'

He was still laughing when she marched away, slamming the door behind her.

Judy stopped off at the flower stall to see Lynda, mainly because she needed to sit down, her limbs were shaking so much. Lynda watched with some concern as she stumbled and half collapsed on to an upturned orange box. 'By heck, you look in need of a mug of strong tea, or happen a double brandy.'

'I'm moving out. I'm leaving Sam and taking the children with me.'

Lynda stared at her friend in total shock. 'Heaven help me, I never thought to hear you say such a thing. Where would you go?'

'I don't know yet. I have . . .' she glanced at her wrist-watch . . . 'four hours to find us somewhere and pack a few things before I pick up the children from school.'

'You're serious, aren't you?'

'Never more so. Do you want to come with me? We could prop each other up, you escaping Ewan, me running from Sam. And I could do with your help, to be honest.'

There was sheer agony in Lynda's face. 'Oh, I'd love to say yes, but I can't leave the house with Mam still in hospital. Nor could I leave all her things to—' she'd been about to say to the mercy of the man who put her there, but pride prevented her . . . 'and leave me dad on his own. It wouldn't be right.'

'Oh, Lynda, I forgot for the moment about all your troubles. How is Betty? Is she making a good recovery?'

Lynda's face took on an anxious look. 'She's been there weeks and still can't walk. The doctors say it's too soon to know if she'll ever walk again.'

'That's awful. I didn't realise it was so bad. And all from falling down the stairs.'

'Yes.' No one knew the full story and Lynda certainly wasn't going to be the one to tell, not if Mam didn't want her to.

'I must call in and see her. I haven't been for a while and I do miss seeing her cheery face on the market every morning. Anyway, I've decided. I'm leaving Sam. I have to do this, Lynda.'

'I can see you've made up your mind. But don't go far away, I need to know you're around.' The thought of losing her best friend made Lynda feel sick. Life was difficult enough right now. A thought occurred to her. 'Look, what about that little bed-sit overlooking the fish market? Would that do for a start? Speak to Amy George. She and Chris lived there for a while during the first traumatic weeks of their marriage when they were in the middle of that family feud, and before them Dena Dobson once occupied it with her illegitimate baby.'

'Oh, Lynda, that would be perfect. I'll go this very minute. Say a little prayer for me, will you?' And she was gone, leaving Lynda staring after her friend in deep distress.

The bedsit was small and cramped, one of several in a tall three-storeyed Victorian house that overlooked the fish market, and a little too close to home for comfort. Yet it felt like a small refuge from her pain. It would do for now, Judy thought, until she could find something bigger and better. She would have to get a job. Her small amount of savings wouldn't last long, that's for sure.

At least Lynda would be able to pop in most days for a chat or a cuppa, so she wouldn't feel totally isolated. And as long as a satisfactory agreement could be reached between herself and Sam, the children could continue to see their father.

Ruth and Tom, however, were far from happy about the change, something Judy had half expected and resolved to deal with firmly and cheerfully.

'Daddy and I aren't getting on too well at the moment so we've decided we need some time apart,' she explained, as she led them up the stairs with its grubby brown carpet and, on reaching the first landing, unlocked the door that was to be their new home.

Tom looked at her wide eyed and asked if his daddy would still be taking him fishing at the canal on Sunday. When Judy agreed that of course he would, that his daddy still loved him, he seemed perfectly content and ran off to explore cupboards and see if the wireless worked. But then, apart from the fishing, Tom tended to find his father somewhat intimidating, and since the bullying incident had been even more circumspect and withdrawn towards him, and even more clingy with Judy.

Ruth was another matter entirely. 'You mean we can't live at home any more? What about all my things, my clothes, my books and stuff?'

'I've packed everything I think you'll need for now, but if I've forgotten anything important I'll go back and get if for you tomorrow. The rest of our things will have to wait until we have more space in which to put it.'

Judy smiled brightly but Ruth looked about her in shock, a look of appalled disbelief on her young face. 'You can't be serious! You can't expect us all to sleep here, in this one room, in one bed? It's impossible, I shall hate it.'

'I'm sorry, love, but I'm afraid we'll just have to put up with it for a while. At least until I can find us something better.'

Judy could see the conflict in her daughter's eyes, like a private war going on in her head. A part of her longed to rage at her mother, to blame her for depriving them of their home, and of

Ruth's own precious bedroom as well as her beloved father, but another part of her mind remembered the ruin of Judy's lovely pictures, including the one of herself and Tom.

'It's not *fair*! Why should Tom and me suffer because you and Daddy have had a falling-out? If you *must* live apart while you sulk, why doesn't *he* have this nasty little room then *we* could all stay at home? There are three of us and we need more space than him. It's not fair,' she said again, for good measure.

'Life isn't fair, my darling,' Judy said, kissing her brow and instantly worrying about how hot it was. 'Don't get yourself in a state about things you can't control. It'll be fun, you'll see. We can eat fish and chips in bed tonight, if you like?'

Tom giggled. 'Ooh, yes please.'

'And then will we go home tomorrow when Dad has stopped being in a temper and you've stopped sulking,' Ruth insisted.

'No, darling, I don't really see how I can.' Whereupon the girl burst into tears. As Judy gathered her weeping child in her arms, Tom standing anxiously by, it came to her that building a new life for them all was going to be much harder than she'd thought.

25

Lynda

Easter was drawing near and Champion Street Market was bright with craft stalls selling gaudily painted Easter eggs and fluffy chickens, prettily painted silk scarves, and on the Higginsons' stall a captivating display of straw panamas, flirty little summer hats and Easter bonnets.

Yet Lynda could take no pleasure in the scene. Her life had changed completely. To everyone else Ewan Hemley was charm itself but her mother was crippled, her brother had disappeared and she was trapped in a living nightmare.

He would sit in his chair and do nothing but complain and criticise, constantly making her do things over and over again. She wanted to protest, to do battle, but how could she? Ewan Hemley had a nasty habit of getting his own way.

Only this morning she'd been rushing round cooking his breakfast, checking what was needed for a meal that night, worrying about how many daffs to buy at market while ironing a shirt at the same time. She should have done it the night before but had gone to bed at eight o'clock, absolutely exhausted.

Lynda had handed him the shirt, all white and neatly pressed and he'd examined it carefully. 'What do you call this? Looks like the cat has slept on it.' Then he'd crumpled it into a ball and tossed it onto the floor.

Close to tears, she'd gone back to the kitchen to damp it down and iron it all over again. But then she'd found coal dust on the cuffs, knew that it would need washing again and very nearly burst into tears, over a stupid shirt.

Yet she said nothing; what was a crumpled shirt in comparison with what poor Mam was having to endure?

At the end of the day Lynda washed the empty flower buckets, swept and scrubbed the duck boards and stowed these and all the remaining flowers away in the lock-up at closing time. She decided that before going home, she'd call in to see how Judy was getting on, make sure she was settling in all right. She'd been in the bedsit just over a week and at least concern for her friend and the children distracted Lynda from her own worries.

The little bedsit was round the corner of the market hall close by the fish market and she saw at once that something was happening as a crowd had gathered with half of Champion Street coming to their doors to watch.

Lynda broke into a run and as she drew nearer realised it was Sam hammering on the door and shouting his head off.

'Open this bloody door this minute before I break it down!'

Lynda could see Judy at the window, and the fearful faces of the children beside her. Without a thought for her own safety she rushed up to Sam.

'What the bleeding hell do you think you're doing? This is no way to behave, making a public exhibition of yourself and frightening your lovely kids.'

Sam stared at her, his eyes empty of emotion, of any expression whatsoever. Ignoring her he reached down to pick up a pebble and Lynda kicked it away.

'No, you flaming don't.' For a moment she thought he might be about to hit her as rage bristled in every muscle, his fists clenched, and the glare he gave her should have shrivelled her on the spot.

Then he put his face in his clawed hands and his shoulders started to shake. Dear lord, surely this big strong man wasn't going to cry? But then he straightened up and she saw it wasn't tears at all but cold fury that caused him to shake and quiver like that. Lynda felt a shiver run down her spine. For a man as disciplined as Sam Beckett to lose control seemed somehow even more chilling.

She stretched out tentative fingers, spoke softly to him. 'Sam! Don't do this. Look at yourself, man: unshaved, unwashed, unkempt, behaving like a lunatic. Go home, have a cup of tea and think things through. You need to calm down, then you and Judy can talk sensibly and quietly, but that's not going to happen with you raging around like a mad bull. What will Ruth and Tom think of all this? They'll not be able to sleep in their beds tonight if they see their dad behaving like . . .'

He interrupted her, furious contempt in his tone as he spoke through gritted teeth. 'Don't lecture me, woman! You know nowt.' And then, to her great relief, he turned on his heel and strode away.

Lynda let out a great sigh and, catching sight of the huddled crowd, the watchful eyes and hushed whispers, shouted across to them. 'All right, show's over. You can go inside now and make your teas.'

Doors slammed, curtains were drawn and the street was empty within seconds. Lynda glanced up at the bedsit window. 'You can let me in now, Jude. He's gone!'

It took Lynda hours to calm her friend down after Sam had left. She made egg and bacon for the children and helped her friend to put them to bed, making sure they were happy and unafraid.

Then the two girls sat by the light of a small lamp and Judy told her in halting whispers that this wasn't the first time Sam had disturbed them. 'He keeps on coming round every night, creating the same sort of rumpus, shouting and throwing stones at the window, ordering me to come home and return his children to him. Oh, Lynda, what am I to do? The first time I rushed downstairs to tell him to shut up but he takes not a blind bit of notice.'

'You know what Betty would say? Stand up for yourself, girl.'

'How?'

'Go and see Constable Nuttall, or better still a solicitor. Get the law on your side.' It seemed so easy to offer advice to others, but why, Lynda thought, wasn't she able to do the same for herself? 'I must go. I'm late as it is and Ewan won't be pleased that there's still no tea on the table.'

'You are all right with him on your own, aren't you, Lynda?' Judy asked, a slight frown creasing her brow. 'I'm so wrapped up in my own troubles I keep forgetting yours.'

'I'm fine. No need to worry about me.'

But then the moment she walked through her own front door Lynda knew that she wasn't fine at all. Something was badly wrong.

While she'd been busy ministering to her friend the place had been ransacked. Drawers had been flung open, chairs overturned, and stuff thrown everywhere.

'Oh, my God!' Her first instinct was to run and pull up the rug to check that her mother's secret hoard was safe, only to discover that the floorboard had been smashed and the stash of money had indeed gone. Someone had stolen it, and it didn't take a genius to work out who. Lynda was quite certain the culprit must be Ewan. Wasn't he constantly complaining of being short of cash and asking her to lend him a bob or two?

But then she remembered Jake's little run-in with Constable Nuttall. Her brother was no saint and it occurred to her that since she hadn't seen him since her mother's alleged 'accident', he must be living rough with no money coming in to feed himself. It was perfectly possible that Mam had been robbed by her own son.

Betty came home the following week and Lynda could see at once that all the fight had gone out of her. She spent her days largely confined to a wheelchair, occasionally lifting herself into the big winged chair when Ewan was out, sitting with her leg in its huge plaster cast propped on a stool. She showed little interest in anything, not even her precious flower stall.

She would sit staring into the fire for hour upon hour, saying nothing, not even reading the *Woman's Weekly* Lynda regularly bought her.

Even friends calling round with gifts failed to cheer her, and she grumbled when Saturday morning came and the Salvation Army started playing 'O Perfect Love'.

'That'll be the day,' was her acid comment. She seemed to have lost her resilience, the sheer exuberance of spirit that had kept her going all these long years.

Worst of all she couldn't get up the stairs to her own bedroom any more and a bed had to be made up in the living room for her. Ewan moved into her old room, and very smug he looked about it.

But then smug was the best way to describe Ewan nowadays. Following the break-in, which Lynda still hadn't told her mother about, nor anyone else for that matter, certainly not Constable Nuttall, there'd been a definite change in his demeanour. He looked very much like the cat who had swallowed the cream and Lynda was feeling ashamed at having accused her own brother of the crime. She was quite certain now that Ewan must have discovered her mother's secret hoard and helped himself to it, attempting to make it look like an ordinary burglary.

Far too afraid to call in the police and risk arousing his temper still further, Lynda had simply tidied the place up as best she could. And when he'd returned later that evening to find her doing just that, Ewan had made no comment at all save to say he was going out again and she needn't bother making him a meal.

Just as well, she'd thought, as I'd be sorely tempted to put rat poison in his food.

All through her childhood Lynda had pined for a father, and now she had one she was rapidly growing to hate and fear him. Any hope that Betty might summon the energy to make him leave was now a distant dream.

Jake still hadn't returned home although she'd recently heard tales of him having been seen sleeping rough under the railway arches, and staying the odd night or two with a friend. Lynda kept an eye out for him everywhere she went, hoping to spot her young brother and persuade him to come home, but in the end she knew she'd just have to wait until he felt ready.

Meanwhile, Ewan's bullying was growing worse.

After collecting the fresh flowers at six she would then have to fry him a breakfast, every single morning. The first time he'd demanded this Lynda had objected.

'I haven't time. Have you any idea how much is involved in setting up a flower stall? All the flowers have to be prepared and set out in the rows of buckets, displays made in some of the baskets, and the potted plants set out and watered, as well as the stall itself needing to be set up with its awning and duck boards. I certainly don't have time to wait on you as well.'

'Now that would be a pity, chuck, if I had to make me own breakfast, because I'm not very good at it, d'you see?' Ewan walked into the kitchen and taking an egg from the wooden holder cracked it on the edge of the table letting the yolk and white drop onto the floor.

Lynda bit back a protest and watched in horror as, one by one, he did the same with the rest of the eggs until he'd cracked and dropped the entire dozen.

'See how clumsy I am? Just a helpless male. Now you're going to have to find time to go out and buy some fresh so's you can make my brekkers. I'd like scrambled eggs on toast this morning, if you please, so buy some fresh bread while you're at it. This heel of crust isn't fit for the mice to eat.'

No, Lynda thought, but it would certainly suit a rat like you. But she said nothing. She went out and bought the bread and another dozen eggs and did exactly as she was told. What other choice did she have?

It was all too evident that she was slipping more and more under Ewan's control and instinct warned her that she could end up like poor Judy, all pathetic and downtrodden, yet she felt helpless to protest.

No one could accuse Ewan Hemley of being the clean and tidy sort yet he would make her polish the linoleum every single day, then walk all over it in his filthy boots and make her do it again. The windows too had to be washed daily instead of their usual once-a-week wipe, and the doorstep scrubbed and rubbed with donkey stone. Then she had to clean out the fire grate and fill all the coal buckets, sweep and clean and polish. Ewan was pitiless, constantly thinking up other chores for her to do, or making her repeat the ones she'd already done.

By the time Lynda got round to helping her mother to wash and dress, she'd be shaking with nerves and close to exhaustion before even the day had begun. Yet she learned to grit her teeth and bear these humiliations in silence, carrying out his every bidding without complaint. How was it possible for her to do otherwise?

Much as she might wish to resist Ewan's bullying there seemed no alternative but to do his every bidding, otherwise he would take his ill temper out on Betty. A risk she dare not take.

Lynda hadn't the first idea how to cope: how to protect her mother, how to find her brother, how to keep the flower stall going on her own, and most important of all how to manoeuvre Ewan Hemley out of their lives. Her situation seemed impossible and her sense of insecurity worse than ever.

And as if all that wasn't enough to worry about, she was missing Terry badly. Once it had seemed as if her dream of finding a man to love was coming true but how could she risk taking up with him again until she'd resolved the problem of Ewan?

It didn't help that she saw Terry regularly around the market, so near and yet so far. She longed to run up to him, to throw herself into his arms and tell him that she was wrong, that she couldn't live without him. But always she managed to restrain herself at the last moment, to lift her chin high and walk away.

Yet sitting at home every night was far too depressing. At least Ewan was usually out at the pub but Lynda felt far too young to bury herself in her parents' misery.

Even Betty saw that. 'You don't have to stop in for me.'

'I don't like to leave you.'

'Nay, I'll be fine here by the fire with Queenie and me *Woman's Weekly*. And "Dick Barton" is on in a minute. Go on, you get out and enjoy yourself, chuck.'

'All right, I'll just pop out for an hour or so, see how Jude is getting on.'

'Give the lass my love and tell her to take good care of them babbies.'

'I will.'

Lynda went round to see Judy and the two girls spent the evening offering pathetic words of comfort to each other.

'Have you been to see a solicitor?'

'Not yet.'

'You should.'

'And you should go out more,' Judy told her. 'Sitting at home brooding over Terry isn't going to help. Why did you finish with him, anyway? I thought you and he were, you know, like that?' She wound two fingers together and smiled.

Lynda shrugged her shoulders and fussed with her auburn curls while carefully avoiding her friend's penetrating gaze. 'Oh, you know me. Can't be satisfied for more than five minutes with a bloke. Who knows, a Tab Hunter lookalike might come strolling over the horizon any minute. I wouldn't want to miss that, now would I?'

But Judy did have a point. Lynda was desperate for some fun in her life, something to make her feel alive again.

The next day she sauntered around the market and let drop the hint that she was fancy free again, and was instantly asked for a date by Kevin Ramsay. The day after that she accepted an invitation from one of the Bertalone boys, and so it went on. Every night a different man. It wasn't that Lynda particularly liked any of them, or was even enjoying herself, but she would laugh at their jokes, smile and sparkle and give every impression of having a good time even when she wasn't.

Knowing smiles were exchanged among her neighbours, heads shaken and lips pursed. Lynda was back to her bad old ways of man hunting, of shallow pretence and teasing flirtations, except that this time there was absolutely no hanky-panky of any sort. Her heart was still with Terry.

And then just when she thought things couldn't possibly get

any worse, one night, with her mother asleep in the bed downstairs, Ewan came to her room.

Lynda was horrified. She'd been reading in bed when he'd walked
in, and she instinctively shrank away from him as he approached.
He'd never behaved towards her as a real father should and now,
whenever he came near, she went all cold and shaky inside.

'You're a right bonny lass,' he said, sitting on the edge of the
bed. 'But then you always were,' and he began to stroke her hair,
tracing his fingers over each cheek, her nose, each eyelid, as if
exploring her face in painstaking detail.

Then he let his gaze travel downwards over the rise and fall
of her breast and Lynda stifled a shiver of disquiet. This couldn't
be right. Was this what loving fathers did? She was wearing her
only baby-doll nightdress and felt oddly exposed beneath his
gaze. She drew the sheet closer to her chin. He was staring at
her in a fixed sort of way, a strange glitter in his eye as he grazed
a hand over the swell of her breast and stomach, causing her to
jerk with shock.

'Hey, what are you doing?'

In answer to her startled question he pressed one tobacco
stained thumb against her mouth as if ordering her to remain
silent. Then his other hand suddenly whipped back the sheet and
grasped her breast, iron hard against the softness of warm flesh
through the nylon. Ignoring her distressed whimpers he fondled
and massaged at his leisure, first one and then the other. His
other hand was firmly clasped against her mouth now, the nico-
tine stench of it making her gag and a sick crawling fear curdled
in her stomach as a single tear rolled down her cheek.

He did nothing more. He didn't touch her private parts, or
interfere with her in any other way. He just smiled at her then
got up and left.

After he'd gone Lynda leaped from the bed to crouch shiv-
ering in the corner of her room for what seemed like hours,
crying softly to herself and far too afraid even to return to her
bed. Her dreams and hopes for a loving relationship with her

father had been utterly destroyed. Not only that but she felt invaded, as if her sanctuary, the only safe place she had left in the world, had been taken rudely from her.

His message was clear. There was no escape from him anywhere, not even in her own bed. Ewan Hemley could do with her as he willed, any time he chose.

26

Judy

'WOMAN are still considered to be the dependants of men, I'm afraid, so far as the law is concerned,' the young solicitor blithely informed Judy. 'And maintenance is not automatic. We may be fortunate and make him pay up, although I have to say that would be unusual as most husbands manage to wriggle out of it. In my experience it can be a constant battle getting them to keep up regular payments year after year. But should he marry again and have another family any money paid to you, his first wife, would be reduced.'

'That isn't fair!' Judy heard her own voice sounding very like Ruth's and hated herself for it. 'What I mean is, they are his children too, surely he is equally responsible for them?'

'Do you have an income of any sort?' the solicitor enquired in that tired voice which indicated he'd been through this conversation more times than he cared to recall. 'You can apply for legal aid, of course, to pay my bill you understand, but they will conduct a means test to ascertain how much your contribution will be. You can pay monthly, of course.'

Judy was horrified. She'd not even thought that far. Striving to remain calm, she said, 'I've very little in the way of savings and only a small income from my stall where I sell my pictures. But the profit I make after I've paid for canvasses and paint is just enough to get by. Unfortunately, in a fit of rage, my husband destroyed all my pictures because I refused to give it up. He's very controlling. So I don't even have anything to sell at the moment.'

'Hmm, well his unreasonable behaviour might help your case somewhat, assuming it can be proved as such. Were the children well cared for while you were working? No accidents, illnesses, problems?'

Judy swallowed on a sudden fit of nervousness. 'No-o . . .'

'You sound doubtful. It's best if you tell me everything, Mrs Beckett. It wouldn't be wise to hold back at this stage.'

'Well, Tom was once bullied on his way home from school. I was delayed by a customer for only a few moments but it made me late picking him up. He should have waited for me at the school gate but . . .'

He made a note on his legal pad. 'I think we won't pursue the line of your husband's unreasonable behaviour. Best not to risk it, in the circumstances. It could very easily back-fire on us. But I'm afraid you will have to find yourself a job, Mrs Beckett.' His tone was brisk now, almost dismissive.

'I'm not qualified for anything. I've always been a housewife.'

'Then you'll have to acquire some new skills.' He smiled at her with a weary patience. 'You do realise that by leaving your husband you not only lose the roof over your head but also any hope of a share in his state pension. You'll have to make your own contributions from now on. I would strongly advise you to consider carefully whether this is the right course of action for you to take. Has he ever been violent towards you?'

'No.'

'Kept you short of money?'

'No.'

'So the grounds would be strictly that of adultery? Do you have proof of this third party? Does he admit to being the guilty party?'

Judy was forced to admit that she did not know the identity of the latest 'other woman'. 'There have been so many.'

'Ah, and you were aware of their existence, were you?'

'Oh, yes, he made no secret of the fact.'

The young solicitor shook his head in sadness. 'The court may view that as complicity, that you'd accepted your husband's straying as part of your marriage, which would make it extremely difficult for his adultery to be considered as grounds now. There are many judges who would see that as collusion. Have you ever taken a lover yourself?'

'No!' Judy was affronted by the very suggestion.

'Excellent! If you were ever tempted you have to appreciate that you would run the risk of being classed as an unfit mother.'

'So *he* is allowed to stray, but not me?'

A shrug of the shoulders. 'Strictly speaking that's not what I said, Mrs Beckett but, in effect, yes you're right. If you have tolerated his infidelity in the past that most definitely weakens your case, and your own would not be tolerated by a judge at all. I assume the marital home was in his name?' the solicitor went on, while Judy was still gasping over that one.

She agreed that it was. There was a cold feeling growing inside and it frightened her. Somehow Judy had imagined that once she'd plucked up the courage to actually leave Sam, all her troubles would be over. But it seemed they were only just beginning.

'If your husband isn't willing to provide evidence of his guilt, in other words if it is not an undefended action, then I have to advise you that your case is not a strong one and divorce could be denied. He could, of course, sue for custody of the children, particularly if you have no means of providing for them. The judge will wish to see evidence that you can fully support them, so that must be your first priority. You need secure employment, a decent home for them other than a one-roomed bedsit overlooking the fish market where you are all sleeping in one bed, I'm afraid. Come and see me again when you have all of that in place.'

He stood up, thereby terminating the interview, and Judy did likewise although her head was still buzzing with questions. Just as she was leaving the young solicitor said, 'Oh, just one more thing. It's always best if access can be amicably agreed between the parties. Otherwise, things can get very nasty.'

'Access?'

'To the children. You need to agree with your husband times when they can visit him, or he can take them out.'

'Oh, I see.' Judy rapidly thought this through, panic growing inside her. 'But what if he should decide not to return them?'

'Do you think that likely?'

'As a weapon against me, yes, I do. What security do I have that he'll keep to any hours or rules I might set?'

The lawyer was already pressing the bell to call in his next client, having satisfied himself that he'd offered all the advice he could for this one. 'I'm sure you are worrying unnecessarily, Mrs Beckett. Talk to your husband. It's important to keep lines of communication open. The division of the marital spoils, and provision for the children are much better resolved before you go to court. As I said, come back and see me once you are in a position to pursue the case from a position of strength.'

A position of strength! And how was she ever to achieve that if Sam was holding all the cards? Throughout their marriage he'd never allowed her the slightest independence, or to work outside of the home. Sam had expected and demanded utter obedience in this and Judy had complied for the sake of peace, and for her children, at least until the end. Now she was to be punished for that fact.

Judy was in despair. Finding somewhere better for them to live was proving impossible on the few savings she had left. Over the next two weeks she applied for countless jobs, but, considering that she couldn't type, had no experience of retailing, and with the kind of scrappy here-today-gone-tomorrow education that had left her with no exams to her name, the only employment she could find was washing up in Belle's café. It paid a pittance but she gladly took it, but Belle still wasn't keen on allowing her to have her stall back.

'Sam's ironmongery business is an important part of this market. I can't risk losing that, and he's sworn he'll up-sticks and move it elsewhere if I let you come back.'

'But that's not . . .'

'Fair? Life never is, pet,' Belle told her, exactly as Judy had told Ruth.

The night Sam had come round and created an embarrassing scene in the street had been one of the worst of Judy's life. On another occasion she arrived back at the bedsit, after a particularly wearing and fruitless search for employment around the department stores of Manchester, to find that her landlord had actually let her husband in.

One swift glance told Judy that Sam had removed all her precious belongings, taken the children's toys and clothes, their books and bicycles, the few pots and pans she'd brought with her from home, even the sheets and pillows off the bed. Her own clothes lay in shreds on the carpet. Judy fell to her knees and wept.

She would never have expected him to be so cruel, so utterly heartless. He seemed determined to destroy everything she possessed. But any anger and grief she might feel on her own account for the loss of these things was as nothing to the pain she felt on behalf of her children.

Tom was bemused, not understanding why his father should deprive him of his tipper lorry, his *Beano* comics and his favourite *Thomas the Tank Engine* books. Ruth was inconsolable and turned on her mother in a veritable tantrum of fury.

'What have you done to Daddy now?'

'Nothing! I've done nothing to him.'

'He wouldn't be so nasty to us if you hadn't annoyed him. Have you been asking him for money or something?'

'Well, yes, we do need money to live on and he is still your father and therefore equally responsible for your well-being. Look, I went to see a solicitor, that's all.'

Ruth's eyes snapped open wide in accusation. 'A *solicitor*? *Why*? Are you going to take Daddy to court or something?'

Sighing, Judy tried to calm the child sufficiently to explain her decision to seek a divorce. Ruth wasn't in the mood to listen.

'You *can't* divorce him! I won't let you. Only bad people get divorced.'

'That's not true, Ruth.'

'Yes it is! Stop sulking, Mummy, and make up. Isn't that what you tell Tom and me when we've had a quarrel? Why can't you and Daddy do that?'

'It's not that sort of quarrel. Mummy and Daddy have big problems that can't be resolved by kissing and making up. I'm sorry, Ruth, but you must understand that we both still love *you*, even if we don't any longer love each other. And the last thing we want is for either you or Tom to be hurt in all of this.'

'Well, we *are* being hurt,' the young girl screamed. 'I want my clothes back, my *Little Women Dressing Dolls*, my *things*, and I don't want to live in this *awful* dustbin of a room!' Whereupon, she flung herself out of the door and clattered down the stairs, sobbing noisily as she went.

'Oh, Tom, stay here, stay here, darling. Don't move an inch. I must go after her.'

By the time Judy had reached the front door there was no sign of Ruth and she spent a frantic half-hour searching every corner of the market before finding her sitting by the rubbish bins sobbing her heart out.

'Oh, Ruth, sweetheart.'

'I tried to go home but the door's locked. *Can't* we go home, Mummy? I *hate* that horrible flat.'

Judy put her arms around her daughter and rocked her lovingly. 'Me too, but we must be brave till I manage to find us something better. Everything will be all right in the end, I promise.'

Ruth looked up, her face grubby and tear stained. 'Why are you doing this to us? Why can't you just go home to Daddy so that things can be like they used to be?'

Judy drew in a slow, trembling breath. How could she explain to this child who worshipped her father, what he was really like? Would she even believe Judy if she told her about his string of affairs with other women, or simply assume she was trying to blacken his name? Could she, young as she was, comprehend such things as a woman's rights and the need for a personal life of her own? Judy wasn't certain and was deeply fearful of making matters worse. She shook her head. 'I can't tell you everything just now, love. Maybe later, when you're old enough to understand. Or you could ask your father. Perhaps he should be the one to explain, not me.'

A decision she was later to come to regret.

On the question of access Judy and Sam agreed, in a most awkward and difficult discussion standing on neutral ground in the middle of Champion Street, that Sam would have the children on Sundays and Wednesday afternoons when he took a half day off from his ironmonger's shop. Judy tried to explain to him that both children, Ruth in particular, were finding the situation difficult and it was their duty as responsible parents to make things as easy as possible for them.

'Oh, and can I please have their things back. Mine too, if you don't mind. It was rather petty of you to take them, don't you think?'

'They wouldn't need to even be in that poky little flat if you'd only see sense and come home. This isn't going to do you any good, Judy. You aren't going to win. Remember, I have far more weapons at my disposal than you.'

'You talk as if we're fighting a military campaign.'

'We wouldn't be in this situation if it weren't for your histrionics. I, for one, am perfectly willing to go on as we were.'

'Oh, Sam, don't start. If you aren't prepared to make a single concession how can we possibly go on as we were? And sniping at each other won't help, nor carrying out malicious reprisals by throwing stones at my window or ripping up my clothes. Accept it, our marriage is over. The important thing now is to make it clear to the children that they are still loved by us both.'

As she walked away she caught a glimpse of Leo Catlow standing on the corner watching her. He half lifted one hand as if about to wave to her, then his wife came out of their front door and he changed his mind, redirecting his smile to her instead. Judy felt the loss of that smile like a physical pain in her heart.

The first time Sam collected the children it felt odd, as if she were losing them in some way. Sam himself seemed like a stranger to her and not her husband any longer.

Judy sat alone all that long Sunday in the little bedsit watching the clock and waiting for their return, terrified they might not even come.

Emotions were running high by the time Sam did actually arrive, an hour late, as if to prove he was still in control.

The situation didn't improve the following week either and by the third Sunday at the end of May, Judy was still sitting with her hands clenched between her knees, for all she should be used to it by this time. All she could hear was silence, not even with the reassuringly normal everyday sounds of the market to comfort her.

How was she to survive? How was she ever to break free? Actually getting a divorce was proving to be far more difficult than she'd expected. She had no money in her purse, scarcely any food in the larder and the landlord was threatening to put the rent up. And now the children were late home yet again.

The moment she heard the hammering on the street door Judy flew down the stairs and flung it open on a sign of relief.

'Hello, my darlings.'

Dressed in khaki shorts and jersey, still wearing his school cap and blazer, and loaded down with fishing tackle, Tom looked somehow very small and vulnerable. Head bent, he walked past her and up the stairs. He always seemed oddly withdrawn and quiet after a day out with his father, which worried Judy immensely as she could find no reason for it.

'Did you have a good day, darling?' she asked his retreating back. The little boy hunched his shoulders and nodded.

'And Ruth?' Judy said, turning to look around, then frowning in puzzlement up at her husband. 'Where is she? Where's Ruth?'

'She's with my mother. Ruth has decided to stay on with me.'

27

Betty

By the first week in June Betty was back at her flower stall, although still in a wheelchair. Her loss of mobility meant she found great difficulty in dealing with the displays but she was happy to be there amongst her lovely gladioli, zinnias, snapdragons and sweet-scented stock. Lynda had done her best in her absence but was clearly in need of more guidance. This morning Betty was trying to explain to her daughter about choosing contrasting or complementary colours for the basket displays, how to vary the shape and heights and add just the right amount of greenery without overwhelming the final picture, but she didn't seem to be properly listening.

Lynda had become rather withdrawn of late, and strangely quiet. Betty guessed she was worrying about Jake, as was she. Oh, how she missed that daft lad of hers and wished he would come home, or at least write to let them know he was well.

If only she could turn back the clock. If only she'd shown more sense as a girl and not got herself involved with Ewan Hemley in the first place. If only pigs could fly!

'You made your decisions and you can't go back and change the past, so live with it, girl.'

'Glad to see you're talking to yourself again, Betty,' Judy teased, coming over to say hello and give the older woman a kiss on each chubby cheek. 'Welcome back.'

'By heck, but you're a sight for sore eyes. I've missed seeing you, chuck.'

'And I you. Unfortunately, I can't afford to buy my usual

flowers this morning, even if it is a Friday. I expect Lynda told you that I've left Sam? Well, I can hardly afford the electricity on the bedsit let alone flowers.' She gave a rueful little smile.

'I hope you've arranged for him to pay maintenance. Don't let the bugger get off scot-free.'

Judy frowned. 'I've made a start to try and put it all on an official footing but it isn't easy. I'm just so glad to get away, to be free of the agony of wondering who he's with and what he's up to.'

'Eeh, I remember that feeling right enough.' Betty thought she wouldn't mind experiencing it again right now.

'Our situation is not ideal, and the children particularly find the bedsit cramped and difficult. But at least I can paint again, if only on the kitchen table, now that Sam isn't around to stop me. The trouble is, Belle Garside won't allow me to start up the stall again because Sam is set against it. She's taking his side, I'm afraid, and finding any other sort of job has so far eluded me, apart from the odd bit of washing-up in Belle's café. I've no training you see, not like you, Betty. I'm just a plain, boring housewife who's been out of the job market for far too long.'

'I can't say I knew much about flowers when I first started, but I soon learned, and you do have a skill at your fingertips already. Your painting. Don't let anyone say otherwise or try stopping you from doing whatever it is you fancy. It's a free country, or was last time I looked since we did win the flaming war. Here, have this bunch of lily-of-the-valley on me. They have a lovely scent.'

Judy firmly shook her head. 'I wouldn't hear of it. You can't afford to give me flowers when you have your own problems.'

It was true that Betty couldn't afford to be too generous with her gifts. Lynda had done her best to keep things going but the flower stall didn't seem to be as financially sound as it once had been. Betty suspected that Ewan was running up debts. Even so, she loved this young lass like a second daughter and since her own parents were abroad, in the army or some such, who else was there to keep an eye on her?

'Go on, lass, take them. One bunch won't break the bank, and they'll brighten up your window sill. Anyroad, lily-of-the-valley are for a return of happiness, so they'll happen bring you luck.'

'Betty, I love you. You're a national treasure, truly you are.'

And the older woman blushed with pleasure.

Betty's next visitor to the stall didn't speak in quite such glowing terms. Constable Nuttall bluntly informed her that although he realised she'd done her best to bring up her son with a proper sense of right and wrong, he had no option but to tell her that she'd failed.

'Do you know where that lad of yours has been all these long weeks?'

'Living rough, I shouldn't wonder,' Betty said. 'Why, do you know where he is?'

'He's been up to no good, that's what. And these last few days he's been up before the beak and spent a night in t'clink, and there wasn't a damn thing I could do to stop it.'

Betty put a hand to her mouth in silent distress. All she could think of was that the last thirteen years of her life had been a complete waste of time. She hadn't escaped from Ewan Hemley at all. He was not only back in her life and beating her up like he used to, had taken over *her* bedroom and was ruling *her* house as if he owned the place, but was also leading her son along the same dangerous path of criminal activity as himself.

'I'd have come and told you sooner, only I didn't know till this morning when they let him out,' Constable Nuttall was saying. 'I took the opportunity to see him home personally.'

And indeed there was Jake, looking thinner and bonier than ever but with an anxious, uncertain grin on his face. 'You're out of Germsville I see, Mam?'

'Jake!' She wanted to leap to her feet and clutch him to her breast, but how could she when she couldn't even get out of this damn chair? Instead, Betty slapped him just as he bent to kiss her. 'What the hell have you been up to?'

'Only hanging out wi' me mates.' He held a hand to his burning cheek, his expression sullen, just like when he was a young boy kicking against her shins because she insisted he go to bed early.

Constable Nuttall said, 'Sorry to interrupt this touching reunion but the lad has got himself mixed up with an even worse gang of hooligans and he's now managed to acquire a criminal record. They were only done for shop-lifting, mind, for which we should be thankful for small mercies. It could have been much worse. But he's on probation so he'll have to keep his nose clean. It won't be just his local bobby keeping an eye on him in future. Anyway, I thought you should know, Betty, and I certainly didn't trust young Jake to tell you.'

Betty's heart sank. All her life she'd fought against this very possibility. Now she considered her son with deep disappointment. He even looked different, something to do with a change of hair-style. He'd adopted a Teddy Boy jelly roll, curling it up even higher at the sides so that it came together in a coil right over his fore-head. And the shoulders on his Edwardian-style jacket were so grotesquely wide they sloped steeply downwards, hanging over Jake's own narrow shoulders as if he still carried the coat hanger inside. Worst of all it was a bright, luminous green with black velvet lapels. She'd have laughed out loud if the situation weren't so dreadfully serious. Her whole life seemed to be falling apart.

'Oh, Jake, how could you?' was all Betty managed, and when he shrugged his shoulders in the ridiculous jacket she could easily have slapped him again.

Clenching her fists and holding on to her temper, Betty thanked the constable, again assuring him that she'd keep a better eye on her son in future. Though how she was going to manage that strapped into this flaming wheel-chair, Betty really didn't have the first idea.

'Was it you who burgled Mam's house?' Lynda demanded of her brother. She was relieved to see Jake safely home again but condemning of his behaviour that had led him to being locked up in a police cell. 'Pity it wasn't longer. It might have knocked some sense into that daft noddle of yours.'

'Why don't you drop dead twice,' Jake shouted back at her.

'And end up looking like you? So, did you do our place over, or not?'

'No, I didn't. That's not the sort of gig I would get involved with so don't come over all frosted with me. Why would I steal from Mam, anyroad?'

'As revenge against this supposed damage she did to you when she chucked your precious father out the door all those years ago. You've spent all your flipping life blaming her for that, just 'cause she wanted a bit of peace in her life.'

Jake flushed. He'd been having second thoughts about that too recently, particularly since Ewan had attacked his mam; having second thoughts about a lot of things, in fact, but he wasn't yet ready to admit as much to his sister. He steadfastly maintained his innocence, saying he'd done nothing wrong and claiming he'd been too occupied trying to find what had happened to his car.

'It's still where you parked it.'

'Not now it isn't. I reckon someone nicked it a week or two back,' he mourned.

'There is justice in the world then,' Lynda said. 'I just hope you've learned your lesson, that's all. Mam has enough on her plate without you making things worse for her.'

'Oh, cut the gas,' Jake muttered, and stormed off in a huff.

Ewan had no intention of ever leaving Champion Street. Why would he when he had nowhere else to go? He was desperately hard up and had spent the time Betty was in hospital setting himself up as a fence. He'd put out a few feelers from contacts he'd made, letting it be known that he was in the business of disposing of unwanted goods, with all due discretion of course.

The money he'd found carefully secreted under the floorboard had helped to get the enterprise launched.

It amused him that Betty still hid her money in exactly the same place as she had in the other house. Did it never occur to her that under the floorboards would be the first place he'd look? Sadly there hadn't been quite as much cash in her tin box as he'd hoped for, no more than twenty quid or so, and he needed considerably more than that if he was ever to make something of his life. Still, it had helped to get him going, a bit of capital always being useful at the start of a new business.

Ewan was tired of having no money in his pocket and he also owed a packet on gambling losses. Nor was Billy Quinn, the local bookie, one to put up with such heavy losses for long before he called in the debt. Stories of what he did to people who welshed on their debts were apocryphal in this neck of the woods. Big Molly, for one, could certainly tell a tale or two about the time her own daughters were kidnapped by Quinn because she'd got behind with her payments. Not wishing to find himself in the same sort of bother, Ewan had decided to take action.

He'd also found it necessary to sell one or two other items he'd found in his ex-wife's house, like the gold clock she kept on her dresser, and one or two pieces of good china. So far Betty didn't seem to have noticed, being too sunk in her own pain and misery, but if she ever missed them she'd assume they were stolen during the burglary. Which they were, in a way, Ewan chuckled.

Lynda had noticed, he could tell by the look in her eye whenever she dusted the dresser or went to a cupboard to fetch something and found it had vanished. She was doing it now, picking up an ornament, dusting under it, then slamming it down again with a heavy hand.

'You're making a hell of a din back there. If you've summat to say, get it off yer chest but don't take it out on that pot dog.'

Lynda stared at her father with his feet up on the mantelshelf in his customary position, reading his *Sporting Life* as if he hadn't a care in the world. 'It was you, wasn't it? I thought it might be our Jake, but it was you who robbed Mam. Don't try to deny it because I know you're guilty.' Lynda put her duster away and got the ironing board out, banging it about in her growing temper. She still had a few shirts to iron and then the tea make. Life was all work these days.

'Ooh, hoity-toity. Got proof, have you?'

She spit on the iron to check the temperature then reached

for the first shirt. 'Our Jake denies selling Mam's precious bits and pieces, and I believe him. He'd never do such a thing.' She was feeling braver suddenly, now that Jake was back home and her mother on the road to recovery. It wouldn't be long before they'd persuaded this dreadful man to leave. 'But you wouldn't think twice, would you?'

Ewan carefully put down his paper and stared at her, his face expressionless. 'So what are you going to do about it?'

'I'm going to see Constable Nuttall, first chance I get.'

'I don't think so, Lynda. I don't reckon that would be at all wise.'

But thinking of her brave friend, Lynda stuck her nose in the air and said, 'Watch me!' She slammed the iron back and forth along the crumpled sleeve.

Ewan got up out of his chair and came over to inspect what she was doing. 'Don't you know you should iron the collar first? Didn't your mother teach you anything? Let me show you.' Snatching the iron out of her hand he grabbed her wrist and pressed the hot iron on her hand. Lynda screamed as the pain seared her skin.

'There you are. A little lesson for you in how to iron, and how to keep your bleeding mouth shut.'

Ewan was delighted to have his son back home. Jake, he decided, could make a very useful go-between by helping to spread the word for this new business of his. But when Ewan outlined to the lad what it was he wanted him to do, Jake simply looked blank.

'What sort of stuff are you talking about?'

'Stuff!'

'You mean like all them bits of engine parts and boxes of records you've got stacked in Mam's bedroom?'

'It's not your mam's room any longer, son, it's mine, and what the bleedin' hell were you doing in it?'

'I forgot, and went looking for her to mend this hole in t'pocket of me trousers.'

'Aye, well, you might ask her to stitch up the hole in your head at the same time.'

'What hole in me head?'

'Never mind. Not the brightest star in the night sky, are you, lad? Listen carefully and I'll explain again. What I want you to do is let them mates of yours know that should they come across anything interesting in their travels, to give me first refusal. I could well be interested in making a little purchase from them which could be beneficial to us both.'

Nothing registered in Jake's expression beyond blank puzzlement. 'They don't go in much for travel don't my mates. They tend to hang around their own pad.'

Ewan sighed, feeling a great urge to tear out his hair, or more likely Jake's. Instead, he adopted the kind of tone one might use with a very small child. 'But they do sometimes visit other people's pads, don't they, when they haven't even been invited?'

Light slowly dawned. 'Oh, yeah, I see what you're driving at, Daddy-O.'

'Don't call me that, son, I don't like it. Just plain Dad will do fine.'

'But it's only a saying, like cool, ya know?'

Ewan gritted his teeth, clenching and unclenching his bony fists which he had a great urge to plant on the boy's stupid face. 'Just try to concentrate on what I'm telling you. Should they ever come across owt interesting in these places they visit, let me know, right?'

Jake grinned, then tapped the side of his nose with one finger. 'Gotcha.' Right now he'd do anything to keep this father of his happy. Maybe then he'd stop bullying his Mam and Lynda.

'Thank God for that,' Ewan said, on a sigh of relief. 'We've got a deal then?'

'Made in the shade.'

'What? Never mind, don't bother explaining, I don't want to know what that might mean.'

Almost at once a frown again appeared. 'Won't Mam object? I mean, she threatened to shop me to Constable Nuttall if I ever did owt wrong again.'

'Ah, but your mam won't know, will she? You're certainly not going to tell her, are you? And I'd be daft to, so there we are, you'll be quite safe.'

'Aw, right, I suppose I would.' Jake still didn't look convinced and Ewan gave it one last push.

'So you'll pass the word around then? It's quite simple, lad, first we find stuff that nobody wants, or folk have found lying about like, then we sell it and share the profits. What could be simpler? Sound good to you?'

'Yeah,' Jake quickly agreed, thinking of his lost motor. 'I need to buy meself a new set of wheels then I can go burn some rubber.'

'Course you do, lad, and I'll help you get one.'

'Rightio, Daddy-O. You're on. I'll go and ask them now, shall I?'

'That's a good idea,' Ewan agreed with barely restrained patience. 'No time like the present.'

'OK, see you later, alligator.' And Jake gladly escaped, though he still wasn't entirely sure what he was supposed to do, or what tricks his father was up to.

28

Judy and Leo

Judy rushed round to see Sam and collect Ruth first thing the next morning.

'She's not here,' he told her. 'She's gone to school.'

'Oh!' Of course she had. So had Tom. How foolish of her to imagine otherwise. But then Judy wasn't thinking too clearly.

She'd hardly slept since Sam had delivered Tom after their day out, a fear growing inside her that he was poisoning the children's minds against her. Tom had been strangely quiet over breakfast and although Judy had been reluctant to interrogate him about his afternoon out with his father, yet she'd found herself asking a few leading questions beneath the usual 'Did you have a good time?'

She wanted to know if anyone else had been there, without actually saying that she meant another woman. If their father taking them back to their old home had made them long to return to their own bedrooms and the life they'd used to know? Judy was quite sure that it must be hard for the children to leave again to return to this grotty bedsit.

She recalled how Lynda often talked of her sense of abandonment and loss, something Judy didn't want to happen to her own kids. She felt it was important that Tom still saw his father; a boy needed a male figure around to look up to and pit himself against. She wanted him to have the chance to love Sam, as she knew Sam loved Tom. She wondered if the little boy was feeling jealous of Ruth because she'd chosen to stay, yet felt disloyal to his mother for wanting to stay too.

Judy was aware that Ruth was anxious about the changes a divorce would make to her own life. 'Will I still be able to see my friends?' she'd asked and Judy had assured her that she would.

'I can't deny that it won't change your life, darling, even after I've found us somewhere decent to live. But you'll still be able to attend the same school, so why wouldn't you keep the same friends?' Unless she couldn't afford a flat or house in this neighbourhood and was forced to move to a cheaper one. Judy tried not to consider such an option.

Now Judy confronted her husband and told him she would pick up Ruth from school as usual and be back later that day to collect her things. Sam looked unshaven and unkempt, as if he hadn't slept any better than she. Judy pushed aside any feelings of pity for him, along with the last remnants of her love for him. He had brought this situation about by his betrayal and infidelity, and his rigid control of her life. 'I don't want the children involved in our quarrel.'

'Of course they're involved.'

'I'll pick her up at four.'

But when four o'clock came round, it was only Tom who walked across the playground towards her, moving like a boy with his feet planted in treacle.

Judy ran to meet him. 'Where's Ruth? Where's your sister?'

He shook his head, his small mouth compressed into a small tight bud of anger and to her horror Judy saw a single tear roll down his pale cheek. She knelt before him, desperately trying to curb the fear that was running through her veins, not wanting to alarm the child.

'Where is she, Tom? Tell me.'

'Daddy came for her at play-time. He didn't want me, only Ruth,' and the lower lip began to tremble just a little. 'Ruth says it's because Daddy loves her best.'

Hot temper brought a red mist before her eyes but just as swiftly as it came, it dissipated. Ruth was only a little girl, being silly and cocky, showing off to her younger brother. She didn't understand. She said as much to Tom. 'Ruth doesn't mean it.

She's angry with me because she's had to give up her big girl's bedroom. Of course Daddy loves you, but you're both going to live with me.'

'Do we have to choose, Mummy? Can't we live with both of you?'

There was such a pitiful expression in his pale pinched face, Judy thought her heart might break. Gathering her son in her arms she tried to tell him how she knew it was hard for him right now, but that it would get better in time. 'Let's go and get Ruth.'

'She won't come. She says Daddy has promised her ice cream for tea every day if she stays with him.'

Bribery, Judy thought. How utterly despicable.

Judy hammered on the door. 'Open this door, Sam. I know you're in there.'

The door opened almost at once and Sam stood before her, his expression filled with cold contempt, one hand firmly placed on either side of the doorjamb, blocking her entrance as she struggled to get past him.

'Let me through. I've come to collect Ruth.'

'She's chosen to stay with me.'

'I'm not staging a battle for my own child on my own doorstep. Let me through!'

'This isn't your doorstep any longer. You'll have to fight for her through the courts.'

'Stop thinking about yourself for once. This isn't fair on Tom to split them up. How dare you separate him from his sister on top of everything he's having to cope with right now. Or sink to bribery to persuade your daughter to stay. *Let me through!*' Judy slapped at him, pushed hard against the unyielding plain of his chest, and Sam simply laughed at her, holding her back easily with one hand. But it was the closest they'd ever come to a physical fight.

Tom began to cry. 'Stop it! Stop it! Mummy, *stop it!*' Then he turned on his heels and began to run. He ran right across the street without even looking. Sam and Judy heard the high-pitched squeal of breaks, the scream of tyres and reacted at the same instant.

'Christ!' Sam was after him in seconds, Judy hard on his heels. Fortunately the car had managed to stop in time, and Tom was standing frozen with shock just inches from it.

Judy gathered Tom in her arms on a gasp of relief, eyes blazing with fury as she turned to face her husband. 'This is all *your* fault! Using the children as a weapon against me is the lowest thing you've ever done, and you've done some pretty low things in your time. Tom nearly got himself killed just now, because you'd taken his sister away from him, as well as his comics and his favourite toys. How could you *do* such a thing?'

It was clear from his expression that Sam was shaken. He reached out a tentative hand to ruffle his son's hair. 'I'm sorry, son. I didn't think.' Tom was clinging to his mother, sobbing as if his heart would break. Out of nowhere, Ruth appeared at his elbow.

'Is he going to be all right? I saw it all from my bedroom. It was horrible! I thought he was . . . Oh, I'm so sorry, Mummy. I thought if I went back home, you'd come home as well.' And Ruth too began to cry.

'Oh, for God's sake, I'll get her things.'

And as Judy knelt on the pavement soothing her distressed children, Sam stormed into the house. Minutes later he was back with two cardboard boxes and Ruth's weekend bag. 'OK, there you are, every flaming Beano comic I can find, Ruth's dressing doll books and Thomas the flaming Tank Engine.'

The children rewarded him with tremulous smiles.

Sam wagged an accusing finger at Judy. 'But don't think for one minute that you've won. This is only the start. I'll see you in court.'

Leo was doing his utmost to avoid Judy Beckett. He'd noticed that she was no longer running her little art stall on the farmer's market, yet somehow she seemed to be everywhere. He only had to cross the street and he would see her, perhaps taking her children to school, or helping her friend Lynda on the flower stall.

Often he'd see her speaking to one of the stallholders. He would see how they would sadly shake their head and it occurred to him that she might be seeking work. Few on this market could afford to employ an assistant. If anyone needed a break during the day they would ask a neighbouring stallholder to watch their pitch, and a day off was out of the question as that would necessitate not putting up the stall.

He was aware that gossip had it Judy had left her husband, yet Leo knew he could do nothing. It would be very dangerous for him to get involved.

He glanced about him now, as if half expecting to spot her, but it was barely seven in the morning with few shoppers around. Despite the early hour the street was a hum of activity, with stalls being erected, vans and lorries arriving every five minutes loaded with the everyday sort of flowers and vegetables grown on farms nearby or bringing goods bought at Smithfield, the wholesale market.

'Morning, Mr Catlow.'

'Morning, Jimmy.'

'It's a bonny one, eh?'

'It certainly is.'

Leo always enjoyed this exchange of pleasantries with his neighbours, loved to linger and watch the activity for a while, and blessed the day his parents bought this house in such a lively spot.

Not that Helen approved, naturally, of their living here amongst it all, and was constantly nagging him to move. Helen considered they lived much too close to the market which she dubbed grimy and smelly. She saw no pleasure in watching the fishmongers gutting fish, plunging a basketful of lobsters into boiling water or dishing out Morecambe shrimps. She found no joy in the colourful array of goods, the way the man selling lino would smack it to draw attention to himself, the clever dexterity of the man juggling plates as he drove down the price of his own china, or Betty over there, hammering the stems of her roses.

Yet Leo did. Leo loved it.

And for the first time in his life he knew that he loved a woman other than his own wife.

As he walked along Hardman Street and turned into Water Street, heading for the warehouse, he still couldn't get her out of his mind. Should he offer her a job? But even if Judy possessed the skills to work in an office environment, he was nervous of having her in his sight day after day. There was something about her which was so appealing, so fragile and special, and whenever they talked it felt so right, as if she were the missing part of himself, the half he'd been seeking all his life. No matter how much Helen might provoke him, or accuse him of infidelity, he was innocent of that crime. So far.

But he was surely allowed to be concerned about her, and Leo wondered if perhaps he could speak to one or two of his colleagues. Even if it wouldn't be wise for him to employ her himself, he might be able to help find her a job with someone else. In order to do that effectively, of course, he would need to know much more about her, to discover what skills and qualifications she possessed.

Leo smiled to himself as he crossed the bridge over the River Irwell. Was that an excuse to see her, to speak to her? Perhaps so, but surely he was only being neighbourly, and she was so utterly irresistible.

It was the following day when Leo came home for his dinner that he saw her again. He'd found the house empty, with only a note from Helen saying she'd taken his mother for a drive in the country. This was something of a surprise, as his wife was not known for her thoughtfulness in the care of her mother-in-law. Should he see this as a good sign, a rapprochement between them, or something further to concern him?

He picked at the plate of cold meats Helen had left for him then abandoned it and decided to call in for a pint of beer and a pie at the Dog and Duck. That's when he spotted her.

Judy was talking to Lynda at the flower stall, smiling as her friend wrapped a potted hydrangea for a customer. Leo's heart leaped at sight of her. She looked wan and far too thin and it was all he could do not to rush over and gather her in his arms.

Losing his appetite for the pie and pint, he hung around by the market hall entrance, watching like some sort of love-sick schoolboy while the two women finished their conversation. It looked a very serious one, Judy's face appearing taut and strained. Then they hugged and said their farewells. As she came around the corner, she was clearly startled to bump into him.

Leo put out his hands to steady her. 'Mrs Beckett, what a surprise! It seems ages since I've seen you. How are things?'

'Okay, thanks.' She sounded hesitant, which didn't surprise him in the least.

'I can't tell you how sorry I am to hear how badly things have turned out for you. I hope you've settled into your new place? Are the children all right?' He was prattling, overdoing it, sounding like an inane idiot. He took a breath then smiled wryly at her bemused expression. 'Would you care for a coffee? I promise not to give you the third degree but I would so welcome your company.'

She smiled up at him then, a bewitching, enchanting smile that warmed him right down to his toes in his suede loafers. 'I'd love to.'

They didn't go to Belle's place, far too risky, but to a small coffee bar close by London Road railway station. They walked there in comparative silence, pretending to be absorbed with the pleasures of seeing the brightly painted barges in the canal basin on this lovely summer's day, yet Leo knew she was acutely aware of his closeness, as he was of hers. Her perfume was light and flowery, her steps perfectly paced with his own.

With a coffee and doughnut before her Leo asked what had gone wrong. 'What happened to your wonderful stall? My mother, for one, keeps asking when it's going to open again. We miss seeing you there.'

Again that smile. 'Your mother was one of my first customers. I'm grateful for that.' But then a shadow crossed her face.

'Tell me about it.'

'I expected too much, that's all. I thought I could have a life of my own as well as being a wife and mother. I was wrong. And now I have nothing: no job, no home, no future, and may even lose my children if I can't provide these things.' Her eyes filled with tears. 'I'm hopeless.'

'I don't believe that. I think you're wonderful.'

She looked at him and gave a tremulous smile that twisted his heart. Perhaps inspired by what she saw in his eyes, Judy began to talk. 'I'm not a wonderful mum at all,' deliberately misunderstanding him. 'I nearly did lose Ruth. She stayed over with her father one Sunday and I thought she might never come home again.'

It was such a relief to let it all pour out. She'd used to find comfort from talking to Lynda, but her friend seemed increasingly distracted with her own concerns these days, and no wonder with Betty in such a state. Judy tried to listen, to understand and be sympathetic, but couldn't bring herself to burden her friend with yet more problems.

'Thank God I got her back the next day, not without a bit of a tussle with Sam, mind. But I could so easily have lost her. He's now threatening to take them from me for good if I don't get myself sorted out. But how can *I* fight him? I can do nothing! He's the one with the house, the business and the money.'

'You can do a great deal, an intelligent, beautiful woman like you.'

She looked up at him, her eyes clouded with pain. 'That's the trouble, you see. I no longer believe that I am. I seem to have lost all confidence in myself.'

'Then somebody needs to put it back,' Leo gently told her.

The pair of them talked for a long time, far longer than they should as Judy told him all about Sam's rigid control, the itineraries he made for her and the children, the immaculate accounts and inventories she was expected to keep. She described her experience with the solicitor, her lack of skills and success in job-hunting, and Leo confided his long-held desire to have a family which Helen had persistently denied him.

It was the market clock striking in the distance that brought them back to reality. 'Heavens, I've a client to see at two and I'm going to be late.' He jumped to his feet but just as quickly sat down again to grasp her hands in his.

'I want to see you again, Judy. May I see you again? Please don't say that I can't.'

They looked into each other's eyes and nothing existed for either of them in that moment except what they found there. 'You know that we shouldn't.'

'I know that we must. It's meant. Tell me you feel it too.'

Judy's cheeks grew pink under the intensity of his gaze but she couldn't speak, only bite her lip and gaze at him in wonder.

Leo smiled. 'I'll see you here tomorrow, same time.' Then he gently squeezed her fingers and left. Judy remained where she was for a long time, listening to the beat of her heart.

29

Betty and Lynda

'Larkspur, I'd say, will suit you nicely, Lizzie love, seeing as how you're so tall and slender. They're blue to match your eyes, and meant for lightness and levity. Whenever I see you serving those delicious chocolates from your cabin, you always look so happy and full of life. A real ray of sunshine.'

Lizzie Pringle chuckled. 'Why wouldn't I be happy with such a wonderful job? I love making my chocolates every bit as much as I enjoy selling them. But I have to say, Betty, appearances are not always what they seem.'

'Don't tell me you're another suffering from problems of the heart. I've enough of those with our Lynda. Are you married, chuck?'

Lizzie shook her head. 'Nope. Single but not entirely fancy free. I live in hope.'

'Ooh, that sounds interesting. What shall we put with the lark-spur then, with the lightness and levity? Now let me think. Hope? No, wrong time of year for snowdrops, or for almond blossom. How about a few roses then for love, and for grace and beauty which you have in plenty, or carnations which say "alas for my poor heart", or how about snapdragons for presumption – on my part I mean?'

Lizzie was laughing long and hard by this time. 'We've so missed having you around, Betty. How would we know what's going on in our lives without you to tell us, or offer advice?'

Betty put a hand to her plump breast in mock imitation of a Victorian maiden, eyelashes fluttering furiously. 'Such kind words set me all of a dither. I believe you compare me to the sweetness of a peach whose charms are also without equal.'

'Well, that's certainly true, you're a one-off, Betty Hemley, and no one can deny it. Which flower represents timidity, because you could never be accused of having that?' Lizzie asked, blue eyes sparkling with amusement.

'Amaryllis. Now I'm with you there,' Betty said, brow creased in puzzlement. 'Nobody could call the amaryllis timid either, could they, since it's so flamboyant? Though some books do say the flower also represents pride, and I have that in spades, so maybe we would be a match after all,' and she grinned happily at Lizzie as she wrapped the chosen selection of flowers.

'Here, lass, put your signature on me pot leg. I'm getting everyone on the market to autograph it for me, then if I ever get lost they'll know where I come from, won't they?'

Lizzie wiped the tears of laughter from her eyes as she signed her name on the plaster cast. 'When are they taking it off?'

'Shouldn't be long now, doc says. Eeh, that's grand. I'm going to stick this bit plaster on my bedroom wall, once I can get up them flaming stairs.'

'I've every faith you'll do it too.'

Betty's good humour dipped a little as Lizzie went on her way, worrying over what the future might indeed hold, but then she dismissed it with an impatient slap of her hand on the arm of the wheelchair. 'Never cross a bridge till you come to it, girl,' she scolded herself. 'We're not beaten yet.'

Oh, but it felt good to be back at work, to be chatting to folk and poking her nose in their affairs as she so loved to do. She could see Big Molly Poulson laying down the law to young Fran, wagging her finger like a good 'un. No doubt wanting to know where she's been hiding herself this time.

Youngsters, such a problem. They think they know everything when really they know nowt, not in Betty's humble opinion.

And there was Leo Catlow, walking out with his mother on this fine summer's morning, which was good to see. Oh, and here was the wife, watching them go. Was she about to join them?

Betty wondered, watching with interest. Apparently not. Leo and
Dulcie had turned the corner arm in arm, perhaps off to the
warehouse or merely to take a stroll by the canal. Madam Helen
turned in entirely the opposite direction and headed for the market.

Now where would she be aiming for? Hall's music? A nice
hat from the Higginson sisters? No, the ironmongery shop. By
heck, Betty thought, I never saw *Mrs* Catlow as the sort to be
in need of hammer and nails, unless she was after a bit of rope
to hang her mother-in-law with. Common gossip had it that the
two didn't get on.

At that moment Sam Beckett appeared at the door of his little
shop, and, looking quickly to right and left, grasped Helen's arm
and pulled her hastily inside. The next instant he turned the sign
to closed and pulled down the blind.

'Now that is interesting,' Betty said to herself. 'Very interesting
indeed.'

As the warm days of June merged into the heat of summer and
Betty grew ever busier at her stall, constantly spraying her precious
flowers with cool water, and busily selling dahlias, delphiniums,
sweet william and bunches and bunches of sweet peas which
more than suited their characteristic of delicate pleasures, she
did her best to keep a close eye on her son.

She also kept an even sharper eye on his pestilential father,
her ex-husband, and became increasingly certain that Ewan was
up to something, though she couldn't quite summon up the
energy to find out what it was. Anyroad, what did she care?
Nothing would give her greater pleasure if he got into trouble
with the law.

But Betty no longer felt able to talk to her old friend Constable
Nuttall, not with all these lies and deceit hanging between them.
The policeman was still under the impression that she'd broken
her leg by tripping and falling down the stairs, and how could
she disillusion him on that score without putting Lynda and Jake
in danger?

Ewan was out for revenge and if she turned it into a vendetta, then her life would get worse, not better. In fact, none of their lives would be worth living. Ewan might only be a petty crook but he could turn pretty nasty if pushed, so best not to challenge him too much.

Betty just hoped and prayed she'd be out of this chair before too long. The doctors had warned her it would be months not weeks, and that she must be patient. Once she was out of the plaster they'd promised to give her exercises and physiotherapy to build up the muscles and help get her back on her feet. They hadn't promised she'd make it, that she would in fact walk again, but she was bloody determined to try. In the meantime, Betty hoped and prayed that Ewan would get bored, or hard up, and go off to make a bit of brass for himself some place other than Champion Street. When had he ever stayed in a place for long?

Trouble was, there was little sign of that happening.

When Betty wheeled herself home later that day, her spirits sank to rock bottom because there he still was, her ex, sprawled all over her little house as if he flaming owned it. And there was Lynda scurrying back and forth, ironing his shirts, putting coal on the fire, fetching his slippers and generally toadying to the horrible old sod.

There'd been a troubling incident a week or two back when Lynda had been suffering from a worrying burn. She'd claimed to have ironed her hand by accident, because she'd been in a hurry, but Betty found the injury disturbing, since it carried echoes of similar incidents in her own life. Since then, she'd made a mental note to keep a closer watch on what was going on before her very eyes.

She glared at her husband with his feet up on the mantel. Something was different but she couldn't quite put her finger on what it was. 'Do you ever get off your backside and do summat useful?'

'Why should I when I've got two women at me beck and call. Lynda, this tea is cold, pet, get me another will you?'

Lynda picked up the mug and marched to the kitchen, refilled the kettle and put it on to boil. Rage boiled up in her too, making a red mist swim before her eyes. She was so tired, near exhausted. It would have to be an easy tea, she decided, opening a tin of stewed beef and scooping the contents into a pan. She'd just peel a few potatoes for some mash.

'I can't go on like this, I really can't,' she said to Jake who was cleaning his shoes by the sink. 'You could help a bit more. Peel some of these spuds, or open a tin of peas for me, at least.'

He cast her an anxious glance. 'Don't let him get to you, sis. Stay cool, Daddy-o.'

'Oh shut up! Why do you always stick up for him? Why can't you feel a bit of sympathy for me, for once.' She thrust her brother out of the way so that she could reach the tap to wash the potatoes, and in her rush to do so knocked the pan of stewing beef all over the floor. Lynda burst into tears.

Looking alarmed, Jake dropped his precious suede-soled shoe in the sink among the potato peelings, then flapped his arms about as if he wanted to take his sister in his arms but didn't quite know how.

'Nay, Lynda, don't take on. Hush, don't cry. I can't stand to see you cry.' He rushed to close the kitchen door, poured a cup of water for her and urged her to sit down at the table. 'Hush, hush, he'll hear you.'

Their mother's voice rose in anguish from the living room. 'Lynda, will you fetch me a fresh cuppa an' all. Your father has just chucked my tea at the cat.'

Brother and sister looked at each other in complete and utter despair. 'We have to do as he says,' Jake whispered, 'for Mam's sake. God knows what he'll do next if we don't.'

Lynda saw then that her brother wasn't unfeeling and insensitive at all; he was just every bit as scared as she was.

A few days later Ewan again approached his son. 'Nothing's come my way so far. What you playing at? Have you set your mates on the job, or not?'

'Yeah, we're cookin',' Jake said, meaning they were working on it.

Not fast enough so far as Ewan was concerned. He took hold of his son by the scruff of his neck and lifted him to the tips of his toes. Jake was tall but Ewan was taller, and where the boy was skinny the man was broad. 'If I don't see some results soon you'll be the one who's cooked.'

'I'm doin' me best,' Jake whined. In truth he'd not even mentioned the plan to his pals, fearful of becoming involved in Ewan's schemes, and frightened that Constable Nuttall might get wind of what he was up to and slap him in the clink again.

'Your best, lad, might not be good enough. I need better than your best in this business. If you and me are going to make some real dosh we need merchandise to sell. And not cheap rubbish either. Radios, cigarettes, booze. You know the sort of stuff I mean, and be quick about it. I have obligations, so if you was thinking of sliding out of this commitment, lad, I'd think again, if I were you. You wouldn't want to upset me, now would you? That wouldn't help your mam to make a good recovery, would it, if I were put in a foul mood, and all because of you.'

'What d'you mean? What has me mam got to do with any business between us?'

Ewan smiled at his son and it was not a pleasant sight. 'Chicken out of the deal and you'll soon find out. She'll be nursing two broken legs then, instead of one.'

Jake was appalled. He could feel all the blood draining from his long lean body, leaving him cold and frozen as an icicle. 'You wouldn't hurt me mam, not again?'

'Want to bet? I'll do whatever I have to do to make my way in the world. That's the difference between us, lad. You talk about being a success; I get on with the job.'

Deeply distressed by the mess he seemed to be embroiled in, Jake tried one more time to stand up to this bully, this so-called father of his whom he'd longed to meet all his life. 'Aye, right, so successful you spent half your bleedin' life in t'nick. Why would I want to do owt that'll land me in t'same hole?'

Ewan punched his son on the nose and while blood spurted, growled at him, 'I've told you why, you daft bugger. Wash out your cloth ears. Bring me summat good to sell by the end of the week or we'll send your mam back into that hospital for a bit longer. You've got five days to prove you're a man. Generous to a fault, I am.'

30

Helen, Leo and Judy

When Leo arrived home, tired and restless and no nearer to resolving his dilemma of whether or not he should do anything to help Judy, he discovered that the Barfords were due to arrive shortly for supper. Leo was hard put not to show his impatience. In his opinion, David Barford was a bumptious, conceited twit who had no other topic of conversation beyond himself and politics, and his wife was a mouse, unsurprisingly.

'I hope this isn't evidence of more manipulation on your part, Helen, because I have made my position clear. I'm aware the by elections are over for this year, but don't think Barford can twist my arm for future years. I will not be putting myself forward as a possible parliamentary candidate, not ever. I hope that is clear. In fact, I've been speaking to Ted Dixon and he sees no reason why I shouldn't serve on the city council. Local affairs are much more in my line.'

Helen was seated at her dressing table, hair brush frozen in mid-air as she stared at him in stunned surprise. 'You've made these arrangements behind my back?'

Leo gave a small click of impatience in his throat. 'It's *my* business, Helen, to decide on these matters, not yours.'

'I'm your *wife!*' The hair brush crashed down, making the glass powder bowls and perfume sprays shiver and chink against each other.

'That doesn't put you in charge of every facet of my life. If I wish to hear your opinion on the subject, I shall ask for it.'

'I expect you ask for *hers* all the time.'

Leo turned away, reached for his tie and began to knot it, determined not to rise to her challenge.

'You don't like the Barfords because David's loyal little wife doesn't fawn at your feet as all the other women do. Oh, I understand you perfectly, Leo. You think if you're top dog in the city you can have your pick of sexy little floosies.'

Leo actually laughed at that. 'Now you're being ridiculous. Were I to be so inclined, party politics would be a far richer field for dalliance, I should imagine. Even prime ministers have been known to keep mistresses. I, however, as I have constantly assured you, my darling, do not!'

As he picked up his cuff links he caught the look of triumph in her face and could have kicked himself. Why did he constantly allow her to provoke him?

When they were first married he'd found her jealousy amusing, even flattering. But as it grew worse over the years it became only irritating and stifling. He understood why she was this way. Her father had neglected both Helen and her mother, dallying with any bit of skirt who chanced by, and had cruelly criticised and belittled them both so that Helen came to believe herself plain and unattractive, instead of the rare beauty she truly was. Although its freshness was fading now, hardened by bitterness and discontent. Her self-esteem had been low even when they'd first met but he'd believed he could change all of that with the right sort of affection. How wrong he was.

She again picked up the brush and began to drag it with such ferocity through the pale fronds of her hair it looked as if she might tear it from her scalp. 'I can see that *I* must be entirely unlovable. How can dull little me hope to hold on to Leo Catlow, the most handsome man in Castlefield?'

'Stop that, Helen! You know that's utter nonsense, and only your own insecurity talking.'

He went to her then, to put his hands on her shoulder, his deep brown eyes warm with sympathy and understanding. 'I want you to put an end to this foolish jealousy. I'm not prepared to play this stupid game any more, nor am I willing to involve myself in tangled arguments because that would sound like an excuse or an apology, and I have nothing to apologise for. I understand what causes you to feel this way, but you cannot go on forever blaming me for what your father did.'

'*Get out! Get out of my room this minute!*'

He heard the sound of the perfume bottle hitting the door even as he closed it.

Leo was into his second glass of whisky by the time she joined him. Alcohol, he knew, was not the answer to a failing marriage but he needed something to sustain him through the evening ahead. Dulcie was happily enjoying her usual gin and tonic, looking quite pink cheeked and perky. He only hoped Helen would do nothing to spoil that happy state of affairs.

Yet again he was disappointed. Helen took her revenge by fawning all over David Barford, making his poor wife squirm with embarrassment, and mocking poor Dulcie over everything she did.

'Use the other glass, Mother-in-law. That one is for *red* wine, not white. Social etiquette has moved on a pace since you used to have your boring little tea parties here.'

'Oh, dear, how foolish of me. But I think I'd really prefer water, if you don't mind, dear. That gin has quite gone to my head.'

'Not surprising, since there's nothing in it to begin with,' Helen remarked, with an acid sweet smile.

Leo issued her with a warning look and poured his mother a glass of water. In her panic, Dulcie then inadvertently picked up the wrong knife.

'The fish knife, for goodness sake! This is trout, and we haven't got to the main course yet. Don't you know anything?'

Sheila Barford, mouse or not, recognised a bully when she saw one and bravely rushed to Dulcie's support. 'Oh, don't worry, Mrs Catlow, I constantly make silly mistakes with cutlery. And it is indeed beautiful, finest silver plate I should think,' attempting to appease her hostess at the same time. 'You are

such a wonderful cook, Helen, I really don't know how you find
the time.'

'What else would I do since my husband is rarely home to
entertain me? You really don't know how fortunate you are that
he has deigned to make an appearance here this evening.'

'My wife does so enjoy her little jokes,' Leo snapped, a grim
smile stretching his lips to the point of pain.

David Barford said, 'Leo will be home even less, Helen, should
he decide to enter politics.'

'That isn't going to happen,' Leo responded, attempting to
keep his tone pleasant and conversational. 'I've more than enough
work running my distribution business and am also becoming
heavily involved in community affairs. I prefer to leave national
politics to those with greater ambitions than I. I've chosen to
stand for the city council.' He avoided glancing at his wife, aware
of the daggered looks she was sending him.

Barford said, 'How interesting. Doesn't offer as much power
of course, but it has it uses.'

Leo glanced sharply at him. 'It isn't power I seek, merely to
put back something into the community that has served me –
and my parents –,' he smiled at Dulcie, '– so well over the years.'

'It's a point of view, old chap, but don't ever forget number
one.'

'I'm sure *you* don't.'

Helen got quickly to her feet. 'Time for the duck, I think. And
before you say you prefer roast beef and Yorkshire pudding,
Mother-in-law, let me assure you I have provided for your more
working-class tastes with a dish of beef stew.'

There was a short, embarrassed silence.

Pink cheeked, Dulcie thanked her daughter-in-law with
commendable grace. 'How kind of you. I think I shall take it to
my room, I'm feeling rather tired suddenly.'

And so the evening dragged on, with Helen seeking every
opportunity to make jibes, Sheila Barford trying to keep her head
down, her husband boring on about the current success of the
party, and getting himself intoxicated on Leo's expensive wines,

while Dulcie felt obliged to make a hasty and early retreat to her bedroom. Happy families indeed!

Judy and Leo began to meet regularly at the little coffee shop. She tried to resist but they both knew that something special was growing between them, and Judy felt utterly helpless beneath the tide of this new emotion that swept over her. Helpless to prevent it. Leo Catlow was the voice of comfort and reason that kept her sane, the attentive admirer who made her feel like an attractive woman again.

She didn't care what Sam might think if ever he were to find out. Judy justified the growing friendship between them by telling herself that if her husband could enjoy his 'other women', surely she was entitled to one male friend.

And that's all they were – friends – not lovers in any sense of the word. Because they did no more than talk over a cup of coffee Judy convinced herself that they were doing nothing wrong, that it was all perfectly innocent, although in her heart of hearts she knew it wasn't anything of the sort.

The glances they exchanged, the heady excitement that soared through her veins if their fingers touched as they both reached for the sugar at the same time, the way they hunched close over the table and confided their deepest secrets to each other, told a different story.

Judy didn't even consider how it might affect her chances of a divorce if this dangerous relationship became known.

When they were together they talked and laughed as if they had known each other all their life. Leo seemed to understand things about her without Judy even needing to explain. And when they were apart she was consumed by the memory of their time together, aching for the next meeting. She loved his deep-set brown eyes, his wide smiling mouth and strong square chin, the way he gently rubbed her shoulder whenever she was upset or worrying about the children. Sensitive, as well as strong, he was also far too loyal to a selfish, uncaring wife.

And there was the crux of their problem. They were both still

married to other people and their liaison was unwise and bound
to lead to unhappiness. Yet since he offered sympathy, compan-
ionship and practical assistance in the form of employment, she
tried not to think about the long-term implications, or possible
troubled waters ahead.

Leo had found her a job operating the labelling machine in a
local jam factory which belonged to a colleague of his. Judy could
only work part time, because of the children, but it was such a
relief to have money coming in regularly again.

She revelled in her new-found freedom and independence and
set about seeking better accommodation for them all with a
renewed confidence. She couldn't afford to buy canvasses so
asked around on the market begging scraps of wood and hard-
board to paint on instead, and in the evenings when the children were asleep, she borrowed her daughter's water colours and
would sit at the kitchen table and absorb herself utterly in her
painting.

Leo constantly worried about her, something which Judy found
quite enchanting. 'You're still far too thin,' he would say. 'Are
you eating properly? You look so pale, so fragile.'

He offered to take her for a drive in the country, to bring
some colour to her cheeks. Never, in all her life had she known
what it was to be cared for by a man, to feel so treasured. But
it was risky. Should she accept? There were dangers, not least
the pain she might suffer if, having set her back on her feet, he
then walked away.

But how long was it since she'd experienced the smallest degree
of happiness? How long since she'd enjoyed a bit of carefree
fun? Too long. Sam certainly wouldn't be depriving himself.
When had he ever? So why should she? She was still young, still
pretty, why couldn't she have some pleasure too? Judy was quite
sure nothing untoward would happen between them. Leo Catlow
was a gentleman, a person to be trusted. It would all be perfectly
safe and above board, not least because the children would be
there too. He made that quite clear.

'We could have a lovely day out, a picnic in some quiet spot in the Ribble Valley. I mean all of you, Tom and Ruth too,' he assured her.

'To act as chaperones, you mean?'

He chuckled at that. 'In a way, I suppose, but I promise, Judy, it will all be most respectable.' A slight pause. 'You can assure Sam of that too.'

'You know I won't tell him.'

'I thought you never kept secrets from your husband?'

'I think I'd better keep this one.'

'Does that mean you agree to come?' His voice lifted, rather like a small boy filled with the anticipation of some promised treat.

And without giving a thought to the advice her solicitor had so painstakingly given her, Judy found herself laughing up at him as if she hadn't a care in the world. 'How could I refuse?'

31

Betty and Lynda

'Na then, Jimmy, what can I do for you, lad?' Betty smiled up at her customer who seemed bigger than ever from this angle.

Jimmy Ramsay wiped his hands on his butcher's apron then tugged his white trilby hat by way of acknowledgement. 'I need a nice bucket for my Maggie. She's been in the hospital for a bit of an op. Women's business, you know.'

Betty nodded. 'I hope she's feeling better.'

'Oh, aye, much improved, thanks. I'm going to see her this aft', so I thought I'd tek her a nice bucket.'

'I'm sorry to say we don't sell buckets, Jimmy lad, only bouquets.'

He grinned at her, showing all his crooked teeth. 'I'm glad to see you back on form, Betty lass, even if you are still confined to that thing.'

'Our Jake quite envies me. He's desperate for a new set of wheels. Na then, Jimmy, what'll it be? Roses? Carnations?'

'She doesn't like a lot of show,' said Jimmy, panicking slightly as he thought of the expense.

'Sweet peas then, the very thing, for delicate pleasures which I'm sure she'll be enjoying again soon, once she's recovered.'

'Aye, aye, course she will,' her husband agreed, blushing furiously.

'Shall I wrap them or would you prefer a little basket? I reckon you can dig deep enough in them capacious pockets of yours to run to a proper arrangement, or have you stitched them up?'

'Is your Lynda not going out with that Terry Hall any more?' The question seemed to come out of nowhere and Betty was surprised.

'Nay, how would I know what our Lynda is doing? I'm only her mother.'

'I only ask because our Kevin's been out with her recently once or twice, and he's seriously smitten.'

Betty smiled. 'As are half the men in Manchester. Don't ask *me* what she's up to, Jimmy. I don't get myself involved in my daughter's love life and neither should you.'

'Aye, you're probably right. It's just that I wouldn't like to see him hurt.'

'Life's all about getting hurt and learning how to deal with it,' Betty bitterly commented.

Before he left, well pleased with his purchase, Jimmy told her of a meeting that evening for the market committee. 'It's to be at the Poulsons' as Big Molly has offered to put on a potato-pie supper. Why don't you come round, if you feel up to it. Time you got back into the swing of things.'

Betty brightened. 'Thanks, Jimmy, that'd be grand. I'm fair sick of stopping in.'

'I could come round and give you a push if you need it, or happen your ex will be happy to do that for you.'

'I'd like to give my ex a push, right into the Irwell,' Betty muttered. 'But don't tell him I said so.'

Jimmy frowned. 'I thought you and him were all cosy again?'

Betty's eyebrows shot up. 'If I ever start to cosy up with that man you have leave to shove *me* in the Irwell yourself, Jimmy lad. I'm doing me utmost to get rid of him, but it isn't working, not so far. Anyroad, that's my problem, not yours, me own bit of hurt I have to deal with. I'll see you all tonight. And give Maggie my love.'

With her mother out for the evening and feeling in need of a bit of company herself, Lynda invited a few friends round. She was lonely, missing Terry badly and the string of dates with several different men had not satisfied her nearly as much as she'd hoped. They'd taken her out a time or two but any flicker of passion would quickly fizzle out. Either she lost interest, or they did. Even Kevin Ramsay, who'd been hot for her once, had refused her offer of a fourth date.

'I don't think so, Lynda, let's call it a day, huh?'

'Why, what's wrong?' She'd felt hurt and abandoned yet again. Hadn't she let him kiss her, fondle her a little, because she knew that was what lads liked? And he'd seemed so keen.

'There's nowt wrong and I still fancy you like crazy, but you're not really there half the time, if you know what I mean. Your attention always seems to be elsewhere. If you ask me, I reckon you're still hung up on Terry.'

'Rubbish. I was over him long since.' The band of pain around her heart threatened to choke her on the lie.

'We can still be good friends though, eh?'

Lynda was thinking that she really mustn't allow herself to even think about Terry. She had to get over him, and what better way than to go out with other guys? Terry had never been near since she dumped him; not called her, not even strolled over to share a coffee with her. Didn't even look her way or say hello if she saw him on the market. He'd obviously forgotten all about her by now, Lynda thought, rather unfairly, so why should she care?

'I said we'll just stay friends then. Right?' Kevin repeated, gently reminding her that he was still waiting for her answer.

'Oh, right. Okay, Kevin. Whatever you say.'

And they had remained friends, although she could tell he was still secretly nursing the hope that they might one day be much more. With the others it had never progressed beyond the first date. She loved men, so what was going wrong? It was disappointing that they didn't ask her out again when she'd put so much effort into trying to please them: dressing in snazzy clothes, laughing at their pathetic jokes, letting them paw and kiss her on the back seat at the pictures. Yet nothing ever came of these sessions. She supposed Kevin was right, she just wasn't interested. All the fun seemed to have gone out of her life.

So with Ewan safely out of the way, drinking with his mates at the Dog and Duck, Lynda and her friends sat around playing records. Kevin of course was there, and a few of his mates including a lad called Pete whom she didn't know very well but who was really quite dishy, and a couple of Lynda's girl-friends.

They sat sipping Coca Cola, singing away to 'Tom Dooley,' bopping to 'The Purple People Eater' and laughing at Kevin doing an hilarious take-off of the Everly Brothers singing 'All I have To Do is Dream'.

As the evening progressed the numbers in the little living room mysteriously swelled. Who all these people were or where they came from Lynda hadn't the first idea, but they'd obviously heard the music and the laughter and wanted to join the party.

Someone brought in a few crates of beer and bottles of cider to replace the Coco Cola they'd drunk, and soon they were all bopping and rocking 'n' rolling, shrieking with laughter over nothing in particular. Lynda had on her favourite tangerine and green checked dress with a three-inch-wide white belt, can-can petticoat, and white stilettos, and she felt pretty and attractive. It was the best evening she'd enjoyed in a long time. It felt wonderful to push all her worries aside and be young again.

She swayed to Pat Boone's 'Love Letters in the Sand' in the arms of the delicious Pete and he was holding her excitingly close, his cheek against hers, the even sound of his breathing in her ear. Lynda felt almighty pleased with herself as he must be the best-looking guy in the room. He was tall too, with dark mysterious eyes. Then his lips were on her ear, a flicker of his tongue and Lynda jerked away to look up at him, one eyebrow raised.

'Hey, what was all that about?'

He grinned down at her and winked. 'Not going to turn all prissy on me, are you, Lynda love? I thought you were fancy free these days, now you've given Terry the push.'

Even the mention of his name brought a sharp jolt of pain to her heart. Lynda ignored it, resolutely pinning a bright smile to her face. 'Course I am. Just a good-time girl, that's me.'

'Well then, let's have a good time then. Long past time you experienced a real man.' He began to kiss her, all mouth and tongue, and what his hands were doing she really didn't care to think but she'd had several shandies and nor did she care. Lynda was hurting inside, eaten up with loneliness, worried over her mam and hating the fact that the return of a father into her life had not lived up to the dream. She revelled in the pleasure of being kissed and petted. Right at that moment any show of affection, even from a stranger, felt good.

The noise from the party was getting more and more raucous and when Pete suggested they slip upstairs for a little more privacy, Lynda was not against the idea.

'Only for a bit of necking,' she told him.

'Course. What else?'

They ran up the stairs giggling and sat on the bed because there was nowhere else to sit. Pete barely stopped kissing her even to let her breathe and his hands were everywhere, touching and fondling and teasing. He must have half a dozen more than any other man she knew, Lynda thought, doing her best to keep track of their progress.

His fingers had found her suspenders beneath the froth of rainbow net and with a neat flick had them undone in seconds.

'Here, not so fast, lover-boy.'

'Hmm, you're scrumptious, babe, I could eat you all up.' He was peeling off her stockings with a touch that sent shivers down her spine. How long was it since she'd made love? She couldn't remember. Terry had always said he respected her too much to go that far, which was one of the things Lynda had loved most about him, his gentleness, and his consideration for others. Pete here was a different kettle of fish altogether. He was getting really rather excited.

Lynda found she was lying on the bed now, and though her head might be a bit woozy she knew this shouldn't be happening. He was hot and heavy lying on top of her, his breathing quick and shallow and those wicked hands of his were now seeking her knickers. Lynda made a grab for one.

'Hey, cut it out. What do you think I am?'

'You're gorgeous. Scrumptious. I want to lick you all over.' And lifting up her skirt he began to do just that on the soft mound of her bare belly. Lynda squealed, partly with laughter because it tickled, but also out of sheer panic.

'Stop it. Stop this right now. You're going too fast. I only agreed on necking not—'

Her words were devoured by his mouth, his tongue dancing with hers. What happened next took her completely by surprise. he grabbed both her wrists and pinned her back on the bed while with his other hand he returned to the problem of her under-wear. Lynda's head cleared in an instant.

'Get the hell off me!' She was struggling now, fighting him with all her strength but he was still all over her, all hands and arms and legs and grunting passion.

'Come on, don't pretend yer Miss Goody-Two-Shoes. I know everyone else has had you. Now it's my turn.'

'What? Everyone *hasn't* had me. *Get off me this minute!*' But he didn't seem to be listening and her knickers were now on the floor. There was only one thing to be done. Lynda brought her knee up to his groin. Hard.

'What the fuck—'

'Get *out*!' She was screaming at him, not caring if anyone heard, but she was at least off the bed and he was crumpled up on the floor, swearing like a trooper.

The bedroom door burst open and Lynda turned to it on a gasp of relief. 'Kevin, get this so-called friend of yours out of—'

She got no further because it wasn't Kevin come to rescue her at all. It was Ewan.

Everyone had gone, including the odious Pete, a much chas-tened Kevin and all her other friends. Lynda doubted they would ever come to her home again. Mam was still at Big Molly's and she was alone in the house with her father.

He walked to the front door and locked it. 'So this is what you get up to when my back is turned?'

Lynda gave a little laugh, desperate to lighten the atmosphere, but it didn't come out right. Not surprisingly as Ewan's face was black as thunder. 'It was just a bit of fun. An impromptu party, what's wrong with that?'

When Ewan had dragged Pete down the stairs and ordered her friends out, he'd told her to stay put in the bedroom. Lynda had welcomed the opportunity to quickly dress herself and make herself neat and tidy, though annoyingly, she'd caught her stiletto heel in the rainbow net petticoat, ripping it a little. Cursing softly, she'd rushed back downstairs anxious to apologise to her friends for the party ending so disastrously.

Now she was beginning to wonder if maybe she'd been safer with the rampant Pete, judging by the darkening fury on her father's face. She felt cold inside and more frightened than she could ever remember being in her entire life.

He just stood there staring at her in grim silence, swaying slightly from all the drink he'd consumed, stinking of beer and tobacco, his thumbs hooked in that big leather belt of his.

Lynda tried a tremulous smile. 'Look, I'm sorry if we were making too much noise but don't get the wrong impression about me. I wasn't encouraging that guy. It was supposed to be just a bit of necking but it got a bit out of hand. He'd drunk one too many beers. You can sympathise with that, I'm sure. Anyroad, nothing would've happened. I can look after myself, ta very much. I was dealing with it. Now I'm off to bed, nighty-night.'

He stepped before her, blocking her exit. 'I could see you were dealing with it. You're a naughty girl, Lynda, and naughty girls have to be punished.'

'What?' Lynda tried to laugh that off but her voice cracked, coming out all weak and nervous. Yet she'd no intention of being bullied. Damn it, she wouldn't allow him to do that to her ever again. Trying not to think of the incident with the iron, Lynda pushed back her hair and bravely faced him. 'It's a bit late in life to start playing the heavy parent. I'm twenty-six, for God's sake, not some daft teenager. If I want a bit of fun with a man I'm perfectly entitled to have it. That would be my choice, right?

And if one gets a bit too randy, then, like I say, I can handle it. I certainly don't need a heavy-handed father to step in and take charge.'

Ewan didn't answer. He just stared at her as he unfastened the buckle of his belt. Lynda watched him for a moment in disbelief.

'Hey, what the hell are you doing?'

'What I should've done long ago. You've been spoiled, girl, and it's long past time you did have a father to teach you what's what.'

He pushed her down over the arm of Betty's new green moquette sofa, and when he brought the leather belt down hard on to her small round buttocks, Lynda screamed.

'You're a whore, a *tart*! That's what you are, girl. I'll make you sorry for throwing yourself at men.'

The fabric of her summer dress was far too thin to offer any sort of protection. With every lick of the belt's tip her skin stung and burned, and Lynda screamed again and again. But there was no one to hear her, no one to help. The neighbours had shut their ears to the sounds emanating from the Hemley household long since.

Her last thought before she fainted and darkness claimed her was that she must deserve this because nobody loved her, not even her own father. And she'd even cheated on her lovely Terry.

32

Lynda

Lynda had come to a decision. After a long and miserable, largely sleepless night spent lying on her stomach stuffing the corner of the sheet in her mouth so that her mother wouldn't hear her sobs, she'd finally calmed down sufficiently to think clearly. She needed help. They both did, Mam too. Lynda couldn't see her own backside but guessed it must be striped purple, judging by the pain. They couldn't go on like this. Something had to be done to get this horrible man out of their lives.

The only person she could think of who might be of some use was Constable Nuttall. Surely assaulting your adult daughter was a criminal offence? If so, then Lynda intended to get him locked up for it. It was time to put an end to dreams and face reality.

'Don't you want any breakfast?' Betty was saying. 'You haven't even sat down for a cup of tea this morning, chuck. What were you up to last night? You're looking a bit green round the gills.'

'I'm all right, I just feel a bit sick this morning.'

'An hang-over or what? Oh, hecky thump not . . . !'

Lynda gave her mother a warning look. 'Don't even think it. It's probably me period coming on, and no I didn't drink last night. I stuck to Coca Cola. Pity a few others didn't an' all.' She took a gulp of tea. 'Anyroad, I don't want to sit down. I haven't time.'

Lynda was thankful Ewan was still sleeping, no doubt *he* was still in a drunken stupor after his night out with his mates. 'I have to go and pick up the flowers, and I'm running late. Barry will be wondering where I've got to.' She took one last mouthful of tea and headed for the door.

Betty called after her, 'I'll get me tin box out later and see if we can afford to buy another van, then you can drive yourself to Smithfield.'

Lynda stopped dead. She still hadn't told Mam about the burglary but it was looking as if she could avoid it no longer. Betty had already asked what happened to her clock and Lynda had made excuses, saying it'd stopped working so they'd taken it to be repaired. Fortunately the dresser was too cluttered with other ornaments for her to miss one or two items.

'We'll talk about it tonight, Mam, I have to go. Don't you try lifting that floorboard on your own.'

'Hold on a minute. What is it you're not telling me? I can tell there's summat. There always is when you get that look on your face.'

Lynda sighed and came to crouch down beside her mother's wheelchair. 'All right, I'll come clean. The fact is, we were burgled while you were in hospital, and yes, whoever it was did find your tin box under the floorboards, I'm afraid. They took everything. We're skint.'

After a beat, Betty said, 'It's not hard to guess who the flaming burglar was then, is it?'

Lynda squeezed her hand. 'Let's leave it, shall we? There's nothing to be done. We've more to worry about than a few quid,' getting stiffly back to her feet.

'True enough,' Betty murmured, rubbing her sore knee. The plaster cast had been sawn off a week or two back but she was still stuck with the wheelchair. They didn't want her to even try to walk, not just yet. An ambulance came for her once a week to take her in for physiotherapy, but she was supposed to do exercises every day, morning and night. Fat chance. When did she have time for such nonsense? Besides, her leg hurt too much to risk moving it.

Eeh, but she'd enjoyed her evening out the night before. She and Big Molly had quite a heart-to-heart. She was a one, was Moll, full of bright ideas.

'At least Jake's back safe and sound,' Lynda said, giving her mother a kiss. 'And we have each other.'

'Aye, love, we do.' Then pulling her daughter close, Betty whispered against her ear, 'We also have a bit money put by somewhere else. I'm not as green as I'm cabbage looking. I guessed Ewan would find my hiding place because that's where I always kept my stash, under the floorboards. But it isn't all there. The rest is nicely tucked away in my post office savings account.'

'Oh, Mam, what a treasure you are. Should we do a runner?' Lynda was smiling, feeling almost light-hearted.

'Pity our Jake hasn't still got the pink jalopy, or we could run off with the hot-rod crowd.' Betty let out a heavy sigh before patting her daughter's arm. 'Go and fetch them flowers, chuck. We still have our living to make. We'll talk later about this other problem,' lifting her eyes to the ceiling from which emanated loud snores.

'Don't worry, Mam. You take it easy and come over to the stall when you feel up to it.'

It was a day or two later before Lynda spotted Constable Nuttall doing his rounds. A quick glance about to make sure no one was looking then she casually sidled over. After exchanging a few pleasantries and the usual stuff about the weather Lynda came to what was really on her mind.

'If someone had been assaulted what do you reckon they should do about it?'

Constable Nuttall rubbed his chin and considered Lynda carefully before answering. 'And who would this someone be, exactly?'

'Oh, just a friend of mine. I said I'd ask you for advice.'

The policeman wasn't fooled but was happy to go along with the tale. 'Ah, I see. So how was she assaulted, this friend? By whom?'

'Does it matter? I don't know . . . a man she knows. The point is should she report him? I mean, would it be safe for her report him? Would he be arrested or summat?'

'He'd be taken in for questioning certainly. Were there any witnesses to this alleged assault?'

Lynda shook her head.

'Hmm, that's a shame. It's only her word against his then.'

'Does that matter? He beat her up.'

'So were there any bruises?'

'Of course there were . . . hell yes, loads of bruises. She can hardly sit down.' Instinctively, Lynda put a hand to her own tender rear. The gesture did not escape Constable Nuttall's eagle eye.

'Ah, so this beating was on a delicate part of her anatomy? And who was he, this man? Anyone I know? Would I know your friend? I take it she does live round here?'

Lynda's cheeks coloured slightly. 'The problem is that this friend of mine has a sick mother . . . relative, I mean. And she's afraid that . . . well, that . . .'

'She's afraid that this man, the one who assaulted her, might take it out on her mam if she reported him to the coppers.'

Lynda nodded, finding herself quite unable to speak as she gazed up into the policeman's kindly face.

He rested a gentle hand on her shoulder. 'Would you like me to have a quiet word with this man?'

'But you don't know who he is.'

'I reckon I can make an educated guess, don't you? Would you like me to have a word, Lynda love, without mentioning any names, of course?'

'Take him in for questioning you mean? Yes, please. Oh, I'd appreciate that, but don't say I told you. Say you've had complaints about the noise or summat. I had a few friends round the other night and it all got a bit out of hand. Oh . . .' She clapped a hand to her mouth.

Now she'd as good as admitted it, really let the cat out of the bag. But the policeman was smiling and Lynda gave a mental shrug realising he'd guessed anyway, and what did it matter so long as he marched Ewan off to jail?

'I did hear something of the sort, so I'd be bound to follow it up, wouldn't I?'

'Thanks.' For the first time in ages Lynda felt almost buoyant, heady with relief. Constable Nuttall would sort Ewan out and they'd soon be free of this stranglehold he had over them all. He'd be back in jail where he belonged in no time.

Constable Nuttall called at the house at around two o'clock by which time he guessed Ewan Hemley would be rising from his drunken slumbers and considering putting an illegal bet on the two-thirty. He came to the door in his vest and a pair of filthy old trousers, braces hanging down and his hair standing on end. The stink of the man's unwashed body and the lingering odour of stale whisky made the policeman take a step back. And he'd thought himself immune after dealing with tramps and suchlike under the railway arches.

'We've had a few complaints about noise coming from this establishment,' the constable began. 'I wondered if we could have a word.'

'I'm listening but make it quick, I haven't had me breakfast yet.'

'Happen we should talk inside, away from prying neighbours.'

'I've never invited a copper into my house in me life and I don't intend to start now. Say what you have to say, then bugger off.'

Constable Nuttall took a deep breath and launched into his spiel on the mythical complaints he'd allegedly received, not only about a rowdy party but also concern over some screams, heard later in the evening. 'I'm reliably informed that there was only you and young Lynda in the house at the time. Is that right? Because if so, I'd be interested to know what you were up to?'

'If it's any of your business, which to my mind it isn't since I'm her dad and it's my place to see she behaves, aye yer right, we were on us own and I did find it necessary to chastise her. But, as you say, she'd no right to hold a flaming party, let alone allow it to get out of hand. I made that very clear.'

'How?'

'I tanned her backside.'

'With your hand or some other implement?'

A slight pause while Ewan leaned against the door jamb and picked his nose. 'I took me belt to her, as my old dad used to do with me. So what? It never did me any harm.'

Constable Nuttall stiffened. He didn't like the man's attitude; he was a nasty piece of work if ever there was one. It surprised him that Betty tolerated having him in the house, though there was no accounting for tastes. Ah, he remembered now, she'd once asked him how to make Ewan leave, but the man had wanted to spend time getting to know his kids which Constable Nuttall had believed to be quite reasonable. Well, this wasn't the way to go about it, and he meant to make that very plain. 'Aye but Lynda isn't a lad though, is she? She's a woman and you can't inflict corporal punishment of that sort on a young lady.'

'I found her romping on the bed with a man she didn't even know. What would you have done if she'd been your daughter?'

Constable Nuttall was struck dumb by this image, a fact young Lynda had failed to mention but was surely relevant. The policeman didn't have a daughter, wasn't even married having devoted his life to the police force, and found such conversations embarrassing so he blustered a little.

'Well, I can understand you might be a bit put out, but she's still a grown woman, and surely free to make her own decisions. I'll let you off this time but consider this as a warning. If I hear of you being so heavy-handed again I'll march you straight down to the station. Is that clear?'

'As crystal.'

'Right, well then, see that doesn't happen. She's a grand lass is our Lynda, if a bit over-enthusiastic where boy-friends are concerned. We'll say no more about the matter but I'll be keeping my eye on you in future. Remember that.'

'I'm shaking at the knees.' Whereupon, Ewan closed the door in his face.

Constable Nuttall was left standing on the doorstep suffering from a few pangs of guilt. But what more could he do? Ewan Hemley was still her father, when all was said and done. He'd make himself into a laughing stock if he hauled a man down the nick for smacking his own daughter. His sergeant would accuse him of wasting police time. No, he'd issued a warning, which was fair enough. There was nothing more to be done.

When Lynda got home that evening, she half expected to find the deed done, her father carted off to jail and the house empty. Instead, she was shocked to find Ewan seated with his booted feet propped up on the mantelpiece, as per usual, newspapers littered about the floor and various plates of half-eaten food left lying about. Nothing had changed at all.

She stood stock-still, staring at him dumb-struck, quite unable to move or think.

He didn't even turn his head to look at her, merely sucked on his pipe and spoke through gritted teeth. 'Your friend the constable and I had quite a chat earlier. Gave me the old lecture about how I should be grateful for having such a lovely daughter but that I shouldn't be too heavy handed. He let me off with a warning so I'm giving you the same.'

He turned to look at her then and the coldness in those dark eyes sent shivers down her spine.

'If you ever grass on me to the law again, girl, you'll have more to worry about than a few bruises on your backside or your mam's broken knee. You'll be swimming in the Irwell in a pair of lead-lined boots.'

33

Judy, Leo and Helen

Leo took them to Clitheroe Castle, that majestic edifice that stands high on a limestone hill above the market town of the same name and Tom listened wide eyed to tales of jousting knights as they climbed up to the ruined walls, and of how the area had once been covered in forest which belonged to the lords of the manor, the de Lacy family. How if a tenant in medieval times were caught stealing a deer they would find themselves incarcerated within the castle's thick walls.

'Chained in the dungeon, you mean?' Tom wanted to know, eyes bright with excitement.

'Something of the sort I imagine,' Leo agreed with a smile.

From this old Norman stronghold they stood looking out over the wide valley to the green hills and woods beyond, to the thick blue ribbon of the River Ribble leading ultimately to the sea. The sun was warm on Judy's neck, Tom's hand in hers but acutely aware of Leo standing relaxed behind her, hands in his trouser pockets.

In that instant she felt so alive, and yet so at peace with the world that she could have wept with happiness.

Leo explained how he'd been born and brought up in the town, and as a small boy had loved to hear tales of the Civil War, of Prince Rupert coming by way of Manchester and Bolton to marshal his forces in Clitheroe before marching over the Pennines to Yorkshire to fight the battle of Marston Moor. Of Cromwell taking refuge at nearby Stonyhurst Hall, yet unable to take to his bed because he feared assassination in the house of a Catholic.

Beguiled by his charm, just as Tom was, Judy listened entranced to Leo's tales, smiling as Tom peppered him with questions.

'Who won the battle? Was Prince Rupert killed? Who knocked down the castle?'

Ruth, less interested in history, adopted a bored expression. She refused to explore the keep, watched in disgust as Tom raced about the swathe of green lawns and scrambled over crumbling stone walls. Nor would she speak to Leo, or even walk beside him, sulkily trunding along several paces behind them all.

Judy observed this behaviour with increasing anxiety, but then the girl had been against the trip from the start, had pointedly asked her mother if she thought it such a good idea.

'What will Daddy say if he finds out?'

'Perhaps he won't.'

Ruth had been appalled. 'You aren't seriously asking us to keep it a secret, are you, because Tom couldn't keep a secret to save his life.'

'No, of course not. We're not doing anything wrong. In any case, I'm free to do as I please now. Leo is just a friend being kind. He wants to give us a day out of the city as a treat. It's just a picnic, a summer outing. Where is the harm in that?'

But Judy could tell her daughter was unconvinced. 'You fancy him, don't you?'

'Don't be silly. I'm not even going to answer that question.' But Judy had been unable to meet her daughter's penetrating gaze as she gave the lie.

Now Ruth scowled and complained of being hungry. 'I've seen enough old stones, thanks very much, aren't there any decent shops in this little village?'

'Of course. How about an ice cream?' Leo suggested, which catapulted Tom back to his side in seconds.

Judy couldn't help but laugh. 'Never misses that word, even at fifty paces.'

The children got their ice creams while the adults enjoyed tea and cakes, the four of them seated at a table in a small tea shop just like a real family.

Tom said, 'Daddy never takes me to see castles, does he, Mummy?'

Ruth answered before Judy had collected her wits. 'That's because Dad wasn't born in a posh town like Clitheroe but in Salford, and then he was in the war for years and years. Were you in the war, Mr Catlow? Did you fight for your country?' Ruth challenged him, a hint of sarcasm in her tone.

'I did, yes. I flew aeroplanes.'

Ruth looked almost disappointed. It was clear she would have preferred him to have done something much less heroic, then she could have found a real reason for her scorn. Tom became more excited, wanting to know all about what sort of planes he flew while Ruth took her ill temper out by crumbling a cream cake all over her plate without eating a scrap of it.

Judy didn't resent her daughter's loyalty to Sam, or regret bringing her and Tom along, even as she ached for some time alone with this man. There was no shame in her now. Leo wasn't happy in his marriage, and hers was over. So if this was their chance of happiness, where was the wrong in it? They meant to see each other somehow, any way they could, no matter how difficult the circumstances. Today, Judy was happy simply to be near him.

Later they took their picnic in the lee of Pendle Hill, that massive hump which overlooked the pretty village of Downham while Leo regaled them with the myths and legends of old Mother Demdike and Anne Chattox, the so-called Pendle witches.

Even Ruth became interested in this tale, listening closely to how through gossip, ill fortune, dubious evidence and the malice of one young girl, these two women, along with many other innocents, ended up in Lancaster jail where they were hanged by the neck until dead.

'The moral of the story being one should never listen to gossip, or fall out with your neighbour,' Leo said, attempting to strike a note of good humour.

'Or believe in witches,' Judy added with a smile, and their glances had met, danced deliciously together for an instant before each had turned quickly away.

If they'd hoped for a few private moments while the children paddled in a nearby stream they were to be disappointed. Tom was eager enough to take off his sandals and dabble, but Ruth remained steadfast in her refusal, sitting between them with arms wrapped about her bare knees and an expression of black misery on her young face, as impenetrable as a brick wall. All they could do was sit and smile regretfully at each other over the child's head.

'Not perhaps quite as successful a day as I'd hoped for,' Leo whispered to Judy later as they stood at the foot of the stairs by the open front door, the children already upstairs and under strict orders to get ready for bed. 'I didn't mean to give a history lesson but felt surprisingly nervous with your children.'

'Tom loved it.' Judy felt suddenly shy and awkward, noting how the lamp-light burnished his dark brown hair almost to a fiery red. 'I'm sorry about Ruth. She's a bit mixed up at the moment, not surprisingly.'

'I'm sure she is, as are we all. I wish I could wave a magic wand and make all these problems and difficulties disappear.' He gazed at her then with such a solemn expression on his handsome face that Judy's heart seemed to turn over. 'I hope *you* enjoyed the day, at least. You caught some sun, I see. Your cheeks are all pink.' He brushed one finger against her cheek, setting the fire in them to an even greater heat.

'That's because you are staring at me. You're making me blush.'

'I can't take my eyes off you. Don't you know how very attractive you are? How very beautiful?'

'You mustn't say such things.'

'Why mustn't I, when it's true?'

He cupped her face with his hands, gazing into her eyes with such intensity it made her blush still more. 'You know that I'm falling love with you. I never meant to, but I am.'

And before Judy could even think how to react to this whispered confession, he'd pulled her gently into his arms and kissed her. The kiss consumed her, being both tender and demanding all at the same time. She didn't want it to end and when he put her from him neither could think of a thing to say. Judy couldn't ever remember feeling so confused, so utterly glorious and happy inside with not a shred of remorse.

'Tomorrow?' he asked, his voice low and thick with emotion. 'At the coffee shop, as usual?'

Judy glanced back up the stairs, then smiled at the pleading in his voice. 'If I can.'

After he'd gone Judy stood leaning against the closed door, heart racing, for some long moments, till finally she asked herself the one question she'd avoided thus far: 'What the hell do you think you're doing, girl?'

No answer came.

She was grateful that Ruth had turned off the light when she got back up the stairs to the bedsit. Judy sat in the darkness going over the day again in every minute detail, reliving every precious moment they'd spent together. Hugging herself with happiness she gazed wide-eyed at the moon, far from sleep and reluctant to allow the day to end. It had been truly wonderful and whatever happened next, she would never regret having accepted the invitation.

However unwise it might have been, and despite Ruth's sulky rebellion, Judy didn't feel the least bit sorry, not in the slightest, and she wasn't going to stop seeing him. Leo Catlow had lit a spark of rebellion within her and whatever the risk, she had no intention of ignoring it.

Unaware that her husband had at last betrayed her, Helen was happily continuing with her own sordid little affair with Sam, still revelling in every grubby little moment. Her dalliance with Barford was also progressing quite nicely.

The fact that men other than Leo wanted her brought a glorious sense of triumph, proof that she was the one who held all the cards, the one in the position of power in the marriage because she was the one with the exciting secrets. She knew everything about Leo, but he didn't understand her at all.

Helen glanced impatiently at her gold watch. Sam was late and she was none too pleased. Since it was a warm, summer's evening with the scent of honeysuckle in the air Helen was down by the canal, but she'd long since grown bored of watching the brightly painted barges glide slowly past. Helen wasn't a woman who enjoyed being kept waiting. She wanted him here. Now!

In a way it was really Leo she wanted but her husband was at the warehouse. He'd been there all day despite it being a Saturday and really she was growing tired of this obsession he had with work. But then he'd been increasingly distracted lately, hardly noticing she was even in the house. Sometimes he would seem surprised to find she was actually speaking to him, and would jerk out of some private reverie.

'What is it?' she would ask. 'What were you thinking about that you even forgot I was here?'

'Nothing.' Then he would shake his head and walk away from her.

Helen hated Leo to have private thoughts. He should think and do only what she told him to. Not that this was easy, not with a man like Leo Catlow. He was his own man, which was perhaps what she loved most about him, and the reason she so enjoyed trying to manipulate and control him.

How Helen loved to see him squirm when she'd made some particularly cutting remark. In her view a comment couldn't be considered cruel if it struck home, and it surely only did that if it were true. She'd so often seen her own mother reduced to tears by the casual neglect of her husband. Helen sincerely believed that if her own beloved father could treat marriage with such contempt, what hope was there for anyone? Right from the start of her marriage with Leo, she'd been determined to protect herself. No man would make a doormat out of her.

Men were not to be trusted or relied upon. Women could depend only upon themselves. Her mother had taught her that much and Helen agreed. She certainly had no wish to end up like her sister Harriet, all her clothes ruined by breast milk and with huge tired bruises beneath her eyes.

Leo could take his pleasures where he chose, but she would take more, *and* win any verbal battle between them every single time. Leo was too much the gentleman, a natural pacifier, and would always withdraw from an argument when it began to get nasty, which Helen found highly amusing. She never saw this as a tactical retreat, only capitulation.

'Have it your own way,' he'd told her only this morning at breakfast when she'd accused him of attending that party Lynda Hemley had thrown the other evening. That blithe look of innocence he wore irritated the hell out of her. Why couldn't he simply admit that the woman was his mistress?

'The whole street could hear the noise they were making, and you certainly weren't at home, or at the office. I rang your secretary to check if you were working late and she didn't think you were.'

'I don't tell my secretary everything. Jean left at her normal time of five o'clock. I returned later, after she'd gone.'

'So you say.'

'Believe what you will, Helen.'

She waited for him to apologise, to come and put his arms about her and assure her that she was the only woman in the world he truly loved, that she should stop fretting about other women. He made no move to do so. 'Is that all you're going to say? This Lynda person is the woman you were drooling over in the pub that time. Don't think I've forgotten. Aren't you going to even deny it and plead with me to believe you?'

'No, I don't think so.'

Rage boiled in her, hot and sour. 'Because you don't care that you hurt me?'

'Because there's little point when you don't believe a word I say.' And he'd lapsed into that unshakeable, impenetrable silence, surely proving that she'd caught him out in a lie yet again. He must imagine she was stupid or naïve to believe him innocent.

Now she sighed and glanced at her watch again. Where *was* Sam?

Recognising herself as a domineering woman, it was a constant surprise to Helen that when it came to sexual romps she was quite the opposite. She longed to be owned, to be possessed. It was an interesting quirk of her personality: David Barford was something of a disappointment to her in this respect, being rather unimaginative and really rather clumsy in his love-making. Probably because he was nervous of his wife discovering that their secret little meetings had nothing to do with politics at all.

Sam was always much more adventurous.

At that moment she saw him striding towards her. He never walked, always strode or marched, a typical soldier. The very sight of those broad shoulders and narrow hips set her pulses racing.

'Where the hell have you been?' She was wearing a strapless red floral sundress and Helen smiled as his gaze slid over her in open appreciation. He almost licked his lips.

'Busy,' he said. 'I couldn't get away earlier. Some of us have work to do, *Mrs* Catlow.'

'Ooh, been that sort of a day, has it? I love it when you sound so grumpy and formal.' She leaned against him, sliding her hand between his legs to cup him. 'Shall I make you feel better?'

His eyes glittered. 'You can try.'

'Nothing would give me greater pleasure.'

'I might be able to think of something in return to pleasure you.'

'Ooh, I can't wait to find out what it is.'

They were so compatible, it was amazing.

They crept into the shadows under the bridge where she let him tie her to the railings with a chain more normally used for tying up the canal barges. Then he grabbed her hair, twisting and pushing her back into the tussocks of dusty grass while he took his time unbuttoning his flies.

Desire slid through her, making her feel lazy and soporific, eyelids drooping closed as if she'd been drugged. Helen loved

feeling this way, so submissive, so needy, craving to be domi-
nated and used. And use her he did, brutally, forcefully, thrusting
all the harder whenever she cried out. But then she welcomed
the pain, which always changed into an entirely different sensation altogether.

She had red marks on her wrists from the chains, and her
backside was sore from being rubbed so hard against the rough
ground, but Helen welcomed these discomforts. These were secret
proof of her pleasure.

When it was over Sam adjusted his clothing. There had been
no conversation between them beyond those first few challenging
remarks. There never was. He glanced down at her where she
sat on the canal bank slipping on her leopard-skin mules.

Helen smiled up at him, her cool grey eyes calm and compla-
cent beneath the pencilled winged brows. 'I have plans for the
rest of this week. How are you fixed for Friday?'

'This was the last time.'

'I beg your pardon?'

He fastened the last button on his shirt, casually flicked away
a few stalks of grass. 'I'm calling an end to it. It has to stop now.'

Helen got slowly to her feet, tugging at the strapless top of
her cotton sundress as it threatened to slide south. 'I can't believe
I'm hearing this. Is there a problem?' Anger was churning deep
inside her, revealing itself only in the clipped tones, the sparks
in her ice-clear gaze. Helen wasn't accustomed to being dumped.
Affairs continued until she called an end to them, not the other
way around.

'Sorry, love, but it can't be helped,' Sam said, deliberately using
a familiar term he knew she didn't like. 'I've got the custody case
coming up soon, so this has to stop, at least until all of that's
sorted.'

'Custody? You're not telling me that you actually *want* to get
your children back?'

He looked at her then as if she were mad. 'They're mine, and
nobody takes anything that belongs to me, not even my bloody
wife. I'll get them back all right. No question. And you, lady, are

history. Thanks for the memories.' And turning on his heel Sam strode away without a backward glance.

Helen took off a leopard-skin mule and threw it at him. Unfortunately, it fell short and plopped into the canal, whereupon she burst into tears. She'd really been very fond of those sandals.

34

Judy and Dulcie

The case for custody was coming up any day now and Judy was nervous. She couldn't say, hand on heart, that access was going well. Sam continued to bring the children home late and once returned to say they weren't coming home at all, that they were staying with his mother for the night. His excuse was that despite having got herself a job she still hadn't found them anywhere decent to live.

'As a matter of fact, I have,' Judy told him. 'I've found a two-bedroom house in Back Quay Street, not the prettiest house in the world admittedly but with a bit of work and a lick of paint it'll be fine. I hope to move in a week or two.'

He scowled, as if this were unwelcome news, which made Judy smile. 'You see, I can manage on my own, Sam, and I really have no wish to quarrel with you. That wouldn't help the kids one bit. Let's go our separate ways in dignity, shall we?'

He grunted, saying nothing, but as he turned to go Judy called after him. 'And tell Lillian I'll come round to collect Ruth and Tom's things in my dinner break tomorrow. Okay?'

The following morning Judy went to work as usual in the jam factory. It wasn't particularly well-paid work and so boring there were times when she thought she was going out of her mind. But they were a cheerful group of girls, the hours were regular, and at least she could now afford a better place for them to live, even if was only a two-up-and-two-down in Back Quay Street. She'd already bought some wallpaper and cream emulsion paint, preparatory to doing it up the minute they moved in. Meanwhile they could cope a bit longer in the fish flat.

She kept her mind occupied by mentally planning any shopping she needed to do when she dashed over to collect the children's things. She would make a cheese and onion pie for tea, as a treat. Money was still tight but if she mixed some mashed potato with the cheese it would go further.

Once these decisions had been made she happily let her mind drift to the latest picture she was painting. It was only in water colour using a cheap tin of Ruth's paints on the back of some scraps of wallpaper she'd found in a cupboard, but it was better than nothing. Judy always felt as if a part of her were missing if she couldn't paint.

'Mrs Beckett, there's someone calling for you outside. Your name is Judy, isn't it?'

The foreman's voice bellowing in her ear above the general din of the workroom made Judy jump.

'Oh, someone for me?'

'They're making a helluva noise. The boss would be obliged if you'd go and see to them afore he calls the police.'

Judy ran, heart beating furiously. There must be some problem with the kids. What could it be? An accident at school? Oh, God, let them be all right. She couldn't bear it if anything happened to either of them.

She heard Sam's voice long before she reached him. He was shouting her name at the top of his voice. '*Judy!* Judy, come out here. *Judy, I need you out here now!*'

When she did catch sight of him through the factory window she was shocked. Never in all her life had she seen him so furious. Her heart leaped into her mouth and she came over all faint, thinking her knees might buckle beneath her. It must be even worse than she'd thought.

'Are you all right?' The boss's secretary looked alarmed, as if fearing she might keel over any minute.

'Yes, yes, I'm fine.' Judy ran out to Sam. 'What is it? What's happened.'

'About bloody time. What the hell are you doing here when you should be with the kids?'

'The children are at school. At least I thought they were. Why are you here, yelling and shouting and frightening the whole neighbourhood. What's happened? Are the children all right? Has there been an accident? Oh, Sam, tell me what's wrong.'

By way of an answer he grabbed her arm and shook her. The gesture shocked her by its violence, since he was usually such a controlled man. 'You should behave like a proper mother, that's what's wrong. Tom vomited all over his desk and where were you? In this place sticking labels on bloody jam pots. What sort of a mother does that?'

'One who needs to earn an honest living.' Judy was beginning to calm down. Maybe the crisis was only in Sam's head. 'I expect he's picked up a tummy bug, that's all. I'll collect him in my dinner hour and see if I can get the afternoon off. Unless Lillian is willing to look after him?'

'It's not my mother's responsibility to mind the children, it's yours.'

'I just thought, since she had Ruth and Tom last night, a few more hours wouldn't make much difference.'

'Right, that's it. You're coming home with me this minute. We're having no more of this silly nonsense about divorce and custody battles, and you working. You're *my* wife, they're *my* kids and I'm taking you back home where you belong.' So saying, he grabbed hold of her arm and began to drag her down the street.

Judy tried to resist. 'No, Sam. No, I'm not coming. Stop that, Sam, I have work to do. I can't just leave in the middle of the morning. Stop it, I tell you! Let me go!'

He wasn't shouting and yelling now. He had himself back under control but was still propelling her down the street with a grip like iron. Judy was the one doing the shouting now, struggling furiously and trying to kick him in the shins or the ankle as he dragged her along. How she broke free she would afterwards never remember, but somehow she managed it.

Calm at last they came to a halt, breathing hard and glaring at each other in silent fury. Judy drew in a trembling breath then, very quietly, and with a voice little more than a cracked whisper, she told him to go home and pour himself a stiff whisky.

'Tom will be fine, I'm sure. I'll ring the school and tell them I'll come to pick him up shortly, in my dinner hour. Don't worry so much, and don't ever come round to my workplace creating this sort of havoc ever again, do you hear? You can't order me about any more. You and me are finished, Sam. It's over! Get that into your head once and for all.'

And turning smartly on her heel she walked briskly away. But by the time she got back to the work's office the secretary had an envelope waiting for her and sympathy in her gentle brown eyes. 'Sorry, love, but it's your cards, and the wages that are due to you. The boss says he can't have this sort of carry-on, it's bad for business.'

Judy's jaw dropped open. 'You mean I've got the sack because my husband came round kicking up a fuss?'

'I'm afraid so. I'm sorry, but there it is. As from this minute, you're out of a job.'

Dulcie had decided that it was time to speak to her son. She'd nursed suspicions for some time, now she was certain that she was right.

Unbeknown to Helen, Dulcie had watched her daughter-in-law set out on her walk quite late on Saturday afternoon, and when, thirty minutes later, she'd seen Sam Beckett close his little shop and set off in the same direction, she'd known instantly what they were up to.

She hadn't dared to follow him, not being quite so agile or fleet of foot as she once had been, yet the signs were all there. Helen was involved in an affair, Dulcie was quite certain of it. She was making a fool out of her lovely boy.

And when she'd seen the state of Helen as she came limping home, Dulcie hadn't been able to resist challenging her on the matter. 'My dear, what *have* you been doing? Your pretty dress is covered in grass stains, and you've lost one of your sandals. Have you been involved in an accident?'

'No, Dulcie, I haven't. I went for a walk by the canal and lost my sandal, so what?'

Helen limped past her into the house. She was still seething inside from the humiliation of being dumped, and really had no wish to be interrogated. All she wanted was a long soak in a hot bath.

Dulcie followed her up the stairs, eyes wide with curiosity but saying nothing until she reached the bathroom door. 'Were you walking with someone, down by the canal?'

'What possible business is it of yours?' Helen snapped.

'None whatsoever, dear,' Dulcie sweetly commented. 'I merely wondered, that's all. I'll go and put the kettle on for a cup of tea, shall I? You look as if you need one.'

She'd spent several silent days mulling over the situation but finally, one afternoon, Dulcie had come to her decision. She put on her coat and hat over her twin-set and pearls and headed for the warehouse.

How she loved coming down to the docks. It reminded her of happier days when her dear Jonty had been alive and the pair of them had been running the business together. It was a pity, in Dulcie's view, that Helen didn't show an equal interest.

As she walked through the gates many of the men recognised her and waved a greeting.

'Hey-up, Mrs Catlow. How yer keeping?'

'Gradely,' she said, laughing.

'I must say you're looking quite spry,' said another.

'I'm feeling on top of the world, Joe. How's yourself?'

'Champion.'

Oh, it was good to be back. Just being in Manchester made her fizz with new vigour. She'd loved her husband, still did for all he was no longer with her, but caring for him had been exhausting. Dulcie hadn't been able to think straight.

She remembered coming to the yard when she was a new bride of just twenty. The Ship Canal had been operational for less than ten years at that time and she'd found it so exciting to stand beside her husband in this great enterprise of his, as if she were making history. In those early days the trippers had loved to view the Canal and the docks, accommodated on the *Firefly* which would also demonstrate its water hoses since it was the fireboat. Dulcie smiled as she recalled getting soaked on one such trip herself.

She would never forget the thrill of seeing the huge ships sail into the wharf, the dangers involved in the loading and unloading, the troop ships during the Great War and the strikes in the thirties. She and Jonty had worked side by side through two world wars but despite the air raids they'd done their bit to help keep the docks going.

Dulcie had been fifty-six in 1939, an age when many women would have been looking forward to retirement, but she'd felt proud to serve King and country throughout the hostilities. Even during the Christmas Blitz when one of the grain elevators had been bombed, buildings had collapsed and grain had smouldered and burned for days afterwards they hadn't flinched from carrying on and doing their duty.

Many warehouses, including their own, had suffered fire damage, and Dulcie remembered Catlows had been full of foodstuffs, the lard melting and running down the street. Jonty had been so brave, so strong, determined that despite great losses they would soldier on.

'We'll make do and mend and not let Hitler defeat us,' was his constant cry. And so they had until they were able to rebuild after the war.

Now her son, her lovely boy, was cut from the same cloth, which was probably why he and his father had constantly rubbed each other up the wrong way. If only he had a wife at his side who understood and supported him as she had his father.

Dulcie had done her best to get along with her daughter-in-law over the years but it hadn't been easy and she was no nearer to achieving the sort of relationship she would have liked now than she had been on their wedding day. The woman was an enigma. Dulcie was quite certain that Helen had seen Leo as her ticket to respectability and riches, yet for some reason had set out to constantly undermine him, even stand against him. Not good wife material at all.

And now Dulcie needed to tell her son that his wife had betrayed him in the worst possible way.

35

Judy

From the first moment Judy entered the witness box and stood before the magistrates she knew she was in for a rough ride. The very first question was whether she felt able to support her children and Judy was obliged to admit that she'd lost her job at the jam factory. She could tell this didn't go down well and she tried to explain about Sam's panic over Tom being sick, to put the blame on to him but Sam's lawyer interrupted with other questions and she barely got the chance.

This led to the inadequacy of accommodation that she could provide for her children and Judy protested. 'I *have* found a better house and I'm quite sure I'll find myself a better job. I'm looking hard, and willing to work at anything.'

An interrogation followed about who would care for them if she succeeded. Did Mrs Beckett have a mother perhaps who lived near by, as Mr Beckett did?

No, Judy admitted, her parents lived abroad but she had friends, and she was sure she could manage. The magistrate frowned at her, clearly unconvinced.

'If only Sam would stop harassing me, I could cope,' she told them, sounding bitter and angry. His lawyer simply smiled, as if pleased that he'd riled her. Judy knew she was giving a bad impression and strived to calm herself.

'It will do you no good at all to allow your desperation to show,' her own solicitor had warned her beforehand. 'You must at all times be calm and reasonable. This isn't yet the divorce hearing. All we are doing is applying for a separation order and custody of the children. The magistrates have to be certain that you are a fit mother.'

'Isn't it true you could only ever do part-time work, because of the need to collect the children from school?' Sam's lawyer asked her, and before she'd had a chance to reply, continued, 'And isn't it also true that you are sometimes somewhat dilatory in carrying out this duty which led, on one occasion, to your son being bullied and beaten up?'

Judy's explanation and protests of innocence were met with silent disapproval.

Sam's lawyer then changed tack. 'These friends you mention, Mrs Beckett, do they include men?'

Shock struck her momentarily silent. Judy didn't have the first idea how to answer.

'Well? It's a perfectly simply question. Do you have any men among these friends of yours?'

Judy cleared her throat. 'One or two. Some of them, like Jimmy Ramsay and Alec Hall, work on the market close to my bedsit. They keep an eye out for me.'

'It wasn't the stallholders particularly that I was referring to. I was interested more in your personal acquaintances. Isn't it true that you have a special friendship with . . .' he consulted his notes '. . . Leo Catlow?'

Who has told him this? Judy stared across at Sam, unable to believe what she was hearing. How did he know? Had he been following her, watching her from afar? A slow beat of fear started up somewhere deep in her belly. This was all going wrong. 'I do know Leo Catlow, yes,' she admitted, in a small voice.

'Good, I'm glad I've managed to jog your memory. And did you accompany Mr Catlow on a trip to the Ribble Valley a few weeks ago? Did he take you, and the children, out for the day?'

'Yes.'

'And isn't this Leo Catlow a married man?'

'Yes . . . he is.'

'Did his wife accompany you on this trip, this picnic?'

Judy shook her head.

'Would you please speak up so that their worships can hear?'

'No.'

'Is he your lover?'

'*No!*'

Sam's solicitor smirked. 'We must take your word for that, I suppose. Although the magistrates may find it hard to believe in the innocence of a respectable married woman spending time alone with a man who is not her husband. Do you not think so, Mrs Beckett?'

Misery ate into her soul. 'I am innocent . . . we are simply friends.'

The solicitor leaned forward, his penetrating gaze cutting into hers. 'And is he your only man-friend, or are there others?'

'No, of course there aren't.' Judy was appalled by the line of questioning and not at all sure how to deal with it. From the corner of her eye she could see her own solicitor sitting with his head in his hands. It was not a comforting sight. 'We're just good friends. Leo wanted to give the children a little treat, that's all, because this whole situation has been so upsetting for them. It was very generous of him. He was just being kind.' She stopped speaking, thinking perhaps she'd said too much, and there was a small tight silence in which all eyes seemed to be upon her.

At length, Sam's solicitor gave a little facial shrug. 'Most generous, as you say. Nothing but a perfectly innocent outing with another man's wife, which you unfortunately forgot to mention to your own husband. But we must believe in your innocence, must we not, since you *are* a respectable woman and a good mother to your children?'

'Yes.' On stronger ground now, Judy met his quizzical gaze with stout courage, even repeated herself. 'Yes, I am.'

But by the time Sam himself took the stand her courage had utterly evaporated. Earlier, she'd nursed fond hopes that her own lawyer would pull him to shreds, draw from him a confession of the unreasonable behaviour which had led her to leave him in the first place. No such questions, apparently, were to be asked. The reasons for the separation were of little interest to the magistrates at this stage. Their remit was more directly concerned with the practical, custodial and financial arrangements for the failed marriage, not the causes.

'Have the household goods been suitably divided between you?' her solicitor asked. 'Are you satisfied that you've got your share?'

'I let her have her personal things, the ones she'd brought into the marriage,' Sam said. 'Various kitchen stuff that women like, and the children's things naturally. I'd provided everything else, the furniture was mine and the house is only rented.'

Judy leaned forward and whispered furiously into her solicitor's ear, '*He came and took them all back again.*'

He got to his feet, an air of weariness about him. 'Didn't you remove some later?'

Sam looked genuinely surprised by the question. 'My wife can have anything she wants. She knows that. I've told her so. I admit that I did make a bit of a fuss at first, but it was only because I didn't want her to leave. I don't want this divorce, I want her to come back home and be my wife again.' Tears filled his eyes and he took out a handkerchief to blow his nose.

'Quite so, quite so,' murmured the magistrates.

'I don't believe this,' Judy muttered. 'Tears from this most controlled, unemotional of men?' But it was too late. The magistrates politely waited until Sam had himself under control again.

Again her solicitor tried a question, though to what purpose Judy wasn't sure. 'Has access been agreed between you, and are you happy that it is working satisfactorily? You are seeing your children regularly, are you not?'

'There are times when I feel I'm no longer a part of their lives. I get little more than a few hours with my kids as my wife keeps a stop-watch on me. I once let them stay overnight and she made a right fuss. That's what the argument was all about in front of the factory, the real reason she got sacked. She started it by being difficult over the children, not me.'

Judy gasped. She longed to leap up and say that wasn't true, that she might already have found herself another job, as a waitress in a café but was still waiting to hear. Except that it wasn't her turn to speak and she could only sit there in stunned silence while the magistrates stared at her, their faces blank.

Other matters were discussed, the fact that Sam's mother, whom the children adored, was happy to mind them if necessary. Judy was barely listening. She felt as if her whole life were collapsing around her. Everything had been twisted, the balance of blame between them cleverly shifted.

Next followed a lengthy description of Sam's financial situation. His solicitor carefully focused the magistrates' attention on the soundness of his business, Sam's lack of debts and his respectability in the neighbourhood.

Judy prodded her own solicitor in the back. 'Ask him how much money he spends on his other women.'

He ignored her and the magistrates withdrew. On their return only moments later Judy knew at once by the tightness of their closed faces that she had lost, even before their judgment was announced.

Temporary custody had been granted to the father as Mr Beckett was clearly in a better position to care for them. Case closed.

36

Helen

'I can't believe I'm hearing this. Let me get this right. *You* are accusing *me* of having an affair?'

'I'm not accusing you of anything. I'm asking a question: is something going on that I should know about?'

Helen's laugh sounded hollow even to her own ears but somehow she held on to her composure. This was the last thing she'd expected, to be accused of infidelity by a serial womaniser such as her own husband. Hadn't Leo himself enjoyed a string of mistresses over the years, despite his constant protestations to the contrary?

'No, nothing is going on that you should know about.'

This was true, in a way, Helen told herself with a secret smile, since Sam had in fact ended their relationship and she hadn't seen David Barford in an age. She allowed the smile to show, lips curling with delectable sweetness as she lay back upon the pillows. She flung one arm back above her head so that he could enjoy the ripe fullness of her breast beneath the cream silk night-gown. That would surely serve to take Leo's mind off whatever little interrogation he'd been planning. 'Who is it exactly I'm supposed to be favouring with my charms?'

Leo was hanging on to his temper with some difficulty. No amount of pouting, smiling or posturing on his wife's part would convince him of her innocence. His mother had been absolutely certain that she was right and, to his shame, he'd felt a leap of hope as if he'd been shown a way out. Leo hadn't realised until that moment how very much he longed to escape the misery of this marriage.

But what if Mother was wrong? What if she'd suffered one of her moments of confusion? Well then, if he asked the right questions, he'd find out, wouldn't he? Stiffening his resolve he said, 'Sam Beckett.'

'*Sam Beckett*? You can't be serious.' Helen allowed herself the luxury of laughing out loud. It seemed the appropriate thing to do. 'You think I'd fall for a rough type like *Sam Beckett*?'

Leo didn't want to even be here having this silly quarrel, but he had to know the truth. 'I long since gave up trying to understand what kind of man you like, Helen. It certainly isn't me. You're quite happy to occupy my bed, but that's as far as it goes. You've never shown the least sign of affection towards me, or the slightest degree of trust. You barely seem to tolerate my presence except on your terms, which usually involves furthering *your* ambitions thinly disguised as being for *my* benefit. You've never really taken the time to get to know and understand the kind of man I really am, not in all the years of our marriage.'

'Heavens, you sound just like your mother,' Helen sneered, and then sat up suddenly. 'This all comes from Dulcie, doesn't it? She's the one who has planted these nasty suspicions in your head.'

'I hardly think it matters where I heard the rumours. All you have to tell me is if they are true.'

Helen was no longer listening. Blood boiling she had but one thought in her head: to demolish her mother-in-law. Kneeling on the bed she screamed at Leo. 'That blasted woman has been out to get her own back on me ever since your father died! She's a vindictive old bat.'

He put out a hand, palm uppermost, in an attempt to placate her. 'Helen, calm yourself. I don't like you using such words about my mother. I know you're upset but losing control won't solve anything.'

'It might stop me from losing you! She knows I never wanted her here, that I valued our privacy, our *marriage* too highly, and she's been seeking any opportunity to put me in a bad light ever since.'

'I think not.' Leo felt cold as ice inside, and his voice sounded as if it came from a great distance, echoing in the empty chamber of his marriage. 'My mother doesn't have an unkind thought in her head. She's a sweet, gentle old lady whose only crime perhaps is to be over-protective of her only son. If she's wrong in her suspicions, fine. We'll say no more on the subject.' He turned to leave but Helen flung back the covers and threw herself into his arms.

'Don't let her do this to us! Don't let her destroy us.'

Leo stifled a powerful urge to shake her and force her to tell him the truth, but instead he gently put Helen from him. She was still his wife, after all, even if her tantrums and her insincerity did sicken him. 'Dulcie isn't trying to destroy us. Perhaps she's been a touch over-zealous, and maybe she has been listening to gossip, I wouldn't know. You tell me. Is it true? Are you having an affair?'

'With Sam Beckett? Of course it's not true. Dammit, what do you take me for? Some sort of cheap harlot that would sleep with any Tom, Dick or Harry?'

He looked at her hard, studying every flicker of muscle in her face, every darting movement of her eyes, trying to decide if she was telling the truth or not. It was hard to imagine that she would consider doing such a thing, that she would sink so low. But then if Helen had successfully conducted an affair without his knowledge, while accusing him unfairly of doing exactly the same thing, she must by now be skilled in the art of lying.

And then quite unexpectedly her eyes filled with tears and she began to weep. 'How can you think such a thing? How can you believe your stupid mother and not me, your own wife? Dulcie hasn't the first idea what she's doing or where she is half the time. Why would you listen to malicious gossip rather than believe in my innocence? How can you be so cruel?'

Her voice rose on the familiar tide of growing hysteria and Leo inwardly groaned, anticipating all too accurately what was coming.

'You want to divorce me and marry your latest mistress, that's the reason for all of this, isn't it?' she shrieked. 'Who is she? Just tell me that. Who is that you love more than me? Is it that little tart, Lynda Hemley?'

How was it, Leo wondered, that whenever they attempted to have a sensible discussion about the state of their marriage, or Helen's own inadequacies as a wife and potential mother, the conversation always ended with the blame being put squarely upon himself.

And yet, on this occasion, didn't she perhaps have a point? If Judy wasn't exactly his mistress, he couldn't deny that he loved and wanted her. Hadn't he seen Helen's alleged betrayal as a means to an end? If only he could be free, he'd thought, then Judy and he could be together. What would Helen say if she knew that he'd taken Judy Beckett, and her children, for a day out into the country on a day he'd claimed to be working? Wouldn't that confirm all she'd ever accused him of over the years? What's more, he'd enjoyed every moment of that day and had never wanted it to end.

Guilt made him turn from her now to take his favourite stance by the window, where he could stare out into the dark night and Helen couldn't see the shame in his eyes.

'Let's say no more on the subject. I've no wish to upset you. No doubt you're right and Dulcie has simply been listening to silly gossip.'

As she came to him on a sigh of relief, Leo moved briskly away. 'I have some papers that need attention before I come to bed. Don't wait up for me,' and he walked from the room, desperately anxious to escape the accusation in her penetrating gaze.

The moment he left the room Helen began to search. Although this was a regular habit of hers, nevertheless she kept an anxious eye on the door, in case he should return unexpectedly. She went through every pocket in every suit that hung in his wardrobe. She riffled through the letters and papers that he'd left lying on his bedside table. Helen even examined every card and note in his wallet which Leo always kept in the top drawer of the tall-boy overnight. But she found nothing!

Who was she, this dratted woman who had come between them and ruined their marriage? Helen gave no thought to her own infidelities, as if they were of no account. She didn't consider for a moment that her husband might have been entirely loyal throughout the years of their marriage, or that it was her jealousy which had driven a wedge between them. In her eyes, it was this woman, Leo's imagined mistress, who was the source of their problems, and one way or another she meant to discover who she was.

Exhausted, and with nowhere left to search Helen flopped back on to the bed, but even then she couldn't sleep. Her mind was too busily occupied trying to decide how to deal with Dulcie.

Ever since the bloody woman had moved in Helen had felt that her life was falling apart. First Dulcie would lecture her on not doing her duty by providing the required heir, then she hung pictures on walls that no longer belonged to her, and she made the place look untidy scattering her *Manchester Guardian* and her *Woman's Weekly* all over the place, not to mention embarrassing her in front of her friends.

Now she was spreading lies about her, well not lies exactly, but certainly stirring up suspicions that Leo would never even have considered without his mother's interference. The woman was quite impossible.

Helen had expected Dulcie to stay for no more than a few weeks; instead she appeared to have taken up permanent residence. She'd taken up again with all her old friends, no doubt relishing the opportunity to spread malicious gossip about her daughter-in-law behind Helen's back. She'd even got herself elected as President of some local Ladies' Luncheon Club or other. Preposterous!

How could the old dear possibly be capable of such a task when she could barely remember where she'd put down the magazine she was reading, or remember to switch off Helen's new electric kettle. Dulcie might claim that it was no more than an honorary position with no work attached, since that was all done by the secretary and chairman, but it put Helen in a bad light. Here she was going around telling everyone that her mother-in-law was growing increasingly senile, and there *she* was proving her wrong by appearing both sociable and capable.

This latest move on her mother-in-law's part seemed to indicate that she was hell-bent on destroying her son's marriage. Well, it wasn't going to happen. Not if Helen could destroy her first.

Helen bided her time, waited until one afternoon when Dulcie was in the kitchen baking scones, as she so loved to do. The woman lived to entertain her friends. She was constantly inviting people in for jolly little tea parties or coffee mornings, without even asking Helen's permission.

'Let her enjoy herself,' Leo would say. 'What harm is she doing?'

Every harm, Helen thought, just by being here, by insinuating herself into *my* kitchen, into *our* lives.

Helen sat quietly in the lounge flicking through *Vogue* and patiently waiting until she was done. The smell of freshly baked scones drifted through the house, making even her own mouth water. It would be a different story very soon.

'Aren't they ready yet?' Helen asked, stepping into the kitchen to peer over her mother-in-law's shoulder.

'Not yet. Five more minutes. That's why I'm waiting here, dear, so that I can keep track of the time.'

'Not easy, for a woman of your age,' Helen dryly remarked. 'I'm sure you do your best, Dulcie, but why put yourself through all of this. You could quite easily buy a dozen perfectly good scones at Georges' bakery.'

'Bought scones are nowhere near as good as home made. Leo will tell you that. He always appreciates my baking.'

'He eats what you bake without complaint, certainly. But that's not quite the same thing, is it? I know he feels it wouldn't be polite to do otherwise, if you've gone to all the trouble of making whatever it is.' Helen smiled into Dulcie's horrified face. 'Leo has acquired a more educated taste these days, I'm afraid. Well, I'll leave you to it. See that you remember to switch off the oven when they are done. We don't want any little accidents, do we?'

'I'm not quite in my dotage,' Dulcie snapped, hurt by the thought that even her own son might be growing tired of her baking, or perhaps of having her around. She saw now that it had been a mistake to stay this long. She should have gone back to Lytham weeks ago.

Impossible as it may seem, relations between the two women had, if anything, worsened since Dulcie had taken her suspicions to Leo. They barely spoke a word to each other, and Dulcie had taken to eating all her meals alone in her room unless Leo were present to act as a buffer between them. In fact, this was the longest conversation they'd enjoyed in quite a while, if that was the right word.

Helen returned to her seat on the sofa and picked up her magazine, while Dulcie stood in the kitchen miserably waiting for her scones to cook.

An hour later Helen saw Dulcie putting on her coat and hat to go for her usual afternoon stroll. The scones were stacked on a cooling tray, waiting for the proposed tea which would take place at four o'clock precisely. Helen immediately set aside her magazine and headed for the stairs.

'I shall take my shower and nap while you're out walking. Do try not to get lost this time, Mother-in-law, because I won't be in a position to come and look for you.'

'I'm sure I can manage. I've lived in Castlefield a good deal longer than you, dear.'

'I'm aware of that,' Helen icily responded. But not for much longer, she added silently to herself as she went upstairs to her room and quietly closed the door. She made no move to undress or to lie down, but stood listening to the sounds of her mother-in-law leaving the house. Her plan was risky but then nothing was gained without taking chances.

Five or six minutes after Dulcie had gone, Helen was clad in her dressing gown, ready to put the plan into effect. She made her way back down to the kitchen.

After lighting the gas burner on the stove Helen took a tea towel which Dulcie had set to dry on the rack and put it to the flame. It caught instantly, filling the small room with smoke in seconds as the flames leaped and danced. Helen held her nerve for as long as she dared, watching as the smoke blackened, the flames travelled and caught the blue check curtains that hung at the kitchen window. She was tired of those curtains in any case, and these kitchen cupboards. Only when she judged sufficient damage had been done did she turn on the cold water tap and begin to fill the washing-up bowl. It seemed about the right time to have smelled smoke, rushed downstairs and to start throwing water about.

But somehow the fire had taken a greater hold far quicker than she'd expected. Filling and flinging bowlfuls of water didn't seem to be having much effect on damping it down. In genuine distress now, Helen ran to the phone to call for the fire brigade.

37

'Your usual, is it, for your lovely mam?' Betty glanced up at Leo, and wondered how a man who had it all could look so tired and depressed. He made no reply so she kept on talking, as was her wont. 'Carnations are lovely just now. Red for 'alas my poor heart', yellow for disdain, pink for a woman's love. I've some garden ones here, shorter stems but with a wonderful scent. Course, standard carnations, or dianthus, as we should rightly call them, don't have any scent. But they'll last three weeks if you look after them properly. Are you not feeling too well, might I ask?'

Leo forced a smile. Last evening at six o'clock he'd witnessed the removal of Judy's children from her care. He'd been hovering around the market, hoping to speak to her and discover the outcome of the case when Sam had arrived in his van and the children and all their goods and chattels had been loaded on board. He'd kept well back in the shadows, silently watching and his heart had gone out to her because he could see at once this wasn't an example of Sam's visiting rights. This was something much more permanent.

Judy had stood at the door white-faced, steadfastly brave for the sake of her children. He thought he had never seen such courage, and such stark despair, in his life before. The bleak terror in her eyes had chilled him, and the silence in the street when the van had driven off in a cloud of dust would echo forever in his soul.

He'd hurried straight across to her but she'd regarded him as if he were a stranger and uttered just two words: 'Stay away!'

'Judy, let me help, for God's sake. I heard about your losing the job. If you've lost the children too, let me help you get them back.'

Wild-eyed, she'd screamed at him. '*Haven't you done enough? Keep away from me!*' And she'd rushed inside and slammed the door.

'I've got the black dog on my shoulder this morning,' Leo admitted now to Betty. 'Feeling a bit low, though not as low as some. You've heard about Judy . . . Mrs Beckett, I suppose. She lost custody.'

'Oh, my giddy aunt!' Betty put a hand to her mouth. 'I'll send our Lynda round right away, though she hasn't been too well lately either.' Betty frowned. 'Nay, what's happening to the world? It's sick, that's what it is, taking babbies away from their mother.'

They discussed the case for a while, and Leo managed to get the message across that he could do little to help without compromising her and Betty promised to keep a motherly eye on Judy. 'I'll take her some flowers,' which brought their attention back to the carnations for Dulcie.

'How is the good lady, well, I trust? Haven't seen her around lately. I heard you had a bit of a fire. That must've been scary. Not too much damage, I hope?'

Leo shook his head. 'Not too much, no.' Except to his poor mother who hadn't stopped weeping since, swearing she clearly remembered turning off the gas jets, *and* the oven. But the evidence was there for them all to see. Helen had been upstairs in the shower at the time and there'd been no one else in the house, so what else could it be but Dulcie's forgetfulness which caused the accident? He'd finally had to accept that Helen was right. It was time for his mother to go into a residential home where she would be given the care and attention she needed. Hence the need for the flowers. It was today he was taking her and felt he had to make her new room as welcoming as possible.

'Well, at least you're looking more yourself, Betty. More lively than I've seen you in a long while.' He smiled at her in a distracted sort of way as he fished in his pocket for his wallet, and Betty grinned back.

'Oh, aye, and I can nearly dance a jig now.' She pulled herself out of her chair and shuffled a few steps with the help of two sticks.

Leo laughed, though he was hardly even looking at her, too busy counting out notes. 'The exercises are paying off then. Good for you. I must go. How much do I owe you?'

The fact he asked the price told Betty that something must be badly wrong in that household.

Things weren't too good in her own household either, did Betty but know it. Lynda had made a startling discovery. She'd been cleaning Jake's room, collecting the dirty clothes that he generally left lying all over the floor, and the tea mugs with mould growing in the bottom of them, hanging up his jazzy Teddy-boy jackets and his string ties.

It was when she was putting his crepe-soled shoes away in the cupboard that she came across the boxes. Any number of them, which Lynda had never seen before. Curious to know what they contained, Lynda opened one. It was full of transistor radios. Frowning, she opened another. Cigarettes. Beginning to sweat, she opened a third. This one contained cartons of Imperial leather soap, jars of Pond's face cream, and any number of bottles of Blue Grass perfume.

'Oh, God. Now he's really done it.'

As if controlled by some will other than her own, Lynda got up from her knees and the next moment found herself standing at Ewan's bedroom door. She never went in here. It was forbidden territory. Ever since her mam had come home from the hospital and Ewan had taken up residence of the room in her place she hadn't come near, not even to clean it, making it very clear from the start that it was his responsibility.

But this morning he was out, so it was now or never.

Lynda grasped the handle and pushed open the door. What she saw made her gasp. The small room was stacked from floor to ceiling with boxes, exactly like the ones she'd found in Jake's cupboard. A few frantic moments later, she knew all she needed to know. Her father was handling stolen goods. He was carrying out his criminal activities from their own home.

Lynda heard the sound of the front door opening and her heart leaped into her mouth. Fast as she could she closed up the boxes again, although she couldn't replace the sticky-backed paper tape she'd peeled off. Instead she shunted another box on top to cover the damning evidence then fled to her own room where she sat on the bed, heart beating like a mad thing.

'Lynda, are you in, love? Judy's in trouble and needs you to go round.'

Lynda closed her eyes on a sigh of relief, drew in a deep shaky breath to steady her nerves and shouted down the stairs, 'I'm coming, Mam.'

Talking to her friend was traumatic, the most difficult thing Lynda had ever done. What comfort could she offer? Lynda said all the expected things about how she would soon find another job and get the children back but Judy didn't seem to be listening. She looked shattered, a broken woman, all the confidence knocked out of her.

Lynda could sympathise with that all right. She felt very much the same herself.

'I have to get away from here,' Judy was saying. 'I've lost my marriage, my job, the house in Back Quay Street we were about to move in to, and now my kids. Leo came round yesterday, trying to help, and I just screamed at him.' Her voice sounded strangely matter of fact, her eyes fixed on some inner pain. 'I love him, you see, and if I stayed on Champion Street I'd need to be with him. I wouldn't be able to help myself. But then I'd never see my children again. Sam has made that very clear.'

She wasn't even crying, which troubled Lynda greatly. Her friend simply sat with her hands in her lap, clenching and unclenching, her face a tight mask of grief.

'You mustn't give up on happiness completely, Jude love.

Maybe later, when you've got the children back, which I'm sure you will do, it'll be different. Once the divorce is finalised I mean, you and Leo can . . .'

'When will I get them back, that's the question? And how? It could take months . . . years, I don't know how long. Forever! I can't bear it.'

A long silence followed in which both girls sat on the big bed that nearly filled the small room, arms wrapped around each other. 'Where will you go?'

'I'm not sure. I'll make some enquiries tomorrow. A room is all I need, now that there's only me, at least until I find a decent job and get a bit of money behind me. Then I'll get something more suitable for the kids.'

'Didn't they make Sam pay maintenance to you?'

'Oh yes, a couple of quid a week for my rent, but without custody of the children it's really up to me now, isn't it?' Judy's voice sounded remote and strangely detached.

Lynda helped her friend pack her few precious belongings all the while urging her not to do anything hasty that she might regret. 'Why don't you sleep on it for a bit, give it more thought. I really can't bear to think of you going away.' A selfish thought, Lynda knew, nevertheless it was true.

'I can't bear to think of it either,' Judy said, and then both girls were crying, stroking each other's hair and clinging to each other, drawing strength from their mutual misery.

'Promise me that you won't do anything in a hurry?' Lynda said again as she left, heart-sore and her face still blotched with tears.

Judy didn't reply but the next day when Lynda went round to the fish flat, she found the bedsit empty. Her friend, and all her belongings, had gone.

Judy had left without saying goodbye, without even leaving a forwarding address.

Betty saw Leo again later that day. She'd seen him set off in his Jaguar with old Mrs Catlow in the back seat. Now he returned alone, parking the car at his front door and looking even more dejected than he had earlier. And there was the younger Mrs Catlow, the elegant Helen, waiting for him on the doorstep and looking mighty pleased with herself. Now what did that mean?

She wondered if Leo realised how friendly his wife was with Sam Beckett, and if she should perhaps casually drop a few hints that she'd seen them locked up cosily together in his little shop the other day? But then Betty changed her mind. What business was it of hers? Didn't she have enough troubles on her plate without adding other folk's?

'Where are you off to at this time of night?' Lynda demanded of her brother. He hadn't been in the house more than fifteen minutes and in that time he'd wrecked the bathroom, leaving towels and puddles of water all over the floor and a dirty ring around the bath, strewn rejected shirts and ties all over his bed and left greasy fingerprints on his clean shiny mirror from all the gunge he put on his hair. Now he placed the egg and bacon Lynda had fried for him between two slices of bread and was heading for the front door.

'Wait a minute, I want a word with you. What the hangment have you been up to lately?'

One hand on the front door knob and his cheeks bulging with sandwich, Jake froze, looking instantly guilty, a tell-tale flush creeping up his neck. 'Nowt, 'cept to get meself a new chariot. It's an old MG sports, real hip this one.'

Lynda frowned, at once filled with suspicion. 'And how did you find the money to buy one of those?'

Jake gave a little swagger. 'Don't underestimate me, sis. I've got meself a job. Two, in fact, helping out Barry Holmes and doing deliveries for a guy on Smithfield wholesale market, so don't look down yer nose at me. I'm making a few nuggets. Anyroad, I can't talk now. I'm off out to the passion pit.'

'Passion pit?' Lynda looked blank and Jake rolled his eyes.

'To the pictures, babe.' He smirked. 'Me and Derek are taking a couple of chicks so don't expect me home early. Mine's called

Brenda and she's gorgeous, I'm real gone on this one. We might take them for a spin after, and play a bit of back-seat bingo.'

'I won't even ask what that is,' Lynda said and grabbing hold of her brother's arm she pushed and dragged him up the stairs, ignoring his vociferous protests. 'But I need to talk to you *now*, chummy, so you're going nowhere till you've explained to me what them boxes are doing in your cupboard. Start talking.'

Having been shoved unceremoniously into his bedroom, Jake's face now lost all its bright crimson hue and turned ashen while he blabbered some nonsense about the boxes being part of his deliveries.

Hands on hips Lynda glared at him. 'Don't try telling porkies to me. I wasn't brought in with the morning fish. Why would you bring them here, to your room, if they're deliveries? You've nicked these trannies and fags, haven't you?'

Panic showed in his eyes. 'No, I swear it, Lynda, I haven't. I wouldn't.'

'Then where have they come from?' She wagged an accusing finger. 'And before you start making up any more lies, let me just mention that I've found dozens more in Ewan's room, which convinces me summat illegal is going on.'

When still he remained silent, anxiously chewing on his lip, the egg and bacon sandwich forgotten, and bouncing from foot to foot in an agitated way, Lynda showed not a shred of sympathy. She ploughed relentlessly on, borrowing some of her brother's favourite slang.

'Well, are you going to tell me or what? Because if you don't, Daddy-o, you're cruising for a bruising, get it, man? Once I tell Mam about all of this, she'll go ape. Isn't that what your hip mates would call it?'

'Naw, please don't say owt to Mam, she'll kill me. And if she doesn't, Dad will.'

Jake spilled out the whole sorry tale then: how Ewan had insisted he spread the word among his mates that he was on the look-out for stolen goods for which he was willing to pay good prices before selling on. 'I didn't want to do it, our Lynda, and

I told him so.' He sounded just as he had as a young boy when he'd been caught scrumping apples or nicking a bar of chocolate from Woolies.

'So why did you? Why didn't you just say no?'

Jake looked blank. 'How could I?'

Lynda took a firm hold of her brother's ridiculously wide padded shoulders and gave him a little shake. 'I know Ewan scares the shit out of you. He does me too. But we have to stand up to him. We can't let him bully us. If you don't start using what few brains you do have a bit better, lad, you'll find yourself careering down the same slippery slope that landed your father *in jail*. Is that what you want? Do you want to be a chip off a not-too-nice block? Do you fancy spending half your life in prison with a lot of low-lifes and perverts?'

'Heck, no.' Jake looked bewildered, as if such a likelihood had never occurred to him.

'Well then, start thinking and taking control of your own life. Tell Ewan you aren't going to do it any more. Tell your mates the same. Clean up your act, Daddy-o, or it'll be the slammer for you.'

38

Judy and Helen

Judy was desperately trying to gain access to Ruth and Tom,
begging Sam to allow her to take them back. He was having
none of it. And despite access being granted to her by the magistrates, she still hadn't seen them since the court case. Either he
claimed one or other of the children wasn't feeling well or else
Judy would arrive to find that his mother had taken them out
for the day – to cheer them up – or some such excuse. It didn't
matter how much she protested that it was her job to care for
Ruth and Tom, not his mother's, Sam would simply shrug and
refuse to cooperate.

'Not only do you not have a fit place to take my children but
neither are you a fit mother. How do you think *I* felt once I
realised that you were having it off with that Leo Catlow?'

'I wasn't having it off with him, it was a perfectly innocent
friendship.' Judy knew in her heart that a great deal more could
have grown between herself and Leo. In truth she ached for him,
longed for his support and friendship. The merest glimpse of
him on the market would set her heart racing while at the same
time send her running for cover, afraid she might give herself
away if they ever met up again. She'd had to leave, for that reason
alone. Yet not for the world would she reveal any of this emotional
upheaval to Sam. 'Obviously, ordinary friendship between a man
and woman is beyond your comprehension since you've spent
our entire married life chasing women and trying to get inside
their knickers.'

'Don't be vulgar, Judy, it doesn't suit you.'

Arguing with him did no good either. He was the one with the house, the business, the money. Consequently the magistrates had put the children into his care, and he was keeping them.

'At least let me see them. I do have rights as their mother and *they* need to see me.' Judy felt close to despair, almost on the brink of hysteria.

Not being able to even see her children was having a terribly debilitating effect upon her. She couldn't sleep, couldn't concentrate, could do no more than pick at her food when she remembered to eat at all. All she'd found by way of employment was dishing out bacon butties in a snack bar. Judy knew she should be applying for jobs with better prospects, or signing herself on to a training scheme for typing or book-keeping, but couldn't seem to motivate herself to do so, perhaps fearing that whatever she did, Sam would only ruin everything for her again. He definitely seemed to have the whip hand.

'Where are you living?'

'I'm not going to tell you. I'm renting a room in the house of a respectable widow. It's not Buckingham Palace but it's okay, temporarily. I'm hoping soon to move into a flat.' She certainly had no intention of telling him that the flat was in Salford. He'd go bananas.

'When have I heard that before?' Sam sneered. 'I shall need to check it out before I allow you to take *my* children there. I'm not having Ruth and Tom contaminated by some cheap dive in the slums, and it obviously isn't anywhere *too* respectable or you'd tell me where it was. There's clearly something you're hiding.'

Everything she said and did seemed to land her in a worse mire. Yet Judy was determined to hold her nerve, telling herself that he was deliberately using these bully-boy tactics in order to force her to give up and go back to him, something she had no intention of doing. He could get one of his women to skivvy for him and follow his obsessive rules in future. She'd had enough.

'I'm not telling you because you've already lost me one set of lodgings, *and* a good job. I don't want you coming round and creating mayhem so that I lose another. You seem to take great pleasure in knocking me down every time I put a foot on the ladder.'

He laughed at that, seeming to think it amusing. 'Let's see if you can climb higher than the first rung without me there to back you up. Now *that* I would like to see.'

Judy ground her teeth together in an effort to hold on to her patience. Not for the world would she allow him to see the depth of her despair, the panic that was building up inside her. 'I'll come round on Sunday around ten. I'd like to take them to the park for a picnic. Please have them ready on time.'

He rubbed one hand over a bristly chin, looking doubtful. 'They have a pretty full routine, homework to do and so on, but I'll see if we can accommodate you.'

He made this very normal request seem unreasonable, as if she were some maiden aunt or distant relative, and not Ruth and Tom's mother at all. 'Please don't make me beg to see my own children, Sam. I might have made mistakes. I might truly be what you term an unfit mother, but if that's the case, what sort of a father are you? Ask yourself that.'

When Sunday came round only Tom was ready and waiting for her in his school blazer and cap, looking unusually sad and serious. Judy hugged the little boy, risking embarrassing her son by giving him a big kiss.

He clung to her for a moment, winding his arms tightly about her neck while he whispered, 'Mummy, I've missed you.'

A great lump came into her throat and Judy feared she might be about to disgrace herself by crying, but managed to control herself just in time. Ruth, Sam informed her, had no wish to come.

Judy's heart plummeted. 'I don't believe you. Let me see her, please. I haven't seen or spoken to my daughter in weeks. She needs to know how much I love her, how I'm doing my best to make things right. Let me at least speak to her.'

Sam shook his head, his face taking on that blank, expressionless detachment that she knew so well. 'She doesn't want to see you. Have Tom back by four o'clock, on the dot. I've no wish to call out the police and charge you with kidnapping.' Then he shut the door in her face.

It continued in this fashion over the following weeks, the Wednesdays and Sunday afternoons she was supposedly to be allowed with both children being reduced to an hour or two at most. More often than not Wednesdays were inconvenient as it was his afternoon off from the market, and he wasn't willing to substitute this day with another. On Sundays, very often Judy would travel the two miles from her digs to Sam's house by bus or even on foot in order to save herself the fare, only to find the door locked fast and no answer to her knocking.

She would hang around the market for hours, hoping they would return from wherever it was he'd spirited them off to. On occasions he'd roll up eventually in the van looking surprised, as if he'd forgotten that it was her afternoon for visiting, which would make Judy very angry.

'This really is too much, Sam. You aren't playing fair.' But where was the point in standing around arguing when it was already gone three o'clock and he insisted she had them back by four?

Tom continued to be excessively clingy and Ruth rarely joined them in their outings. If she did agree to come it was with ill grace, often refusing to even speak to her mother.

'It's all *your* fault we're in this mess,' she insisted, when Judy ventured to question her on the matter. 'How can you be so mean to poor Daddy when he's tried so hard to make you happy? You've just left him all on his own, for no other reason than you fancy working instead of looking after us as a proper mum would. *And* you've got yourself a boy-friend.'

Evidently, Sam was not only keeping the children from her, but poisoning their minds against her.

Finally, in desperation, Judy went back to see her solicitor and told him exactly what was happening.

'It just isn't working. I seem to have no rights at all. Sam is being extremely difficult, cutting my access times to the bone and sometimes I don't get to see them at all. Can't we go back to the magistrates and complain that my husband is being unreasonable?'

Instead of sharing her concern and offering to speak for her in court, the lawyer raised a pair of dark eyebrows and looked down his beak of a nose at her in surprise. 'Complaining won't help. I'm afraid you did yourself no service, Mrs Beckett, forming an attachment with a man-friend at this juncture in the proceedings. Far better you concentrate your efforts on securing yourself worthwhile employment, a decent home and child-care for your children. Otherwise, I see little hope of you ever getting them back.'

It was not at all what she'd wanted to hear.

Helen sensed that Leo had changed in some indefinable way. He seemed more distant, more withdrawn and was rarely even interested in sex these days. They hadn't made love in weeks, which was unusual, and most worrying.

She was feeling particularly low, in any case. Since Sam had called off their little affair Helen had found life really rather dull. Even ridding herself of her mother-in-law and incarcerating the old bat in a home, which was surely where she should have gone months ago, had proved less satisfactory than she'd hoped. Largely because Leo continued to visit her, not simply on a Saturday as had been the case when Dulcie had lived in Lytham St Anne's, but regular and frequent visits, sometimes as often as three or four times a week. It was most infuriating.

When she'd remonstrated with him, pointing out that this was quite unnecessary now that Dulcie was no longer his responsibility, he'd glared coldly at her.

'She's my mother. I visit her because I want to, because I care about her, not out of necessity or a sense of responsibility.'

'But *we* don't have any time together any more. Wasn't that partly the reason you agreed she should go into the residential home, so that we could regain our privacy?'

'It was not *my* reason. It might well have been *yours*. Are you saying that it wasn't simply because you believed my mother to be a danger to herself when she started that fire? Am I missing something here?' He regarded her quizzically, and for once in her life Helen found herself blushing. The last thing she wanted was for Leo to grow suspicious.

'I'm simply saying that you make no effort to please me or make me happy, none whatsoever.' Whatever little control she'd been able to exercise over him in the past, often through deviousness or clever manipulation, no longer seemed to work. Leo simply wasn't interested in going along with her games.

'Indeed? Did you make any effort, Helen, to comfort my mother after losing her husband, or make her feel welcome in what had once been her own home? Do you ever make *me* feel welcome in this house, as your husband, unless I jump through whatever hoops you've set out for me.'

Helen clicked her tongue with annoyance. 'I don't understand you, Leo. You're not at all yourself these days. I really don't understand what it is you are accusing me of.'

'No, you don't, do you? Maybe that's the trouble. You're far too selfish to ever notice that other people might have needs too.' He looked at her with such sadness Helen's heart turned over. It felt almost as if he were about to bid her goodbye, which was the last thing she wanted.

'We could have had so much fun, you and I. Love, happiness, good sex, children, a comfortable life with a sound income and a house in the country, but no, that wasn't enough for you. Your ambitions reached even higher, clawing desperately for more and more power, and never did involve homely things like babies, or a willingness to include a sweet, gentle mother-in-law in your life, someone who was absolutely no trouble to have around and caused no problems for anyone.'

'Not for you perhaps, but the woman drove me *mad. And I don't like babies!*'

'I'm going out.'

'Where?' Helen ran after him as he strode to the door.

Turning, hand on the brass knob, he regarded her without any sign of emotion in his handsome face, not a glimmer of his usual concern. 'Do you know, I haven't decided. Somewhere I can be with people who smile and laugh and make me happy. Somewhere I can get very, very drunk, maybe.'

'Don't you dare! You've no right to speak to me like this, Leo. No right to be so cruel! You're going to see *her*, aren't you? Your *mistress*. That's what this is all about.' She was screaming at him now, stamping her feet and on the verge of a fine old tantrum.

Leo pushed his face down to within an inch of Helen's own. 'Do you know, I just might do that. All these long years of our marriage I've behaved impeccably towards you, Helen, with absolute loyalty and never once – not *once* – have you believed me, or appreciated that fact. This overwhelming jealousy that festers within you has destroyed us. It's eaten away at all the trust and love there used to be between us till there's nothing left but bitterness, and I'm tired of it. I can't stand any more, so yes, maybe I will find myself a mistress. Why not? I may as well since you believe me guilty anyway.' And so saying, Leo stormed out of the house, slamming the door behind him, oblivious to Helen's screams of fury.

While Leo sat in the Dog and Duck, sunk in contemplative misery, Judy sat in her single room gazing out over the bleak chimney tops of Salford and wondering what she had come to in her life to be so alone and without hope.

Her landlady was kind enough and it wasn't the place that was the problem, it was her. The city was thriving, new houses and improvements being built all around. Salford was undergoing a renaissance for an area which had once been one of the bleakest and most deprived. Bombed-out sites and the Victorian slums from the city's dark industrial past were being cleared away; old churches, cinemas and other redundant or dangerous buildings were closing down at a startling rate and rapid progress was being made in the city's rehousing schemes. Two new secondary modern schools had opened their doors this month already. Modern industries were springing up on the site of defunct cotton mills, and there was talk of Salford becoming a smokeless zone within a decade.

Even the housing shortage was well on its way to being solved with tenants being presented with the keys to new flats and maisonettes almost every week. Judy had been down to the council offices and put herself on the list.

'How many children do you have?' asked the young woman, pen poised over a lengthy form.

'Two.'

'And where are you living at the moment with your children?'

'Well, it's not quite that simple,' Judy admitted. By the time she'd finished explaining her circumstances, the woman behind the desk was pursing her lips and trying to appear sympathetic, promising to do her best but not particularly optimistic. It really was a chicken and egg situation: without the children Judy had little hope of being granted council accommodation, and yet without a home, she had little hope of winning back her children. Throat aching and blocked by emotion, eyes shining with withheld tears, Judy thanked the young woman and promised to return next week – every week if necessary – to check on progress.

It felt somehow easier to rejuvenate a whole city rather than the justice system. What justice had she seen, with Sam winning hands down? And did she possess the energy to carry on fighting him?

But without her children, without even Leo, what alternative did she have?

39

Lynda

Autumn was coming and the scarlet berries of the rowan were as bright as drops of blood against the white chrysanthemum blooms as Lynda made up a bouquet and carefully wrapped it. The starkness of the arrangement seemed to suit her mood perfectly, as if they were drops of her own blood fallen upon the white tissue paper. She tried to smile as she handed the flowers over to the customer but her face felt stiff and awkward.

Smiling had become alien to her. But then there seemed to be so much else to worry about. Her mother's health for one thing. Betty did her exercises, when she remembered, and was making surprisingly good progress. The doctors were pleased with her. She could pull herself out of her wheelchair and even walk a few steps with the aid of her crutches or a walking stick. She was getting out and about a bit more and often spent time round at Big Molly's, a right old pair of gossiping biddies they were.

But she wasn't supposed to overdo it, and Lynda had insisted she take the morning off since she'd been working hard lately.

As for Ewan, judging by what she'd recently discovered, Lynda was convinced that he was planning something illegal, and that her brother was involved in some way. The worst of it was that Jake didn't seem to have any better idea how to deal with their father than she did. Like her, he was scared witless.

Lynda felt like one of those old turtles carrying the troubles of all the world on its back. A hundred and fifty years old, not just turned twenty-seven. Lynda sighed, thinking back with nostalgia to the time when she'd felt young and attractive, when men had queued up to take her out and her only concern had been to decide what shade of lipstick to wear. Was that really only twelve months ago?

If only she had something good to look forward to, had someone who cared about her and had the strength to protect her? But Ewan, her own father for goodness' sake, had made certain that she had no friends, that she possessed nothing of any value, not even her own self-esteem.

His greatest pleasure in life was to ridicule and poke fun at her, to criticise and carp and complain. Whatever meal she cooked for him he'd complain that the meat wasn't cooked properly or he didn't care for fish, or cheese or whatever; always something wrong even when he'd eaten every scrap. And no matter how much care she took over ironing his shirts or tidying and cleaning the house, he would always find some reason to make her do it over again.

Lynda had said nothing to him about the boxes of transistor radios and cigarettes she'd found in his room, afraid of what he might do if he ever became aware that she'd been snooping. Nor had she told anyone else, other than Jake. If Constable Nuttall had ever been of any help to either her or her mam in the past, Lynda might well have gone to him, but no doubt he'd just give Ewan a stern little lecture and do nothing more about it.

Every now and then Lynda would remind her stupid brother to stay well clear of whatever game their father was currently playing. She'd glare or wink at him across the room, warning him to scarper if she thought Ewan was about to start in on him. Consequently, Jake had been noticeable by his absence from the house lately. Lynda hoped her brother was keeping himself out of trouble, trying to keep his nose clean, as she had instructed.

And then there was her best friend Judy. Where had she gone? How was she coping without her precious children? Would she ever find happiness with the man of her choice? Oh, what a mess marriage could make of your life.

Later that morning Terry came strolling by in that casual way he had and it was as if time itself stood still; certainly Lynda's heart did. Usually he stayed well away but now here he was, standing right before her, his expression solemn, hands thrust deep in the pockets of his customary black jeans, dark curls ruffled by a brisk breeze, asking her how she was keeping these days.

In that moment Lynda knew that even after all these months of silence between them, she still wanted him. Oh, why did life have to be so complicated? Whatever she said by way of reply, and it was all such a blur that afterwards Lynda really couldn't remember, Terry nodded and smiled that dazzling smile of his and Lynda's insides just melted.

'I haven't seen you around the market much lately, or out at the dances,' he said.

'That's because I haven't been out much lately.'

There followed one of those long aching silences which usually filled her with embarrassment, but now Lynda used it as an opportunity to glance up at him from beneath her lashes. He looked just the same, every bit as handsome and her fingers itched to run through those wiry dark curls. She longed to nibble that full lower lip, to feel her tongue dance with his.

Lynda shut down the thought. This would do her no good at all.

Then quite out of the blue, as if he'd been examining her in much the same way, Terry asked point blank if her refusal to see him had anything to do with her mother's accident.

Shocked by the unexpectedness of the question, Lynda couldn't think of a thing to say but he asked her again, louder this time. 'Tell me, I want to know, and I'll keep on asking till I get an answer. If I thought you were happy about this decision not to see each other any more I'd leave you alone, but you're not happy, any fool can see that. I want to know the truth about why you dumped me. I deserve that, at least.'

'Oh, Terry, please don't do this. Just take it from me that it was better we did finish. I couldn't ever see you again – don't *want* to see you again.'

'I didn't believe that the first time you said it, and I don't believe it now.' He glanced back over his shoulder then came a step or two closer. 'You know what *I* think. I reckon you *do* want to see me again, very much. I can see it in those lovely hazel eyes of yours. I think that's why you won't ever look at me properly, and why you run away whenever you spot me around the market.'

'I do not!' She did look at him then, her expression resolutely cool in an effort to appear totally unaffected by his pain. But the words that blurted out of her mouth, quite of their own accord, told a different story. 'Don't make things any harder for me, Terry, please. I daren't go against my father's wishes and there's an end of the matter.'

Terry's face seemed to light up, as if she'd said something to cheer him. 'I *knew* it. I knew finishing with me wasn't your decision.' Then he pulled up an orange box beside her, and perching himself upon it insisted she tell him everything.

Oh lord, she'd done it now. His long legs were spread wide apart, encircling her, his knees almost touching hers and Lynda found her gaze transfixed by the sight of those tightly clad thighs. Quite against her better judgement she sat down beside him and began to talk. It felt such a relief to let it all pour out, to share the burden of her troubles. Lynda told Terry everything, couldn't seem to help herself.

'I guess I shouldn't be surprised Ewan hasn't turned out to be the father I'd hoped for. Even before he attacked Mam, and that was after he'd thumped our Jake, he made it very clear to me that I mustn't ever see you again. It *was* Ewan who beat you up, wasn't it? Go on, admit it.'

'I didn't want you to know that. I was trying to protect you.'

Lynda sniffed back the tears, slapping them from her eyes. 'Well, there's no point in trying to do that any more, is there?'

'If I'd knocked him out cold you might never have spoken to

me again. How could I fight back and stand up for myself when it was your dad who was doing the punching?'

'Oh, I know exactly how that feels. I can't stand up to him either. If I did, he'd take it out on Mam.'

'If that's the kind of power he has over you, then he's won. He's totally in control.'

Lynda looked steadily into those delicious chocolate-brown eyes with the long curling lashes. 'Yes, I think he has won, and there's not a damn thing we can do about it because we're all too afraid of him.' Misery clogged Lynda's throat, threatening to choke her.

Terry said, 'The truth is that at the time I didn't reckon on him insisting you finish with me. I thought he just wanted to make sure I didn't get you into trouble, you know, up the duff.' He gave a sheepish grin and Lynda groaned.

'He doesn't know how innocent we were, what a good girl I'd been since I was trying so hard to impress you.'

'You've been out with other guys since though.'

Lynda gave a shrug. 'Once or twice, nothing serious, nothing . . . like us.' Then as if she must blurt the words out before they choked her, 'He would've hurt you badly if he'd ever caught us together again. I couldn't take that risk. I've seen what he can do . . . see it every day, every night.' She shuddered.

Terry's faced closed in tight anger. 'Are you saying he's hurt you, because if he has . . .'

Panic hit her. 'No, I'm not saying anything of the sort. I can look after myself.' The last thing she wanted was for Terry to come charging round like a bull in a china shop. 'But I still can't see you. He wouldn't allow it.'

They digested this unpleasant fact for some long minutes before Lynda risked a sideways glance at Terry, eyes filled with tears.

'You'd better go before he comes out of the Dog and Duck and sees us talking. You do understand why I had to finish with you, don't you?' Lynda fully expected him to agree that of course he did, that it was just as well in the circumstances because really he didn't care one way or the other. Instead, he put his arms about her and hugged her tight.

'I do, aye. But I'm pretty cheesed off about it, I can tell you. I've had enough of that man telling us what to do with our lives. I'm not giving you up, Lynda. I'd cut off me right arm sooner.'

'Oh, Terry, love. Don't say such crazy things. Ewan Hemley is much nastier than I'd ever bargained for.' There, she'd said it at last, openly confessed that the father of her dreams was nothing more than a myth. But Terry wasn't really listening. He was chuckling softly into her neck while he kissed it.

'I'll tell you summat for nowt, love. If that so-called father of yours ever tries to do me over again, I won't be so reticent about socking him one next time.'

It felt so good to have Terry kiss her again Lynda instinctively turned her face up to his for more of the same. 'But it's still over, right? You do understand that nothing's changed, and I for one don't want him making mincemeat of you, as he's promised to do. I can be brave for myself, but not for you, or for Mam. He put her in a wheelchair for heaven's sake, just over our Jake being late for his tea. God knows what he'd do if we made him really angry. We're finished, Terry. Now go away and find your-self a new girl.'

'Never! No chance.' His long lingering kiss by way of reply stirred up all that damped-down emotion inside and left her shiv-ering with desire. Oh, she still fancied him all right, still loved him like crazy.

Terry stood up, her hand still in his as he stroked each finger, each shell-like nail. He was shaking his head, a smile wreathing his face. 'I can wait, either till Ewan Hemley has upped and gone, or until your mam is better. We can only hope that eventually he'll get bored and leave. In the meantime you and me will do as we please. We're not going to be dictated to by a nasty old sod like him.'

Seeing the fear spring into her eyes, Terry cupped her face between his two hands. 'Don't worry, love, we'll keep our meetings secret, at least for a while, long enough for me to get a licence and us to nip down to the registry office and get wed. How would that do? Once you're my wife, there's not a damned thing he could do to stop us being together.'

'Oh, Terry!' Lynda felt as if all the roses on her mam's stall had just burst into bloom.

'Until that happy day, if he gives you any more trouble, Lynda love, don't hesitate to give me a shout. If he ever lays so much as a finger on you, I'll sort the bugger out good and proper.'

What would Terry say if he knew that her father already had laid more than a finger on her, had burned her hand, beaten her backside black and blue and even fondled her breasts. Thankfully, he'd never come to her room since but Lynda lived in constant fear that he might. There was no peace anywhere, certainly not in her bedroom despite the chair she stuck under the door handle every night, or the chest of drawers she drew across it.

She did as much that night before climbing into bed, hugging the memory of Terry's proposal to her heart. She'd found him, her Mr Right, her lovely Terry. He was definitely the man for her. She loved him to bits, and nothing Ewan Hemley said or did would prevent her from marrying him.

No sooner had the thought come into her head than she heard the sneck on her bedroom door lift. He was coming! Oh God, had he seen them together in the street? Had he come to take his revenge?

A tap on the door, the sound of his voice, all maudlin and wheedling. 'Lynda love, open the door, I just want a word. I'm feeling all lonely tonight. Come and have a little chat with your old pa.'

Lynda bit down hard on her lower lip just in case her mouth might open and obey him of its own accord. The sneck rattled some more and the door shook but the chest of drawers was firmly wedged and it remained shut. Finally he gave up and went away.

With a sigh of relief, Lynda buried her head under the covers and tried to get some sleep. She'd be out of here soon, married to Terry and happy at last. He'd even promised to care for her mam as well. They were going to look at some of the new flats and find one for them all to live in, so the whole family would be safe, free of Ewan Hemley at last.

40

Judy and Helen

'Is that you, Judy?' Leo half walked, half ran across the cobbles to almost snatch her up in his arms before thinking better of it. 'I can't believe it, after all this time. I've been looking for you everywhere. I want to hold you . . . touch you.' He glanced about at the crowds milling around the market. 'Can we go somewhere so that we can talk?'

Christmas was drawing near and the rousing strains of 'Good King Wencelas' echoed along the street, wreaths of holly and mistletoe were strung around every lamp post and fairy lights twinkled high in the rafters of the market hall. But images of Santa Claus and his galloping reindeer painted on every window did little to lighten Leo's heart. He had never in his life felt less like celebrating the season of goodwill.

Judy still hadn't spoken and Leo waited anxiously for her agreement. She gave a little shake of her head, not trusting herself to speak, deliberately dropping her gaze when she saw the desolation come into his face.

'Please?'

'Don't you understand? You must stay away from me. I was just returning the children. We've been out for the afternoon but you mustn't speak to me. Leave me alone!'

She looked so frail, so ill, with big purple bruises beneath each eye, that he ached to gather her up into his arms and carry her away to some safe place where he could make her better. 'I'm so sorry about the children. That was a horrible decision on the part of the magistrates. I assume you're fighting

Sam over it. He's no right to take them away from you like that.'

'Apparently he does. Sam is their father, and in a far better position than I to care for them. I was also accused of having a man-friend . . . a lover . . . you!'

Now he understood why she'd been avoiding him. Of course, how stupid of him. He should have thought of that before. Even as Leo stared at her in stunned disbelief he could appreciate at last the reason for her anger. 'Heaven help me, I didn't realise. But we didn't . . . we're not.'

'*I* know that. *You* know that. But how can we prove it? He obviously found out about our day in Clitheroe. I expect the children told him.' She sounded weary, resigned, all the fight drained out of her. Leo on the other hand was pulsating with fury, would have beaten Sam Beckett to a pulp there and then, given half a chance.

'Or else he had you followed. Damnation, whatever and however he learned of our day out, that's a wicked trick to pull. Sam is the one who can't keep his trousers on, not you.'

Judy winced at the image this evoked. Ignoring her, Leo raged on. 'Which magistrates were sitting that day? I'll write to the Justice of the Clerk's office. We can get this sorted out.'

A kind of terror came into her eyes and she pushed him away from her, punching his chest with two clenched fists. 'No, no, no! You mustn't do any such thing. You'll only make matters worse.'

When she would've turned and run from him Leo caught her by the wrist, holding on to her despite sensing her fragility. His heart ached to see how her shoulders shook, to hear her small hiccupping sobs. 'Please don't cry. I hate it when you're unhappy. I hate having these terrible things happen to you. I just want to help. I love you, Judy. Always remember that I love you.'

She gave a low groan. 'Please don't say such things. Don't even think it.'

'Why not, if it's true?'

'Someone might hear.'

He wanted to say let them, that he would happily swing from

the fairy lights and shout his feelings from the rooftops but common sense prevailed. 'Where are you living? Can we at least meet for coffee some time?'

But she was wriggling free of his restraining hand, dashing the tears from her eyes. 'Stay away from me, Leo. Leave me in peace. I have another custody hearing coming up soon and having you around won't help. Just leave me alone!'

As she hurried away, Leo couldn't do any such thing. He followed her. Not so close that she could spot him tailing her, but he needed to know where she was living. He simply couldn't bear to lose her.

Unbeknown to Leo, he in turn was being followed. Helen had sat in her new Ford car and watched her husband talk in frantic hushed tones with Judy Beckett, watched her walk away and Leo follow several paces behind.

She'd hardly been able to believe what she was seeing, but their body language said it all.

Now she started up the engine and, keeping a discreet distance between herself and the pair of them, edged her way along the street. It was a long, slow journey since they walked and she drove, but at least Helen could take refuge in her car, pausing occasionally so that she didn't catch up and get too close.

Eventually she saw Judy skip up the steps of a tall terraced house some distance from the market beyond Pomona Docks on the outskirts of Salford. Leo, she noticed, stood undecided for some moments before turning on his heel to make his way back to Champion Street, fortunately choosing a different route through the network of passages and bridges that linked the docks, and not passing her car.

When he had gone, Helen sat back in her seat with an expression of cold fury on her face. So now, at last, she knew the identity of her husband's mistress. It struck her as particularly galling that he was bedding her own ex-lover's wife.

By way of retaliation Helen turned her attention to Barford. He was not so exciting a lover as Sam Beckett but he would certainly help to alleviate her boredom until she came up with someone better. And there was always the chance that together they might be able to devise some scheme to further Leo's ambitions, even if it was against his better judgement.

Unlike Sam, Barford preferred to enjoy his sexual adventures in comfort, and they'd spent the afternoon ensconced in a pleasant little hotel room somewhere in deepest Cheshire. Helen had insisted her new motor be parked in an anonymous country lane a short distance away, so that no one would see their two vehicles cheek-by-jowl in the hotel car park. Yet here they were, very much together in this delicious little room. Perfect.

She watched him walk back from the shower and pull on his vest which he'd left neatly folded on a chair. Helen didn't usually care for men who wore vests, and Sam would've been far too eager to bed her to waste time on such niceties as folding his clothing. She stifled a sigh. Such a pity that little romp was over. They'd had such fun together, but throughout her little liaison with Sam they'd neither of them been aware of what was going on right in front of their noses, with their own respective spouses. Helen didn't know whether to laugh or cry. In reality she was far too angry to do either.

David Barford was tying the shoe laces on his highly polished tan brogues. Helen propped herself on one elbow to watch him. No doubt he was off for a round of golf before returning home to his angelic, patient little wife, his halo still in place on his handsome, arrogant head. It was sad too that all the plans and schemes they'd devised together to thrust Leo into the forefront of power had come to nothing. Her life seemed to be falling apart, everything going wrong before her eyes.

'I was just thinking that now Leo is on the city council, there's very little hope of him ever turning his attention to party politics, as we once hoped,' Helen commented, expressing her thoughts aloud.

Barford glanced up and allowed his gaze to trail over the curve of her hip, the narrowness of her waist and the way her full breasts pillowed out above the sheet she was holding with one elegant hand. He half wished he didn't have to rush away and could take her all over again, while a part of him regretted ever becoming involved with Helen Catlow in the first place.

She wasn't an easy woman to please and he hadn't managed to get what he'd wanted out of the relationship, certainly not politically. Creating useful links in powerful places was what he did best. It was a skill he'd perfected over the years and used many times to his advantage. Unfortunately, on this occasion, the woman's husband had proved to be strangely obstinate and refused to play along.

But then a thought occurred to him and Barford allowed himself a rare smile. 'The city council, of course, I was forgetting Leo was involved with that. Now there's a thought. He'll have access to planning applications, will he not?'

Helen shrugged. 'How would I know?' She never troubled herself with the trifling details of what her husband actually did with his life, only with what benefits he could provide for her.

Barford stood up and took his jacket from the hanger in the wardrobe where he'd placed it. 'That could prove useful. The city re-development programme is gathering pace and there's money to be made out of it.'

He came to sit beside her on the bed, kissing her shoulder and possessively fondling her breast before going on to explain how he'd recently purchased an old Methodist chapel at auction.

'My intention was to turn it into flats but then I decided to demolish it and sell it on for development instead, with planning permission to build a whole modern apartment block in its place. A far more lucrative proposition, but the powers-that-be are proving difficult. They say it's too close to the proposed site of a new motorway, as if that mattered. I stand to make a fortune if I can sell this land; otherwise, taking into account the cost of conversion, two or three flats won't make me anywhere near as much profit. How would it be if I let you have a copy of the plans and you persuade good old Leo to swing the vote my way? You can do that for me, surely?'

Helen brushed his probing hand aside and sank back upon

the pillows on a light laugh. 'Don't be foolish. I've already explained, Leo isn't listening to me any more. I'm fighting hard just to keep my marriage alive.'

Barford's smile was chilling. 'Well then, you wouldn't want anything to destabilise it further, would you, and risk losing access to all his lovely money by somebody spilling the beans about our little activities here, for instance.'

Helen became very still. 'You would never do such a thing?'

Barford stood up, adjusted his tie and picked up his briefcase. From it he drew out a sheaf of papers and tossed them on to the bed. 'Let's hope it never becomes necessary but I can't emphasise enough, Helen, how very important it is for me to push this scheme through.'

'That's blackmail.'

'I dislike such nasty words but you owe me, Helen dear, for the risks I've taken on your behalf. Promises, promises, that's all I've ever had from you in return. Now I'm calling in the debt. I'll ring you next week, see how you've got on.'

Then he walked out of the room and left her, not even bothering to bring her car round for her.

Helen was not used to being so ill treated, to having someone else call the shots. Yet despite her dislike of being put in an untenable position, she did her utmost to persuade Leo to support the planning permission application. She pointed out all the benefits Barford had mentioned, even adding a few of her own, including the possibility that he might permit Leo to join him in the deal and make a few thousand for himself. That had apparently been the wrong thing to say.

'You want me to cheat, to commit a crime for a few measly quid?'

'Barford will make nearer a million before he's done. He's going places, Leo. You should listen to him more.'

'I'd rather listen to my conscience.'

No further discussion on the subject was allowed. Leo was adamant that he would never do anything remotely illegal.

Fortunately, he wasn't in the least suspicious about how she came by this information, but he certainly wasn't any longer listening to her. In fact, he seemed to be totally absorbed in a world of his own, and Helen felt a terrifying sensation start up inside her, it was as if she were sliding down a slippery slope and was helpless to prevent herself from falling off a cliff. She realised it was going to take every ounce of her undoubtedly clever wits to turn this disaster around.

At Judy's insistence, her solicitor had made a further application for custody but once again it was refused. The children were settled, the magistrates said, were well provided for by their father and being properly looked after by their grandmother whenever he was at work. A perfectly agreeable arrangement. The mother could continue to have reasonable access but the fact that Judy now had employment in a snack bar and her name on the housing list, cut no ice at all.

'Come back when your name reaches the top of the list,' was what they told her. 'When you have a home of your own to offer.' Besides all of this, the magistrates were not entirely convinced that the alleged lover wasn't still around.

Sam reinforced this belief. 'Leo Catlow is often seen about the market with my wife. They were spotted talking vehemently together only the other day, so are undoubtedly still a couple.'

Nothing Judy said could convince them otherwise. She might well be free of Sam and her claustrophobic soul-destroying marriage, free of his rules and orders, and his strange punishments, and free of the humiliation of wondering which woman he'd slept with before climbing into bed with her. But the price had been high. Sam had been determined from the outset that she would pay for her independence by losing her children. Now he'd turned that into a reality.

Later that evening, following this insensitive verdict, Leo returned to the Victorian terraced house beyond Pomona Docks that he'd seen Judy enter. Having made it his business to discover that the case was to be heard today, he was determined to be there for her. Either to console her disappointment if the worst happened, or ready to vanish out of her life completely if the news was good.

Judy dragged herself from the bed where she'd lain sobbing her heart out for hour upon hour, took one look at him standing in the rain and, hoping the landlady wouldn't notice, allowed him to gather her in his arms and join her in it.

She gave herself up to his loving on an emotional tide of pain and joy. It felt like bliss, like coming home, just as if she belonged there. Leo made love to her as Sam had never done, with passion and tenderness, with a slow caring sensitivity and on a rising crescendo of desire so that neither could have prevented what followed, even had they wished to.

But what did it matter? What more did she have to lose?

The very next evening when the day's work was done and they were sitting at the dinner table supposedly enjoying a civilised meal together, Leo calmly asked Helen for a divorce. He gave no explanation but simply and politely made his request, claiming their marriage was nothing but a sham and it was time they put it to rest.

Helen sat frozen for a whole half-second and then picked up her glass of red wine and flung it in her husband's face. Fortunately he ducked and it hit the imitation Chinese silk wallpaper instead, leaving a dreadful stain that would surely never come out. Helen didn't even notice.

Pushing back her chair she got shakily to her feet and faced him with ice-cold dignity, so controlled and collected that Leo should have been concerned. As it was he was too busily engaged sweeping a few stray droplets of red wine from his best tweed jacket.

'Don't imagine for one minute that I'm completely stupid, or ignorant of the identity of this mistress of yours. I know who she is. You've been sleeping with Judy Beckett, haven't you? That's the reason she's lost her children, because of *you*.'

Leo took a breath, somewhat surprised and shaken by the

accusation but determined not to be thrown by it. 'I'm afraid that's true, although I wasn't sleeping with her at the time,' and then devastated his wife by adding, 'although I am now.'

By way of response Helen picked up the fruit salad and Leo leapt from the table, holding up his hands as some sort of inadequate shield.

'Hey, I am at least being honest with you, as I have been throughout our married life. I want you to know, Helen, that I was totally loyal until last night. But your jealousy, your manipulations, your determination to take, take, take, and never give of yourself or show any sign of affection is what has brought an end to this marriage, not my sleeping with Judy. You can't blame her for this, or me for that matter, much as you might like to. You can only blame yourself.'

Leo braced himself for the tirade, for her rage and fury, for her to fly at him with talons outstretched, with or without the dratted fruit salad. Instead, after a long and telling pause in which she was clearly considering her options, Helen placed the cut-glass bowl carefully back upon the mat and smiled serenely at him.

'I'm so sorry. My nerves are somewhat jangled at present, not surprisingly. I believe it is quite common for a woman in my condition.'

A deathly pause. 'Your *condition*?'

'Yes, my darling. You say that I take, take, take, well that's not strictly true. I do listen to your heartfelt requests occasionally. In fact, I've done more than that. There is one thing I'm about to give you, with all my love and joy. I'm having a baby, Leo. You're going to be a father at last.'

41

Leo

Betty had always enjoyed Christmas. She loved the cold crisp days, the general feeling of anticipation in the air as people chose gifts for their loved ones. She always did a roaring trade selling mistletoe and holly, all the while grumbling that she'd do better if the gypsies didn't steal so much of her trade by undercutting her.

Her stall this morning was bright with pots of azaleas and cyclamen, hyacinth and of course roses and her favourite chrysants. She could hear the Salvation Army playing 'While Shepherds Watched Their Flocks By Night', and Lynda happily singing silly words to the tune. It was good to see her daughter more cheerful, but her mood swings were very worrying. She was up and down like a yo-yo.

'Your good mood couldn't have summat to do with that young man who keeps winking at you, could it?' Betty suddenly asked, her face a picture of innocence.

Lynda flushed bright red, knowing full well that her mother was referring to Terry who seemed to be constantly hovering on the periphery of her vision. She really must speak to him about that. It would never do for Ewan to notice and have his suspicions aroused.

'I can't think what you're talking about,' Lynda said, but she cast her mother a sideways smile which spoke volumes. Betty simply chuckled.

Belle Garside interrupted them at that moment to say that the committee had decided to put up a Christmas tree, as usual, in the market hall, and could Betty order one from her own supplier?

'I know we're late in making the decision, Betty, but we're a bit strapped for cash and there was a row about whether we could afford to have a tree this year. Anyway, it's finally been agreed that the market hall has to be decked out properly or else trade will suffer. And being late, we're in a bit of a hurry now, of course. Can you organise it?'

Betty agreed that she could, would in fact send Lynda round to Smithfield this very minute. 'I'd go myself but these wheels don't have an engine attached and although I can hobble a bit now, it might be next Christmas before I got there.'

Belle laughed. 'I'm disappointed in you, Betty love. I'd've thought you'd be jet-propelled by this time.'

'Nay, I'm training for the next Olympics, doing the hundred-yard dash on me crutches.'

'You'd win too, nobody can keep our Betty down for long.'

Betty turned to her daughter, her expression giving nothing away. 'Do you want our Jake to take you to Smithfield in that fancy car of his, or can you cadge a lift with someone? Ask them to deliver the tree first thing in the morning, if they can.'

Lynda hid a smile. Good old Mam, never missed a trick. 'Oh, I reckon I can cadge meself a lift, thanks. I'll see to it, Belle. Leave it with me.'

'No need to hurry back,' Betty said, 'I can manage.' She winked at her daughter, then Betty sent Lynda on her way, having issued a long list of instructions about what to look for and how not to be fobbed off with any old rubbish.

'And take care. Don't let your father catch you or he might send you off doing all sorts of jobs for him.' Their eyes met, exchanging the kind of signals which indicated they were both aware Betty was issuing a different warning entirely. It was a dangerous path Lynda trod in re-establishing her friendship with Terry, and if they were to have any peace it was vital Ewan didn't discover what they were up to.

Belle said, 'Your ex still giving you trouble then, Betty?'

'Not for much longer. I've got a plan. If he isn't out of here by Christmas I'm going to put weed killer in his trifle.'

Belle went away chuckling, and the moment she'd gone Betty was inundated with customers, Leo Catlow among them. 'Why is it when there's two of us here we're sat twiddling our thumbs, and the minute I'm on me own I'm rushed off me feet? Mind you, I dare say my feet could do with the exercise.'

'Does anything rob you of your sense of humour, Betty?' Leo asked and Betty pretended to give due consideration to the question.

'Can't think of owt offhand.'

Leo smilingly offered her a piece of advice. 'I happened to overhear what you said to Belle, and I have to warn you that divorce is more practical than poison, and far less dangerous.'

'Aye, I tried that once and it didn't work. Don't worry, Ewan Hemley will outlive us all. The good lord is in no hurry to have him come calling. Only the good die young, more's the pity. How about you? You've been having it a bit rough lately too, from what I can gather. Got that new kitchen fitted, have you? Bet it cost a packet.'

They enjoyed their usual chat about his mother and the fire and the renovations, and how Dulcie was settling into the home while Betty made up a bouquet of carnations for the old lady. But her mind was elsewhere and she kept lapsing into silence.

'Spit it out,' Leo said at last. 'I can see something is bothering you.'

Betty smiled brightly up at him. 'I was just thinking about the things I see sitting here in this chair of mine. People coming and going, talking, gossiping, making assignations, having rows. I've sat here so long they no longer see me, if you catch my drift, so they sometimes reveal things about themselves without realising.'

Leo was frowning. 'I suppose they do. Were you thinking of anybody in particular?'

'Well now, that'd be telling, wouldn't it? And you know I'm not one to gossip, not like some round here. Anyroad, if a bloke takes a married lady into his shop then shuts the door and puts up the closed sign, who am I to say what's going on?'

A small silence followed in which Leo fixed her with his penetrating gaze for a long moment before allowing it to drift over the market. There weren't many actual shops, just a few on the periphery of the market hall. A tobacconist and Alec Hall's music shop among others, and the ironmongery belonging to Sam Beckett. Was she hinting at something to do with Lynda and Terry, or something else entirely?

Leo looked back at Betty, eyebrows raised in enquiry, but she only smiled up at him.

'How about a potted hyacinth for your lady wife? Hyakinthos was a handsome young Greek loved by Apollo, the sun god. Trouble was, the god of the west wind loved Apollo and he didn't much care for his adored to turn his attention elsewhere. He was bitterly jealous. Anyroad, one day while they were all practising discus-throwing the god of the west wind became so overcome with jealousy he blew the discus right back and it killed poor Hyakinthos. From his blood grew this lovely flower which Apollo named after him.'

Leo said, 'A tragic tale, Betty, but why are you telling me this?'

Betty shrugged, her face devoid of expression. 'I was just thinking that jealousy can be a wicked thing. It can destroy a marriage, or prove fatal for some poor victim, if you don't watch out.'

'Yes,' Leo thoughtfully agreed. 'I suppose it can.'

'And often those who are most jealous, like the west wind, have least reason to be. Maybe he was just misguided, overcome by his jealousy but some people, in the real world I mean, aren't always as innocent as they make out. They might be involved in secret affairs of their own, and put the blame for the failure of their marriage on to their spouse, as part of a cover-up.'

Betty smiled benignly up at Leo, allowing the silence to develop before continuing, 'But, as you say, it's nobbut a Greek love tangle, a myth, nowt to do with reality. So, what about a hyacinth then for your good lady wife? Bring a beautiful perfume into her lounge for Christmas.'

Leo accepted the suggestion though he said nothing more, and as he walked away with his flowers he lapsed into deep thought.

Judy stared at Leo transfixed, unable to believe what she was hearing. She'd found him waiting for her when she'd got home from the snack bar and had run to him in joy, eager to show that she held no regrets over what had happened the previous night.

Judy had made up her mind that she would fight Sam all the way, that she would go through with the divorce, then she and Leo could apply to adopt the children, as man and wife, just as they'd discussed last night. Judy's heart was filled with happiness and new hope at the prospect. Everything was going to be all right, she knew it.

Now she stared at him in disbelief. 'Helen is pregnant? But . . . I thought she didn't want children? I mean, I thought you and she were no longer . . .'

'We aren't. We haven't slept together – had sex – in several weeks.' The deep-set dark brown eyes brooded more sombrely than ever, and a crease appeared between the winged eyebrows as Leo attempted to calculate dates. 'Though probably there was the odd occasion in the last three months, while I was still trying to make a go of it. I can't remember.' He looked at her then with such agony in his eyes Judy could hardly bear it. 'You know what this means, don't you?'

She couldn't bring herself to think, to view a life without either her children or Leo, not now when they'd both admitted how they felt about each other. 'Don't say it. Please don't say what I think you're going to say.'

'I'm so sorry, love, so desperately sorry but I can't leave her now, not when she's having my child.' Leo captured Judy's face in his hands to look deep into her blue eyes. 'I'd give my soul for it not to be true. All these years I've longed, ached for a family. There was nothing I wanted more than to father a child of my own, but not like this when my marriage is in tatters and I've found you.'

Judy had to say it. It seemed that she was constantly driven to fight for the people she loved. 'What if it isn't yours?'

He paused then, wondered if those convoluted hints Betty had dropped had something to do with Helen having an affair? He couldn't be sure, of course but they certainly tallied with what his mother had told him. And if the child were indeed Sam Beckett's, or some other lover? How would he feel about that, even if he could prove it?

Leo dropped his hands to his side on a sigh, and shook his head. 'She's my wife so I have to assume the child is mine, which it may well be. In any case, for the child's sake, if nothing else, I have to assume that it is.'

There was a silence, one far too deep for either of them to break. Leo cradled her in his arms while Judy wept quietly on his shoulder. She drank in the familiar scent of him, savoured the warmth of his body, the strength of his arms about her, so newly learned and now to be lost forever. The embrace did nothing to quench the pain in her heart which was surely breaking inside, nor to stem the tide of emotion that threatened to overwhelm her. With reluctance he set her from him.

'I have to go.' Leo held her chin between his thumb and fingers, kissed her softly on the mouth. 'Take care, Judy, my love. Fight Sam for those lovely children of yours. Don't let him win. And remember that I love you. Always remember that.' Then there was nothing but a blast of cold air as the door closed behind him.

42

Lynda

Lynda visited the wholesale market with Terry, and having placed her order for the tree, they spent the rest of the afternoon filling in forms for a marriage licence and enjoying a cappuccino and a sandwich in Lewis's department store. It felt so good to be together again, as if it were right, like slipping a hand into a well-loved glove.

Mam had told her not to hurry back, allowing them a little time together, so they went for a leisurely walk. Not by the canal where the narrow boats cruise which used to be a favourite walk of theirs but beyond Castlefield, over towards Ordsall where Terry had heard there were new flats to let. He was keen to find a place quickly, so they could get married.

He suggested that since they'd consistently failed to persuade Ewan to move out, then the rest of the family should do so instead, lock, stock and barrel. Terry was more than willing to share their future home with his mother-in-law, Jake too if it meant he could protect the woman he loved. And as luck would have it, they found one. Three bedrooms and a bathroom fit for a queen, together with a spacious living room and kitchen, and all on the ground floor so it would be perfect for her mam.

Lynda was itching to tell Betty her good news when she got home, but didn't get the reaction she'd hoped for.

Betty was shocked. 'I'm not moving. This is my home, has been ever since I came to Champion Street at the start of the war, and they'll carry me out of here in a box. I'm certainly not going to be chased out by that no-good ex-husband of mine.'

'But wouldn't you rather live with me and Terry in a lovely new flat? Then you'd be free of him for good.'

'No, I don't want to live in a lovely new flat with you and Terry, nor do I want to move from the market. Ordsall wouldn't be at all convenient, and you have your own lives to live. I like it here in Champion Street close to my stall, and I certainly have no intention of handing my house over to *him*. Never!'

So that was the end of Terry's plan. Lynda wasn't sure she could bring herself to leave her mother alone with Ewan, but if she didn't how could she and Terry ever hope to be together? Oh, it was all so difficult. She'd just have to hope that she could win her mother round in the end, perhaps when she went to see the new flat.

'Eeh, but I'm right thrilled for you, chuck. I'm so pleased yer getting wed. He's such a grand lad,' and mother and daughter hugged each other in a rare moment of joy.

'Terry will look after you, and I want you to be safe. But don't you worry about me. I'll be all right here.'

'But I do worry about you, I worry a great deal. I can't leave you two on your own, there'd be blue murder done.'

'I'll have our Jake. Anyroad, I've thought of a scheme to get rid of his lordship,' Betty said, lowering her voice and tapping the side of her nose with one finger. 'It's risky, but it might work.'

Lynda got her mother into bed and made them each a mug of cocoa, Queenie in pride of place on Betty's feet. They enjoyed a bit of gossip but she absolutely refused to say any more about this so-called scheme of hers.

'Not yet, chuck. I have to finalise a few details. I'll let you know when the time is right.'

When Betty started to nod off, Lynda washed the mugs and locked up. It was ten o'clock and Jake was still out with his mates. When she'd seen her mother safely into bed, Lynda crept up the stairs, shoes in hand so as not to disturb her.

Lynda took her time getting ready for bed, happily spinning delicious plans for her future with Terry as she undressed and went to the bathroom. She didn't mind in the least having a register office wedding. All she wanted was to be with Terry, the man she loved.

She'd maybe treat herself to a new suit for the ceremony, or one of those shift dresses in cream wool. And she could ask Patsy to make her a hat to match. Lynda wondered if Judy would be her matron-of-honour, if she could find her in time. Would Sam know where her friend was living now, she wondered? Probably not. But she couldn't be far away, because of the children. Maybe Ruth knew. Why hadn't she thought to ask before?

Warmly wrapped in her dressing gown, Lynda sat at her dressing table and began to write out a few invitations.

Mam had made it plain that she wasn't entirely happy about the arrangements, not wishing her daughter to have a hole-in-the-corner wedding, yet they both knew absolute secrecy was vital. Lynda had reluctantly agreed to invite a few relatives, her Aunt Marjorie and Uncle Joe, a couple of her favourite cousins who lived in Blackburn, and one or two old school friends who lived far enough away not to come into contact with Ewan Hemley.

After that she started work on a list of jobs which needed to be done before the Big Day. It was all so exciting.

She lost track of time as she sat there, entirely engrossed in making these delightful plans. Then she smoothed cream over her face and plucked her eyebrows, wanting to stay beautiful for Terry, and only became aware she was no longer alone when she heard the bedroom door click shut.

Whirling round in alarm she was shocked to discover Ewan standing with his back against it, his nasty little eyes glittering in the half-light from her bedside lamp, and a leering grin on his ferret face.

Thinking he was still out, she hadn't got around to blocking it off. Lynda felt a flutter of nervousness in the pit of her stomach. The last thing she wanted was to provoke an argument, nevertheless she was determined not to show her fear.

Striving to keep her voice pleasant and calm, Lynda calmly

remarked, 'You're back earlier than usual. Do you want a cuppa before you go to bed? Only, I'd rather you didn't come into my room if you don't mind. I've told you already, it's strictly private.'

'That's not a nice attitude to take with your old dad.' He came up behind her, wobbling slightly as he picked up her hair brush. The stink of beer and unwashed sweat emanating from him almost made her faint. 'I thought happen I'd help you get ready for bed, since you're my little girl. Read you a story, brush your hair like, or help you into your jammy-jamas.'

Lynda felt sick at the thought but again warned herself not to antagonise him. 'I can manage perfectly well, thanks. You look more in need of a lie down. Go on, get yourself off to bed before you fall down.'

Instead he began to brush her hair, slowly stroking the soft auburn curls, making her shudder so that it took all her will-power not to shove him away. Lynda tried to think what she could do. She was on her own with no one to help. Her mother might be on the mend at last, but didn't have the strength to come running upstairs and take on this brute.

Ewan was shaking his head. The movement caused him to burp loudly and he laughed, as if he'd done something clever, then his tone became maudlin with drink.

'You wanted a father and here I am, ready and willing to make up for lost time. We could be good mates, you and me, keep each other company like. So be nice to your lonely old dad, eh? Where's the harm in a bit of a cuddle so long as we keep it in the family? You're a bonny lass and . . .'

'. . . You're drunk, you don't know what you're saying.' Frantic now, Lynda leaped from her seat and backed away, although there was no escape, nowhere to run. Ewan stood between herself and the closed bedroom door and the way his gaze was roving over her was sending chills down her spine. Lynda tugged the chord of her dressing gown tighter.

'Oh, aye, I do indeed know what I'm saying.' His voice dropped to a hushed calm, chillingly vicious as he grinned at her with a lop-sided leer. 'We can't let that Terry have all the fun, now can we? Wouldn't be right when I have first call. Oh, don't you fret, I know where you've been today and who you've been with. I make sure I keep a beady eye on what's rightly mine.'

Desperation rose in her throat as sour as bile, and as he began to smooth a hand over her neck Lynda slapped it away.

'I don't *belong* to you, or to anyone else for that matter. I'm not some sort of possession. All right, so Terry gave me a lift to Smithfield market today to order the Christmas tree, so what?'

His mouth curled with distaste. 'I spotted you on the back of his motor bike. Now where's she off to now, I wondered? But you didn't come home when you'd done your errand, did you?'

Cold fear was growing inside her. How did he know all of this? Should she risk calling out for Mam? But then what could she do? Betty could hardly pound upstairs and beat her ex-husband over the head with her crutches, could she? Lynda had no choice but to stand up to him and deal with this herself.

'I have my spies,' he said, as if reading her thoughts. 'Didn't I tell you to stay away from that lad? I don't remember giving you permission to start seeing him again, or any other chap for that matter.'

Lynda lifted her chin in a gesture of defiance. 'I've no idea what you've got against Terry, and I don't care because it's none of your business. He loves me and I love him.' She'd meant to remain calm and not let him upset her but Lynda could hear her voice rising, filled with indignant anger. 'In fact, you might as well know that we're going to be married. If you really have followed us today you'll probably already have guessed that we've organised a marriage licence, *and* found ourselves somewhere to live, somewhere for all of us, Mam and Jake too. We're leaving. So you can put that in your flaming pipe and smoke it.'

'You're going nowhere without my permission, and you're certainly not bloody getting wed!'

Lynda knew he would hit her even before she saw him raise his fist. But while she'd been shouting at him she'd also been scrabbling quietly behind her back on her dressing table, desperately searching for something, *anything*, with which to defend herself. Her fingers closed over a pair of scissors.

Now she lurched forward, scissors held high, although whether she might actually have used them she could never afterwards be sure for at that moment came a piercing scream from downstairs.

'Lynda, Lynda, come quick . . .'

They both froze, but, fearing her mother was having a heart attack or something equally dreadful, Lynda was the first to react. She dropped the scissors, thrust Ewan to one side and flew down the stairs to find Betty on her knees in the kitchen with the cat in her arms. It was soaking wet through, its body ominously limp. Betty brought her anguished gaze up to her daughter's, tears rolling down her fat cheeks.

'It's our Queenie. I found her in the kitchen sink when I went to get meself a drink of water. Some bugger has drowned her.'

As one, their combined gaze swivelled towards Ewan where he stood at the bottom of the stairs. He gave a snort of laughter as if this were all the funniest thing imaginable, and again burped loudly before attempting to speak.

'I did warn you, Lynda love, that you'd regret it if you went out with a young man without my permission. You've only yourself to blame. You just won't do as you're told, either of you, and I can't have that. I *won't* have it.'

43

Leo and Judy

Dulcie seemed to be surprisingly content in the home. She had a pleasant room with her own things about her, had made many new friends and Leo thought on his recent visits that she was much less lonely and confused.

On this occasion when he called she was sitting with a group of ladies in the conservatory playing bridge. She was smartly dressed in her favourite pale blue twin-set and pearls and matching tweed skirt, her white hair shining with health and her round face pink with happiness as she triumphantly claimed the rubber. She jumped up at the sight of him and came at once to kiss him. Leo apologised for not having brought her any flowers but he'd come to see her on an impulse, in need of some advice.

'Doesn't matter, son, I'm always delighted to see you.' Her face clouded over. 'Something is bothering you, I can always tell. Let me ask Janice to fetch us some tea then we'll sit and chat.'

As they sat sipping tea together in the winter sunshine that filtered in through the conservatory windows, Leo tried to smile. 'Actually it's good news. Helen is pregnant, would you believe?'

Dulcie said nothing. She sat unmoving, cup poised inches from her lips, then set it down on the table untouched. 'Well now, that is a surprise.'

'Isn't it?'

'I suppose . . .' Dulcie cleared her throat then started again. 'May I ask a rather impertinent question?'

'Mother, you never usually ask my permission to interfere in my affairs so why start now?' But he was smiling, to show that he didn't object.

'It's more your wife's affairs that are concerning me, Leo. Are you sure, hand on heart, that this child is yours?'

Her question, so closely echoing Judy's own, made him gasp. 'What makes you say such a thing?'

'You remember my telling you that I suspected she was having an affair with that ironmonger, Beckett, is he called? I once saw her coming home, arms full of shopping yet she claimed she'd been to the warehouse which was in quite the opposite direction, and then I spotted Beckett's car. I'm quite sure he'd given her a lift from town.'

'That's hardly proof of a love affair.'

Dulcie pursed her lips. 'I asked her but she denied it. Why do that if she was innocent? So I watched her, to see if my suspicions were correct. She would slip out to see him several times a week. They'd meet either in his shop or she'd go off up some back alley. I followed her once and saw them together. It wasn't a pleasant sight. Despite her possessiveness and the furious jealousy I know she exhibits over you, dear, she is by no means innocent herself. I did warn you once before, Leo, and I stand by what I've observed.'

Leo was struck into stunned silence. Was he being deliberately blind, perhaps anxious to convince himself that it couldn't possibly be true? It seemed impossible for a woman so consumed by jealousy over her husband's imagined affairs to be guilty of the very same crime herself. And yet perhaps she had become entangled in an affair herself as some sort of perverted vengeance.

'Would it shock you very much, Mother, if I told you that I was no longer quite so innocent either? Throughout my married life I've remained loyal and steadfast, but Helen's jealousy ate away at me and eventually destroyed whatever it was we had together. She seems incapable of showing affection and that too has taken its toll.'

Dulcie said, 'I've been aware for some time that you weren't happy, dear. Your father and I used to talk about it often. You've perhaps been too loyal, Leo, too generous-hearted, as you always were as a child.'

Leo smiled at this typical example of maternal pride, but could he accept that Helen had played him false? 'Even if what you say is true, Mother, Helen and I are still man and wife and this child will need a father. How can I deny it one when it might still be mine?'

'But are you absolutely certain? And if you're not, can you face taking responsibility for what may well be another man's child? It wouldn't be easy. You'd always be asking yourself that question.'

'Not if I came to love the child as my own.'

Dulcie gazed upon her son with real sympathy in her faded blue-grey eyes. All these years Leo had longed not simply for a son to inherit the business, but for a family of his own. He'd always wanted to be a father, and to have this doubt hanging over the paternity of this unexpected offspring was sad to say the least. 'When did Helen discover she was pregnant?'

Leo shook his head. 'I don't know. She told me the other night. I'd asked her for a divorce, having finally given up all hope of us ever being happy. That's when she told me. It was a real bolt from the blue, I can tell you.'

Dulcie gasped. 'My dear Leo, you are an innocent indeed. Didn't it occur to you that she might be lying, that she could be faking this so-called pregnancy simply in order to prevent a divorce and hang on to her failing marriage?'

Leo looked stunned. 'That had not occurred to me, no. But surely, even Helen wouldn't stoop so low. How could she hope to get away with it? I'd be bound to find out eventually, obviously, when no baby came, no bump even.'

'She wouldn't be the first wife to play that trick and later fake a miscarriage. By which time she would hope you'd have lost your new lady-friend and the pair of you would be reconciled once more.'

'God, what a naïve fool I've been!'

'I'm simply asking, dear, if you have any proof that she is indeed pregnant? Have you spoken to her doctor?'

Leo shook his head. 'Why would I? It would look as if I didn't trust my wife.'

'But it's true, you don't. Neither do I.' Dulcie took a sip of her tea, found it cold and set it to one side. 'Leo, there is something else I need to discuss with you. I realise I've been having a few problems lately over forgetting things, and still do when I get upset or stressed. Caring for your father was very difficult and for much of the time I was exhausted. He could be particularly demanding at times.'

Leo snorted with laughter. 'Don't I know it.'

'But I'm not quite senile, not yet anyway. Maybe I'll end up that way,' she added with a smile, 'but it's perfectly normal to get a bit forgetful when you're older, particularly in a distressing situation. No, don't interrupt, I must say this. I'm very happy here in this lovely private home. The staff are delightful and very friendly and there are plenty of other widowed ladies here rather like myself. We have quite a good time and I still keep in touch with my old friends. Most of all I have no wish to be a burden to you, Leo, but Helen went about getting rid of me in quite the wrong way.

'The fact is, my dear, she lied. *I* did not start that fire, *she* did. Helen reminded me to turn off the cooker and of course I did. I've been cooking for over fifty years and it's automatic to turn off the heat when something is cooked. I never used the gas jets at all as I was baking scones. I then went out for my walk and Helen went upstairs for her shower. But she must have come back down again the moment I'd gone and started the fire herself.'

Leo was aghast. 'Why would she do such a thing?'

'She wanted me out of her house, *your* house. She'd made several attempts to persuade me to return to Lytham because she's jealous of me and wanted to have you all to herself. Helen is a sick woman, Leo, with no sense of moral rectitude.'

Leo might have smiled at his mother's quaint turn of phrase had not the matter been so serious.

'Ask yourself,' Dulcie continued, 'how would a tea towel catch fire, which is what she claims must have happened, when we hang them up by the sink to dry, nowhere near the cooker? I'm quite certain I wouldn't foolishly leave a tea towel by a lighted gas jet, and, as I say, you bake scones inside the oven, not on top of it. Helen started that fire in order to force you to agree to putting me in a home.'

And here Dulcie gave one of her sweetly patient smiles. 'I'll admit that it has turned out for the best, even if I disagree with the method she used to achieve it. Perhaps I should have volunteered to go of my own free will. It was wrong of me to try to cling on to the past by staying in my old home close to the market, and to cling on to you. But ask her, Leo, what *really* happened that day. I beg you, please don't believe everything she tells you simply because she is your wife. Helen will tell any lie that suits her own ends.'

Leo was seething with anger by the time he left, his first instinct being to rush back to Judy and discuss this new possibility with her, but then decided against doing so until he was certain of his facts. It would be cruel to raise her hopes that they might have a future together after all, only to have them dashed by incontrovertible evidence his wife was indeed pregnant. So far Leo had no proof, nothing more than gossip and innuendo from a couple of old dears, his mother and Betty Hemley. Hardly reliable sources.

He judged it wise to say nothing to Helen immediately. Leo felt that he needed to digest what his mother had told him, watch her for a while and check for himself if what Dulcie accused her of might possibly be true.

Weren't pregnant women sick in a morning, or exhibited other symptoms of pregnancy such as strange cravings and aching legs? He'd watch and wait.

He considered ringing the doctor but how would that sound, if Helen really was pregnant? Did he want the whole world to know at this stage that he no longer trusted his wife and believed she was either lying over this alleged pregnancy, or was guilty of having an affair?

Leo really had no wish to broadcast his marriage difficulties to all and sundry. In any case, old Doc Mitchell might not answer the question. Wasn't there something called patient confidentiality?

Best to wait. If Helen was lying, she couldn't keep it up for long. He'd give her a week or two. In the meantime if he spotted old Mitchell, socially as it were, he might casually bring up the subject of Helen's pregnancy in a chatty sort of way, just to judge his reaction to the news.

As for the fire, to imagine his wife capable of such malice was quite beyond him. There were ways he could check, he supposed, by asking some questions of the fire brigade. They could tell him the seat of the fire, though not who had started it even if it did look like arson.

Once he knew the truth for certain, and *if* his mother was proved right, *then* he would go to Judy.

44

Lynda

The morning following poor Queenie's demise, Lynda came downstairs to find that Betty had already left. Ewan wasn't there either, although he could still be upstairs in bed snoring his head off for all she knew. Jake was standing in the middle of the kitchen munching Marmite on toast and sipping a glass of milk. He was in his blue work overalls, hair all over the place, looking as if he hadn't even been to bed.

'What time is it? Have I overslept?' Lynda peered bleary-eyed at the clock on the mantelpiece. It said ten minutes to six. She rubbed her eyes, looked again in disbelief then once again addressed her brother. 'Where's Mam? She can't have gone to the market already?'

'I dunno,' Jake shrugged. 'How would I know?'

'Has she got a lift with Barry Holmes to Smithfield? If so, that's very naughty of her. She does too much already. Though Barry will help her, I suppose. Anyroad, I wish she'd told me then I could've had a bit of a lie-in. I'm worn out after our late night dealing with . . .' Lynda drew in a sharp breath . . . 'our poor Queenie.'

Betty had insisted they bury the cat there and then, declaring she couldn't possibly sleep a wink knowing its little body was lying dead in the kitchen. Jake had arrived while they were still weeping over it and he and Lynda had wrapped the cat up in a towel and buried her under a tree in a corner of the churchyard, which seemed appropriate.

Lynda moaned. 'I feel dreadful, almost as bad as you look. Did you have a bad night too?'

Jake finished slapping Marmite on his second slice of toast and headed for the door. 'See ya.'

'Jake, I'm talking to you!' But the only answer was the slam of the front door. Her brother was behaving even more oddly than usual.

Since Mam had already gone there seemed to be no great rush and Lynda dragged herself back upstairs and slept for another hour, then took her time over breakfast, dreamily going over her wedding plans as she washed the dishes and tidied up. Consequently it was almost nine o'clock by the time she got to the market.

But as she approached the corner where the flower stall usually stood she could see no sign of it, nor of Betty. Lynda quickened her pace, looking about her in startled disbelief.

'Oh, there you are, lass,' Jimmy Ramsay said as she passed his butcher's stall. 'I were wondering where you were. Had a lie-in, eh?'

'Where's Mam, have you seen her?'

'No, not a sign.'

Lynda's heart slowed to a dragging, fearful beat. Then where was she? Why wasn't she here setting out her flowers and chatting to people from her chair, as she always was. Lynda spotted Barry Holmes stacking apples on his stall, and hurried over. 'Am I glad to see you. Where's Mam?'

Barry turned on his heel to look at her, a quizzical expression on his face. 'I beg your pardon? Why would I know where Betty is?'

The heartbeat was gradually increasing in pace now, thudding in her ears like a drum so that Lynda could barely hear herself think. 'Didn't you give her a lift to Smithfield this morning?'

Barry shook his head. 'Is it her morning for going? She generally goes on Mondays, Wednesdays and Fridays, same as me. It's only Thursday today.'

'Oh, lord, course it is. I'm losing track.' Lynda took a moment to catch her breath. 'Sorry, I wasn't thinking.'

She looked frantically about her, some instinct warning her not to raise the alarm, not just yet. There had to be a perfectly innocent explanation, if only she could think of one.

'Have you lost her then?' Barry was asking, a smile on his face.

Lynda managed a little laugh. 'No, no, she can't have gone far, can she? Not in her wheelchair, and she's even slower on them crutches. The cat died last night, that's all it is.'

'What, your Queenie? Eeh, I am sorry. Well then, I expect she's in a corner grieving somewhere, you know how potty she was about that cat.'

'I expect she is. Thanks, Barry,' and Lynda walked calmly away, but after twenty paces her calmness evaporated and her walk turned into a run. If Mam wasn't in the house, or on the market then Barry was right, there was only one place she could be.

But minutes later when Lynda arrived at the churchyard it was to find it empty with no sign of Betty, nor a single flower on the small unmarked hump of ground beneath the beech tree. So where the hell was she?

Terry offered to help organise a search. All the stallholders were worried by this time and started to make helpful suggestions. Jimmy Ramsay thought Betty might have gone back to the hospital to show off her new skills with her crutches. Alec Hall, Terry's father, believed they shouldn't overlook the obvious and offered to call some of her friends.

'She might just be visiting someone.'

Belle Garside said, 'She could've done a runner, metaphorically speaking. I know she wasn't getting on with her ex and joked about poisoning his trifle this Christmas. You might be fond of your father, Lynda, but Betty found it less easy to deal with him.'

'Don't I know it, but where would she run to? Champion Street is her home and she has no relatives or other family around, not that I know of.'

'Happen you don't know everything, girl. Children don't.'

Terry visited each stall and small shop, asking everyone to keep an eye out for her, while Lynda knocked on every door. They pointed out that Lynda was afraid she might have fallen somewhere, since she was still unsteady on her feet.

On hearing the news, Big Molly at once put on her hat and coat. 'Right, I'm coming with you, lass. We have to find the poor cow, she's me best mate. Come on, our Ossie, wake up and get yoursel' out of that chair, there's work to be done. I know that's an alien concept to you but for once hearken to what I say to thee, lad. You and me is going hunting for our pal Betty.'

And for once Ossie put on his boots and his raincoat, and his flat cap, and willingly followed his wife on a trek that was to last for much of the rest of that day. His dog naturally must come too, perhaps in the hope that he might sniff her out.

All Betty's friends, the people who were her regular customers – Joyce from the hairdressing salon, Patsy and the Higginson sisters, Amy George, Dena Dobson and the rest, even Winnie Holmes – were equally devastated to hear that Betty was missing.

'Nay, don't let's panic,' Winnie kept saying, showing her usual stout common sense. 'She could fall in a midden could our Betty and come out smelling of roses.'

Chris George and Barry Holmes collected together a deputation of men and volunteered to search under the railway arches and down by the canal basin. Winnie couldn't help but dryly remark upon this. 'Trust the chaps to offer themselves up for that duty. See you don't get up to any shenanigans with that Maureen, Barry Holmes, or I'll have your guts for garters. If she offers you a cup of tea, say no, or you might get more than a custard cream with your Tetley's.'

Barry simply grinned and then flustered Winnie by kissing her on the cheek right in front of everyone. 'Why would I want any other woman when I've got you to come home to every night, with or without a custard cream?'

'I wish Mam would come home,' Lynda groaned. 'I really

don't understand where she can have got to, or how she comes to be missing at all. I've a bad feeling about this, real bad.'

'Isn't Ewan missing an' all?' Barry asked.

Lynda tossed her head, making her curls dance in a crackling fury. 'I don't give a monkey's about him, it's Mam what matters. She's the one on crutches, the one who's in trouble. I just know it.'

Lynda spotted Constable Nuttall as she was on her way back to the house later that same day. She was in a hurry, wanting to check if Betty had gone quietly home when no one was looking but she paused to wait for him, hoping the policeman might have heard something.

Where could she be? Her mother couldn't simply vanish off the face of the earth. It was all very worrying.

Lynda recalled that, worryingly enough, Jake's bed hadn't even looked as if it'd been slept in when she'd left that morning. She should have suspected something was wrong the minute she'd set eyes on him. He'd turned into such a dandy recently Lynda realised that she should also have been suspicious to see him looking so rough.

Perhaps he'd been out and about on Ewan's nefarious business last night although she hadn't even knocked on her father's door to check if he was still in bed. But then she never did. Lynda preferred to steer well clear of Ewan's room. She was wondering how to knock some sense into her young brother's head when the policeman approached.

'Hello, love, can we go inside for a minute? I wanted a word.'

Lynda stared at Constable Nuttall, a hollow ache suddenly swelling and expanding inside, threatening to overwhelm her with fresh pain. 'Oh no, it's me mam, isn't it? Where is she? Have you found her? Has she had an accident?'

'I think we'd best go inside, if you don't mind.'

Only when Lynda had finally agreed to go inside the house and sit down, did Constable Nuttall finally speak. 'The truth is, Lynda love, we didn't even know your mam was missing, but we're a bit concerned because we've found her wheelchair.'

'What?'

'Now I know she's getting back on her feet again, doing them exercises and practising little walks and so on. I've seen her once or twice out and about but finding the chair without her in it doesn't seem quite right, does it?'

'Oh God! Where did you find it?'

Constable Nuttall paused to clear his throat before he answered with painstaking slowness. 'I'm sorry to say it was down by the canal basin. We're arranging to have it dragged, but don't upset yourself over that, Lynda love, it's only a matter of form. I'm quite sure your mam wouldn't be so daft as to fall in.'

The thought that came unbidden into Lynda's terrified mind was: No, but somebody might have pushed her.

45

Lynda

Lynda told Constable Nuttall all about how Ewan had done for poor Queenie in retaliation for her continuing to see Terry when he'd told her not to. 'It's all about power. He just likes to lord it over us.'

Her hazel eyes were filled with fear but the policeman made no comment. He simply pressed his lips together in thoughtful disapproval and went on listening, clearly used to hearing tales of family squabbles.

'Fathers can be a bit over-protective when it comes to their daughters. That's something which will seem a bit odd to you, I expect, not being used to having a father around when you were growing up, but I'm sure I would be just the same with mine, were I fortunate enough to have a family. Only, I will accept that drowning the cat is going a bit far.'

Lynda said, 'So are you prepared to start listening to me at last?'

Constable Nuttall only shook his head in resignation. 'That's ex-cons for you. Different set of morals altogether.' Then he went on to tell her not to worry, that soon she'd be married with babies of her own and come to understand how you have to watch them every minute of the time.

'But I'm not a baby, I'm a grown woman, and I can please myself who I go out with. Terry's a lovely man.'

'I'm sure he is, Lynda love, but I expect your father's only concerned about the age difference between you so's you don't get hurt, or else for Terry's reputation for whizzing about on that motor bike of his. Dangerous vehicles they are.'

Abandoning hope of the policeman ever understanding her point of view, Lynda did at least succeed in making him promise that the police would carry on searching the docks and water-front as well as the canal itself, just in case Betty had wandered too far in her grief and fallen somewhere.

But he wasn't optimistic. Neither was Lynda. She was deeply afraid something terrible had happened to her mam.

If Ewan had done something to hurt her then she mustn't let the trembling fear she felt inside overwhelm her. Lynda knew she couldn't afford to fall into a heap, but neither could she convince the policeman that her mother might have been done in by her own ex-husband, just like the flaming cat. She had no proof, although everyone was aware that the pair were at logger-heads. Somehow she had to make him understand what kind of man Ewan Hemley was.

That's when the solution came to her.

'Come with me, Constable, there's something I want to show you, something which should be brought to your attention.'

Lynda led the curious policeman up the stairs to Ewan's room and, flinging open the door, stood back to allow him to enter. 'There you are, what do you think of that?'

Constable Nuttall stepped into the room and looked about him, clearly somewhat perplexed. Lynda sighed with satisfaction. There, she'd proved her point at last and got her own back for all Ewan's nasty violent outbursts. She'd shopped him to the coppers just as her mam had done all those years ago.

The constable said, 'Very nice, Lynda love. Exactly the kind of tidy bedroom I'd expect to see in an ex-con. Few possessions and all neatly aligned.'

'Tidy, what are you talking about? What about all those boxes?' Lynda stepped into the room after him and gasped. It was empty, not a box in sight. All swept out and neat as a new pin. She ran to her brother's room, flung open the wardrobe doors, pulled out ever drawer but that too was clean. Every single box, every item of stolen goods had vanished. Not even a stray sock out of place.

Lynda was horrified. 'They must have moved the stuff, perhaps sold it on already.'

'What stuff? You're not making any sense, Lynda love.'

She glared at the policeman as if this were all his fault, and then all the energy drained out of her and she felt weak, and sick. Ewan had won again. He'd anticipated that she would tell on him following his drowning of the cat, so he'd kept Jake up all night moving the damn stuff out.

Lynda took a shaky breath. 'You have to believe me but Ewan Hemley, my father, is acting as a . . . what do you call it . . . a fence for stolen goods. And he's got our Jake involved . . .'

It instantly flashed into Lynda's mind that she should be careful not to get her brother into too much trouble, so modified her explanation a little. 'Only fetching and carrying, mind, but you know how thick he is, he'll do anything for an easy life. We all have to toe the line where Ewan Hemley is concerned. But can you do something to stop him? Can you find Ewan and arrest him?'

'Not without proof, Lynda love. We can keep an eye on him, certainly, and I'm quite prepared to believe what you say but there's nowt I can do without proof. Does he have a lock-up that he might have moved the gear to?'

Lynda put her hands to her mouth in a gesture of despair and shook her head. She was so consumed by anger she could hardly speak. Ewan Hemley, the father she'd always dreamed about and longed for had walked into their lives and destroyed them. She'd never forgive him if he hurt her mam. Never! Lynda fought to regain control, fists clenched, eyes dry and hot.

'I don't know, do I? Jake might know. I could go and find him and ask him. He's working at Smithfield market this morning.'

'Right, you go and see what you can find out there. We'll keep searching for your mam. And don't fret, I'm sure she'll turn up any minute. She'll come hobbing down the street large as life and twice as lively.'

'I hope you're right. And you'll keep a look-out for Ewan too?' Lynda warned. 'He's up to summat, I know he is.'

Sadly a long day of searching ended in failure. No one had seen a sign of Betty Hemley anywhere since yesterday morning when she was selling flowers on her stall as usual, and Lynda hadn't the first idea where to look next.

Jake knew nothing about any lock-up, nor had he seen his father that morning.

Lynda groaned. 'Well, where is he? They can't both be missing. Have they murdered each other, do you reckon?'

Her brother looked horrified. 'Don't even joke about such things, sis, it's not funny.'

Lynda knew he was right. Something was wrong, badly wrong, and she couldn't begin to think what it might be. 'So tell me what you did with all that stuff last night? And don't try to deny you were involved, I can tell when you're lying. Where did you stash it?'

Jake fidgeted, shifting his feet about in their huge crepe-soled shoes, then lit himself a cigarette, drew on it hard and began to cough.

'When did you take up smoking?'

'I were given a few packets last night for a job well done. So what? Everybody smokes these days.'

'And if everybody set fire to themselves would you do that as well? Oh, never mind, answer the question. Where did you take the stolen gear?'

Jake sulked, studiously not meeting his sister's eye. 'We loaded it on board an Irish ship, if you want to know. I don't know which one, what it were called or owt. It were dark and I just did the job and cut out, ya know?'

'I do wish you'd cut out that daft lingo. Which dock, which wharf?'

But no matter how closely she interrogated him, Lynda got no decent answers. All she got were excuses, that he was only following orders. The truth was that he hadn't paid proper attention, but then when did he ever? He'd stacked everything in a van that Ewan had borrowed and drove till he was told to stop then loaded all the boxes on board ship. 'That's it. End of story. He gave me a chunk of bread and I was out of there.'

'A chunk of bread? What were you doing eating bread on the docks in the middle of the night?'

'Bread. Money. Do you dig me?'

'Actually, I reckon I should have dug a hole big enough for you an' all when we buried our Queenie.' Seeing his shocked face she patted her brother's cheek. 'I'm only joking.'

'Look, I didn't have no choice. It was a real front burner, hot, you know, unreal, so I didn't hang around to eyeball what was going on around me. I cut loose before I got a knuckle sandwich from anyone. There were some real bruisers on that boat. Didn't much care for any of them.'

'And what about Mam? Where was she when all of this was going on?'

Jake shrugged. 'Still at home, so far as I know.'

Lynda was struggling to hold on to her patience, her fingers itching to slap her stupid brother round his cloth ears. She almost spelled out the words for him. 'Was – she – there – when – you – got – back?'

Jake shook his head to indicate he had no idea, eyes so wide and innocent Lynda had to believe him. 'I never went in the living room, I just crept upstairs to bed though it was nearly dawn, lay on top of the covers and crashed out for an hour or two. She were gone when I come down an hour or two later.'

Lynda frowned. This wasn't helping at all, but she believed Jake to be telling the truth. 'I can only hope this will be a lesson to you, and you'll stay well clear of Ewan's mischief in future. In the meantime, you can come and help me look for Mam. She must be somewhere.'

Jake came readily enough, as anxious to find his mother as Lynda was, but even though they checked again, Betty still wasn't in the churchyard. They searched every place they could think of, every lock-up that belonged to the stallholders, every warehouse within walking distance, every old shed and garage. They found no sign of her.

Lynda was in tears by this time and Jake was feeling decidedly sick, filled with guilt for all the hassle he'd given his mother over the years. He'd never meant her any harm, not in a million years. She was an old fuss-pot but he loved her, right? She was his Mam for God's sake!

In the end, close to exhaustion, Lynda suggested they went back home for a bite to eat. 'Happen she'll have turned up by now. You never know.'

But the only person in the house was Ewan himself. He smiled grimly at the pair of them as they came through the door, took the pipe from between his clenched teeth and knocked it out on the corner of the mantelpiece, sending hot ash scattering all over the hearth-rug. Lynda stamped it out on a burst of anger at his carelessness.

'Where the hell have you been? Have you seen Mam? We've been looking for her all day. Do you know where she's gone? Have you hurt her? I'll kill you if you have. I'll knock you from here to the middle of next week.'

He considered her for some moments, a look she could only describe as low cunning on his face. 'That's a lot of questions in one breath, girl. And not a few threats.'

'Answer me. I'm not in the mood for your nasty little games.'

'If Betty is missing, why assume I have owt to do with it?'

'Why do you think? Because you're a piece of shit and I hate you.'

Jake sank into a chair on hearing his sister use such foul words, striving to make himself invisible.

Ewan got up to stand threateningly close to her, a smirk of satisfaction on his ugly ferret face. 'And what if I were to admit that mebbe I do know where your mam is?'

'I knew it. So where is she? What little game are you playing now?'

'Oh, it's no game, chuck. But I'm sure she's safe and well. All I'm saying is that should you ever want to see her again, you and your dozy ape of a brother here had better start doing exactly as I tell you. I need your help in a little enterprise I'm planning and if you don't cooperate, our lovely Betty will be dog-meat. Got that? Plain enough for you, is it? You can stop messing me about, the pair of you, and give me the obedience I deserve. Then when the job is over, I'll be out of your lives for good and all. Otherwise, it won't be a cat who's drowned next time, it'll be your bloody mother.'

46

Helen, Leo and Judy

Helen fully anticipated this Festive Season being the worst
ever. Dulcie would come for Christmas lunch, of course,
which wouldn't be easy as relations between them were so frosty
they were barely speaking. But Leo absolutely refused to allow
her to invite any other guests, which might have made the whole
thing more bearable, insisting she take things quietly because of
her condition.

He was constantly making remarks of this nature and the
curtailment to Helen's social calendar was beginning to gall her.

Nevertheless she felt quietly triumphant. She was quite certain
that she'd won, though how long she could keep up this myth
of a pregnancy was another matter. Long enough to screw up
Leo's little affair with the Beckett woman, that was for sure, and
until Helen herself felt more sure of him.

There had been a certain rapprochement between herself and
Leo. He was behaving as Helen would expect any caring husband
to behave. He would urge her to put her feet up, bring her a
cushion, or whatever took her fancy and Helen began to really
quite enjoy the extra attention. It might almost be worth having
a child if this was the kind of treatment she could expect.

And then she would remember her sister Harriet and her brood
of noisy infants, and shudder with distaste. Playing a part was
one thing, reality quite another thing entirely.

Oh, but she meant to win him back one way or another. She'd
have him eating out of her hands in no time, just as he'd done
in the early days of their marriage.

For her own part, Helen went through the motions of reconciliation, making every attempt to appear less critical, but she was bored out of her mind. But as she sat listening to Cliff Richard sing 'Living Doll' on her new stereophonic radiogram, Helen was beginning to feel jaded and even rather old. Her life seemed so dull, so unexciting, despite all her best efforts to spice it up.

They seemed to have fallen into monotonous routine: Leo working long hours at the warehouse, still visiting his mother several afternoons a week, generally alone, although occasionally Helen would accompany him for form's sake. Each evening they would sit and eat dinner in comparative silence, exchanging little more than cool pleasantries, and information regarding their respective schedules.

Helen would tell him of meetings she had attended, gossip she'd acquired from among her social set. Several times she mentioned Barford and tried to engage Leo's interest in her lover's plans for property development, but when still she got absolutely no response, she gave up.

Helen finally abandoned all hope of turning her strictly moral husband into the kind of entrepreneur capable of ever taking risks and bribes which others took for granted in their quest to make serious money. Unfortunately, Leo seemed to be shackled by too many scruples. In any case, what did it matter if Barford did spill the beans over their little liaison? Leo wouldn't leave her now, not with the baby coming.

Sometimes Helen almost forgot that this baby wasn't real, so convincingly did she play her part. Naturally it would become clear eventually that she'd lied, or at least been mistaken about the pregnancy. Surely she could manufacture a convincing miscarriage when her next period started?

Helen worried that if relations between them didn't improve, she might be compelled to reconsider and actually produce a child. A drastic measure she intended to avoid at all costs, but nor did she have any wish to lose access to her husband's lovely money. It was all most vexing.

But it did occur to her that perhaps it wasn't going to be quite as easy as she'd first thought. Something had changed in him. He was no longer the man she'd married. *That* Leo had been attentive because he loved her, because he wanted to make her happy. *This* Leo was simply going through the motions and didn't really seem to care. *This* Leo loved another woman, and Helen hated him for that, the jealousy eating away at her like a greedy worm. Their marriage had turned into nothing more than a sham, a sad and bitter union. They were drifting further and further apart and she could find no way to stop it.

How dare he prove her right and have a mistress after all?

Leo had grown tired of waiting. Helen seemed perfectly well with little sign of morning sickness, yet it was surely early days yet. If only he knew one way or the other? On impulse he made up his mind to speak to Judy. Leo felt a great need to discuss his doubts about this alleged pregnancy, on the grounds that perhaps Judy might be able to advise him on what other signs he should look for which would prove or disprove her condition. Pregnancy was something Judy would obviously understood a good deal better than he, having gone through it herself.

Besides, he really missed her and was desperate to see her lovely face again. He missed her dazzling smile, her pert nose that he loved to kiss, and the soft silkiness of her skin.

Unfortunately when he got to the tall terraced house beyond the Pomona Docks where she'd been staying, he found her gone and the room where they'd made love now let to somebody else. More worrying still, the landlady had no forwarding address, no idea where she'd gone.

He urged himself not to panic. Surely she couldn't be far away. Her need to keep in touch with the children necessitated her remaining in the area.

And then he recalled how Betty Hemley had said that Judy was like a second daughter to her, and Leo knew Judy to be close friends with Betty's daughter Lynda. He headed for the flower stall in case the older woman might have some idea where Judy might be, but was surprised to find that the stall wasn't there.

Leo was upset, hoping Betty hadn't suffered another accident, or was sick. As none of the other stallholders could tell him exactly when Betty and her flower stall would be back he went to her house to ask Lynda for help in finding Judy. She too was also desperately worried about her friend.

Lynda stood on her front doorstep looking really rather unwell, Leo thought, although he made no comment upon it. She'd always appeared to him such an attractive woman, but now her hair was tousled and she appeared pale and fraught, older in some indefinable way. She didn't seem to be in the mood for a chat, being fidgety, almost nervous. Nor did she ask him inside but at least made an effort to console Leo. 'I don't think Judy is missing as such. More likely hiding away, perhaps out of misery and depression over losing her lovely children.'

'And even *I* let her down by telling her that I didn't see how I could possibly get a divorce from Helen. Now I think there might be hope for us after all, although I'm not certain, not yet.'

'Then leave her alone until you are,' Lynda warned in a tired sort of way. 'She's been hurt enough already.'

Leo felt ashamed suddenly for being so selfish as to rush around looking for Judy on the pretext of needing her advice, when really he was simply anxious to see her again, to touch her, to love her. He missed her so badly.

Just before he walked away, resignedly accepting that Lynda was probably right, Leo asked, 'Where's Betty? I looked for the stall but it wasn't there. She's not ill I hope?'

Lynda didn't answer immediately, seeming distressed by the question and again glanced anxiously behind her into the house. 'Mam has been overdoing it a bit recently. I'll talk to you later, right?' and she shut the door in his face.

This was so unusual, the stallholders of Champion Street Market generally being a helpful, friendly bunch, that Leo was puzzled. But he had more personal worries on his mind so moments later he'd forgotten all about Betty Hemley.

Unable to persuade himself to give up, Leo trekked up and down streets, searching Castlefield high and low in the hope that he might spot Judy, perhaps on her way home having found a job in a shop or factory, or simply out and about shopping. He even went to Ruth and Tom's school, watching from a distance in the hope that he might spot them and get the chance to ask where their mother was.

He did indeed see them being collected by an elderly woman but he hesitated about intruding, and then desperation overcame common sense and Leo quickly crossed the street and politely tapped the woman on the shoulder.

'Excuse me, but I'm trying to locate Judy Beckett. I don't suppose you would know where she is, would you?'

The old woman scowled at him. 'Who wants to know? What's Judy got to do with you?'

Tom beamed up at him. 'Hello, Mr Catlow. It's all right, Gran, this is the man who once saved me from some bullies. He's nice.'

'No, he's not,' Ruth sulkily interrupted her brother. 'He's the one who's caused all this trouble between Mum and Dad. He's her fancy man.'

Leo saw then that he'd made a bad mistake. He'd underestimated the anger that even her children, her daughter anyway, might feel against him. And how could he deny that he had indeed created problems for her? Was it any excuse at all that he loved her?

'It wasn't quite like that, Ruth. Sadly your parents' marriage was over long before I appeared on the scene.'

'And then you left her,' Ruth cried, her child-woman eyes rounded in accusation.

'No, it wasn't like that at all. I love her. I couldn't help it, I . . .' But it was too late, impossible to explain to this young girl with her idealistic view of life how he'd tried to do the right thing by everyone and it had all turned out wrong. Nor was he given the opportunity.

By this time the old woman was wielding her umbrella, shouting at him to be off before she called the constabulary; that she hadn't the first idea where her daughter-in-law was living but if she ever saw her again it would be too soon. And Leo could do nothing but apologise for troubling them and step back out of their path to allow them to go on their way.

Perhaps it was this painful encounter with her children, seeing the possible hurt he had done them as well as being unable to find Judy that decided him, but Leo went straight home and rang his wife's GP. He didn't get through immediately but intended to keep trying. He also made up his mind to speak to the fire brigade about what exactly they had found on the day of the kitchen fire. It seemed sensible to gather a few salient facts, which he probably should have done ages ago. Depending on the answers he got to his enquiries, he would then decide what course of action he should take.

Judy was struggling. She'd found herself a two-bedroom flat but the window frames were parting company with the walls, as was the wallpaper in the living room. Mould flourished everywhere and the kitchen was so small it contained only one Bellman cooker, one kitchen dresser painted a sickly green, and a sink. There was no room even for a table let alone a washing machine. Not that she had one of those any more.

Judy was forced to use the communal wash house at the public baths. She took a bath there too, since hot water was rarely available at home. The flat was six floors up from the street, there was no lift, and there was nowhere to dry clothes except by stringing them out of the window and hoping they didn't blow away in a howling gale.

From her window that looked out over the rapidly changing vista of Salford in the throes of modernisation, she could see swathes of bombed-out houses and decrepit air-raid shelters. The city had little land available for new development so had opted for tower blocks, and even then slum areas had to be cleared first. Judy rather thought the tenement block she was living in ought to be next.

In the street directly below, the setts glistening in the rain, she could see the wreck of an abandoned car and a small girl taking her younger sibling for a walk in her pram, clattering along in her mother's high heels. Judy wondered if the child was quite safe to be out there in the street by herself. No one took any notice of her, hurrying by with their faces buried in their coat collars, looking very much like figures from a Lowry painting.

The image made Judy think of her own children and a tear slid down her cheek. Who would look out for them now that she wasn't there to care for them and love them? Sam and his mother, she supposed, which surely wasn't quite the same. She missed them so much it felt as someone had stuck a knife in her heart and left it there.

Oh, and she missed her friends too, and the liveliness of the market. Judy hadn't realised how much she loved Champion Street until she'd left it. She missed the people, the smells and noise of the place, the women rooting through the second-hand clothes stalls looking for cheap cardies, mufflers, kecks and nebbers, the latter being a flat cap for their husband.

And she missed their banter. 'Nay, it's chuckin' it down this morning, I'm fair frozzed. Sell us that brolly, luv. Call that a bargain? Gene Kelly would pay less.'

Not that Judy had any money to go shopping with these days, even for bargains on a market. There was a pawnbroker's on the corner, which was handy. Ticketed suits hung in the window, rolls of carpet stood at the door and inside it smelled of cat pee, stale sweat and lost hope. She'd already pledged her gold watch and wedding ring. What need did she have of such things now?

Did Tom and Ruth blame her for what had happened? Did they believe that she had deserted them? Judy couldn't bear it if that were the case.

Ruth was just about as angry as a ten-year-old child could be. Her brown eyes seemed to have no iris left around the black pupil, as if she hadn't slept in weeks, with twin patches of colour on each cheek. 'I hope Daddy finds a new mummy because you're no good any more. How could you just let us go like that, without even trying? You didn't even *care!*'

These were the sort of accusations the girl constantly threw at her mother following the magistrates' heartbreaking decision. Judy hadn't the first idea how to answer them without criticising Sam, which she didn't feel would be wise, in the circumstances. Apart from the fact it would make him very angry, starting a slanging match via the children was no solution, in Judy's opinion. Yet she couldn't allow her children to feel abandoned or neglected.

'I did my utmost, darling, I promise you. I love you so much but your father is stronger than me. He has the money to fight for you, a business and a lovely home for you to live in, which I don't.' Judy put her arm about her daughter to pull her close in the bus seat but Ruth shook it off. They were on their way to Buile Hill Park yet again, and she'd been hoping for a peaceful afternoon.

'Can't you get more money?' Tom asked, big round eyes filling with tears.

How could she explain how difficult that would be without any skills or training, and far too many years confined to the kitchen sink. Judy tried to sound bright and optimistic. 'Of course I will, lovey, but it will take a little time. I've made a good start by getting myself a job in a snack bar serving sausage sand-wiches,' trying to make it sound fun. Tom was impressed. Sausages were his favourite food.

Ruth was scathing. 'Fat lot of good that will do. Tom keeps crying, and he's getting all his sums wrong. *I* probably won't pass the eleven-plus because I've got too far behind, and it's all *your* fault. Daddy can't even cook, and there are lists everywhere of what we're supposed to do.'

Judy detected a note of panic in her daughter's voice and again put her arm about her and gave her hunched shoulders a little squeeze, relieved to find that this time Ruth didn't shrug it off. 'I'm sure you will pass the exam, darling, because you are clever as well as pretty. Look, this is our stop,' Judy said, ushering them off the bus on to the pavement. 'And the sun is shining so let's not think of unpleasant things today.'

'Oh, no, not the museum again. Can't we go and see "Pillow Talk"? Museums are so *boring*.' Ruth trailed unenthusiastically behind her mother and Tom.

'At least it will be warm,' Judy joked, 'and they serve tea and iced buns.'

Tom, who rather liked iced buns, turned on his sister, his small face quite cross. 'Do stop moaning, Ruth. Mummy's told you she doesn't have any money yet. Anyway, I like museums, Mummy. Do they have dinosaurs?'

47

Lynda

Christmas was rapidly approaching and Lynda was running the flower stall alone, struggling to take her mother's place, which wasn't easy. All the pleasure seemed to have gone out of life and working the stall wasn't fun any more. Not that she had any choice in the matter. Ewan insisted she continue working as it brought in good money, and he was very much in charge these days. It also kept her out of the house of a morning while he did his bit of business.

Since Betty's disappearance her home had become a centre for fenced goods, about which Lynda dare say nothing. There was no question now of revealing the loot to Constable Nuttall, even though boxes filled every bedroom and lined the stairs. She was far too much under Ewan's control. Lynda cleaned the house, cooked his meals, minded her flower stall and kept her head down.

At least having to deal with the stall allowed Lynda a sort of escape for a while and helped to keep her mind off her grief.

This morning she was struggling to make holly wreaths, incorporating ruscus, which had heart-shaped leaves with a prickle on the end. It was a plant that grew wild in Cornwall and was ideal for a Christmas wreath but Lynda didn't possess her mother's skill so she was all fingers and thumbs. Nor did she have Betty's knowledge of flowers to be able to match the right bloom to the right person.

She looked it up in her little book and discovered that holly was for foresight, which Lynda fervently wished she'd had more of when Ewan had moved in; and mistletoe for surmounting difficulties. She'd certainly need to do plenty of that. But when she'd tried to sell Winnie Holmes a potted azalea the other day, on the grounds that it was for temperance, the woman had taken offence, refused to buy it and had not been near the stall since.

Sometimes one of the other stallholders would wander over and ask if there was any news of Betty, or to express their regret over her loss.

'Eeh, I do miss your mam's cheery face, and her lovely sense of humour,' they would say.

Big Molly, for one, was never away, constantly fussing over Lynda and offering her potato pies to keep her strength up. 'Don't give up hope, chuck. She could pop up out of the woodwork one day, who knows? You can't keep a good woman down, not one like our Betty.'

Clara Higginson would remind Lynda on a daily basis, as did many of her other friends and neighbours, that she must pop in any time if she felt like a bit of company. Ewan would never permit Lynda to indulge in tittle-tattle, but she was grateful for the offers and glad to know they were there.

She did her best to smile as the comments were meant only out of kindness but inside Lynda felt frozen and strangely numb. She'd even lost interest in her secret wedding. How could she even consider such a thing with her mother missing, feared dead?

A group of mummers were playing out St George and the Dragon on the market-place cobbles, and Lynda paused in her labours to watch their antics.

She could see Terry through the window of his father's music shop and her heart leaped at sight of him, as it always did. He was laughing and joking as he served a customer with a record, maybe Bobby Darin's 'Mack The Knife', which was in the charts right now, or Adam Faith's 'What Do You Want'? Lynda certainly knew what she wanted. She wanted Terry. She wanted to be happy. She wanted to be normal!

Terry hadn't minded postponing the wedding, so long as it wasn't for too long, although he was even more concerned for her safety. Lynda didn't care about herself any more, she was far too concerned about her mother. Every morning when she opened her eyes, her first thought was to wonder where she was, and what had happened. And each day she half expected a visit from Constable Nuttall to tell her that Betty's body had been found washed up somewhere.

It might almost be a relief if he did. At least they'd know then, one way or the other, and not be constantly worrying and wondering. Hard as that would be to deal with, at least Lynda would then be free to leave and start living her own life with Terry. And Jake could find himself a decent job and go straight.

But until they were absolutely certain that Ewan didn't have Betty locked up somewhere, frightened and alone, doing God knows what to her, they daren't take the risk of standing up to him.

Lynda was haunted by this thought.

She would ask herself ten, twenty, a hundred times a day. If it was right what he'd said, that her mother was still alive and well somewhere, where could he have hidden her?

Night after night she and Terry would search the alley-ways and back streets of Castlefield, hoping for some clue, a sighting, or news of where Betty might be. Terry had made posters and stuck these up all around town. Lynda even persuaded the editor of the *Manchester Guardian* to put a picture of her in the paper with a piece about her mysterious disappearance, hoping against hope for some sort of response. There was none. Clearly no one had seen her mother anywhere.

Ewan read the articles in the press and laughed himself hoarse.

What she couldn't understand was why Ewan would go to all this trouble. Why would he bother to kidnap and lock up his ex-wife? Was it in order to take control of her home, her business and her children?

Jake's theory was that Ewan's activities as a fence was only a small part of his plan, that he had something else up his sleeve, something big, and that he needed their help to carry it out.

'The only way he can force us to be a part of it is to threaten to hurt Mam if we don't go along with his nasty scheme, whatever it is.'

If only they could find her before that.

Jake spent every waking minute running errands for his father, taking messages, fetching and carrying stolen goods, loading and unloading on the docks in the dead of night. Like it or not the poor boy was up to his neck in criminal activity. She herself had turned into a complete drudge, become a shadow of her former confident self and grieved for the warmth of the love she'd once enjoyed with her mother.

On the other hand this could all be a tissue of lies and really he'd drowned her on the same night as he'd done for poor Queenie. Lynda knew that he was perfectly capable of taking advantage of their grief to wield an even greater hold over them.

But the police had dragged as much of the canal basin as seemed feasible, searched many of the surrounding waterways and found no sign of her.

There was one occasion when they came and took Ewan away for questioning but could find no evidence against him. No blood in the house, no body, no evidence at all of any crime being committed, only an empty wheelchair by the canal. In the end they came to the conclusion that Betty Hemley had met with an accident and they'd let him go.

Until they did find Betty, either dead or alive, both brother and sister were entirely at Ewan's beck and call, and there wasn't a damn thing they could do about it.

The noise of the market seemed to wash over her as if she weren't really a part of it, as if she were separated from it by a shield of frosted glass. She could hear the lively banter: 'I'm not asking ten shillings, I'm not even asking five . . .'

'I should think not, mate. I wouldn't give you tuppence for it.' But none of this brought forth a smile. These days Lynda had a permanent sick feeling in the pit of her stomach, and an icy chill running along every nerve ending.

The wicked dragon in the Mummers' play had finally been vanquished and recovered sufficiently to quaff a gill of ale along

with the rest of the lively cast, and everyone was clapping and
cheering having enjoyed the entertainment. All perfectly normal
fun. If only Lynda's own life were normal, if only she was able
to vanquish Ewan from their lives half as easily, then they wouldn't
be in this dreadful mess.

Christmas proved to be even more of a nightmare than she'd
feared. There was no hope of seeing Terry over the holiday and
Lynda certainly wasn't in the mood for a turkey dinner with all
the trimmings although Ewan insisted upon it and she had no
choice but to obey. She sweated for hours cooking the meal all
alone in the kitchen, aching for her mam to be there beside her
joking and laughing and exchanging gifts, as they'd used to in
the old days. At least Jake ate every scrap even if the lad did look
hollow-eyed, and conversation between the three of them was at
an all-time low.

Feeling brave after a glass or two of port and lemon, Lynda
demanded to know who was providing her mother with food on
this special day of the year, if she really was locked up somewhere.

'Where is she? Where's Mam? What have you done with her?'
Tears filled her eyes but yet she persisted. 'Did you really kidnap
her and lock her up in some dirty hole by the docks? It's a rabbit
warren down there. You know we'd never find her without help.
Tell me the truth, you cruel bastard, I want to know!'

But her courage earned Lynda no answers, only another
beating. Ewan knocked her off her chair with the flat of his hand,
and when she lay crying on the floor, kicked her in the back and
stomach till she stifled her tears and finally shut up.

Jake sat like a stone throughout, seemingly dazed by events,
unable to bring himself to react or even defend his sister.

Then Ewan dragged Lynda upstairs and locked her in her
room. He'd bought a padlock for the purpose and whenever he
considered she was getting out of hand, or irritated him with her
constant litany of questions, Ewan would lock her up, sometimes
for hours, not letting her out until it was time for her to go back
to work.

Even so, Lynda continued to take the precaution of blocking the door from her own side as well, using the chest of drawers as a barrier since Ewan kept the key.

The reality was that she'd become a prisoner in her own home, allowed out only to run the flower stall, under strict orders to behave as normally as possible in public. And Lynda was far too afraid to do anything but obey. She couldn't tell anyone about what was going on behind closed doors because somewhere her mother too could well be a prisoner, and Betty's safety, her very life depended upon her son and daughter doing exactly as Ewan said.

From time to time in the week before Christmas and the days after, Constable Nuttall would call at the house to tell Lynda how their search was progressing. She always looked startled when she saw him, half expecting bad news. Finally he came to warn her that she must accept the fact Betty was dead and gone, just like poor old Queenie.

'I'm sorry to say that it's highly unlikely your mam will be coming back, Lynda love. She's a goner for sure. The poor lady must have slipped in the canal when she was out doing her morning exercise. I told her to take care on them slippy wet cobbles, but when did she ever listen to advice?'

This annoyed Lynda so much that for once she came out of her shell of misery and shouted at the policeman. 'She wouldn't have got into this mess in the first place if *you'd* ever listened to what *she* had to say. Where were you when my so-called father was moving in and making himself at home and Mam wanted rid?'

Constable Nuttall looked stricken by guilt, as well he might. 'It's not easy getting involved in a domestic, or in a situation concerning divorce.'

'Utter rubbish! You abandoned her, abandoned us all. Nobody had ever given a monkey's, not the police, not the social, not even the flaming doctor. They've none of them ever lifted so much as a finger to help her, not in all of her life. They just turn a blind eye, talk a load of nonsense about their hands being tied, about it being a private matter between husband and wife, as if a woman has no rights to safety, even in her own home. Sometimes I think Mam was absolutely right in her opinion of men. When have they ever treated women well? Bullies and cads the lot of them.'

'Nay, Lynda love, that's not true. There are some good apples in the barrel. We're not all bad.'

'Oh? And what did you do to help when Ewan put her in hospital with a broken leg?'

'Ewan did what? I thought Betty fell downstairs?'

And as Lynda froze, realising her temper had taken her too far, a voice at her elbow said, 'She did fall. You must forgive my daughter, constable, but she's got herself into a right state over losing her mam, she's distraught, you know? Gone a bit loopy. It's understandable, of course, but her imagination is running riot and she really shouldn't say things which aren't true.'

'Aye,' said Constable Nuttall, his tone thoughtful as he watched Ewan Hemley draw the girl back into the house and start to close the door. 'I can see she's a bit upset, and has every reason to be. I'll keep popping in, Lynda love, just to see how you are.'

But by this time he was speaking to a closed door.

Lynda's careless mistake earned her another beating and she spent all the next day locked in her room, even though it meant losing valuable trade on the market. Ewan was always circumspect as he dealt out the blows, making sure there were no bruises on her face but Lynda ached in every limb, vomiting into her wash bowl from the pains in her belly.

She cried for a long time after the policeman had gone, so filled with misery she couldn't sleep, couldn't eat, couldn't concentrate on anything. She yearned for someone to help her, for Terry to come and rescue her and be her St George.

This was all her fault, Lynda told herself over and over. She'd brought about this terrible situation by being so desperate for a father that she'd insisted on inviting Ewan in for that fateful Sunday lunch. If only she'd listened to her mother.

Now Betty was gone and Lynda had no one. Even Terry didn't seem able to help but then he didn't know the half of what was going on. She'd told him very little and he knew only that her mother was missing, probably as a result of an accident. But in the depth of her despair, and somewhat unrealistically, Lynda felt that if he truly loved her he ought to be doing more. She longed for Terry to beat up Ewan and force him to divulge the information about what he'd done to Betty.

Why didn't somebody guess what was going on and offer to help? Why didn't her daffy brother do something? Why did Constable Nuttall never believe a word she said to him?

That was men for you, as her mother would so often say, always choosing the easy path. Bullies and cowards the lot of them.

Lynda began to sob all over again, knowing deep in her heart that she was being unfair, particularly to Terry, but she had to blame someone for this dreadful predicament. It was all very well for people to say she could call on them if she ever needed help, but she needed it now, and where were they?

48

Leo

It was January, snow was thick on the ground and Leo was on his way to see his mother, as usual. A bouquet of carnations lay on the passenger seat beside him which he'd bought from Lynda's stall, Betty still not having reappeared. He couldn't find Judy either. It was the start of a new decade yet nothing had changed.

He and Helen were barely even talking and she appeared as slender and elegant as ever with no sign of a thickening waist-line despite continuing to maintain that she was pregnant. Leo was feeling deeply frustrated and depressed. His life was a mess and he couldn't find a way to put it right.

He suddenly realised that the traffic lights ahead were against him and he slammed on the brakes, the car going into a sickening skid before sliding to a halt.

A woman who'd been about to cross the road cast him a fierce glare and a man shook a fist at him.

My God, he'd nearly caused an accident, could have killed someone. What was he thinking of? Not concentrating on his driving, that was the problem. Leo came to a sudden decision. The roads were unsafe and he was unfit to drive. He'd give the visit a miss today.

He stopped off at a call box and rang the home, so that his mother wouldn't be anxious. She was perfectly understanding, given the state of the roads.

Leo wasn't sorry about the change of plan. Every time he called to see her these days, Dulcie would be sure to ask if he'd challenged Helen on the subject of her alleged pregnancy, not to mention the fire that had driven his mother into the home in the first place. Time after time he'd promised to try ringing the doctor again because surely Dulcie deserved an answer, as did he. But somehow he'd never got round to it. There seemed little point without Judy in his life any more, although he suspected that a part of him had no wish to face the truth, and the tantrums and acrimony that would surely follow if his wife really was lying.

He had at least made some enquiries of the fire brigade regarding the kitchen fire. The results had been interesting if inconclusive. Only Helen knew the absolute truth, at least her version of it, but Leo's patience was wearing thin.

He was tired of being manipulated, of doing anything for a quiet life by avoiding confrontation. And Helen's own efforts at reconciliation, of behaving like a loving and caring wife were beginning to show signs of strain. Being thrown together over Christmas had revealed the cracks in their relationship for what they were and Leo was once more the subject of a constant litany of complaints over his supposed life-long passion for infidelity.

'Wasn't I right all along? How could you do this to me?' Helen would say twenty times a day. 'How could you be so cruel? How do I know you aren't still seeing that Beckett woman while I'm carrying your child?' And even, 'Haven't I always trusted you?' which they both knew to be absolute nonsense.

Even the way Helen preyed upon his kindness, using him as some sort of slave to fetch and carry cushions and drinks for her, making him pander to her sudden fancies for bunches of grapes or smoked salmon – these cravings generally being of the expensive variety – were beginning to grate upon him, and he missed Judy so badly. He loved her, he needed her. God knows where she was living, or what she was enduring but they surely both deserved the right to find happiness together?

While he was standing in the call box in the snow, Leo came to a sudden decision and, on impulse, rang the family doctor

there and then. After he'd spoken to Doc Mitchell, he put down
the phone, turned the car around and drove straight back home.

Judy was working at a little snack bar for ten solid hours a day,
from eight in the morning till six at night. It was her job to make
and serve bacon sandwiches, fried egg and chips, sausages,
Holland's meat and potato pies and endless cups of sweet tea to
women in headscarves and men who sat silently reading the *Daily
Dispatch*. It wasn't the kind of trendy coffee bar that the young
favoured with frothy coffee served in glass cups, and Elvis Presley
records belting out at top volume from a Juke Box. It was simply
a place where Lancashire folk went for 'summat warm to fill me
belly'.

Strangely enough, Judy found she quite enjoyed the work
because the people who frequented it always seemed to appreciate what she cooked for them.

'Eeh, that's gradely, love,' a chap would say as she set bacon
and eggs before him.

And then at the end of her shift she would return home through
graffiti-decorated stairwells that reeked of urine and boiled
cabbage, rushing up the stairs and locking herself quickly into
her miserable, lonely little one-bedroom flat, where she would
see no one until she went back to the snack bar the next morning
at eight.

Not that any of this mattered one jot. Judy could have endured
anything so long as she had Tom and Ruth with her. But where
was the point even in living if she couldn't be with her children?

Sometimes Sam would be generous and allow her to have
them for an afternoon, although never a whole day, or even every
week. And she always had to tell him in advance exactly where
she was taking them, aware that at some point during the afternoon he would check up on her, to make sure they were exactly
where she said they'd be.

They would be happily playing snowballs in Buile Hill Park,
or huddled in the museum, yet again, because it was winter and
too cold to sit outside listening to the band or to eat a picnic by

the river. Nor could she afford to take them anywhere really exciting like Belle Vue, or the pictures.

And then Judy would suddenly become aware of his presence lurking in the shadows. She was always careful not to react, or to let Sam know that she saw him, too afraid that if she annoyed him he might march over and snatch the children away from her, or not let her have them again.

Judy had discovered that she must obey her husband's strict rules far more now that she was separated from him, than she ever had when she was living with him as his wife.

It might have been different if she and Leo had got together, as they'd once hoped, but she should have realised that was nothing more than a pipe-dream. In truth it would have been far better if she'd never met Leo Catlow, never had coffee with him, never taken him into her bed.

Now she had lost everything, and had nothing left to fight Sam with.

Leo was filled with renewed energy. Fortified by what he had learned from the doctor, he was determined to get some proper answers this time. He strode into the house, opening and closing doors, calling out Helen's name as he went from room to room, searching. Even before he heard the rustles and thumps from the direction of their bedroom, some instinct warned him what he would find. And he was right.

His wife was in bed with David Barford.

'Ah,' Barford said, clearly endeavouring to sound calm despite the crimson flush stealing over his cheekbones. 'Cats out of bags are the words which spring to mind.'

'Leo, this is not how it looks,' Helen whimpered, rather unrealistically, he thought.

He felt a surge of such hatred for her, such rage he could barely speak for a moment. All these years she'd accused him of having a mistress, had screamed at him, hectored and lectured him, searched his pockets for evidence, finding none; interrogating and berating him if he so much as spoke to another woman. And all the time she was the one guilty of infidelity, not he.

'You surely aren't trying to suggest that he took you by force? Don't be ridiculous, Helen. Look at the pair of you . . . stark naked and suffused in guilt. Besides, it would only be yet another of your lies.'

'I think I'd better leave.' Barford slipped quickly from the bed and Leo tossed him his carefully folded shirt, crumpling it in his clenched fists as he did so.

'I won't give you the satisfaction of popping you one, tempting as it might be. As far as I'm concerned you're welcome to her. She's all yours, mate. You can have both my wife and the child.'

Barford went quite pale, pausing in his battle with his underpants, one leg suspended in mid-air. 'Child, what child?'

Helen struggled to her knees on the bed, dragging the sheet with her. 'Leo, this isn't the time or the place. We'll discuss this delicate matter later, in private.'

'No, Helen, we'll discuss it *now*.' Leo stood in the doorway, arms folded, legs astride, face set grim with determination, blocking Barford's exit which the man was clearly anxious to make. 'Haven't you informed your lover that you're pregnant? Or did you decide not to confuse the issue by mentioning it, since I wasn't supposed to realise that I might not be the father? I do wonder if you are in fact pregnant at all, since you look remarkably slim and supple for a mother-to-be. Or could that possibly be a lie too, like the time you blamed my mother for starting that kitchen fire? Fortunately she is happy in the home you banished her too but . . .'

'. . . there you are then, I was right to . . .' Helen began.

Leo kept on talking. '. . . Dulcie is adamant she turned off the oven and never even used any of the top gas jets as she was only baking scones, so how come a tea towel caught fire unless someone did it deliberately? The fire brigade confirm that the seat of the fire was on top of the cooker, so what do you have to say about that?'

To his utter astonishment Helen burst out laughing. 'Fair cop, m'lud. Caught red-handed all round. But what does it matter, I always get my way one way or the other, so why bother arguing? As you said yourself, Leo, Dulcie is perfectly happy in that place and if I did use that silly little fire to help her see sense, wasn't it worth it to be on our own again? Plus, I even got a new kitchen out of the deal, paid for by the insurance company, so where's the problem?'

Leo stared at his wife in total disbelief and was forced to draw a deep steadying breath before he could continue. 'Aside from the fact that you could have burned the house down, as well as leaving an old woman not only homeless but accused of something she didn't even do, our problem now lies in the fact that I can no longer trust you.'

As if to give credence to his words, Leo swivelled his gaze back to Barford, who seemed to be standing frozen in his shirt and underpants, taking all of this in and clearly wishing he were somewhere else so that he wouldn't have to. Leo ignored him and returned his ice-cold gaze to his wife.

'I'll give you ten minutes to pack your things and leave.'

'Leave?' Her beautiful cool grey eyes sparkled up at him in merry laughter, as if he'd made some sort of humorous remark. 'I'm not going anywhere. Why would I?'

'Perhaps because this morning, puzzled by a pregnancy which apparently requires no medical checks whatsoever, presents no difficulties over what you can eat, no morning sickness, no problems of any kind so far as I can see, I finally rang the doctor. I must say Doc Mitchell was surprised to hear that you were pregnant, Helen, although happy for you naturally. It was, apparently, the first he'd heard of it.'

Leo sensed, rather than heard, Barford's sigh of relief but still chose to ignore the man. He knew now that Barford wasn't her only lover, and merely a pawn in whatever little game she was playing. 'If this pregnancy is indeed genuine, how come you haven't even seen a doctor, particularly considering your life-long fear of the condition.'

On this occasion Helen remained silent, merely pouting sulkily at him.

Leo gave a half-smile, though it did not reach his eyes. 'What I suggest is that you get on with your packing rather quickly, so that your lover here can help to carry your cases out to your car.'

For the first time he saw panic in her eyes. 'You can't be serious?'

'Never more so.'

Barford said, 'I say, old boy, that's cutting it a bit rich. Where could she go at this time on a Saturday afternoon?'

'Do you know something, I really don't care. I'm sure you can find her a good hotel, or perhaps your wife could lend her a bed for the night? Actually, I'll pack for her, shall I? Much quicker and easier all round. I'm sure she doesn't need much, and the rest of her considerable wardrobe can be sent on later, or perhaps given to a suitable charity.' Striding over to his wife's wardrobe Leo began to toss dresses, skirts and blouses out on to the bed. Naked, as she was, Helen flew at him.

'Stop that, Leo, stop it at once, do you hear? You're acting like a mad-man. I absolutely refuse to be bullied out of my own home.'

'Indeed? But that is exactly what you did to my mother. You bullied her constantly, over which fork to use, where she could sit to read the paper, whether she could put a picture on the wall, if she should be allowed to stay in what used to be her own house. And no, I haven't gone mad. I'm simply acting like an irate husband who's reached the end of his tether.'

'How dare you accuse me of such horrible things? How *dare* you!'

While Helen flew about the room desperately picking up discarded underwear and clothes and struggling into them, Leo pulled a suitcase down from the top of the wardrobe and began tossing in her Dior suits and Yves St Laurent dresses as if they were old rags. Barford, he noticed, had taken advantage of the fact Leo had left his station by the door, and had beaten a hasty retreat. He couldn't really blame the man for that, even it was rather ungallant of him to leave Helen without either assistance or sympathy. But then she didn't deserve any.

Having found her bra and panties and pulled on a skirt and blouse, Helen came at him again, flailing, punching, screaming and kicking his shins with her bare feet. Leo grasped her by the wrists and flung her back on to the bed.

'Don't tempt me to retaliate. Just tell me the truth for once – *are you pregnant?* Are you carrying my child?'

'*No, I'm not!*' Her screaming response left him in no further doubt that his mother, old and confused at times though she may be, had been absolutely correct. Leo picked up the suitcase he had packed, snapped it shut and, walking to the front door, tossed it out on to the pavement. Then he snatched up a pair of shoes and coat, grabbed his wife's arm and thrust her into the street after it so that she fell in a crumpled heap in the snow.

'Go and live with one of your lovers. I'm sure you have plenty to choose from. Oh, and I recommend you find yourself a good lawyer.'

Her screaming response was drowned by the slamming of the door. Leo leaned back against it feeling cleansed, as if he'd been liberated. But although he'd rid himself of a lying, cheating wife, he was no nearer to finding the woman he loved.

49

Jake and Lynda

Jake was doing his best to help, albeit in his own ineffectual way. He'd searched every alleyway and outbuilding for his mother, including Betty's lock-up where she stored the flowers, and even Barry Holmes's shed on the allotments, though why she would be there he didn't stop to think. But then Jake was not strong on thinking.

It upset him that he couldn't find her, but hoped that if he kept on good terms with Ewan, his father might start trusting him a bit more, might even let slip some vital piece of information which would lead him to her, even after all this time. Not that he was certain he would recognise such a clue, even if one were dropped, but he lived in hope.

She'd been missing for a couple of weeks now, since just before Christmas. Could she still be alive in these sort of temperatures? And if so, what game was his father playing, and why was it taking so long?

The trouble was that Ewan rarely let him out of his sight, save for those occasions when he himself demanded privacy and would send Jake off on some manufactured errand. Yet despite the difficulties, and his own feeling of inadequacy, Jake did manage to keep a close eye on Ewan's activities, sometimes secretly following him for days on end, trying to work out what his plans were.

His father had spent half the morning at Potato Wharf, though Jake hadn't been able to ascertain exactly what he was doing there beyond talking to a group of shady-looking characters. After that he'd gone on to the Dog and Duck for a bite of dinner and to haggle with his mates over where to place his bets for the afternoon races at the dog track.

Jake joined them there, as instructed, and was made welcome enough, but he was careful to say little himself in the hope the men might forget he was present and mention something useful. They never had before but he still lived in hope.

Their conversation was largely concerned with how much they'd won or lost from the bookie, and who was working on which boats down at the docks and Jake soon grew bored.

He found himself lamenting his own loss of freedom to cruise around the neighbourhood in his flash car with his mates, which was now a thing of the past. Nor was he in the mood these days for teasing Lynda with his favourite slang, and he couldn't even go dancing or dating chicks. He'd no money, for a start.

Jake had been forced to give up working at Smithfield. It was either that or start stealing from his employer and he'd absolutely refused to go that far. It was bad enough having to ask his mates to procure items for his father to fence. Ewan had bought an old van and it was scarily nerve-wracking driving the stuff around. He lived in fear that Constable Nuttall might stop him at any time and ask to look inside. But he'd certainly no intention of getting involved in any stealing himself. His terror of getting caught was even greater than his fear of Ewan and so, for once, Jake had stood up to his father's demands.

'No, I'll not do it. You can't make me,' he'd yelled out in sheer panic when Ewan had outlined what he expected from his son. 'I'd be the first they'd suspect if stuff went missing. Anyroad, it's mainly flowers and fruit and veg that I deliver, so where's the profit in nicking that sort of stuff?'

He'd regretted this remark almost the moment it was out of his mouth because Ewan had nodded in thoughtful agreement. 'You're right, son. Why waste time and talent on trivial rubbish, we've enough of that already. Far better to concentrate on summat worthwhile, summat big. Don't worry, I'm on the look out. I'll find something. I can concentrate now I don't have that bloody wife of mine nagging me the whole bleeding time.'

Jake experienced a surge of protective anger on behalf of his mother. He felt certain this was all his fault. If he hadn't wanted his dad back in the first place, if he hadn't been so awful to his mam, or if he hadn't planted the idea in his father's head that he should be looking for bigger fish to fry, happen they might not be in this mess and she'd be sitting on her flower stall like always, chatting to her customers.

'I'm not doing owt more for you unless you let Mam come home.'

It had been a brave remark, perhaps even foolhardy, and Jake's heart had hammered in his chest while he'd said it, but his father had put back his head and laughed as if he'd said something funny.

'I don't think you're in any position to bargain, son. But don't worry, you'll get your share, so long as you do as you're told. Then, who knows, you might be lucky and see your mam again. She might rise like Frankenstein from the deep.'

Fussy and irritating though Betty might be at times Jake really couldn't let that pass. The thought of his mam's possible suffering in some dank cellar gave him the courage to press his case, to forcibly point out that she'd want him to keep his nose clean and stay on the straight and narrow.

'She'd leather me if I did owt wrong. I'm not getting involved in owt illegal. I've an aversion to confined cramped spaces, and I've no wish to spend time in a prison cell, ta very much, so count me out.'

Ewan had stopped laughing by this time and his expression was grim. 'You'll get involved if I say you will, make no mistake about it, so shut your gob or I'll shut it for ya.' He'd accompanied this warning with a punch that knocked out one of Jake's front teeth.

Jake still shivered at the memory of that moment, had sleepless nights over it. Now the sound of raised voices muttering something about Irish narrow boats brought him back to the painful reality that despite his protests events seemed to be escalating like a steam train out of his control. His mam was still missing and he was in the Dog and Duck with his father and a bunch of dodgy blokes planning some big robbery that he'd no wish to be a part of.

Ewan was clapping him on the back, saying something about him being a chip off the old block. 'Or at least you could be if you had a bit more intelligence.'

The other men chuckled, snorting into their pints of Guinness. 'But everyone has their uses and a good fast driver is always useful in these sort of operations.'

'What sort of operation?' Jake asked, hoping Ewan would tap his nose in that sneaky way of his, and tell him that the least he knew the better.

Not this time. On this occasion he told Jake everything and the lad felt sick to his stomach by the time he'd heard it all, sincerely regretting ever having asked the question. Ignorance, and being considered a bit of a dim-wit, Jake decided, was far safer. Because now he was in possession of all the facts, he was going to have to do something about it.

The docks were a hive of activity as always when Jake made his way across the yard, negotiating stacks of timber, iron girders and agricultural machinery in the process of transit. The offices of Catlow and Son were small and surprisingly untidy, situated in a corner of one of the warehouses. Jake kept on glancing nervously over his shoulder, half expecting Ewan to emerge from behind a stack of crates. It'd taken every ounce of courage to escape his father's eagle eye and make it this far. He only hoped he didn't live to regret it.

Jake tapped on the somewhat dilapidated door and walked straight in. A blonde, no doubt a secretary, was typing furiously on a battered Imperial typewriter, the desk piled high with paperwork, with files and dockets, and bills of lading. Another girl in a red checked dress was putting even more paper into an overstuffed filing cabinet while chatting to a young male clerk who was presumably engaged in book-keeping.

It was clearly an operation that devoted most of its time and money on turning the goods around, on loading and unloading, importing and exporting, and wasting few resources on dealing with the massive mounds of paperwork all of that work created. Jake wondered if they were equally careless over security matters.

'Can I help you?' The sound of the clattering keyboard momentarily ceased as the secretary sat, well-manicured hands poised over the keys, finely trimmed eyebrows raised, while she regarded Jake with a piercing gaze over a pair of half-moon spectacles. Her expression clearly stated that she certainly wasn't going to waste any of her precious time on Teddy-Boy types like him so he'd best say what he had to say quickly, and get out.

'Um, I wondered if t'boss were in.'

'By whom you mean Mr Catlow?'

'Aye . . . er, yes, I do.'

'If you're seeking employment he isn't taking anyone on at the moment.'

'No, I weren't. I mean, I'm not. I just need to talk to him about summat.'

'I'm afraid he's in a meeting and cannot be disturbed. May I be of any assistance?'

'Hecky thump, no, it's private.'

'Then you will have to come back later. Let me see . . .' The woman glanced briefly at a diary on the desk beside her typewriter, running a pointed pink fingernail down the page. 'I could make you an appointment for Tuesday week.'

Jake was thrown off balance by this. He'd practised most carefully what he wanted to say, choosing his words with meticulous care. He certainly had no intention of giving the impression that he personally was about to commit a criminal offence. Jake had also made up his mind that Ewan's name could not be mentioned at this juncture, but must remain anonymous since you didn't grass on Ewan Hemley in a hurry. He simply wanted to put Catlow on his guard without getting himself into any bother. Now he looked at the woman in dismay.

'But it's important. I have to see him today.'

'Important to *you* perhaps, but Mr Catlow deals with far more important matters than you could ever imagine each and every day of the week. How could a person of your sort ever hope to understand what a very busy man he is?'

She gave a disapproving sniff and returned to her typing. 'I'm sorry, but if you aren't prepared to give me any clue as to what this matter is about, that's the best I can do.'

Jake glanced frantically about him, spotted a door set in the back wall from which he could detect the murmur of voices and wondered if he should burst it open and charge in. He saw himself as the hero of the hour, surprising Leo Catlow at his meeting by making a bold dramatic announcement that his warehouses were about to be raided in the early hours of Friday morning, and then storming out again before they could catch him and ask how he knew this fact. Or any other awkward questions, any who, why or wherefore. But he could see the young clerk watching him out of narrowed eyes and knew he wouldn't get further than one step from this desk.

Or he could try explaining it all to this woman who was his secretary and just hope she didn't call the police.

'Well?' she said, watching him closely as if trying to read his thought processes. 'What is it to be? I haven't all day.'

Jake looked at her smiling coolly up at him with lipstick on her teeth. 'Stuff it then,' he said, and walked out.

Jake left Potato Wharf and was passing by the Mission Hall along by the canal basin when who should step out in front of him but Ewan Hemley. The sight of his leering smile sent a chill running down Jake's spine.

'Hello, son, and where might you have been on this bright winter's afternoon? Don't look to me like you're engaged in your usual deliveries.'

'I've just made one,' Jake recklessly agreed, impulsively snatching at this possible excuse.

'Indeed, and where to, might I ask? Not Catlow's warehouse by any chance? And while you were there making this mythical delivery without even the help of a hand-cart, did you happen to suggest that he might do well to check out the locks on his gates, or get an alarm system fitted?'

Jake had gone white to the lips, his mouth ash-dry and were he capable of thinking of a suitable reply he couldn't possibly have uttered a single word.

Ewan grabbed him by the throat and shoved him so hard his knees buckled. He tripped over an iron bollard and fell. The next instant Jake was lying on the hard ground with his head and shoulders hanging over the edge of the canal bank, mere inches from the black swirling water beneath, and Ewan still hadn't let go of his throat. ''Cos if you had done owt stupid like that, you know I'd be pretty pissed off about it. I might even do summat really nasty that you'd come to regret. Know what I mean?'

Jake wasn't in a position to nod his agreement. He merely blinked, like a frightened owl.

'And let's not forget your poor mam. Betty is depending on you to keep your end up, so to speak, so's this can all end happily and she can come back to her own hearth and home. Your sister too needs you to hold your nerve. We don't want owt to happen to our lovely Lynda, now do we?'

Jake attempted to shake his head but Ewan's thumb was pressing so hard under his left ear that it started to buzz very loudly. He was quite certain that if he moved an inch he'd slip backwards into the oily depths. And he couldn't even swim.

'All you have to do is follow instructions and drive the van. Right? I reckon we should allow your lovely sister to join our little game. We need her assistance too.' He told the boy what was expected of Lynda and Jake's eyes were nearly popping out of his head by the time he was done.

'You can explain it all to her tonight. And make sure she understands how very important it is for her to follow my instructions to the letter. I don't want any bloody stupid rebellions on this job, or you know what will happen.'

50

Judy

Judy sat huddled by a single bar of the electric fire, somehow unable to shake off the cold that seeped right into her bones. She had it on all the time these days although heaven knows what her electricity bill would be. Sometimes she even slept in here, since there was no heating at all in the damp bedrooms, and not even a power point. It was so cold there was ice on the inside of the windows.

What was happening to her? Why was her life such a misery? Christmas had been a nightmare without the children, Sam insisting she wait until Boxing Day before being allowed even to give them their presents. Not that she could afford much: the *Eagle* Annual for Tom, and *School Friend* Annual for Ruth, plus a box of Bassett's Liquorice All Sorts each.

After the holidays when she'd rung from a local call box to make arrangements for her next visit, Sam had told her that they were staying with his mother until it was time for them to go back to school, and she couldn't see them.

Judy had protested, saying she was their mother and they should be with her, that she surely had a right to see them, but he'd hung up on her leaving her weeping down the phone at the dialling tone.

The visit with the children today, to which she'd looked forward with such eagerness for nearly two whole lonely weeks, had been a complete failure. Ruth had sulked for the entire time and despite Tom's efforts to be brave the small boy had sobbed his heart out when it was time for her to leave.

'I shall see you next Sunday,' she'd assured him, trying to offer comfort. 'That's only a few days to wait.'

'It's a whole *week*! And what if it's longer, like last time? You might forget all about us.'

'Of course I won't forget you . . .'

At which point Sam had intervened, his face utterly devoid of emotion, completely dispassionate and oblivious to her pain. 'It all depends whether you're a good boy, Tom. If you can manage to keep your bedroom tidy and do your homework then perhaps I might allow you to see your mother.'

Judy felt hot rage boil up inside her. Was he using her as some sort of reward for good behaviour? What was it that made Sam behave so cruelly towards her, and to his own children? It seemed to be his only source of pleasure these days. But she refused to give him the satisfaction of rising to his bait.

'I shall come for you next Sunday as usual,' Judy firmly announced to her son's retreating back but as she tried to kiss Ruth goodbye, the young girl brushed her aside and fled indoors, clearly on the brink of tears.

They seemed so unhappy, so desolate, and yet she was power-less to put things right.

Driven by despair, Judy took the decision that if she were careful, she could manage to avoid bumping into Leo Catlow, and hurried straight round to Lynda's house. She felt desperate to see a friendly face, for a heart-to-heart chat with her closest friend. To her surprise it was Jake who answered the door, opening it only wide enough to stick his head around.

'If you're wanting our Lynda she can't come to the door right now, she's busy. Sorry!' And before Judy could ask the reason the door was closed again and his pale face had vanished.

Judy walked home in complete misery, facing yet another week alone, relieved only by hours at the snack bar.

Late one afternoon on her way home from work Judy called in at Hackett's shop, as she often did, for a few groceries. It was the kind of cheap corner shop which sold everything from mouse-traps, which she was constantly in need of, to soap and dolly blue to soak her wash, and Bournvita, bread and potatoes which formed the major part of her diet, along with such everyday necessities as firewood, hammers and nails, Coleman's starch, and donkey stone.

Children would stand at the counter for hours deliberating between aniseed balls, gob-stoppers or sherbert lemons, and Mrs Hackett never hurried them.

Mrs Hackett was a comfortable, motherly sort who'd taken Judy rather under her wing. 'Are you still working in that greasy spoon?' she would ask her at least once a week, and Judy would admit that she was and then Mrs Hackett would tell her she deserved something better.

'You should have a job in a library,' she would say, as if that were the ultimate aspirational place of employment. 'Since you love reading so much.'

Mrs Hackett ran one of the last remaining penny libraries from a range of bookshelves set behind the shop door, which Judy plundered on a regular basis. With no television or radio in her flat, books were her main source of entertainment, particularly now that she no longer had the heart to paint.

Every spare shilling she had left at the end of the week, and there weren't many of those, Judy saved for the day when she would get her children back, and for finding a place to live which would impress the magistrates. Apart from Ruth's old box of water colours Judy didn't even possess any materials. But she did miss creating pictures.

One quiet morning in the snack-bar she'd sketched an old man quietly reading his paper, using a bit of pencil on the back of a paper bag. The result hadn't satisfied her and she'd thrown it away, but the feel of a pencil between her fingers again had lifted her spirits for a moment.

Now, as she approached the little shop her eyes alighted on a sketch-pad in the window. It had obviously been there for some time as there was dust all over it, and a few dead flies, even now in the depths of winter.

Why hadn't she noticed it before? She stood staring at the

sketch-pad for a long time, shoulders hunched against a bitter cold wind. It was large and thick, and paper was expensive. Could she afford to waste money on such an indulgence? Judy still hadn't made up her mind when she opened the door and went inside.

The little bell over the shop door jangled and she braced herself for the usual motherly lecture. But Mrs Hackett, savvy when it came to her customers, asked her quite a different question. 'So what caught your eye in me winder? What have you set yer heart on, love?'

'Oh, nothing. I probably couldn't afford it anyway.'

'Well, unless you tell me what it is, we'll never find out, will we?'

Unable to prevent herself, Judy's eyes swivelled back to the window display and soon the sketch-pad had been brought out, dusted off and laid before her on the counter. It was even larger close to, and of good quality paper, strong enough for water colours and a surprising find in this tiny shop. But then it was that kind of place.

'How much is it?'

'How much have you got?' Mrs Hackett asked right back. 'Look, I'll come clean with you, love. This isn't generally the sort of stuff I'd stock but I got it for a gentleman customer specially like, only he never returned for it. So there I was, lumbered. Make me an offer, I'll not say no.'

Minutes later Judy was outside the shop hugging the precious sketch-pad to her breast. Oh, she hadn't felt this happy in months!

Judy began to draw. She would sit at her window high above the street and draw whatever she saw in the city beyond: the new blocks of flats, the old mill chimneys, parked cars, church towers, the washing strung from windows, a medley of angles and lines on the majestic giant cranes working on the many new building sites.

As the weather improved she would venture out on to the streets, brown paper carrier bag in hand to carry her pad and pencils and Judy would sit on a wall somewhere and sketch the people as they hurried home; a child crying or playing with a hoola-hoop; old men leaning on lamp-posts smoking their cigarettes; mothers nursing their babies as they sat on stools at their front doors, or enjoyed a bit of a craic with their neighbours.

They would watch with open curiosity as she got out her sketch-pad, swiftly capturing the outline of the scene with a few deft strokes. She treated herself to a softer pencil, made a tightly rolled bit of newspaper to use as a stub to blur the shadows she created. Judy had never done this sort of work before, always concentrating on flowers and animals bursting with colour. But there wasn't much evidence of any of that in this industrial scene, so she drew what she saw.

If only she had some oils.

'Who do you think you are, love, Lowry?' they would ask.

'Got an eyeful? Do you want a photo an' all?'

At first Judy would blush and hurry away, embarrassed by their rude remarks, but then as she became more engrossed in the work, she decided to brazen it out. She couldn't afford to waste the paper with half-finished sketches.

After a while they got used to seeing her around and would wander over to see what it was exactly she was drawing. Friends and neighbours would follow and in this way Judy began to collect an audience, sometimes appreciative, at other times astutely critical.

'You've not got his hat quite right, love. It cocks over his eyes a bit more.'

'I like the way you've made the ship look as if it's disappearing in the fog, but that tug in the front needs a bit of smoke coming from its funnel and bring the prow up a bit. Aye, that's better. You're getting it, lass.'

And then one day she brought out Ruth's paint box and added a touch of colour. Her admirers were captivated. 'By heck, you even make me old bicycle look grand, though I would never have thought to paint it pink. Where'd you learn to paint like that? Will you do our Doreen? She's a right bonny lass. I can't pay you owt, though I'd keep you going with bacon butties and cups of tea.'

Judy gratefully accepted the offer. Mostly she'd given her sketches away, to children, to old people, but slowly she began to realise that she might have something worth selling.

Judy preferred to stay well away from Champion Street in case she should chance upon Leo Catlow. Generally Sam would bring the children to her at some pre-arranged spot, and collect them again a few hours later. She always felt bereft after they were gone, every parting a painful one with Tom trying so hard to be brave and Ruth pretending not to care. Afterwards she would usually walk, sometimes for hours, determined to tire herself so that she would sleep.

One Sunday while on one of these lengthy perambulations around the streets of Salford, Judy chanced upon a small art shop which seemed to have only recently opened. She certainly didn't recall having seen it before. It was just off Liverpool Street close to Langworthy Park and she stood before it, entranced.

Its window was full of paintings and sketches by local artists. Studying them, Judy considered that her own efforts compared reasonably favourably with many of the pictures on display. She'd have said better than most were she not so modest and insecure about her work.

The shop was closed, it being a Sunday but the next day Judy found herself sneaking off early from the snack bar and hurrying back to the little shop, anxious to get there before it closed. She took with her a brown paper carrier bag which held a selection of her sketches and water colours.

A young woman sat behind the tiny counter, not much older than Judy herself. She seemed to be working on her accounts. There were tubs of brushes, flat, bright, and round, in squirrel, hog and sable, racks of canvasses, palettes and knives, easels, and an all-pervading smell of oil paint. Judy's mouth was almost watering with her longing to buy.

'You have a wonderful little shop here. Have you been open long?'

'Only a month or two.'

'It's lovely. Very exciting.' Judy browsed for a while, critically examining the pictures, wondering how best to proceed. She could feel her heart beating so loudly the woman must surely hear it. Maybe she should go now before she made a complete fool of herself. She'd reached the door when the woman spoke again.

'Do you know much about art?'

Judy shook her head. 'Not really. I just know what I like.'

The woman gave a vague smile, having heard this one before.

'I wonder if I may see the proprietor?' The words seemed to pop out of Judy's mouth without any thought, and her cheeks fired crimson at her own temerity.

The woman smiled. 'That's me.' Then she glanced at the brown paper carrier bag with an air of resignation, and Judy sensed the woman had already grown weary of would-be artists showing their masterpieces to her in the hope of making a fortune.

Judy set her bag on the counter and drew out a couple of the better water colours and several sketches of people and places she'd drawn. 'They're just sketches, I'm afraid, and a few water colours. Some of them aren't even finished. I much prefer working in oil on canvas but I'm not in a position to buy the materials at present. However . . .' Judy cleared her throat and tried a weak smile. 'I thought . . . I mean, I hoped . . . well, anyway, I'd be interested in your opinion.'

As she hesitantly put forward her request, she was spreading her work out on the top of the counter, covering up the woman's account book and her scribbled notes. The owner of the shop said nothing, just stared at the pictures for a long while.

'If they're no good you can say so. I won't be offended.' Judy gave an embarrassed little laugh. 'Well, not too much.'

She waited for the woman to respond. Instead, she picked up one of the paintings and took it to the window where she could see it in a better light. At length she said, 'How many of these have you done?'

Judy shrugged. 'Oh, lots, but I give most of them away. It's just that I could do with a bit more cash and I wondered . . .' Embarrassment washed over her again and this time she could bear the woman's silence no longer. Judy began to quickly gather the sheets up, slipping them back into the carrier bag.

'What are you doing? I haven't finished looking at them yet. I like your use of colour, it's imaginative and you've managed to bring both light and vigour into what would otherwise be a grey industrial scene. You even catch the droll Lancashire humour in some of these faces. There's so much character there. But you're right, you don't seem entirely comfortable with water colour. It's perhaps a rather insipid medium for pictures that possess such energy and vibrant tones. And of course, far more difficult to control, as I'm sure you've discovered.'

Judy had stopped packing the bag to listen to all of this, beginning to think that maybe the woman might like her work after all.

She smiled at Judy and held out a hand. 'I'm Angie, and you are?'

'Judy.'

'Well, Judy, I'm not making any promises but I think you and I might be able to do business. How about if I lend you a few canvasses and some oils, whatever you need to get going, and you pay me back when I sell your first finished picture.'

'Oh!' Judy gasped, seemingly stuck for words.

And then Angie gave her a lecture on what was wrong with her pictures instead of what was right. Images which appeared rather flat, or the perspective or angles that weren't quite right. 'I do hope that hasn't depressed you.'

'Oh, no, not at all. I appreciate your advice.'

'But can you keep that lovely loose style in oils?'

'I think so. But I tend to use colours that I like, not necessarily what I see, or what seems appropriate.'

Angie smiled at her. 'Like the pink bicycle, and the blue and orange dock scene. Good. That is what's so attractive about your work, the blend of good drawing and an original use of colour.

Come back when you've something more to show me. I look forward to seeing what you can produce.'

Half an hour later Judy left the little shop loaded with palette, easel, brushes and oil paints. How she would manage to get all this stuff back to her little flat on the bus and up six flights of stairs she neither knew nor greatly cared. Her heart was singing and she wore a big foolish grin on her face. She could see the future at last, and it was good.

51

Lynda

It was a couple of nights later and a much subdued Jake sat in silence as the three of them ate the lamb stew Lynda had prepared for supper, but once Ewan had gone off for his evening pint, Jake took her completely by surprise by staying behind to help with the washing-up.

'What's this? Don't tell me you're turning into Goody Two-Shoes?'

'I've found out what he's planning. I know what it is, this big job he's lining up. He's given me all the details.'

Fear sparked in her hazel eyes. 'What? Tell me, because if it's bad, if it's criminal, I can't do it, I just can't.'

Jake looked at his sister, aghast. 'You'll have to, for Mam's sake. Listen, he's told me everything but you haven't to say a word. You have to promise me that, Lynda. He's threatened to kill her, and me too, if a breath of this gets out. And I believe he'd do it too, I do really. He nearly did for me the other day when he suspected me of grassing on him. That's how I lost the tooth.'

Jake grimaced as he revealed the gap to his sister, just as he'd used to do as a young boy, and Lynda felt that familiar chill creep down her spine.

'And did you, grass on him, I mean?'

Jake shook his head. 'Never got the chance, and I wouldn't be daft enough to try again. Neither must you or it'll be curtains for Mam and me both.'

Her stomach lurched so badly Lynda thought she might actually vomit, but managed to somehow hold on. 'Oh, Jake, I'm so frightened I don't think I can take much more of this.'

Then to Lynda's great surprise, her young, self-obsessed, slang-talking, idiot of a brother put his arms about her and gently stroked her hair.

'Don't worry, sis, I'll look after you. It'll be all right, you'll see, and we've really got no choice. He's going to fill me in on the final details tomorrer, but his plan is to steal a large consignment of TVs and radios coming in from Japan on Friday. He's no goof, so I expect he sees a lot of money in it. Televisions are selling like hot cakes these days and they're not cheap. Ewan's plan is to wait till they're all unloaded and all the dockers have gone home, then move in and steal the lot.'

Lynda stared up at her brother, knowing her own face must look as white and strained as his. 'And what's our part in all of this?'

Jake chewed on his finger-nail. The smoking had gone by the board and nail-biting was his latest fetish. Lynda took his hand and patted it. 'At least tell me what you know. You'll be driving the van, I suppose?'

Jake nodded bleakly.

'And what about me? What am I supposed to do in this precious scheme of his?'

Jake swallowed. He knew Lynda wasn't going to like this, not one little bit, but that wasn't his responsibility. He just had to make sure she did as she was told. 'Catlow's employ a night-watchman, big guy, ex-soldier, and your job is to keep him occupied so's he has no inkling of what's going on down on the wharf.'

'What?' Lynda half laughed. 'And how am I supposed to do that?'

'How do you think?'

Lynda looked at him, too stunned to think of a response.

'I tried suggesting they just knock the old guy out, but Ewan said this way would be much more entertaining. It's his way of controlling us. If we're both involved we're not likely to shop him to the cops, are we? And don't even consider not doing as he says, sis. Just think of poor mam locked up in some dark hole some place. Not a word of this to anyone, or God knows what little treat he'd have in store for us. I'm damn sure you'd like that even less.'

Lynda was shaking her head, panic roaring through her veins. 'But I can't do it, I can't, Jake. We have to get out of this somehow. There must be another way.'

Lynda started restlessly roaming about the room, rubbing her arms as if she were cold, and Jake tried to stop her, to calm her down. 'There is no other way, not since we can't find Mam, and she seems to have vanished off the face of the earth. But if Ewan really does have her locked up somewhere, what choice do we have but to obey him?'

'She can't have vanished completely. She must be somewhere. We have to find her.' A feverish brightness came into Lynda's hazel eyes then she took Jake completely by surprise as she spun around and headed for the door. 'And I'm going to find her. I must, I must!'

Lynda ran out of the house and was knocking on their neighbour's door before Jake had time to gather his wits and run after her.

She ran from door to door, hammering on each with her fists, screaming and yelling at the top of her voice, 'Where's Mam? Where's me mam? Has anybody seen Betty? Somebody must know where she is. Tell me where she is, you buggers. You have to help us. You have to help . . .'

Jake did his best to stop her but she was like a wild thing, racing up and down the street like someone demented, knocking over dustbins, flinging open the boots of parked cars, pushing over stacked market stalls with twice her usual strength as she shouted and screamed for Betty.

'*Mam, Mam, where are you?*'

Jake froze, feeling utterly useless, paralysed by panic, and nobody else tried to stop her. The folk of Champion Street emerged from their houses blinking in the lamplight, curious to know what was going on. When they realised it was Lynda Hemley and that she'd completely flipped, and who could wonder at it if she was in the throes of a complete break-down, poor lass, they shook their heads in dismay.

They stood and watched in sympathetic silence as her father came running from the Dog and Duck to gather her in his arms, doing his best to hush the girl and calm her down. Even then she didn't stop screaming, the sound of her frantic terror echoing down the quiet street as Ewan half dragged and half carried her back home, chilling the souls of all those who witnessed the scene.

As Winnie Holmes said to Big Molly, 'By heck, but she's lucky to have found her dad. The poor lass is certainly in need of one now that she's lost her mam.'

Terry went round first thing the next morning to see how she was, bravely risking Ewan's ire by knocking on the door since she wasn't at the flower stall as usual. He hadn't seen Lynda properly since before Christmas. It was almost as if she were deliberately avoiding him, and he worried that what had once seemed so good between them, could have soured yet again. He wasn't allowed to see her, of course, Jake coming to tell him she was resting.

'Well, just tell her I called, will you, Jake? I miss her. Tell Lynda I was worried about her.'

'Aye,' Jake said, glancing back over his shoulder into the silent house. 'We all are.'

Terry said, 'I knew she was upset over losing her mam, but I hadn't realised quite how badly it had affected her. But then is it any wonder? It must have been dreadful for the poor woman to end her days by falling in the canal when she can't even walk properly on dry land. It must be hard for Lynda to live with that fact.'

'She didn't drown,' Jake snapped. 'We've no proof, so don't you go saying she did.'

'Oh, sorry!'

A voice from inside the house called out for him to shut the flaming door, he was causing a draught. Jake jumped and began to do so, but just as it was about to close he stuck his head into the crack and fiercely whispered, '*Tell Leo Catlow to watch out on Friday!*' Then Terry was left staring at the door panel, wondering what that had been all about.

As he walked away he looked for Lynda at her bedroom window, and there she was, quietly weeping into the lace curtain, her pale face blotched with the flush of tears. He waved and blew her a kiss, hoping she'd wave back and for a moment thought she was about to raise the sash window, but then he saw her turn quickly away before vanishing altogether.

Terry was hurt that she could care so little that she didn't even want to speak to him. He stuffed his hands in his pockets and walked sorrowfully away, but couldn't resist keep glancing anxiously back, hoping she'd reappear. She didn't, and his earlier worry had now grown to a deep anxiety.

What had Jake meant by that warning? What was it Leo Catlow had to watch out for exactly, and why on Friday? Why had Jake insisted that Betty hadn't drowned when it was quite plain to all that she must have done. Why had Lynda lost her head in that way last night, which was so unlike her, and why didn't she at least look pleased to see him this morning? It was all very strange.

It then occurred to him that she might not have been alone in her bedroom; that someone, her father perhaps, might have come in and prevented her from acknowledging him, might almost be holding her there against her will.

And what if Ewan Hemley was planning a job, and Jake was involved?

My God, now it all began to make sense.

Back on the market Terry went straight to his father and begged an hour or two off work. His next port of call would be Leo Catlow in the hope that he might be able to make some sense out of Jake's gibberish. Whatever was wrong, Terry was determined to get to the bottom of it.

Friday night found Lynda standing shivering in a corner of Catlow's yard down by the docks wondering if she would even live through this night. It was black dark, the moon covered by a blanket of cloud and she could hear nothing but the faint strains of Radio Caroline coming from the office. The docks themselves were silent, with not even the familiar whirr and grind of machinery to distract her.

Ewan had made it plain what she must do.

'Don't worry, no need to make up any tale about what you're doing there in the middle of the bleeding night. He's expecting you. The night-watchman's palm has been well greased to look the other way while we get on with the job, and you're a part of that payment. You're the bit extra to keep him sweet, and since you're an attractive woman see that you make it worth his while. We don't want no repercussions, no mouthing off afterwards to the police because you didn't deliver. Understand?'

Lynda had listened in silence, understanding only too clearly, but not even commenting on what kind of father sold his daughter to a perfect stranger for the sake of a few televisions and radios.

Now that the moment had actually arrived she felt a numbness creep over her. What did it matter? What did anything matter any more? For all she knew this might all be a waste of time and her mother already dead, but until she had proof of that she had to go along with Ewan's plan.

Either way, Ewan had succeeded in destroying their happiness, and his ex-wife. He'd implicated Jake already in his illegal activities, and now it was her turn. He'd used every method at his disposal: bullying, kidnap, threats and blackmail to get what he wanted, even drowned their lovely Queenie, and Lynda guessed he'd stop at nothing now, not even murder to get his hands on this rich consignment of goods.

He'd told them a dozen times how the load was worth a small fortune, but he'd also added that this was just the beginning, that he was moving up into a new league, leaving the petty stuff behind him and working with the big boys now.

'How can I lose with my family behind me?' He meant that there would be no one to grass on him, as Betty had done all those years before.

Lynda could see her brother chewing on his finger-nails as he sat waiting in the van, knew that Ewan and a couple of his cronies were tucked away in the back of it. There were other members of this make-shift gang in a second van at the other end of the yard, waiting only for her to walk into that office. This would be the signal for them to drive quietly along the wharf, break into the warehouse and start shifting the electrical goods.

'Easy as taking sweets from a baby,' Ewan had told her.

Lynda straightened the short, too-tight skirt she'd been instructed to wear for the occasion, and, turning her back on the van, walked towards the office. The crack of light under the door grew brighter as she approached, the strains of 'What Do You Want To Make Those Eyes At Me For?' playing on Radio Caroline rising to an ear-splitting crescendo, in competition with the hammering of her heart.

She'd vomited up the supper Ewan had made her eat, but was well beyond fear now. Her limbs weren't even shaking and her hand was rock steady as she turned the door handle.

And there he was, the night-watchman she was supposed to entertain, standing before her like a huge lump of blubber, piggy eyes bright with desire in a round, shiny face as he wiped sweaty hands on the back of his trousers. He flapped at her to come in, pushing the door shut behind her and quickly shooting home the bolt.

The sound snapped in her head like the shutting of a trap but somehow Lynda managed to smile up at him, perhaps hoping to charm this fat man into not hurting her. He put out one hand and squeezed her breast, quite hard, and with a jolt of shock Lynda recognised her mistake. She'd secretly hoped that she could talk him out of it, now she saw no chance of that. He'd no doubt been looking forward to this moment all day, and could hardly contain his excitement. One hand was in his trouser pocket, fiddling with something.

'Do you want a drink?' He drew out a whisky bottle, from which he'd obviously already drunk half. Lynda shook her head.

He took a long swig himself, licked his fat lips then swiped one podgy hand across his slobbering mouth, small beady eyes boring into her with lascivious greed. 'Get on with it then.'

'What?' She was startled by his directness, though what exactly she'd expected, Lynda wasn't sure.

'Strip off! I want me money's worth. I want to see the merchandise before I taste it.'

Oh God, this was going to be a thousand times worse than she'd imagined! Lynda felt drained, incapable of reaction or running away, even had there been anywhere to run to. It was as if she were standing outside herself watching what was going on from a great distance as she went through the motions of taking off her jacket, folding it with painstaking care upon a nearby desk. Next she unbuttoned her blouse, let it slip from her shoulders and folded that in the same punctilious way.

She heard him give a low groan as his salacious gaze fastened hungrily upon her breasts, daintily clad in a pretty, lace-trimmed bra.

Lynda hesitated, unwilling to go any further, but again he flapped a hand frantically at her, urging her on and this time her fingers did start to tremble as she reached for the button on her skirt. The horror of her situation was beginning to slowly dawn on her, fear rising like bile in her throat.

Jake and Ewan and the rest of their motley crew must surely have reached the warehouse by this time. How long would it take them to load up the gear? Not that this had any bearing on her own part in the performance, Lynda bitterly reminded herself. She'd been ordered to give satisfaction so that there'd be no come-backs.

Their own getaway in the van driven by Jake had been carefully planned but her own was a much more hazy affair, apparently depending on how long it took her to 'do the business'. Lynda had been instructed to 'slip away into the darkness' when the job was done.

But Ewan had promised that when this night was over her mother could well make a miraculous return. Lynda could only pray that this was true.

The fat man was fiddling with his trousers, had them unbuttoned and was growing increasingly impatient with Lynda's own fumbling attempts to remove the skirt. He seemed to be panting for breath and, reaching out, made a grab for her, causing Lynda to cry out in alarm.

The next moment she was being pushed down on to the office floor, her legs being dragged apart as panic swelled and bloomed inside her, paralysing her with fear as she wondered frantically if she would survive this, or if the fat man's enormous weight would crush her. And then all hell broke loose.

The air was suddenly filled with the sound of police whistles, the roar of engines and car tyres screeching to a halt. An inner door burst open and amazingly there was Leo Catlow, half a dozen pairs of hands dragging the heap of blubber off her, and her own darling Terry gathering her into his arms telling her to stop crying because everything was going to be fine now.

Even Constable Nuttall was grinning at her saying she was perfectly safe, that he hadn't let her down this time.

52

Judy and Lynda

O ne morning at the snack bar Judy was surprised to see Sam walk in. He marched right over to the counter, ignoring an old lady ordering a cup of tea and a sausage roll. 'You have to come home. The children need you.'

Judy stared at him, stunned. 'I don't think this is the time or place to go over all of that again, Sam.'

'I mean, it's an emergency. The kids haven't been well and now my mother has the 'flu an' all, so you'll have to come home to look after them all. They're on the mend but still not fit to return to school yet. You'll have to come at once.'

Judy was already untying her apron and reaching for her coat. Turning to her employer she gave an apologetic smile. 'Sorry, but you heard what my husband said. I'll have to go.'

'Don't expect me to keep the job open for you!' he shouted as Judy followed Sam out of the snack bar.

'Suit yourself but my children must come first.'

Judy took one look at her mother-in-law and instantly called the doctor. Mrs Beckett's 'flu had swiftly deteriorated into pneumonia and she needed to be taken into hospital.

It felt strange to be in her own home again. Sam had simply dropped her at the door and gone straight back to work but Judy loved having Ruth and Tom to herself for the entire day. They played Ludo and Snakes and Ladders by a roaring fire, drank mugs of cocoa and nibbled on chocolate fingers. A delicious, cosy day with her beloved children.

She stayed with them until Sam came home then put on her

coat and prepared to leave. 'Your tea is in the oven, and I'll be back in the morning before you leave for the shop.'

'Where are you going?'

'Home. If I hurry, I'll just catch the six o'clock bus back to Salford.'

Sam had settled in the chair with the newspaper, now he jumped to his feet to protest. 'I don't think so. What if the children are sick during the night?'

'Then you'll have to take care of them.'

'But you know that I always go to the British Legion on a Wednesday evening. You'll have to stay and look after them.'

Judy shook her head. 'Sorry, no can do. I have to go. I couldn't possibly sleep here. It wouldn't be right. Oh, and you'll have to help out a bit more with money, since I lost my job coming here today, not that I mind and I'm sure I can get another once the children are back at school, but in the meantime I have my rent to pay, electricity bills and so on.'

Tom began to cry. 'You aren't leaving us again, Mummy, are you?'

Judy rushed over to the small boy to kiss and hug him. 'Of course not, darling. Don't worry, I'll be back first thing in the morning. I'll be here just the minute you open your eyes.'

Tom instantly brightened and gave his mother a tremulous smile. 'I wish you were there every morning, for ever and ever.'

'Of course he does, and so you should be,' Sam barked at her, furious that he no longer seemed to have the control over her that he'd once enjoyed. 'Stop being so stupid, stop all this nonsense about divorce and come home to your children, where you belong.'

'But nothing has changed, has it?' she challenged him.

There was a short telling silence in which Judy had no wish to ask him, not in front of the children, if he were still seeing Helen Catlow. Though by the guilty flush creeping over his cheeks, she'd guess that he was, or else had some other woman in his sights.

'I thought not.'

Judy kissed Ruth, and, surprisingly her daughter clung to her and hugged her back. 'I'll look after Tom, Mummy. Don't worry, he'll be all right. We'll see you tomorrow, and thank you for a lovely day.'

My goodness, Judy thought, can my little girl be growing up at last?

It proved to be a busy week for Judy as she came each day to care for her children, one in which they were able to grow close again and be a family.

And each evening, on her way home, she would call in at the hospital to see her mother-in-law. The old lady was not at all well, and it looked unlikely she'd be able to cope with a pair of lively children for some considerable time even if she did make a full recovery.

Once the children were fit enough to return to school Judy returned to the snack bar and, amazingly, found that her old job was still available after all. Perhaps nobody else was prepared to work for the pitiful wages her boss paid. But she made him shorten her hours slightly, since she had to pick the children up from school every day in Castlefield now their grandmother wasn't well enough to do that any more.

Oh, but it was so wonderful to spend time with them again, and it had given her hope for the future, that she might one day win them back entirely. The only problem was that part-time work meant a part-time income. Judy knew that she needed much more money and security in her life if she was to prove her worth to the court.

But then she had great hopes for her painting . . .

Lynda stood in the fold of Terry's arms and quietly wept with joy. This was the day she'd dreamed of for so long: the day she became his loving wife. They were married at the local register office, exactly as planned, except that it no longer needed to be kept secret. Everyone was there smiling up at her, the blushing bride, beautifully attired in a cream wool sack dress with matching jacket, a tall walking-stick umbrella and one of Patsy Bowman's wide-brimmed feather hats. Terry had whispered that she looked utterly gorgeous.

It was all over. Everything. That dreadful night was nothing more than a bad memory now.

The police had taken Ewan away in handcuffs, Jake too unfortunately, although Lynda had put in a strong plea for them to go easy with him. 'He didn't have any choice. My brother either had to do what our father said or be beaten senseless, as I was.'

'Don't worry, Lynda love,' Constable Nuttall had assured her. 'All of that will be taken into account, including the fact that he tipped us off about the robbery. Fortunately Mr Catlow guessed at once what Jake was referring to, just as soon as your Terry mentioned Friday. A couple of phone calls and we were ready for him.'

Leo said, 'I can't tell you, Lynda, how very grateful I am that Jake found the courage to do that, at great risk to himself. I've already arranged for my solicitor to be there at the police station ready to represent him.'

Lynda had smiled her gratitude, then turning back to Constable Nuttall, had said, 'I'm sorry for all those names I called you. I realise now that in your own way you *were* keeping an eye on us, there just wasn't anything you could do about it, any more than we could.'

'I did what I could, Lynda love, but I agree it wasn't enough. The law has to be changed. Women have to be better protected, even in their own homes from their own husbands.'

'I might still have a mother, if they'd done that already,' Lynda said, her face a mask of pain. 'He did for her too, didn't he, just like Queenie? She never was locked up anywhere, was she?'

Constable Nuttall looked sorrowful. 'We haven't given up, lass. We're still looking for her. My colleagues are combing the docks and canal basin all over again, even as we speak, checking on anyone connected with this robbery.'

Lynda could hardly swallow the great lump that had come into her throat. 'I wanted to believe so badly that Mam was still alive that I was prepared to go through with all of that, to sell myself, body and soul, to that great lump of blubber.'

'Nay, tha'd have given him a kick in the googlies when the moment came. I wouldn't expect owt less from a daughter of mine.'

'*Mam!*' Lynda flung herself out of Terry's arms and into Betty's. 'I don't believe it! You *are* alive.' She stroked her mother's plump cheeks in disbelief, smoothed her wild mass of grey hair, hugged her tight and looked in danger of never letting go.

'By heck, you're near throttling me, lass. Don't you do for me, when I've managed to survive that great bully.'

Everyone gathered round then, shaking Betty's hand, patting her on the shoulder, saying how good it was to see her walking with the aid of only a stick. Leo Catlow looked pleased as punch, as if he'd organised the entire rescue himself.

'But where were you, Mam?' Lynda wanted to know. 'Where did he put you?'

Her face took on a sheepish look. 'Well, it were a bit of a scam actually. I weren't locked up in no cellar or warehouse, and I didn't drown, as you can see, but I were hoping that everyone would think that I had. Then they'd arrest that bugger, throw him in jail and toss away the key. That was my little scheme. I'm only sorry I had to let you and Jake think I were a gonner. I couldn't do nowt about that if my plan was to work.'

'But the police couldn't arrest him. They couldn't find any evidence.'

'Aye, that were a big disappointment, that were. I'll admit things didn't turn out quite as I expected, or planned. I never wanted you and Jake involved or hurt in any way. But the toe-rag couldn't resist taking advantage of the fact I was missing, presumed drowned, to tighten the screws on you both, and set up a scam of his own. But we got the bugger in the end, eh?'

Everybody laughed. 'We certainly did.'

'Good old Betty,' Leo added with a grin. 'I owe you.'

'Don't worry, I'll charge you double in future for your mother's carnations.'

More laughter but Lynda was still looking puzzled. 'You still haven't told us where you've *been* all this time? We looked every-where.'

'You didn't look under your own nose. I were round at Moll's, hiding in her back bedroom.'

Only then did Lynda become aware of Big Molly standing grinning just behind her mother. Lynda burst out laughing. It was all suddenly so ridiculous she couldn't help it. 'So that's why you've been stuffing me with meat and potato pies, Molly Poulson? You were mothering me in her place.'

'I couldn't let you fade away, chuck. Anyroad, somebody had to keep an eye on you who knew exactly what was going on.'

'Speaking of food, I'm feeling a bit peckish meself right now,' Betty put in. 'I've been well taken care of by Moll and Ossie, but I'll be glad to put me feet up in me own home, knowing we're free of that bastard at last. Come on, Lynda love, let's go put the kettle on.'

Terry said, 'I'm coming too, and I'm going to make you the biggest plate of bacon and eggs you ever saw in your life.'

'Eeh, the man of my dreams: a chap who can cook. Welcome to the family, lad.'

As they were about to go, arms wrapped around each other, Betty turned back to Constable Nuttall, face grim, finger wagging. 'I'm going to give you some bramble to grow in your garden, Bill Nuttall. It's for remorse, and will remind you of your own failings. Or happen hemlock, since you were very nearly the death of me.'

This brought forth a few chuckles but the policeman's eyes were bleak as they regarded her. 'I know I failed you, Betty, but it wasn't entirely my fault. I was only doing my job, inadequate though it might be at times. Lynda and I have already spoken about this and agree police attitude towards domestic violence needs changing. I'm sure it will change eventually. We'll certainly be putting in a report to the Chief Constable pointing out the problems we've encountered in this case. But I hope you and I can still be friends.'

Betty regarded him coldly for a long silent moment, then she clicked her tongue, giving her head a little shake. 'I never could stay angry with you for more than five minutes, you great daft lump. But see that our Jake is home in good time to enjoy his breakfast. You owe me that much at least, Bill Nuttall. You failed to save me from that ex-husband of mine, so the least you can do is give me back my son.'

'Don't worry, Betty. I'll make sure he's there. And I'll also make sure that Ewan Hemley is locked up for a long time and doesn't ever return to Champion Street.'

'Music to my ears. I might spare you the hemlock then.'

And so here they were, all of them, all her friends and neighbours from Champion Street Market, her mam and Jake, all joining Lynda to celebrate her marriage to Terry Hall, and she'd never been so happy in her life.

And by her side as matron-of-honour was her best friend, Judy Beckett. The two girls hugged each other in delight.

'Everything all right with you, Judy love?'

'Oh, yes,' Judy said, eyes shining. 'Everything is just wonderful.'

Mrs Beckett had died of pneumonia and Sam could no longer manage the children without her help. A few weeks after that when Judy had taken her case back to court the magistrates had been much more sympathetic to her case. They decided that the children were happier with their mother and the fact that she only worked part time was a definite point in her favour.

By then Judy had moved to a two-bedroom flat in a much pleasanter area and was regularly selling her paintings, which she was able to work on from home in the afternoons. She was, in fact, beginning to make quite a name for herself. They saw no reason why she shouldn't be granted custody.

Sam was given the usual rights of access and, as Judy now excitedly related to Lynda, since she had her children safely back in her care she would be far more generous with him than he had ever been with her.

Lynda shook her head in despair over her friend's generosity. 'You're a living saint. I've always said as much, now I know it.'

'Sam is still Ruth and Tom's father, and always will be. It's only right that he continues to be a part of their lives. It's not like your own situation, love. Even Sam, for all his controlling, bossy ways, couldn't be compared with Ewan.'

'No,' Lynda ruefully reflected. 'Nobody could. Ewan Hemley is back in clink, where he belongs, and Mam is happily back on her stall, and I'm a good deal older and wiser. I no longer wish for the moon, for the perfect father, or the perfect marriage. Hey, but what about Leo Catlow? Are you and he . . . ?'

Judy smiled. 'Maybe one day, who knows? Right now I need to concentrate on caring for my children and proving myself to be a good mother.'

'And your new career as an artist, don't forget.'

'Yes, that too. Oh, but I'm so pleased about you and Terry. You found your Mr Right after all.'

'Course I did. And we're going to prove the exception. Terry and I are going to live happily ever after with never a cross word . . .'

Judy burst out laughing. 'That'll be the day.'